Of Women, Outcastes, Peasants, and Rebels

A Selection of Bengali Short Stories

EDITED, TRANSLATED,
AND WITH AN
INTRODUCTION BY

Kalpana Bardhan

UNIVERSITY OF CALIFORNIA PRESS

Berkeley · Los Angeles · London

This book is a print-on-demand volume. It is manufactured using toner in place of ink. Type and images may be less sharp than the same material seen in traditionally printed University of California Press editions.

University of California Press
Berkeley and Los Angeles, California

University of California Press, Ltd.
London, England

Library of Congress Cataloging-in-Publication Data

Of women, outcastes, peasants, and rebels: a selection of Bengali
    short stories / edited, translated, and with an introduction by
    Kalpana Bardhan.
        p.   cm.
    Translated from Bengali.
    Bibliography: p.
    ISBN 0-520-06714-2 (pbk.: alk. paper)
    1. Short stories, Bengali—Translations into English.   2. Short
stories, English—Translations from Bengali.   I. Bardhan, Kalpana.
PK1716.04   1990
891'.4430108—dc20   89-35749
                                                                   CIP

Printed in the United States of America

The paper used in this publication meets the minimum requirements of
ANSI/NISO Z39.48-1992 (R 1997) (Permanence of Paper). ∞

CONTENTS

v

ACKNOWLEDGMENTS

I would like to thank several people for granting me permission to publish my translations of the stories in this collection: Jagadindra Bhowmick, director of Visva-Bharati Granthayan Bibhag, for the stories by Rabindranath Thakur; Mrs. Kamala Bandyopadhyay, for those by Manik Bandyopadhyay; Sarit Kumar Banerjee, for those by Tarashankar Bandyopadhyay; Mahasweta Devi; and Hasan Azizul Huq. Mahasweta Devi and Hasan Azizul Huq also offered valuable comments on my translation of their stories.

The translations have gained from the detailed comments and suggestions painstakingly made by Shamik Banerjee and Pranab Bardhan. Karine Schomer read an earlier draft of "Paddy Seeds." The introduction, which went through at least as many drafts as the translations, gained enormously from the comments of the two reviewers of the manuscript and above all from the thorough reading and careful remarks of Lynne Withey, George Hart, and Pranab Bardhan on the penultimate draft and from Eileen McWilliam's copyediting of the final draft. Ina Clausen designed a simple cover uniting the brown of the toiling people, the green of the paddy fields, and the vermilion of hope.

During the three years that I have worked on this manuscript, and especially during the latter half of that period, when I was fully immersed in it, I would not have managed to sustain the effort had I not been able to share with Pranab and Titash my frustration at the setbacks and my joy at the accomplishments, both of which tended to overwhelm me.

INTRODUCTION

Bengali literary prose emerged in its contemporary form in the early nineteenth century. Around the middle of the century, Iswarchandra Vidyasagar
and Bankimchandra Chatterjee among others perfected the idiom of modern
secular writing. Bengali literature, however, has a much longer history, beginning with a lyrical tradition many centuries old. Historians have traced
the origins of two of the streams of this tradition to the Buddhist scholarly
works and hymns (*charyagiti*) written in the tenth century by the Bengali
acharyas, who formed the bridge from eastern India to Tibet, and to the
Brahmanic Sanskrit literature, which reached its peak in Bengal during the
twelfth century.[1] The third and most pervasive stream existed in the early
medieval (tenth- to twelfth-century) folk literature, in the narrative poems
known as *mangalkavyas*; these were based on popular religious myths and
stories that were current during the pre-Brahmanic mercantile era in Bengal
long before the Turks came and set up their sultanate in Delhi. The Buddhist
and the Brahmanic Sanskritic literary influences, which came from outside
Bengal, and the folk lyrical tradition of the *mangalkavyas* converged in the
fifteenth-century poet Jayadeva's *Gitagovinda*, a book of romantic lyrics on the
love of Radha and Krishna. Although *Gitagovinda* was written in Sanskrit, its
tonality, rhythm, and idiom were inspired by Bengal's indigenous tradition
of literature in the popular dialects.[2] The *Vaishnava padavalis*, lyrics celebrating the love of the gods in human terms, descended directly from *Gitagovinda*, though their tone and images tended to be more devotional and less
erotic.[3] In the course of time, the Vaishnava padavalis and the *mangalkavyas*
became the two most important elements in the evolution of a Bengali literary
style and idiom based on folk dialects and Sanskritic infusion (and later on
Persian and Arabic infusions). A final development, which made way for the
secular social orientation of Bengali literature, occurred in the early nineteenth
century, when the language was hammered by a generation of socially con-

1

scious, progressive writers into a form suitable for writing essays and literary fiction relating to the lives of ordinary people. The medium of short stories, for which ease of expression and realism of theme and characters are vital, was shaped and perfected in the late nineteenth century, most of all by Rabindranath Thakur (in anglicized form Tagore), with whom we start this collection.

Bengali literature of the past hundred years is in many ways one of the most significant world literatures. A brilliantly prolific, diverse, and socially sensitive literature, its readership today probably runs to at least 20 million, out of a total of 170 million Bengali speakers. More important than the size of the readership is its sophistication and love of good writing. Educated Bengalis have always been voracious readers and have liked to think of themselves as connoisseurs of good literature. Perhaps their passion for literature is inversely related to their indifference to and even disdain for (as well as lack of success in) trade, business, and agriculture. Perhaps it also stems from the relative overgrowth of the educated urban middle class, which is quite large for a region as poor and as rural as the two Bengals combined. Certainly the Bengalis' interest in literature has much to do with the currents of Bengal's social history during the past hundred years, especially in the decades since the 1920s. This period in Bengal has seen enormous social and political changes and a series of upheavals and crises, and these, as we shall see, have had a significant impact on the literature.

My active interest in translating a selection from Bengali literature began some years ago, inspired mainly by three factors. First, I frequently encountered Western readers interested in non-Western literature who admired how Latin American literature reflected the turmoil of a society in flux. Their view of this relationship as unique seemed to reveal a doubt that such a literature could exist in Bengal, which has also been in much turmoil since the turn of this century. In trying to refute the implicit, and unjustified, doubt, I was frustrated by the lack of good recent translations from the large body of socially focused Bengali literature. Similar feelings may have provoked quite a few others into similar enterprises, for translations of such literature have recently begun to appear, and many more are in process. Second, the insistent curiosity of my non-Bengali Indian friends about how social change and transition have been reflected in Bengali literature, especially compared to the literature in their respective languages, was a more positive incentive that sustained me through the labor of translating. In a country of continental size and great linguistic diversity, a country in which one of the few convenient colonial legacies is the use of English as a common language, the desire for exchanging the cherished fruits of vernacular literature across the language barriers is no small motivation for the many translation projects under way. Third, about five years ago, while working with statistical and ethnographic data on women's socioeconomic status in India, I was increasingly drawn to take stock of and collect Bengali stories dealing in one way or another with the gender aspect of oppression. Struck by the parallels and connections between the forms of oppression—by gender, class, caste, and tribal ethnicity—I sought a collection of stories that represented the interrelated forms and mechanisms of oppression at various levels of society.

I used two primary criteria for selection: first, the story had to move me deeply; and second, its main character had to belong to one or more of the categories in this anthology's title: women, outcastes (or members of an oppressed ethnic group), peasants, and those among them who rebel. Then, to an enormous number of interesting choices meeting these two criteria I applied additional conditions to arrive at an anthology of manageable size with a clearly discernible and meaningful pattern. These secondary criteria, as I will elaborate, reflect currents of social change and events of major social significance, and provide a revealing variety of focus in time, region, and socioeconomic context. Most of the stories I finally selected have not previously been translated into English.[4]

Like many others trying to understand social processes, I turn to the literature of the society I study—Indian generally, Bengali specifically—for insights and for affirmation or negation of observations that have been made with statistical, sociological, and anthropological methods. Literature as social commentary helps me gain valuable insights not only into behavior, but also into the thoughts, beliefs, and motives underlying behavior. Literature helps me understand the microsociology of behavior within the layers of social relations: relations between individuals, between groups variously situated in society, between individuals and the group, and the contradictions in these relations. In a society characterized not only by hierarchical structures of privilege and oppression but also increasingly by class differentiation and class conflict, literature reflects and grapples with the tensions between these structures. These tensions, crucial to understanding social processes, are extremely hard to discern and measure with the standard methods of the social sciences.

The power relations and modes of oppression in society must be seen at multiple levels, in their many-faceted and interconnected patterns. Both oppression and the resistance of the oppressed are structured by gender, class, caste, and ethnicity, usually in combination. If we want to understand the modes of oppression and the modes of resistance and rebellion in relation to each other, then literature is a good place to look. For literary realism, which describes both the mental and the material lives of groups and individuals, is perhaps the only medium capable of revealing the nuances of the relations between the oppressor and the oppressed, between the dominant and the subordinate.[5]

In the course of searching through literature as social commentary, I began to select and translate stories from Bengali, my first language. I decided to use stories (and the authors' biographies for understanding the stories) rather than novels, because I could thereby encompass, within a book of manageable length, several aspects of the social processes seen at different levels and from different angles, and I could also represent the many faces of oppression, of rebellion and quiescence, either strategic or fatalistic. By selecting stories by several major writers in the language, I could construct an interesting set of variations and parallels on the theme that would shed light on oppression at the social, familial, and personal levels and on the forms that resistance and rebellion take in concrete contexts. The subordinated, the oppressed, and the exploited in these stories are women, peasants, landless laborers, and other marginalized and stigmatized groups, in various combinations. In some cases they choose overt rebellion; more often they struggle in either the realm of consciousness or the arena of material means of power, or both. Sometimes they do neither, and the subject then is the disability of consciousness and will, as in "The Unlucky Woman" and "The Daughter and the Oleander," both stories of the indigent and declining sections of the middle class.

Although this collection includes some of the finest examples of the major literary currents, its purpose is not so much to precisely represent modern Bengali literature by way of the short story as to show the faces of oppression, the facets of power relations, and the figures of resistance and rebellion through the stories that I love and that move me deeply again and again. Set at various social levels and at different points of social change, the stories tell us about the ways in which oppression is rejected, passively or actively, in thought or in action, in silence or in tumult, in violence or in peace. The collection also incorporates, both as background and as foreground, some of the mass movements and major traumatic events that Bengal and neighboring areas have experienced in the course of this century.

THE CURRENTS OF SOCIAL CHANGE
REFLECTED IN THE LITERATURE

Some of the complexities of Bengal's social fabric are, on a broad level, shared by other regions in the subcontinent and other parts of the "developing" world. They reflect the contradictions of a society that is both traditionally hierarchical and variously in flux. What modes of dependence and subordination pervade a society that is at once closed and open, static and changing, contained and explosive, hegemonic and pluralistic? Where do we find the oppressed between quiescence and rage, between resistance and rebellion? Bengali literature offers a specific context to elucidate these questions. The stories in this collection describe the conflicts and dynamics of unequal relationships—between men and women, the upper and the lower strata, rebels and those rebelled against, the quiescent who accept hegemonic ideas (or the shrewd who feign acceptance) and the dominant elite. Some stories also describe the relationships between the progressive and the reactionary elites as well as those between the progressive elite and the oppressed—relationships that in fact hold one of the keys to social change.

The particular complexities of Bengal's social culture derive from the unique currents and crosscurrents of its colonial and postcolonial history. One major current, containing several related but distinct subcurrents, was the Bengal Renaissance, which reached its maturity in the late nineteenth century and was followed by the growth of its liberal nationalist subcurrent. Another major current was the consciousness of class exploitation, which fueled peasant struggles from the 1920s through the 1940s that ran parallel to and sometimes intersected the struggle for independence. The devastating famine of 1943 further politicized Bengal's peasantry as well as its intelligentsia, especially the younger generation of writers. The Partition of Bengal in 1947, attended by riots, massacres, and massive displacement of people as refugees, was the single most traumatic event in the history of Bengal. After two decades of quietude following Independence, peasant revolt erupted again in the late 1960s, although it differed from the earlier movement in form as well as in regional distribution. While the peasant revolts were being suppressed in northwest Bengal and in Bihar, the demand for regional autonomy broke out in East Pakistan, where brutal denial and repression led in 1971 to a liberation war that created Bangladesh amid massive casualties and displacement. These currents of social movement profoundly influenced Bengali literary thinking and expression. The tragic events, each with its painful aftermath, each rooted in prior social and political problems, have also shaped Bengal's intellectual, artistic, and folk consciousness, in large measure through the anguish of self-examination. Even the 1943 famine, at least as much man-made disaster as natural calamity, produced deep and lasting effects on the thinking and social consciousness of all Bengalis, not just the intellectuals.

The nineteenth-century Bengal Renaissance brought a number of rationalist humanist changes in intellectual and artistic thinking and in social attitudes and activism—changes that historically shaped the Bengali intelligentsia. These had started in the early nineteenth century, roughly three decades before India's first nationalist revolt—or the 1857 Sepoy Mutiny, as it is termed in the colonial historiography—after which the direct rule of the British Crown replaced the East India Company's mercantile rule. Initially, the renaissance was a product in part of the cross-fertilization of Vedic Hindu spiritualism and Western liberal rationalist ideas, specifically those of the French Revolution and the contemporary British liberal thinking. This creative crossing of ideas was primarily manifested in the social reform campaigns led by scholars like Rammohun Roy (1772–1833) and Iswarchandra Vidyasagar (1820–91).[6] It also appeared in the universalist humanism of the Brahmo (Hindu unitarian) reformation, which involved some but not all the social reformers, and which the more popular and deeply permeating Hindu revivalism of Ramakrishna and Vivekananda eventually eclipsed. The cultural influence of the Brahmo lifestyle persisted nonetheless, especially with respect to women's education and gender relations. The nineteenth-century cultural awakening in Bengal propelled, and was in turn propelled by, the early spread of liberal higher education among both men and women.[7]

A surge of progressive reformism rejecting obscurantist customs, the renaissance was characterized by rationalist and humanist thinking in a number of areas, including literature, academic studies, and methods of education. The combination of rationalist humanist ideas and pride in the best in Indian culture favored social reform, which prompted the hostility of orthodox Hindu society and, later in the nineteenth century, the rise of liberal nationalism.[8] As historian Susobhan Sarkar has noted, within this cultural awakening were two opposite flows, Westernism and Orientalism,

> not unlike the contending streams in the nineteenth-century cultural awakening in Russia. . . . The conflict did not take the form of two clearly divided camps. Rather, it was evident even in the thoughts and vision of single individuals, someone like Rabindranath, for example. . . . The Western affinity, or influence, however one views it, expressed itself in intellectual rationalism and humanist values, and thus in favor of social reform. In competition with this thrust towards rationalist humanism and social reform was a strong inclination to learn and uphold the true glories of the ancient Eastern civilization. . . . Rabindranath's enormous creativity owed much to his success in marrying the best of the opposite worlds into a special kind of cosmopolitan humanism that has enormous appeal to this day.[9](1982, 52–54, 58)

Sarkar sets the duration of this cultural awakening in Bengal at roughly one hundred years, from the time Rammohun Roy started writing and campaigning for social reform (in the 1810s) to the First World War, although he points out that "the creative reverberations of the Bengal Renaissance continued long after, and in many more forms than in the writings of Rabindranath himself and others" (1982, 79–80). David Kopf (1969), however, dates the renaissance from 1773 to 1835, based on the rise and decline of the collaboration between sections of the Calcutta intelligentsia and the British Orientalists centered at Fort William College, which for thirty-five years trained British civil servants in local language and culture and prepared the early textbooks in Bengali for that purpose.[10] This criterion is too limiting. Although the exchanges and the textbook-writing and translating teamwork between the Orientalists and the Sanskrit-Bengali pandits were an important initial element of the creative mixture of alien, opposite intellectual streams, their endeavors encompassed only a few aspects of the renaissance as a bourgeois cultural revolution within Bengali society and among Bengali intellectuals, artists, and writers. Rabindranath, the major literary product of the renaissance, started his writing career nearly fifty years after 1835, the

year of Macaulay's call for English education of Indians instead of Oriental-
ist training of British officers and the end year in Kopf's periodization. As
personal carriers of Westernism in the renaissance, David Hare and Drinkwater Bethune had a greater influence on the spread of secular liberal education and closer interaction with the Bengali intelligentsia in the first half of
the century than did Orientalists like William Carey.[11] Even Henry Derozio,
a Calcutta-born Portuguese-Indian who enjoyed a brief career as a young
agnostic teacher of maverick brilliance at Hindu College before dying in 1831
at twenty-two, inspired a generation of bright young men (known as the
Young Bengal group) to question authority and be patriotic at the same
time. Shibnath Shastri (1847–1918), an astute observer and chronicler of the
renaissance and one of its eminent figures, was firm in his view of the years
1825 to 1845 as the period in which the renaissance emerged out of the clash
between the old and the new (Shastri [1903] 1979, 292). Everything considered, we can regard the period from the 1810s to the 1910s as the time of
unfolding of the renaissance in Bengal, especially in light of our focus on
social change and literature as social commentary. From this standpoint, the
renaissance reached its maturity in the later half of the last century.

University education and Western science, philosophy, and literature
were introduced in Bengal during the early nineteenth century at the initiative of Bengali social reformers and educators, and were later fostered by the
Anglicists after the 1857 Mutiny. The spread of higher education, which
infused the currents of liberal thinking and social change that permeated Western intellectual thought at the time, was accompanied by sustained growth
and creativity in Bengali language and literature, a growth and creativity
that were suffused with new interest and insight in the classics as well as the
living traditions. The process of delving deeper into the purer aspects of
Indian culture, combined with the Western intellectual infusion, produced
much of the modern Bengali language and literary idiom. Higher education
in Bengal—in both Western and Indian subjects—became a powerful tool
for intellectual liberation from obscurantism and ascribed authority and
for fighting prejudice and personal conservatism. The conflict between the
progressive sectors of the middle classes and the reactionary sectors over
social reform issues and social and personal attitudes shaped Bengali urban
middle-class culture and creativity throughout the nineteenth century. Eventually, the liberally educated middle classes stood up against imperialism,
propelled into the freedom struggle by the evolving elements of the renaissance. Then for the first time, initially as part of the *swadeshi* movement, the
middle classes opened their minds toward the masses of the peasantry, who
were engaged in their own struggles against the exactions heaped on them
internally and externally.

Starting in the 1920s, this development generated a second current in
Bengali society and literature: the growing perception of class stratification,

exploitation, and conflict and the perspective of social restructuring through consciousness and organized struggle. Powerful expressions of this perspective were seen not only in the reality of the struggles of Bengal's peasantry during the 1930s and 1940s, but also in the idiom of progressive realism in Bengali literature. The true limitation of the renaissance up to that time had been its lack of sensitivity to the struggles of ordinary people, the rural masses. "The educated community of the nineteenth century failed to understand the exploiting character of the British rule in India," noted Sarkar. "The protagonists of our 'awakening' had little contact with or understanding of the toiling masses who lived in a world apart" (1958, 31). Rammohun Roy was full of admiration for the French Revolution, but his writings contain no mention of any of the revolts that took place in rural Bengal during his lifetime. The indigo growers' agitation and strikes (1778–1800, 1830–1848), for example, receive very little notice in either his works or those of his immediate successors, with the exception of Dinabandhu Mitra's celebrated play *Nil Darpan* (1860). In the second half of the eighteenth and the first half of the nineteenth century, rural Bengal had seen at least two dozen localized revolts among various communities of peasants, tenants, weavers, and tribal people. Progressive intellectuals regarded these revolts with indifference; conservatives with hostility and contempt. The Bengal Renaissance, not unlike the Chinese May Fourth movement and the Russian renaissance, was narrowly confined to the urban and urbane middle class. Moreover, whereas nearly half the population of Bengal in the last century was Muslim, the leading figures in the Bengal Renaissance for the most part were Hindu, and their reformism mostly concerned the Hindu society (Wadud 1958; Joarder 1977). Although the spread of colleges and universities in the latter half of the nineteenth century and the entry of middle-class Muslim men and women into the mainstream of the highly educated had some effects in terms of cultural and literary creativity and gender relations, the ripples beyond the Muslim Bengali middle class were slight.[12]

Rationalist humanist literature generated within a small stratum of society can nonetheless have profound influence and power, far beyond its own time and circle. In spite of its limitations, "our 19th century 'awakening' . . . had a reality of its own, an impact on the country, a real contribution to make to modern Indian culture" (Sarkar 1979, 157). The surge of creativity inspired by Rabindranath's vast works clearly attests to the force of this process, as does the enormous energy later generations of Bengali writers had to exert to move away from the Rabindric style, perspective, and outlook on society.

Manik Bandyopadhyay is the best known of the post-1920s Bengali writers who moved away from the Rabindric perspective and scrutinized life in the huge and increasingly complex lower socioeconomic strata. These writers focused not only on the exploitation and struggles of the rural peasantry but also on both the urban underclass, which by that time had grown enormously, and the sectors of the middle class affected by Calcutta's decline as a commercial center, a decline in employment that was aggravated by the disruption of Bengal's economy by wartime inflation, the 1943 famine, and the riots attending the 1947 Partition.[13] Class consciousness and class struggle were now less obscured and distorted by the religious and sectarian communal prejudices that had channeled the rebellions of the preceding century. The pace of class differentiation had accelerated since the turn of the century. The ranks of the middle classes, variously experiencing instability and downward mobility, were troubled by doubts, a sense of inadequacy, and the chasm between their cherished values and the reality of their compromised lives.

Manik had been a writer for some years when in his late twenties the sharecroppers' Tebhaga movement began to spread through the villages in both East and West Bengal. The movement centered on the twin issues of where and how to divide the harvest between landlord and sharecropper. The peasants demanded a two-thirds share and also that the division take place in their own yards or storages rather than in the landlord's storehouse or barn, where he had the power to lift off a part.[14] The sharecroppers' movement, which had begun in the 1920s, gathered momentum through the 1930s, reemerged after the 1943 famine, and exploded in 1946, the year before the subcontinent was divided for the Independence.

The catastrophic Bengal famine of 1943 shook society at all levels. The tragedy resulted not from any major crop failure but from the deadly combination of administrative negligence, a callous "scorched-earth policy" on the war front near Burma, and rampant speculation in food. The famine killed at least three million, roughly four percent of the population of undivided Bengal at the time, and affected several times as many, making them indigent and disintegrating their lives.

Bengali intellectuals, writers, poets, and artists who were young during the Tebhaga movement, the 1943 famine, and the subsequent food riots and marches became radicalized in consciousness and creative expression. In their work they tried to confront the contradictions between middle-class sentiments and the realities of middle-class life, even within their own lives and surroundings. Manik had started facing those contradictions in his writing some time before these events broke out. More than any other writer of his time, he was troubled by the increasingly unbearable disparity between the changed realities of life and the unchanged literary sentiments. He criticized the shallowness of the work of the new wave of writers that emerged in the 1930s and the 1940s (known as the Kallol group, which included himself to some extent):

How could one talk in the same breath of Hamsun and Gorky? How could one
fail to distinguish between the storm in the emotional sky and the flood racking
life on the ground? . . . Slum life came into literature, but not the reality of slum
dwellers' lives. Nor had the reality of middle-class life really been revealed.
. . . When a middle-class writer does not understand much about the
peasants' struggle, he tends to see the deprivation of peasant life in terms of the
failures of the middle-class life he is familiar with; he tends to see exploitation
and oppression by material means in terms of the mental conflicts of the middle
class.[15]

If we therefore set as a criterion for progressive literature the freedom from
middle-class sentimentality when describing the life of the lower classes,
along with respect for and acceptance of authentic dialect and idiom, we may
consider Mahasweta Devi and Hasan Azizul Huq two of the best living writers
in this particular tradition of literary realism. In an unpublished interview
from 1983, Mahasweta said that although she had seen the momentous
periods of the Tebhaga movement in the 1930s, the food riots of the mid-
1940s, and the Partition, with its Hindu-Muslim killings, she was not a
writer at the time. But at the end of the 1960s, another major social up-
heaval took place—the Naxalite revolt—which she has tried to document
in her writing in as much detail as possible.[16]

The Naxalite revolt (roughly 1967–1971) was in large part a decentralized
revolt of tribal and landless peasantry against landlords and moneylenders in
areas of northern and central West Bengal and southeastern Bihar. The start
of the revolt, and its name, is traced to the armed insurrection of tribal
peasants in a village called Naxalbari in north Bengal. Related to and partly
intersecting it was a militant revolt of radical-left urban youth, which was
ruthlessly suppressed. The youth revolt, its internecine battles, and the
police brutality in its suppression shook the ranks of the urban middle class
in a way that the peasant revolts, both current and previous, could not.
Although Mahasweta's first novel focused on the urban youth revolt, her
subsequent writings described the turmoil in rural areas of Bengal and Bihar,
the more pervasive turmoil that was not confined to the areas where the
Naxalbari-type revolt had actually taken place. Her stories are full of anthro-
pologically detailed narratives of the class-and-caste oppression and of the
ongoing struggles and resistance in the tribal and outcaste hinterlands of
southeastern Bihar and West Bengal.

The shattering experience of the 1947 Partition, accompanied by gang
killings and riots—engineered partly by criminally opportunist politicans
and partly by political nonintervention in a situation of rumor-fueled
distrust—produced massive casualties and streams of refugees who overnight lost home, family, and friends. Moreover, unlike that of the Punjabi
victims of the Partition, the suffering of the Bengali victims was protracted,
like a death by a thousand cuts, by the demoralization and pathology of

living for years in a state of uprootedness, alienation, and stagnation. This protracted suffering features prominently in the writing of Hasan Azizul Huq. So too does the traumatic revelation of the ugly face of ethnic imperialism during the language movement in East Pakistan and the 1971 war of Bangladesh independence, which killed over a million East Bengalis and forced over ten million to flee their homes. Two of the four stories by Hasan Azizul in this volume provide a somewhat different angle on the peasant perception of their own oppression, on their thoughts and acts of resistance; the other two stories explore oppression as a moral crisis within the individual psyche: one in an upwardly mobile middle-class context, the other in a declining middle-class context.

THE AUTHORS, THEIR TIMES, AND THEIR STORIES

The stories in this collection were written over a span of roughly ninety years, from the early 1890s to the early 1980s. This period, as we have noted, has been marked in Bengal by the culmination of the renaissance, the struggle for independence, the galvanizing peasant movements of the years from the 1920s to the 1940s and of the early 1970s, and the traumatic episodes of the famine, the Partition, and the Bangladesh war. The period was one of epochal transition experienced in several related forms, including the decline of the *zamindari* (absentee landlord system) as a significant socioeconomic feature, the growth of both the urban middle classes and the affluent farmers on the one hand and the landless laboring poor on the other, and the exposure of remote rural regions to urban customs, artifacts, and the sometimes violent intrusions of economic development.

When arranged according to the chronology of their writing, the stories show a striking thematic and idiomatic sensitivity to the structural changes in Bengali society over time, the major upheavals and dislocations, and to the related change of sociopolitical focuses in the intellectual psyche of Bengal. The 1930s and the 1940s constituted, in the intensity and rapidity of change and turmoil, the great divide in Bengal's social history. In the stories we see the central characters shift from the middle classes to peasants and slum dwellers, from upper-caste Hindu families to outcaste and tribal communities, from the myth-shrouded closed villages before the "green revolution" to those tribal communities rudely disrupted by economic development. Correspondingly, we see a change from quiescence under hierarchic social order to social conflict, from hegemony to ideological resistance and questioning of oppressive norms. We see a shift from a universal idiom to a subaltern idiom, from the social milieu of the educated middle class (*bhadralok*) to the stark lives of the lower classes (*chhotalok*). And perhaps most interestingly, we see the juxtaposition and interaction of these opposites at the level of both social relations and individual consciousness.

The stories are written by one woman and four men. Among the most important writers in the Bengali language, they represent the main genres of literature as both art and social commentary. As I was preparing this manuscript, someone asked me why I included many more men than women writing on women. Not having given much thought to the gender of each author, I was struck by the question's unstated presumption, which also made me take more conscious note of the delicate, sensitive tone of some of the male authors, especially Rabindranath and Hasan Azizul, and of the strident boldness of Mahasweta. I grew more convinced than ever that Virginia Woolf was right when she spoke, apropos of Coleridge's remark that a great mind is androgynous, of the "man-womanly" and "woman-manly" quality of creative minds.

Rabindranath (1861–1941) grew up and received his education in a family that was like a brilliant constellation of literary and artistic talents, involving itself in a number of journalistic and educational enterprises with the enthusiasm of pioneers. Undoubtedly, Rabindranath was the family's brightest and most prodigious member, bringing many facets of highly original creativity to fruition through his long life, which he lived in a strikingly organized, stable, and steadily focused manner, despite his many personal losses.[17] He himself considered his outlook, family environment, and work very much a product of the time.[18]

Apart from developing a whole new musical tradition by fusing classical and folk music, designing a new format of drama, and establishing in Santiniketan an innovative center of learning from elementary school through college, Rabindranath was a phenomenal literary creator. He was a poet, novelist, essayist, and playwright, as well as the first major writer of modern short stories in Bengali (as distinct from the tales and narrations based on the epics and the *Panchatantra* fables). His short stories, about ordinary people's lives and emotions in real social contexts, shaped and perfected this medium in the Bengali language. Most of his nearly one hundred short stories were written between the 1880s and the 1920s; their themes and tone are sensitive to the ongoing social changes through this fifty-year period, which saw the culmination of the Bengal Renaissance and the rise of nationalist sentiments.

His five stories in this collection were written in 1892–93 and 1914–15; he wrote the first three when he was just over thirty and the last two in his early fifties, when, having lost his wife and two of his children, he was totally occupied with writing, raising his other children, and running the twelve-year-old Santiniketan center. The passage of those twenty years is reflected in the stories in their social situation, the characters and their interactions, and the author's examination of oppression, especially of women, and rebellion. In an early story, "The Living and the Dead," a woman kills herself publicly to prove that she was not dead as assumed. In a later story, "Letter from a Wife," a woman writes her husband a letter of denunciation after leaving her materially comfortable but restrictive and prejudiced marital home. For both women, the catalyst is the power of love for a child or a childlike character, a love she is not allowed to act upon; but the form of rebellion differs according to the time: shaming by suicide in the first, leaving the marital home in the second. It was not uncommon in nineteenth-century Bengal for a man to marry a second time if the first wife was childless, even if he loved her (as in "The Girl in Between"). By the 1920s, however, a middle-class extended family in Calcutta would find it hard to have their son remarried while his wife lived and stayed on, no matter how much they resented her, though they could hasten her death, as in "Haimanti," a method that has persisted in one form or another.

So much has been written in English about Rabindranath's works that we need not go into detail here but simply note some points specifically relating to the five stories in this collection. His storytelling contains a unique blend of opposites. The influence of the romantic-lyrical harmony of the Vaishnava padavalis ("full of freedom in meter and expression," in his own words), which he first read in his precocious early teens ("obtained surreptitiously from the desks of elder brothers"), is pervasive in all his writings, not just his poetry. In short stories, the other influence is Western, especially of Chekhov and Turgenev, and in some of his later stories, of Shaw and Ibsen. The obvious parallel between "Letter from a Wife" and "A Doll's House" has been drawn by Chakravarty (1965) among others; but there are also some very meaningful, more subtle differences, to which I will turn shortly.

The sensitive, androgynous mind of Rabindranath is strikingly presented in the five stories in this collection. These are some of the most sensitive portrayals of the female condition in various situations and at different levels of society that I have come across in my search. I also selected these five for their interesting variation in the source and mode of oppression and the forms in which oppression was experienced and rebelled against or transcended. Four of the protagonists are middle-class women in the early nineteenth century—three in the city and one in a village—and one the wife of a landless laborer. The class aspect of oppression is muted, although other societal aspects of oppression are not. This is partly because, though it existed, the class aspect of social conflict did not quite come into focus for the Bengali intelligentsia before the turn of the century. That focus grew sharper only from the 1920s on, with the rapid increase in the number of landless people as the sharecropping peasantry became destitute, as the agrarian struggles rocked the countryside, and as the 1943 famine produced its devastation.

Class conflict is muted even in the later writings of Rabindranath, though class division is not, partly because of his humanist ideology, his belief in the essential universality of human feelings and thoughts, irrespective of class, creed, and social position. His subject is, above all else, the mind and feelings of the individual in relation to specific circumstances and social mores. Thus his stories are the least bound by time and place, while at the same time they portray a specific time and place in minute detail. They enable anyone to relate to the essentials of the oppression and the rebellion or transcendence. While reading of Chandara's punishment of Chhidam for his unintended insult of their love, we can imagine another headstrong girl in a different class, in a different society; yet we see the monstrous oppression of the girl and her man as something wrought ultimately by the exploitation of the landless peasant in rural Bengal, by the vulnerability of the poor compounded by their illiteracy, and by the oppressive hold of the mores that can make the lips speak what the heart does not mean. Mrinal's reason for leaving her marital home and the autonomy of thought that she asserts in her letter to her husband reveal modern feminist consciousness; but her reference to Meerabai, the sixteenth-century Rajput queen who left her marriage and palace life to be free to sing for the god of her love and who took as her guru a Chamar *bhakti* poet, pulls us back to her time and context. The mature Mrinal was once a village girl married at twelve into an urban family; within its confines she taught herself to read, write, and think, as was quite common in the urban Bengali middle class by the turn of this century, when the initial stirrings of nationalist sentiments inspired interest in biographies of legendary rebel characters. A spirited woman denouncing her narrow-minded husband and even leaving him for that reason is perhaps a little more common today, though today she would probably not have as her inspiration Meerabai's spiritual rebellion. Yet the instances in recent years of the suicide-murder of young wives connected with dowry dispute, and the abetted self-immolation of Roop Kanwar at eighteen on the funeral pyre of her husband in Deorala, Rajasthan, heighten the significance of this story: not only Mrinal's moral outrage at society's cruel indifference to female life, but also her emulation of Meerabai, who gave up her marriage rather than either her spiritual quest or her life. In a society in which marriage is the equivalent of sacrament for women, in which the presence of widows and unwed women is considered inauspicious, and in which leaving one's husband is regarded as sinful, Meerabai's life remains a truly revolutionary counterpoint.[19]

In the five stories by Rabindranath, the oppressor is ultimately some aspect of the cultural ideology and the social situation in which both men and women find themselves trapped because of some socially bred dysfunction of the individual will and psyche. The tragedy lies in the distortions that their personalities and relationships suffer under the tyranny of social mores and beliefs, in the havoc that ingrained ideas can play on human mind and behavior. The climax comes with the realization that habitual notions have led one to blindness, to closed doors, to barriers from more humane choices,

ultimately to becoming one's own jailer. It is then too late to change the
rules, even though the nature of the problem has been perceived. All that
remains is the shattering knowledge that the ideas one has always lived by
are wrong, oppressive, and mindless. The loss, the unraveling of accustomed
life, is often terminal, beyond redemption. Only in "Letter from a Wife" is
there no tragedy of conscience for the protagonist. She loses her battle
against bigotry to protect a helpless girl, but she remains morally undefeated
and resists the formidable powers of intimidation to which others succumb as
a matter of course. She challenges the balance of power between her values
and those of her husband and his family, rejecting the ideology they live by
and their double standards. Mrinal's humane courage contrasts with the
defeatism of her counterpart in the husband of "Haimanti."

The five stories by Rabindranath in this collection are also extraordinary
love stories; the love heightens the tragedy, making poignant the chasms
unexpectedly opened up and unbridgeable. The heroines are each spirited,
bolder than the men, even in the face of great adversity; the source of their
oppression, their consciousness of it, and the nature of their response vary
interestingly and meaningfully among the stories.

Kadambini, the meek and demure childless widow of an extended family
in "The Living and the Dead," is convinced by a strange turn of circumstances that she has "crossed the river of death," that the spirit of her dead
self is somehow stranded with the living. Profoundly alienated in this way
from her regulated life, she suddenly feels freed of all the accustomed rules of
conduct and movement in a way she had never thought possible when she
was "alive." In the end, it is her love for a baby not her own that dispels her
existential disorientation and also liberates her from habitual self-effacement.
After crossing miles of deserted village paths alone on a rainy night to see the
baby, the "ghost" of her timid self confronts the now fearful family and proceeds with uncharacteristic boldness to demonstrate that she is indeed alive.

Mrinal, the daughter-in-law of an affluent conventional family, shelters a
plain orphan girl nobody wants around. Her love for this adolescent child,
her surrogate daughter, mobilizes her courage, consciousness, and integrity
to the fullest; it makes her rise in rebellion against what she is supposed to
obey, or at least acquiesce in, like everybody else; it prompts her to reject all
the rewards for such obedience.

Haimanti's college-student young husband loves and admires her guile-
less humanity and spirited spontaneity, products of an upbringing removed
from the customs and the stifling process of female socialization among the
petty gentry of the nineteenth-century urban Bengal. He loathes the hypocrisy and tyranny of his patriarchal family, which has cramped his own spirit
and personality and is set to crush hers. He is similar to Mrinal in his
humane revulsion for conventional tyranny, but he is her antithesis in his
self-conscious inability to act upon it and defend the one he loves. By failing

to fight to save what he cherishes, he ends up loathing himself, condemned to degenerative and destructive self-pity.

In "The Punishment," a naive poor man, tired after a grueling day of exploited labor and panicked by a terrible situation, inadvertently insults his conjugal love with his unthinking use of the socially programmed line "a wife can be replaced but not a brother," and he loses his wife irrevocably. All his attempts to retrieve the mistake are sharply rejected by the outraged young woman. The story focuses on the devastated young husband as much as on the shocked wife, both victims of the oppressive social hierarchy and the treacherous norms that, internalized through repetition, substitute for thought and violate true feelings. The wife, Chandara, is an ordinary village woman except for her keen resistance of the husband's jealous efforts to control her and her anger at belittlement. This story has been interpreted differently by Sidhanta (1961, 287) as the story of a husband callously willing to let his wife die to save his brother because he could always get another wife. So it has seemed to the wife, and it is one aspect of the reality of their situation. The author, however, dwells on other aspects of the man's emotional reality, the betrayal of feelings by mores and the intimidation of those at the bottom of the social hierarchy, elements that make it a complex story of love and oppressive power relations—the tragedy of a man without social power who seeks the marital power that will allow him to dominate.

"The Girl in Between" is not just about a woman's suffering in polygamy but also about the introspection that leads her from romantic naivete to mature awareness. Harasundari comes to know the pain of recognizing her own emotional deprivation when she was a bride herself and had regarded herself as happy. "Woman serves, but she also reigns. How could it become so polarized that one woman was only a servant and the other only a queen! That took the pride out of one's service and the happiness out of the other's power." Once a believer in the capacity of love to be endlessly generous, she still tries to remain steadfast for her weak-willed, dull husband, despite the pain it causes her and the sad contempt she comes to feel for the unworthy object of her devotion. She faces the consequences of her mistaken premise about love unflinchingly. More than a victim, she is a tragic heroine, poignantly aware of the unexpected forms of human weakness she has unearthed in the ironic course of life as she looks into the depths of her romantic disillusionment and despair.

These five female protagonists are extraordinary characters, in different ways. Interestingly, each one is a childless wife who entered an extended family as a child bride and was removed from her natal family. The deprivation of filial bonds is undoubtedly an important aspect of the oppressiveness of female life in that context. The patriarchal customs of marriage isolate the young woman from her natal home and family by mandating her early marriage into a different clan and community and by requiring her to adapt to the ways of her husband's extended family. The consequences of her abrupt, premature deprivation of filial love and support, long before conjugal solidarity can develop, have been studied by anthropologists and have long formed the staple of female rituals and lores as well as of literature. Rabindranath's wife and the wives of his older brothers entered the family as brides of ten or twelve, and Rabindranath was acutely aware of the wrenching transplantation, the pain and vulnerability of a young girl torn from her own family. One wonders whether the five characters would have been as rebellious in their different ways and as unwilling to conform had they become mothers soon after marriage. The enormous importance of children in women's lives, and the energy and attention that nurturing requires, tends to diffuse and sublimate the oppression and frustration in conjugal life. A young childless wife would be far more inclined than a young mother to value emotional conjugality and to use a higher standard to judge it. The tendency to examine conjugal relations later in life, after the children have grown up, is much less common in India than in the West, because by then women have developed a dense network of relationships within the joint household and with their grown children, even if they live away. The Western type of nuclear family is less common even in urban India today, and after households divide over the family life cycle, strong cohesion is maintained informally, especially with the mother.

Of all the characters, both women and men, in these five stories by Rabindranath, Mrinal is the only one who resolutely refuses to be diminished, suppressed, or destroyed. "To stick by one's own truth is to live. I am going to live." Striving to live at peace with herself, she is uncompromising in her dissent from the hypocritical norms that she has fought but failed to dislodge, refusing to be warped by bigotry, tyranny, and pettiness. Mrinal's polar opposite is Haimanti's husband, who, in his paralysis of the natural human urge to protect the loved one, especially one helplessly dependent on that protection, is not very different from the old man in Hasan Azizul's "The Daughter and the Oleander." In both cases, this paralysis is the most crucial, even if indirect, oppressor—and not just of the primary victim. The cowardice, the knowing passivity, produces a self-oppressed and self-pitying secondary victim whose nonrebellion seems to be a key factor in the pathogenesis of oppression.

Mrinal leaves the wealth and comfort that reward obedience to stay true to her intelligence and her inopportune love, taking her inspiration from the legendary *bhakti* rebel, the queen who became a wanderer to be able to sing the songs the king forbade. Finally, facing the boundless ocean and sky, she writes her husband a letter that starts with the customary "To your lotus feet" but is signed "Mrinal who is torn off the shelter of your feet." The comparison with Ibsen's Nora has often been made, and it is known that Rabindranath read "A Doll's House" sometime before he wrote "Letter from a Wife." Though Mrinal and Nora are similar insofar as they both leave the security and privileges of marriage, there are a number of significant differences between them in personality and motivation. Mrinal's transition from conscious resistance to outright rebellion is a steady, cumulative process; Nora's from docility (or the appearance of docility) to defiance is more sudden. The catalyst for Mrinal is not any mistreatment of her but the family's callousness toward the plight of a pathetic girl, a poor relation she has been trying to shelter; Nora's outrage is at her husband's patronizing condescension toward her. Mrinal never quite plays doll's house; mentally she has always stood a bit apart from her marital home, never quite accepting its norms or adopting its attitudes. She is far more clear than Nora about how she wants to live, what she values. "A Doll's House" ends with Nora slamming the door behind her. "Letter from a Wife" is calmly written some days after Mrinal has left home on the pretext of going on a short trip. Her quarrel is with the place accorded to women in the social order, even though her personal position in it may be privileged and could be comfortable if she were not so "opinionated."

If Rabindranath was the explorer of the rarefied world of emotional sensitivity, Manik Bandyopadhyay (1908–56) was the unsparing reporter of the lower depths—the disintegrating petty bourgeoisie and the proletariat-information. He was an artist of class conflict and the related gender conflict, exposing social pathology, detecting unsuspected sources of hope, though never with any illusion. He wrote also about a period of war, the Second World War, a distant war that nonetheless wrecked Bengal's rural and urban society with a man-made famine, causing massive death, displacement, and degradation.

By the time he died at forty-eight, after a twenty-six-year writing career, Manik had published thirty-nine novels, sixteen collections of stories, and over two hundred other stories scattered in periodicals. While an undergraduate student of mathematics and science, he had decided against writing until he was thirty, because he firmly believed that one must accumulate enough experience as raw material for serious writing and also arrange the material aspects of one's life so as to have time free of the worries of earning a livelihood. Even then, on the daily long walk home from college, he would sit alone for a while by the Ballygunge lake (that was before the lights, the promenades, and the landscaping) and try to evoke images. What appeared in his mind were the faces of his "neighbors, relatives, acquaintances, with their words and gestures, faces etched with the complexities of their life, their anxieties, faces of passengers in buses and commuter trains, faces of porters and vendors, faces of weavers, fishermen and peasants who inhabited the villages near the smaller Calcutta of the time. Those faces kept appearing in my mind, clamoring to speak. Those faces made all my feelings rise to acute sensations" (1957, chap. 1). Then, one day, in an argument with college friends, he took a bet to write a story and have it published within three months in one of the three major literary journals of the time. He won the bet, and the editor asked for more. He dropped everything and started writing, and wrote until he died at forty-eight. He never escaped economic hardship.

Manik stressed the importance of the relationship between his writing and the existing literature and of his own experience.

> I write because I want to convey to others at least a fraction of my mental experience of life around me. . . . Two other elements must be combined with one's total mental experience of daily life, society, and individuals. One is the knowledge of existing literature, and awareness of its influence on one's viewpoint, consciousness of theme and format. No literature has ever arisen without the powerful influence of existing literature. The other element is a perspective from which one can look at one's experience and see what is there and what is not there, what is breaking down and what is building, what is missing and what can be fulfilling. (1957, chap. 2)

After Rabindranath, Manik is one of the most important writers of Bengali fiction, in terms of the influence that his writing style and subjects had at the time and continue to have on generations of Bengali writers. The material that is analyzed most perceptively in his work is conflict and change at the levels of the personal and the social. Most analyses of Manik's works tend to divide them into two groups: his early novels and stories, written in his twenties and thirties, and the writings of his later years.

Rabindranath was in his seventies when Manik was producing most of his early works, which focused on the contradictions and pathological aspects of the middle-class psyche. In the 1930s, there had arisen a wave of neo-realism in Bengali writing, referred to as the Kallol Yug, to which Manik's early work is loosely related.[20] Even among the notable Kallol Yug writers, who were striving to "create literature at the ground level, close to the people, leaving the world of imagination, Manik undoubtedly occupied a very special place, in terms of viewpoint, characters, analysis, and form," remarked the publisher of his collected works. "The two most striking things about his work are: the deemphasizing of storyline and drama in the portrayal of real characters in real life; and the merciless exposing of even the unconscious pretenses and contradictions, bringing to the surface the crisis and duplicity of the 'civilized' life and the degradation as well as the humanity of members of the faceless masses, the underclass."[21] Manik, however, noted that much of the new wave of realism, including his own first novel written at twenty-one, had not managed to shake free from romantic idealism:

> The realism that the Kallol group claimed to have portrayed was a spontaneous expression of the conflict between the ideal and the reality of middle-

class life, the same consciousness that dominated my early youth. That by itself
cannot revolutionize literary tradition. . . . Although the portrayals of villagers'
and coalminers' lives were perfect, they remained portrayals. Their conflict
with the wider society remained uncharted. Instead, the same middle-class
romantic feelings were expressed through the medium of slum life. Nor had the
reality of middle-class life been really revealed. The middle-class ideal of
romantic love, for example, had not been discarded as sham, but lingered on in
another context. (1957, 65–68)

Manik's later works, most of them focused on social conflict, have the clear
imprint of the galvanizing peasant movement and the traumatic events of the
1940s (particularly the devastation wrought by the 1943 famine). The combination of these upheavals profoundly affected the social fabric of Bengal,
radicalized the intelligentsia, and gave strong impetus to class consciousness
and class struggle. Before the 1940s, the time of Manik's later writings on the
subject of social conflict, the literary scene was dominated by Rabindranath
and a number of great writers in the Rabindric tradition of humanism and
individualism.

Manik remarked that his enraged rebellion against middle-class sentimentality forced him to keep looking at what was real. His early perception
of the disparities between the bhadralok and the chhotalok societies, he noted
in his memoirs, sharpened his questions about life in both strata. In the
harsh lives of the uneducated laboring classes, he could see the same realities
out in the open that in the middle classes often stay neatly hidden behind
appearances of gentility. Having recognized the concealing devices constantly used by the latter, he could see in the lives of the extremely poor the
unsatisfied needs, the crushed desires and dreams of all those apparently
happy middle-class families. Two questions grew insistent in his mind: why
and how is it that the false notion of gentility in middle-class life, the bhadralok myths, persist in spite of its reality of conflict, hypocrisy, meanness,
selfishness, pathology, artificiality, and custom-fixation; and why is it that
the less hypocritical, less artificial lives of the peasants, laborers, fisherfolk,
and outcastes find so little place in literature. Increasingly, this gap in literature, the chasm between sentiment and reality, and the deprivation of
ordinary people tormented him. At the same time, he became painfully
aware of the contradictions within himself. Born and brought up in a middle-
class family, socialized into the bhadralok values and ethos, he found himself
in revolt against them:

I was hating expressions of sentimentality at the same time that I was sen-
timental myself. I liked the genteel, cultured life, my middle-class friends, did
not entirely drop my middle-class hopes and aspirations. Yet I felt my mind
constantly poisoned by the narrowness of that life, its meanness, open or dis-
guised, its artificiality. Sometimes, I ran away from my own life to the company
of the chhotalok peasant-laborers just to be able to breathe. Other times, tor-

mented by the relentless harshness of their deprived lives and the uncovered reality of their ruthless daily existence, I ran back to my own life just to be able to breathe.(1957, 23–24).

The four Manik stories included here are good examples of his dual focus: the narrowness and hypocrisy hidden behind the presumed gentility of bhadralok life, and the courage and nobility in the relentless harshness of the deprived chhotalok lives. The stories are about four very ordinary women, ranging in age from a pubescent girl to a very old woman, none with the benefit of any education or cultural sophistication, their lives buffeted by oppressive conditions, weighed down by deprivation and grinding labor. Three of them have come to grips with their situations with the only means they have, namely, their own insight and intuition about their lives and the society they have to live in.

In the aftermath of the 1943 famine in "A Tale of These Days," Mukta, the "lost" wife of an impoverished peasant, is trying to come home with the help of social workers. Like many others, her husband had come back to their village from a futile trip in search of work and food to find his wife driven by hunger to prostitution in town. Together with his side-kicks, the self-styled pillar of this "lower-class" society tries to stir up opinion to stop this desperately poor, broken man from taking back his strayed wife; but the other desperately poor, broken men cannot quite shake their minds free from how similar all their buffeted, battered, terribly compromised lives are. Mukta, returning home in the public glare out of a life of shame, attempts with quiet determination to pick up the pieces of her conjugal life. Also determined to come home is a girl kept away from the village as mistress of the very same pillar of society. The formerly timid girl is enraged when she finds out that her mother is deranged with grief and that her lecherous "keeper" has had the gall to call a village trial to stop the peasant from taking his wife back. She manages to come to the trial. The tired people half-heartedly gathered there sit up electrified when she raises her voice to defend the peasant's wife. She then goes home to her mother, who recognizes her voice but not her ravaged face.

In "The Old Woman," the title character knows the key to survival, having lived through her misfortunes long enough to be jolly at the wedding of her great-grandson. When the bride is widowed within a year, and the family is scheming to get rid of her, the old woman calls her aside and whispers to her the tricks of survival, techniques well tested in her own life.

Young Durga, a bud briefly blooming in the muck of a city slum, faces and resolves her dilemma in "A Female Problem at a Low Level." She is the pubescent daughter of a mechanic who, maimed by a machine, is put out of work and left disabled and penniless, cynical and merciless. Surviving each day is a monumental battle with only the petty earnings of the mother, who, when she is not giving birth, is worn out by the daily round of piece-wage cleaning and washing. Some of the babus of the houses the mother works for are more keen to hire the daughter. As the crunch gets worse, even the formerly protective father starts pressing her to take the offers. Durga thinks she has a choice, a way out in the young factory worker who one day wants to marry her. Out of work now, he could get his job back by collaborating with the recruiter-foreman instead of striking and getting police beatings at the picketline. Durga sees her choice depend on his. Then, as she watches him torn between not wanting to let her down and not wanting to let the strike down, she sees his struggle for dignity as a worker alongside her struggle to survive without hating herself. She sees his choice depend on hers, and comes to a decision of her own.

Unlike these other three women, Kusum in "The Unlucky Woman" is terminally lost, so confused and numbed by the gap between her sentiments and the reality of her life that it all seems incoherent and incomprehensible. Her existential disorientation is a crippling disease, totally disabling the mind and the will. It is not a liberator from accustomed restrictions, not even in the sense it becomes so for Kadambini in "The Living and the Dead." Harried and confused, Kusum merely goes through the motions of life, and in seeking relief from misfortune, she merely sinks deeper into superstition and false sentiments, and the fantasy of dying in a fire like a *sati* joining her dead husband. Her real misfortune, the real source of her oppression, is her inability to grasp the significance of either life or death. This lower-middle-class woman's disease of consciousness is a significant counterpoint to the clear-sighted determination of the slum girl, or the peasant wife, or the girl the old woman once was, to survive in the face of the extremely oppressive conditions of their lives. Unlike Mahasweta's Giribala and funeral wailer, she is not motivated to struggle and hope even for the sake of her children.

Tarashankar Bandyopadhyay (1898–1971) is widely regarded as one of the best fiction writers in Bengal. In his earlier novels he portrayed the epochal transition in the remote rural life of Bengal. His writing is profoundly steeped in the traditional realms of the semi-arid red-soil Rarh region of rural Bengal. He was born into a declining landed family in the village of Labhpur in the Birbhum district. He went to school in Labhpur and to college in Calcutta. During his college years, he was associated with a radical militant youth group and was arrested and interned in his village. In 1930, he joined the Gandhian civil disobedience movement and was jailed. He started writing in the early 1930s after he was released, somewhat late in his life compared to either Rabindranath or Manik, but from then on he wrote continuously, drawing on his experience and the sensations that pervaded and saturated his memory.

He had lived his childhood and much of his youth in his village and the surrounding areas, soaking up the culture of the people of the Rarh region. And he wrote almost entirely about the life and culture of premodern Bengal, the agrarian culture of the Rarh region minutely observed at the ground level. His writings bring to life the variegated rural underclass of snake-charmers, corpse-handlers, outcaste bonded peasants, stick-wielders, potters, witches, Vaishnava minstrels—a great variety of vividly portrayed characters from a world on the brink of disintegration.

"The Witch" is set in a scatter of villages of untouchable communities in a remote, semi-arid area of Birbhum, before the time of roads, buses, movies, the ripples of the "green revolution," and labor contractors coming in to round up young men and women as coolies to build the monuments of economic development. It is a self-contained world, later to vanish with the inexorable advance of modernization. Tarashankar knew that world intimately, with his head and his heart, and the story is steeped in his deep understanding and respect for the feelings and the legends of those people. Throughout his boyhood and youth he had the habit of wandering among the ordinary village folk in the area, carefully listening to how they talked and what they talked about.

"The Witch" is the most acclaimed of Tarashankar's short stories. He worked on several versions of it. The one included here—the one he is known to have been the most satisfied with—was first published in 1940. It is well complemented by a subsequent, less fictionalized account published in 1951, an excerpt from which is given following the 1940 story. Both are based on his personal knowledge of an ostracized, "cursed" old woman who used to live on the edge of his own village. He had heard about her all through his childhood and adolescence, and had seen her a few times. The old witch who was once a young woman with the lovely name Swarna lived alone, away from people and the green paddy fields, in a hut under an old banyan tree on the far end of a large barren stretch of sandy dust. "She herself believed that she was a witch. She believed that her witch power poisoned her love and turned it into a lethal arrow. . . . When she cried, she frantically wiped the tears off her eyes and shuddered if a drop fell on the ground because witch tears would scorch the kindly bosom of mother earth."

Unlike Mahasweta's "Witch-Hunt," which is about social oppression and exploitation, scapegoating and deceit, Tarashankar's witch story is about how belief systems are formed in folk culture and how social oppression is personally internalized in a closed world. The villagers fear the witch, but they can also feel her misfortune. They know, as she does, that she has human feelings but is the helpless host of an evil lodged inside her like a coiled cobra, ready to strike whoever crosses its path. Living away from people's homes, she sits alone all day, gazing at the midday haze over the dusty barren land, recalling how she came to be seen, and see herself, as a witch. The story is about belief as a source of oppression, and the relentless frustration and despair of seeing oppression as inescapable, as "what is written on one's forehead."

And yet, even as she thinks of her oppression as inescapable, she is not convinced of its justice or "naturalness," nor entirely resigned to it. She keeps sorting and resorting the experience of her terrible life in the hope of making sense of the oppressive belief. From time to time she lets her human emotions be expressed to a stranger, perhaps in search of a piece of evidence to falsify the oppressive belief. And although most of the time she regards her witch identity as her fate, which she cannot alter, which not even the gods can alter, she has never failed to use her survival strategies—scaring people to get alms and to keep away her tormentors, and fleeing when things become too intolerable. This story of oppressive belief, the victim's internalization of it and struggle against it within her own mind, is curiously also a moving story of stubborn resistance against the cruellest of society's impositions.

Mahasweta Devi (1926–) moved from East to West Bengal as an adolescent, and studied at Visva-Bharati and Calcutta University. An important literary and political influence on her, in addition to her family,[22] was her early association with the Gananatya, a group of highly accomplished, keenly political actors and writers, who took the revolutionary step of bringing theater to the villages on themes of burning interest in the thirties and forties in rural Bengal. Subsequently, she became a writer and journalist herself, while holding a job as a college teacher in Calcutta. Over a period of years, she has studied and lived among the tribal and outcaste communities in the southwest of West Bengal and the southeast of Bihar, rural areas where capitalist exploitation combines with feudal oppression. She became closely involved as a participant-observer and political-anthropologist in the late 1960s. She continued visiting those areas and collecting information directly from the lives of the rural and urban underclass, and from many who were involved in the Naxalite struggle either as peasants or as urban youths. She transformed her observations of actual situations, persons, dialects, and idioms into her unique style of narrative realism.[23] In 1984, she took early retirement from her teaching position in order to give more time to writing, reporting, and social activism. In all these activities, but especially in her writing, her keen anthropological work has been the primary raw material. She has described her writing of fiction as inseparable from her work as an investigative journalist and editor of a "people's" magazine:

> I have always believed that the real history is made by ordinary people. I constantly come across the reappearance, in various forms, of folklore, ballads, myths and legends, carried by ordinary people across generations. . . . The reason and the inspiration for my writing are those people who are exploited and used, and yet do not accept defeat. For me, the endless source of ingredients for writing is in these amazingly noble, suffering human beings. Why should I look

for my raw materials elsewhere, once I have started knowing them? Sometimes it seems to me that my writing is really their doing.[24]

The first five stories by Mahasweta are set in southeastern Bihar during
the mid-1970s, in a belt of semilandless tribals and untouchables effectively
denied the rights guaranteed by the Constitution, even a legal minimum
wage, and marginalized by the process of economic development. The socioeconomic situation is polarized, agitated, and violent, with the capitalist
forms of exploitation reinforcing the old forms of oppression by high-caste
landlords and moneylenders. Class exploitation has combined with, not replaced, the age-old caste oppression. There are other new elements in the
scene: politicians seeking votes and largesse, officials supposedly protecting
the underdogs, Sarvodaya workers trying to change the exploiters' hearts,
radical city youths trying to forge links with rustic comrades, administrators
of famine relief, an occasional visiting intellectual, perhaps like the author
herself, trying to learn about the modes of rebellion against oppression, both
past and present. The tribals and the untouchables, tyrannized and exploited
by landlords and moneylenders, deceived and let down by double-dealing
officials, patronized by educated radicals, are beginning to wage their own
struggle. Drawing on her years of first-hand observation, Mahasweta writes
these stories in a mixture of tribal or folk dialects and urbane Bengali, whose
marvelous effect in the original cannot fully come across in translation;
the stories remain powerful, however, in their themes and portrayals.[25]

"The Witch-Hunt" is set in a severe drought in a cluster of villages of
tribals and untouchables. Manipulating their myths and beliefs, the priest of
the nearby town temple has planted the witch scare; he is very powerful both
economically and politically (the police officer and the politicians come to
touch his feet and seek his advice). After a series of frenzied witch-hunts,
when the tribesmen come upon the cruel truth about the identity of the
witch, and how they have been manipulated, they try to channel their outrage into revolt. The Oraon chief, whose great-grandfather had once fought
the British and been hanged for treason, decides to end the long period of
quiescence. Out of the witch-hunt are born class consciousness and class
struggle.

In "Paddy Seeds," a storm is gathering and then raging as the land-poor
outcastes demand the legal minimum wage from their Rajput landlord, who
owns hundreds of acres, ten guns, a private army of thugs, and the passive
connivance of the local police. The protagonist, violently jolted from the sideline into the eye of the storm, is "a wizened old man, covered with wrinkled
leathery skin, clad only in a loincloth." His crafty personal battle of wits with
the powerful, his manipulative obsequiousness, is not unlike the strategies of
indirect personal power that women learn to deploy to counteract patriarchal
domination. When he finds himself trapped in the landlord's diabolical

scheme, he finally deploys his cunning, his only tool of personal survival, in a solitary guerrilla war on his personal and class enemy. It is a story of despair as well as hope. It is a story of rebellion against tyranny at several levels, personal and social, economic and cultural.

In "Dhowli," a young outcaste girl has the misfortune of having the Brahman landlord's young son fall in love with her. It is common for a high-caste landlord to have an untouchable mistress and children by her, supported by him to make sure that the "door" once used by "a lion" never receives "the pigs and the sewer rats." What is uncommon is that the boy is too confused to act upon his position of power. The code of honor of the wealthy and powerful, which is not unlike the colonial code of honor, expects him to be her patron. The girl moves from grief and shame to embittered rage, from fearful timidity to emboldened efforts to survive. This the powerful cannot tolerate. They contrive to drive her out of her home and village. She does not weep until she notices how unchanged nature is on the day an innocent girl is crowned with the ignobility of the city whore.

An interesting minor character in the story of Dhowli is Sanichari, the medicine woman. Poor and outcaste, she is sought even by the powerful, who are helpless before her knowledge of their diseases of body and mind. She is indispensable, with her knowledge of medicinal herbs and her help in preventing stillbirth, aborting unwanted fetuses, and holding onto straying husbands. With her informational resources, intelligence, and biting tongue, she keeps crossing back and forth between the worlds of the oppressor and the oppressed, chastising some and shaping the opinion of others. She may not be powerful enough to stop Dhowli's banishment, but she will remain a powerful social presence, someone hard to suppress or ignore, someone who, despite her poverty and low social status, will use her indispensability to confront the most powerful, to voice her views of what is fair and what is not.

The funeral wailer in Mahasweta's third story is also much in demand. She was never able to shed tears when her own loved ones died, as she always had to struggle frantically to stay alive and keep alive what remained of her family. By the time she finally develops a business of funeral wailing, she has no family left. The irony of her situation strikes her, but she is not one to indulge in self-pity. With the demand for her service growing, she decides to train and employ women who have had to become prostitutes to feed themselves, and in the process to retrieve her son's widow, whom earlier she had hated for becoming a whore. The funeral wailer is not yet as articulate, as developed in leadership qualities, as the medicine woman. The process of weathering her terrible personal losses and misfortunes, the alchemy of sorrow and despair, gradually produces in her a positive resolution. She starts fighting for others with the same tenacity with which she has fought all her life for the survival of her family. There seems to be more of Hercules than Sisyphus in this poor, artless woman's determination to nurture what she has left rather than weep for what she has lost. She is the opposite of "The Unlucky Woman," who sheds tears by the bowlful when misfortune strikes.

"Strange Children" is about the prejudice and the condescension of officials and the urban educated toward tribal life and culture. The tribals are the casualties of economic development projects, which disenfranchise them for the benefit of other people in other parts of the country. To this injury is added insult, in the form of the patronizing gentlemen officials. The location is a remote hilly area with barren ferrous soil. Unable and unwilling to till the infertile soil, the community lives its demoralized, ebbing life on food handed out by the government. Underneath the sullen resignation is anger and hatred toward its violators. A new relief officer wants to live up to his reputation for efficient and compassionate service, refusing to follow the bureaucratic line of least initiative. One night the zealous official is faced with a reality that nothing in his training and his life has prepared him for. The shattering of an official provides a little amusement to the grievously and irreversibly wronged; but it does not end the tyranny and condescension of the dominant culture and its official elite.

Mahasweta's sixth story, "Giribala," has a different regional setting from the other five, and in it the source of oppression and the mode of revolt are also different. Giribala grew up as a peasant's daughter in the Murshidabad district, in the north central part of West Bengal. Accustomed to the saying that a daughter born is already gone to husband or death, she sadly but obediently goes to live with her worthless husband and struggles along to bring up her children and build her household—with hard work, not charity or trickery. But it is to trickery that she loses two daughters. Naturally quiet, she is enraged when people try to console her with the same old proverb. She finally does what she has always been told was improper for a woman to do. She rebels—and not just against her husband, but against the norm of wifely compliance, a norm that her mother follows at all cost and she herself has been following until now. Her least verbalized but perhaps profoundest rebellion is against her own mother's fatalistic compliance or acquiescence and passive failure to protect her daughter. In the shock of her grief, she rages at the conventional discounting of daughters and the resignation to their suffering as inevitable. When she cries, she cries from regret for not rebelling earlier, and from anger at all those who can let their children down, whether out of greed or concern for norms of propriety.

In Mahasweta's "Giribala" and "Witch-Hunt," as also in Rabindranath's "Letter from a Wife," the catalyst for the rebellion is the shock of finding out that one can be tricked into letting one's child (or a childlike person) be abused. What seems to spark the grief and the regret for not rebelling earlier is the anger at the terrible price exacted by social and familial conventions as tools of oppression. Compliance has its rewards and costs, but so does rebellion. The mentally liberating and regenerative effect of the rebellion in these three stories contrasts sharply with the degenerative self-pity of the cowardly husband of Haimanti and the hypocritical father in "The Daughter and the Oleander."

Hasan Azizul Huq (1938–), the foremost writer of short stories in Bangladesh in recent years, was born in West Bengal, in Jabagram in the Bardhaman district. He knew the red-soil Rarh region of Bengal and its people that Tarashankar wrote about. After finishing his schooling there, he went in 1954 to study in Khulna in East Pakistan, where his married sister lived, and then to Rajshahi University, where he received his M.A. in philosophy in 1960. The next year, his family moved from their Jabagram home to Khulna, after the long-drawn-out arrangements for the transfer were finally cleared. After a series of college teaching jobs, Hasan Azizul returned to Rajshahi University in 1973 as a professor of philosophy, where he has stayed since.

Although Hasan Azizul cultivated his literary talents from his high school days, the conscious decision to be a literary interpreter of society, of the changes and turmoils that he had observed and experienced, was probably made in 1960 with his highly acclaimed short story "Shakun." The first three stories included here were written in the mid-1960s and published in a 1967 collection that was reprinted several times. It was the second of his eight collections of stories published so far. His short stories are powerful in their treatment of both peasant and urban middle-class culture. The peasant stories are particularly notable for their folk realism and authenticity. "Amrityu Ajiban" ("Through Death and Life") is a marvelous example. A number of his stories study the social and psychological pathology generated by the Partition of Bengal, its immediate impact and aftereffects in the form of disruption and uprooting of ordinary lives, relationships, and hopes. "The Daughter and the Oleander" is one of the best examples in this category. The fourth story, in the context of the Bangladesh war of independence in 1971, was first published in 1975 in a collection with several other stories on related themes.

The fact that Hasan Azizul lived the first sixteen years of his life in West Bengal and spent his early youth through middle age in Bangladesh brings a vital dimension of social perception to his writings. His close familiarity with the social and cultural lives in both Bengals, the friendships he has maintained from his Rarh Bengal days, his experience spanning cultural settings, attitudes, and sociopolitical contexts, different in so many ways yet similar in so many others—all these are reflected in the cross-religious configuration of the characters in many of his stories. The focus on the problems that involve and yet cut across religious identities is indeed a prominent aspect of the post-1940s Bengali literature. The peaceful coexistence of people of different religions is not a mere literary phenomenon; it is neither romanticism nor purposive realism but a reflection of something very real and natural in the ordinary daily lives in ordinary times. In a very real sense, it is the sustained backdrop, the counterweight to the violent eruptions that have threatened it from time to time; it is like a powerful current periodically disturbed, but not eliminated, only modified in the aftermath of each conflagration. In a recent interview, Hasan Azizul notes that the individuals in his writing are not fashioned after abstract humanist ideals in the tradition of Rabindranath.[26] For a writer who has lived through the last four decades and wants to use that experience as raw material, it is hard not to bring to the forefront the oppression and the exploitation, in which communal division is but one factor. Writers, in their belief and personal relationships, may be above sectarianism, but they cannot realistically deny its existence as a force, destructive or otherwise, in the society in which they live. A society's divisions can be neither assumed away, nor steamrolled.[27] The people who make up society in their various relationships are divided by religion and community, by wealth and the lack of it, by education and illiteracy, by the work they do and the work they do not do. In his writing, Hasan Azizul strives to show people as they are, as they behave and interact in their situations, because, he believes, "it is only by examining the intertwined elements of social conflict, strand by strand, that the covers can be pulled away." In this sense, Hasan Azizul is one of the most significant transcommunal writers of Bengal.

The underclass characters in "The Daughter and the Oleander" are both Hindu and Muslim. The story's backdrop is the awkward, hopeless transplantation of a family from its ancestral home and well-rooted life to a different region and setting, something Hasan Azizul's own family experienced. The subject is the pathological disorientation that this can produce, particularly in the older members, when combined with poverty and maladjustment. Hasan Azizul remarks that he has seen these lives, lives like worn-out rags, similar to the old man's in this story. He says the tears of the old man at the end of the story are not so much sorrow or grief as a viscous mixture of frustration, regret, hatred, and misdirected anger, "a mixture similar to the blood and pus that collect inside an abscess." Although the senseless tragedy of the Partition forms the backdrop to the old man's pitiful demoralization, there seems to be something more to his and the young procurer's hopelessness, something that can go terribly wrong in the psyche of the declining sections of the middle class. The backdrop to the moral crisis, the hypocritical pretense of respectability while cynically giving up its substance, could just as well be any external crisis, such as unemployment (which it is for the young man). The opposite of the old man and his submissive wife is Mahasweta's Giribala, and Giribala's husband a vagabond version of the cynical old man. In this collection, among the stories written from the 1930s on, the moral disintegration of the recently impoverished sections of those socialized into the bourgeois values stands out in sharp contrast to the instances of tenacity, even integrity, among the laboring classes struggling to survive in chronic poverty.

Hasan Azizul's stories are alive with insights into the middle-class (or pseudo middle-class) psyche on one side, and peasant culture and symbolism on the other, as the four stories in this collection illustrate. "The Daughter and the Oleander" is about the moral disability of a father, the meek submission of a mother to a daughter's oppression, and the impotent rage of an unemployed youth. The story follows the two-rupee clients, going like thieves in the night for the "smooth golden body" sold inside the home of a displaced family, and focuses on a derelict young man's acute sensation of the winter night, its changing winds and shades of darkness, the cold bloom of the moon, the sleeping homes he walks by, and the lush oleander in the bare yard. The clients and the sellers are terribly impoverished, both economically and morally. "In Search of Happiness," on the other hand, is about a college-educated young woman. Well married by the standards cherished by her and countless middle-class girls like her, she finds herself inexplicably depressed and plagued with headaches, especially in the company of her husband. Surrounded by the material objects of her dream, she is a pathologically alienated victim of a culture that feeds and is fed on female dependence and consumerism. It is the all too familiar culture of the upwardly mobile sections of the lower middle-class. Dolled up inside the doll's house of her fantasy, she stagnates in anomie and withdrawal, which she wonders about but does not quite comprehend. In her inability to deal with the gap between sentiment and reality she is similar to Kusum in "The Unlucky Woman," despite the differences in their education and economic level, and the four decades of modernization and economic growth separating their times.

"Through Death and Life," in contrast with the above two stories by Hasan Azizul, is about the near-landless peasant Karam Ali's life, his stubborn struggle, and his death. The story is permeated with Karam Ali's haunting visions of life and death, symbolized respectively by the coming of the rains and the cobra he has accidentally disturbed. The monsoon has just arrived, and it is time to plow the soil, plant the seeds, and toil toward yet another annual cycle of life. But he loses his bullock. He wants to see the somber beauty of the dark rainclouds, the soft green of the tender seedlings, the wet brown sod about to be turned into growing fields. But the promise of life's renewal, the vision of nature rewarding labor with food, is blocked by the specter of a giant hooded head with bared fangs and a cold fixed stare. In a flash of lightning, he glimpses the village as a whole, his familiar world with its many relentless struggles for survival, including his own, held in the monstrously grown mouth. The snake symbolizes to him not only cruel defeat but the ruthless and inscrutable adversary in the constant battle of life, and therefore also a measure of the courage of those waging the battle undeterred by the prospect of defeat.

"A Day in Bhushan's Life" sees a village marketplace full of small, dark-skinned Bengali peasants gunned down by the big, fair-skinned men of the Pakistani army. The stumpy peasant, who has come to the market to sell a few vegetables and catch his lazy son, hears machine-gunfire for the first time in his life and sees a crowd of stunned villagers killed. In a fleeting scene in the half-daze of Bhushan's last moments, a young mother nestling her baby is trying to reach the cover of a tamarind tree. When the baby is hit, she stops to shout in Bengali at the Urdu-speaking men and challenge them. When Bhushan himself is suddenly within a couple of feet of one of them, the muscles of his peasant hands tighten, and for a second his body is undecided whether to go for the killer's throat or to comfort his dying son. His last deliberate action before certain death is to cradle his dying son like a mother rather than try to smash the head of a viper. The last moments of Bhushan's life illustrate the convergence of the female and the peasant, which is one of the ideas underlying this collection.

This collection, as we have noted, illustrates the similarities, the differences, and the connections between the forms of oppression, and therefore also between the forms of rebellion or nonrebellion. It gives us a glimpse of the dynamics of conflicting pressures in various situations within the culture of oppression. We see the shifts between submission (to oppressive ideology) and rebellion (in the form of subversive or passively defiant counterculture). There are the clever survival strategies of the oppressed as they try to manipulate the contradictions of the system to relieve their disadvantage. There are tragic defeats, the process of defeat itself educative for the defeated. There are also cases of hopelessly passive defeatism and escapist self-pity. Then there are the conscious acts of liberation, of positive rebellion, of rejection of accepted notions. In some stories they occur in severe pain or after great loss, though, as some other stories show, these are neither necessary nor sufficient conditions for revolt.

One reason I put these seemingly diverse stories together is that I have always been struck by the parallels, the connections, and the points of intersection between the oppression of women in India and that of peasants, untouchables, and other stigmatized groups. Class exploitation and social and cultural oppression by gender, caste, or ethnicity often overlap and actually reinforce each other. That gender hierarchy is embedded in other socioeconomic hierarchies supports, and is supported by, my selection of stories. The relentless nature of oppression in society derives precisely from its many facets and interactions. The nexus of oppression—between familial and societal patriarchy, between patriarchy and caste/ethnic hierarchy, between class exploitation and social denigration—is not a theoretical construct but the stuff of constant experience. It is at the core of consciousness for both the oppressed and the oppressors.

I was drawn particularly to the points of intersection and the qualitative similarities between the oppression of women and that of the marginalized, the economically exploited, the socially outcaste, and the "internally colonized," whether they be the tribals in southeastern Bihar or Bengali peasants in pre-1971 Pakistan. In seventeen of the twenty stories, the protagonist is either female or a member of a denigrated (outcaste, tribal, ethnic) community; and in at least four she is both. In six stories, the protagonist is a woman belonging to the middle or upper socioeconomic strata. In six others, she is a member of the laboring classes (peasants, wage laborers), in three cases also an untouchable outcaste. The woman's viewpoint, thoughts, and behavior form the central focus, the direct subject, of thirteen stories. In two or maybe three stories, she is the passive subject. In five or maybe six, she is a tragic heroine, the tragedy arising not from a contradiction within herself in the classical tradition (except perhaps for Harasundari), but from the crushing or dissipation of her personal battle of resistance. In three, she is the counterpoint to the constrictive social and familial patriarchy, from within which she battles: one (Haimanti) is crushed, though not subdued, by it; the other two (Mrinal and Giribala) choose to leave it rather than have their personal integrity either crushed or subdued.

In three of the stories, the oppression of the female is seen through male eyes and reflected in male actions and reactions. The importance of this perspective is pivotal in the perpetuation of or the resistance to patriarchal oppression. The failure of the male to live up to his own self in relation to the female, the recognition of his own defeat and degradation in hers, is a potentially powerful basis of transformation for him. We know that this perspective was important in Bengal in the nineteenth-century male-led reform movement. Haimanti's young educated husband, starting off in high spirits, ends up hating himself for being unable to stand up to the autocratic patriarchy. He mocks himself and the supreme male role model in the Hindu culture: "If I am not to sacrifice my true feelings for what people regard as proper, then what about the ages of social indoctrination running in my blood? . . . Don't you know that on the day the people of Ayodhya demanded the banishment of Sita, I was among them? Those who sang the glory of that sacrifice, generation after countless generation, I was one of them too." In "The Daughter and the Oleander," the hypocritical father suffers a degenerative disease of self-hatred. At the end of "The Witch-Hunt," in contrast, the tribesmen stoning the witch they believe to be responsible for the drought and related calamities silently grieve after discovering their mistake, and then resolve to fight the enemy within that gives the enemy without such a helping hand in oppressing them.

The massacre committed by the Pakistani army to suppress the "puny" Bengalis' demand for autonomy and democratic power-sharing parallels the destruction of a rebellious "lower-class" woman like Dhowli by powerful, socially "superior" men. The mowing down of villagers gathered in the marketplace parallels the brutal killing of landless peasants by gun-toting blue-blooded Rajput landlords in southeastern Bihar in "Paddy Seeds." "A Day in Bhushan's Life," set at the beginning of the Bangladesh war, illustrates the parallel that is often drawn between imperialism and sexual subjugation; the imperialist is outraged the same way the patriarch is when confronted with the demand for independence from those he has always ruled, whose obedience he has always taken for granted. The very gesture of the ruled seeking autonomy produces the maddening anxiety in their rulers, the excessive brutality to teach them a lesson.

Revealing parallels between different forms of oppression is not the only purpose of this anthology. Another is to present various angles on who or what is the real oppressor, offer various perspectives on the mechanisms of oppression. Oppression does not always take the form of outright exploitation, subjugation, and antagonism. Love itself can oppress—when one is slave to false notions of love, like the young couple in "The Punishment" and young Harasundari in "The Girl in Between." Sometimes an idea or belief oppresses, especially when it is internalized by the victim, a process often condescendingly called "false consciousness" or the subconscious means of handling "cognitive dissonance," overused notions that can be mistaken and misleading. Underneath the seeming compliance in many of the cases, under widely different circumstances, exists a variety of struggles, resistance, rebellion, and revolt—at the level of ideology and thought, and sometimes also at the level of action, gesture, and cultural practice.

The stories focus mostly on the thoughts and perceptions of the oppressed, on their reflections on their personal situation and the social order, and on their reactions, which take the form of resistance, revolt, sublimation, or transcendence. At the same time, they offer glimpses of the thoughts of the oppressors and of their accomplices, witting and unwitting. In some of the stories, both sides of the process of oppression exist inside the individual mind—indeed, certain beliefs ultimately hold more oppressive power than either physical or economic coercion. The most crucial step in the rebellion of both Mrinal and Giribala involves actively rejecting an accepted notion and violating a norm. In other cases, brutal force and coercion are formidable deterrents to outright rebellion even when the ideology of hierarchy or the imposition of stigmatized identity is rejected by the subordinate group or individual.[28] Mahasweta's stories illustrate this, and also show when and how fear is finally overcome. In many of the stories the oppressor is clear-cut, black and white. In some, the oppression, the consciousness, and the revolt are clearly class-based, even if they are played out in an individual context. In others, the nominal oppressors are themselves victims of the real oppressor: the oppressive features of the social order, the familial order, and certain social norms.

ON THE FACES OF OPPRESSION AND
THE MODES OF RESISTANCE

The forms of oppression and resistance are particularly complex in a society in which the traditional hierarchies of age, sex, and caste have combined with increasing class stratification. In a context that combines the oppression of feudalism (agrarian, patriarchal) with the exploitation of labor through control of land, capital, organizational power, and the means of coercion, it is practically impossible to separate economic exploitation from sociocultural oppression.[29] By the same argument, it is unrealistic to categorize resistance, struggle, and rebellion by class, caste, ethnicity, and gender. The balance of evidence seems to be that, according to their specific needs, the oppressed groups try to form alliances on the basis of a wide variety of folk beliefs, or what currently is called subaltern ideology.

One reason why neither oppression nor resistance should be divided into categories is that the categories intersect and interact, producing results that are often quite complex. The oppression of a tribal or outcaste peasant woman is a compound of oppression by gender, class, and caste/ethnicity: it is economic, social, cultural, and sexual. Another reason against such categorization is that there are parallels and connections, especially between the oppression of women and the oppression of outcastes or tribals. And these parallels and connections, no matter how they are viewed theoretically or separated for analytical convenience, are actually perceived and experienced as such by the oppressed groups themselves. This comes out quite clearly in ethnographic evidence, as also in this collection of stories.

The nature of gender oppression, for example, varies according to class, caste, and ethnicity. The hold of the patriarchal family in Bengal, and in India for that matter, varies significantly among ethnic communities and across the class strata, both ideologically and in its material basis. Women do not constitute a collectivity cutting across the socioeconomic strata any more than men, because they do not have enough in common in their experience. For women in the subordinate classes, whether land-poor peasants or landless laborers, oppression comes in the form not just of beatings from their husbands, but of sexual exploitation by employers, landlords, labor contractors, merchants, sometimes even the police. Tribal and outcaste women may be dominated as wives, and as women within their own community, as middle-class women also are, but they rightly perceive their own oppression, along with their menfolk's, more in terms of the economic and extraeconomic exaction to which they are subjected by virtue of their subordinate position in society. Their oppression in the arena of class and caste relations is far weightier, objectively and subjectively, than their oppression in the arena of family and community relations. The laboring classes perceive their lack of material assets and education, which results in the appropriation of the fruits of their labor, as far more crucial than the gender-biased distribution of the little they possess. This perception is central to folk feminism in a country like India, or to black feminism in a country like the United States, as distinct from middle-class feminism.[30] It also explains why class struggle so often takes the form of outcaste and tribal ethnic movements that advocate civil rights and oppose social denigration as well as economic exploitation.

In the Indian subcontinent, it is not difficult to see the parallels between gender oppression and caste and ethnic oppression, even when these do not occur together. The ethnic and gender aspects of class exploitation are hard to miss.[31] No one is surprised that the victims of the riots before and after the 1947 Partition were disproportionately the poor. Having the religion of Islam in common was not enough to keep together East and West Pakistan in the face of ethnic domination and an unequal, exploitative economic relationship. Common experience tells us that the kind of oppression that a powerful class/caste/ethnic sector considers intolerable within its own sector it sanctions or at least accepts as normal in its treatment of subordinate groups. The subordinate groups, acutely aware of the double standards and of the hierarchic structure of oppression, see their own strategies for coping not just at the level of resisting material exploitation, but also in ideological terms, at the level of resisting the ideas that legitimize the oppressive hierarchy. "If the 'function' of social ideology is to legitimate existing structures of domination, then power conflict necessarily takes the form also of conflict in the domain of ideology" (Chatterjee 1988, 379).

Mahasweta's "Strange Children" centers around the conflicting ideologies of the Agariya tribals, marginalized and victimized in the development process, and of the state and its modernizing elite—government technicians and administrators. The surviving fugitive Agariyas, who long ago butchered a mineral exploration team for dynamiting a hill they considered to be the abode of their gods, are helped by the later-day Agariya youths. The honest, well-meaning administrator's kindly patronizing does not make the youths forget their primeval ideological loyalty, nor does it persuade them to see the state functionaries as anything other than their exploiters, even though they must depend on government-supplied drought relief. Being reduced to utter dependency on outsiders is especially oppressive and humiliating in the tribal communal ideology. Since they perceive their oppression in the form of the intrusion of government officials contemptuous of their "primitive" beliefs, their revolt is also at the ideological level of refusing to accept the officials' advice and help. We see the primitive state of the Agariyas in a losing battle against the modern state of India, using their tribal beliefs against the Hindu religious beliefs as well as the bourgeois etatist belief in modernization.

In "The Witch-Hunt" too, a drought has brought in relief officials and social workers, but the main oppressive power for the tribal and untouchable villagers in the area is feudal, in the form of the landed upper-caste families, especially the politically and economically powerful temple priest. The tension grows around the priest's contempt for them; the final crisis is their discovery that he has deceived and manipulated them. The ideological conflict is then transformed into a class struggle fueled by their consciousness of how they are exploited. To an urban intellectual whom he has befriended, the tribal chief vows to battle the economic exploitation, using tribal loyalty and the memory of past revolts.

Mahasweta's funeral wailer takes to manipulating the feudal values of her (and her people's) ruthless exploiters when she finds a way to turn their desire for a "status item" (public wailing by poor women at the funeral of a landlord-patron) into a means to fill empty stomachs. Since the landlords recover the losses they incur from the overspending at funerals by exploiting the outcaste and tribal peasants and laborers even more, the funeral wailer's strategy does not quite amount to class struggle. But it does amount to the conscious subversion of hated values of the wealthy powerful by the destitute powerless. It is also an attempt to exact some compensation for the oppression of the outcaste poor women who were formerly patronized but later dumped by the wealthy men.

In "Paddy Seeds," we see wealthy landlords tacitly supported by the state in the conflict with land-poor peasants over higher wages. The period, from the mid-seventies to the late seventies, is significant because it follows the Naxalite peasant movement and is followed by the repressive Emergency rule. The outcaste peasants are highly conscious of the mode of their exploitation; they are also aware that the alignment between the government functionaries and their semifeudal local oppressors is partial and somewhat flexible. They are simultaneously aware of the corruption of the functionaries and on the lookout for any opening for useful alliance, any possibility of having some public institution or functionary as a buffer against the oppression and an ally in their battle for the legal minimum wage. They are oppressed by the police raids, though some have learned to tackle them. They are sarcastic about the Gandhian idea of Bhoodan, or land redistribution through voluntary giving. But they know that to outmaneuver, or at least withstand, their local oppressors they need to take advantage of externally powerful outsiders like the Harijan welfare department officer and the occasional "good" bureaucrat, who wants to implement the law and whom the landlord does not seem to be able to buy off.

In recent years, we have seen increasing attention turned to the "everyday forms of resistance," "subaltern history and ideology," "social consciousness of subordinate classes," and to "elite cognitive failure" as opposed to "subaltern cognitive failure."[32] As Scott puts it, it is important to understand

> what much of the peasantry does "between revolts," . . . the prosaic but constant struggle between the peasantry and those who seek to extract labor, food,

taxes, rents and interest from them, . . . the Brechtian—or Schweikian—forms of class struggle. . . . What is missing from the picture of periodic explosions is the underlying vision of justice that informs them and their specific goals and targets. The explosions themselves, with their mortal risks, normally come only after a protracted struggle on different terrain. (1985, xv–xvi, 29–30, 37)

More than thirty years earlier, Manik Bandyopadhyay, in a Bengali article on what he regarded as progressive realism in literature, remarked:

To think, or give the impression, that the peasants', and other common people's, struggle against oppression is expressed only in the form of confrontation and battle is to deny the very core of their struggle, to reduce their life-permeating resistance to a few discrete, temporally limited events. The reality of their struggle lies in its centrality for their lives and their minds. The peasant's struggle today is not just for two-thirds of the crop he grows, but also in his thinking that it is wrong to treat his wife the way he used to. He may still lower his head to the priest in the temple or the Mullah in the mosque, but he does so with much less conviction. . . . Progressive realism is not just showing the actual battles for land that peasants are engaging in with mere sticks. That would be a narrow, misleading portrayal of the peasants' real, constant struggle. (1957, 114–15)[33]

The moment at which men and women in the economically exploited and socially oppressed group actually decide to fight together against their oppressors is the central event in two of Manik's stories included here: in the perception of Durga in "A Female Problem at a Low Level" and in the quiet determination of a peasant and his wife to confront the bullying of the self-appointed moral guardians in "A Tale of These Days."

Some of Mahasweta's stories, anthropological in idiom and semi-documentary in account, are saturated with the theme of the constant guerrilla tactics of the powerless, the resistance of extreme exploitation by means of what Scott calls "low-profile techniques such as false compliance, foot-dragging, feigned ignorance, dissimulation, slander, gossip, sabotage, and so on" (1985, xvi). Set in rural areas of southeastern Bihar during the seventies, they remind one of Michel Foucault's point that, in Colin Gordon's words, "the category of resistance cannot be made to exclude its (supposedly) 'primitive' or 'lumpen' forms of manifestation; . . . the binary division between resistance and non-resistance is an unreal one. The existence of those who seem not to rebel is a warren of minute, individual, autonomous tactics and strategies which counter and inflect the visible facts of overall domination, and whose purposes and calculations resist any simple division between the political and the apolitical" (1980, 257).

In some of the stories, we also catch a glimpse of the point at which indirect resistance turns into direct rebellion: in "Paddy Seeds," in old Dulan's climactic shift from his usual low-key tactics for personal survival; in "The Witch-Hunt," in the Oraon chief's decision to fight after discovering that he and his people have been manipulated by their oppressor and exploiter. The catalyst for the big step varies, but some similarities stand out: in "The Witch-Hunt," "Giribala," and "Letter from a Wife," the catalyst is the cruel deception of one's helpless child or a childlike figure. Prompted by her realization of how oppressive is the process in which young peasant women become marketplace prostitutes, the old funeral wailer stops thinking of them as bad women and attempts to avenge their wrongs in her limited and indirect way. The turning point from personal to political for Dulan, at the level of consciousness and action for the collectivity, comes when the class struggle going on around him hits him personally, when he has been manipulated into becoming the oppressor's accessory.

Indian peasants, outcastes, and women have long been cited as archetypal examples of fatalism and of the hegemonic hold of elite ideology on the consciousness of the subordinate classes or groups. Barrington Moore, Jr., claims that "all these people felt that their sufferings were unavoidable. For some victims such suffering appeared to a degree inevitable and legitimate. People are evidently inclined to grant legitimacy to anything that is or seems inevitable no matter how painful it may be. Otherwise the pain might be intolerable" (1978, 459). Only in the last few years has this view come under serious criticism. As Scott puts it, one may "claim that the exploited group, because of a hegemonic religion or social ideology, actually accepts its situation as a normal, even justifiable part of social order. . . . This argument asks us to believe that, for subordinate classes, the larger structure of domination is typically experienced in the same way in which a peasant might experience the weather" (1985, 39, 324). In her anthropological study of untouchable communities in South India, Mencher (1980) notes the ways in which they reject or counteract their imposed identity, which they experience as sheer exploitation. That they do not usually act out or express this rejection outwardly must be due at least in part, she points out, to the enormous coercive powers they face and to the ease with which the perpetrators of violence against them go unpunished by the larger society.

Several stories in this collection let us see the tension between these levels of perception, within the consciousness of the subaltern or oppressed group or person, as well as the ways in which the oppressed resist viewing the inescapable as either just or legitimate. As noted earlier, some of the stories also delve into the circumstances under which the seeming acceptance and covert resistance of a dominant ideology may be transformed into open rejection. This is most evident in the subcultures of the socially denigrated untouchable and tribal communities in the stories by Mahasweta, in the dichotomies between consciousness and behavior, between behavior inside the group and behavior outside, and between different levels of awareness the characters traverse under varying circumstances. We see how a politicized community of outcaste peasants or laborers manages to undermine the elite's usual mode of access to their consciousness, even if the movement that politicized them does not reach fruition or the initial gains are subsequently reduced or taken away.

Even the most abject victim, Tarashankar's witch, who is so totally isolated that there is no scope at all for the formation of a divergent subculture and social interaction on the basis of it, can be seen switching to other states of consciousness. At some points, when a new situation or a new person allows her to do so, she rejects her witch identity in feeling and behavior. At other points, when pushed to the extreme, she aggressively acts out her witch image in order to survive. Several times in the course of her life she runs away in order to avoid extreme persecution, and despite her terrible loneliness she survives to a very old age.

Karam Ali in "Through Death and Life" is a peasant constantly living with and battling starvation, a state that extends as far back as he can remember and as far ahead as he can see. Like many other toiling peasants, he is profoundly aware of the enormity of his oppression as well as the enormity of his resistance. The inarticulate Karam Ali's consciousness is permeated with three images. One is that of the giving nature: the rainclouds—the promise of bounty in the paddy-growing wetlands, from which he is not allowed what he needs to live on—and the brown earth he is about to plant. In the second image, the ruthless adversary with whom he struggles for his life is compared to the king cobra, which kills his plow bullock at the very start of plowing season and keeps reappearing before his eyes and in his vision as the symbol of his tenuous existence. The third image is of the courage of humanity's constant battle against the adversary in the struggle for survival, the image of "forever sharpening and resharpening whatever weapons one had and whatever technique one could learn, no matter how many times one was defeated." The cobra is disturbed when he attempts to clear the weeds and reclaim his infertile piece of uncultivated land in order to reduce his dependence on the onerous sharecropping lease. The old Karam Ali, believing "no one could ever kill it," still goes along with the youthful group trying to kill the snake, but when the snake appears with its towering hooded head, they stand transfixed by its cold cruel stare, until it strikes down a small boy in the group. Then, Karam Ali steps forward to bring his hoe down on the middle of the fast slithering form, injuring it but failing to kill it. Constantly moving between fatalistic thoughts and determined attempts to survive against terrible odds, he finally manages to get a loan to buy another plow bullock to retain his annual lease. Although the way he is finally destroyed makes fate appear to have won, Karam Ali has never given up. To him fate is not just cruel defeat and death, but the wily adversary in the constant battle that is life for him and others like him, and hence a measure of their amazing courage.

It is neither the witch nor the illiterate peasant Karam Ali nor the unfortunate funeral wailer who is willing to accept defeat, either morally or in the struggle for survival, but certain middle-class characters: Kusum in "The Unlucky Woman" and the patriarch in "The Daughter and the Oleander," both victims of false sentiments and of the inability to deal with the gap between those sentiments or pretenses and the reality of their lives. Their oppressors are inside their minds, not outside, and they are unequipped, unlike the peasant, to fight them. The untouchable girl Dhowli, in the course of her unusually cruel exploitation, liberates her own mind from her false romantic notions, and even as she is being crushed by her powerful adversaries, she tries to keep her thoughts focused on her newly acquired consciousness. The peasant daughter Giribala eventually rebels against the norms of proper behavior that she has been socialized to follow and that have cost her a great deal. Her decision to fight it out absolutely on her own is not only a wife's rebellion, but also a daughter's rebellion against her mother's compliance with the norms of wifely obedience even at the expense of filial duty. Mrinal's rebellion is partly fueled by the mindless obedience of the family's other daughter-in-law.

In the educated middle-class context in "Letter from a Wife," we see the protagonist expressing ideological rebellion against the oppressive mores and double standards in the family and the social order by drawing inspiration from the spiritual rebel Meerabai. In "Haimanti," the consciousness is voiced by mocking the age-old tradition of praising Rama's banishment of Sita to appease public opinion. For young women and youth in general under patriarchal domination, for those who are oppressed within the middle classes by middle-class mores, it has been possible to battle the role models used for imposing ideological hegemony by invoking as role models rebels from within the elite culture—mythological and historical characters, and religious rebel-leaders persecuted in their own time, like Kabir, the fifteenth-century mystic poet of Hindu-Muslim brotherhood, and his contemporary, Bengal's own Shri Chaitanya, who led a cult of devotion to a personal god with no need for either priests or Brahmanic rituals.

The Gramscian thesis about the crucial role of ideological hegemony in power relations, and therefore the centrality of the struggle to claim autonomy of one's consciousness, seems in the Indian context to be no less relevant for the middle class than for those at the bottom of the socioeconomic hierarchy. Some of the stories in this collection illustrate the struggles in the mind of a middle-class character against the oppressive elements of middle-class socialization and culture, while others illustrate the disability of middle-class consciousness. In the stories focusing on the laboring classes, the rebellion against ideological hegemony is, of course, the key element in the various forms of struggle against material exploitation.

Taken as a whole, the collection reflects two of the most significant aspects of Bengali society and culture in recent times, in all its continuity and discontinuity. One is the process by which the toiling masses of ordinary people have become increasingly politicized in their consciousness of, and resistance to, their social oppression and economic exploitation. The other is the waging of battles within the middle-class life and psyche. The literature reflects the hopes and frustrations of these conflicts, the anguish of self-interrogation and ethical questioning of accepted norms.

Bengali literature of the last hundred years offers a moving study of oppression—within the ranks of the middle class and in their relationships with the dispossessed on one side and the reactionary privileged on the other. The conflicted mind-set of the middle class as both elite and critic of society is particularly prominent in Bengal in large measure because of the extent of downward mobility in its ranks caused by the tragic events and economic stagnation of the last five decades. Middle-class displacement can be utterly demoralizing and degenerative; it can also be liberating and regenerative. These opposite forces, manifest in both life and literature, and the tension between them within the culture, hold the key to the pivotal role of some of the variegated sectors of the Bengali middle class in their relations of conflict and alliance with the laboring classes. Understanding oppression and rebellion within the Bengali middle class helps us assess the undercurrents of change in the structure of social relations, the potential for progress in the state of flux of this class, to which the writers and the readers mostly belong. Only a small sample from the literature, this collection of stories depicts both despair and hope. It sketches the relentless character of oppression at different levels of personal and social life, depicting the separate yet related struggles against it both within the middle classes and by the masses.

NOTES

1. See Roy ([1950] 1980, chap. 13); Chatterji (1926).

2. Roy (1980, 737, 757) notes that while all the words and the grammar of *Gitagovinda* are undoubtedly Sanskrit and the narratives and characters conform to Sanskrit literature, the very life of the lyrics, the mood, the rhythm, and the sentiments are those of the existing folk literature in the local *apavrangsha* dialects, mainly *Shourasheni* and *Gaud-Bangiya* (a variant of *Maithili*). Thematically, too, *Gitagovinda* is a wondrous blend of mythology and popular love lyrics, a blend that profoundly influenced Bengali literature and culture.

3. *Gitagovinda*'s greatly moving projection of romantic human love onto gods inspired the explosion of padavali lyrics that accompanied the spread of the *Vaishnavite* movement of religious humanism in Bengal in the sixteenth century.

4. Four of the five stories by Rabindranath Thakur have been translated before: "Jibita O Mrita" (as "Living or Dead?"), published by the Macmillan Company in 1916, and "Streer Patra" (as "A Wife's Letter"), "Shasti" (as "Punishment"), and "Madhyabartini" (as "The Girl Between") in a volume edited by Amiya Chakravarty and published in 1965 by the Beacon Press. Mahasweta Devi translated "Bich-

han" herself (as "Seeds"), but she liked my translation enough, and found it to be different enough, to give me permission to publish it. Manik Bandyopadhyay's "Aaj Kal Parshur Galpa" ("A Tale of These Days") was translated around the time I translated it in 1987, though I did not discover this until it was published by Thema in Calcutta in 1988. Hasan Azizul Huq mentioned in a letter to me some other translations (which I have not seen) of his "Amrityu Ajiban" ("Through Death and Life"), and he remarked that my translation of it most successfully evoked the harmony (*sushama*) of the original story, which he said is his favorite.

5. Literary realism can be steeped in folklore; it can be centered on universal humanism; it can be focused on conflict and struggle at the social, the interpersonal, and the individual levels. The stories in this collection may be seen in one or more of these categories. The witch's story by Tarashankar, the peasant Karam Ali's story by Hasan Azizul, and two of Mahasweta's stories can be placed in the first category. The five stories by Rabindranath are examples of the second category, and to some extent of the third, insofar as they explore the conflicts inside the individual mind. The stories by Manik and by Mahasweta and two of the four by Hasan Azizul can be viewed largely as belonging in the third category, of social conflict, of oppression and resistance.

6. Rammohun Roy waged his campaign against *sati-daha* (immolation of a widow on the funeral pyre of her dead husband) with scholarly tracts and polemics based on classical Hindu philosophical positions in the *smriti* texts. He published them in papers like *Calcutta Gazette, Reformer*, the *Bengal Herald* and his own *Brahmanical Magazine*. Unlike the social reform campaigns of the late nineteenth century and recent times, his was based not only on humanitarian grounds but on interpreting the religion itself, which he carefully deployed to battle the Hindu orthodoxy of the time, the "vulgar" Hinduism, the obscurantist customs and rigidly ritualistic rules that suppressed spirituality and rational thought. Similarly, Iswarchandra Vidyasagar, in campaigning against child marriage and polygamy and for widow remarriage, used his scriptural knowledge to fight the deepest social prejudice (Sarkar 1979, 35).

7. By 1820, a number of boys' schools and the Hindu College had been established. Girls' schools had an earlier beginning in East Bengal than in Calcutta. But even in Calcutta, several girls' schools were running at full capacity by 1850, including Bethune School (founded in 1849), which in 1888 became the first women's college in India to teach through the M.A. level.

8. The Western influence of liberal humanism was expressed especially in the movement against customs that degraded and oppressed women, customs like child marriage, polygamy, the extreme self-denial prescribed for widows, many of them child widows, and the restrictions on the education and mobility of women. The movement also advocated the establishment of schools to spread secular education in Western science and literature along with Indian languages, literature, and philosophy.

9. In a letter to Sturge Moore on May 1, 1914, Rabindranath wrote, "Literature of a country is not chiefly for its home consumption. Its value lies in the fact that it is imperatively necessary for the lands where it is foreign. I think it has been the good fortune of the West to have the opportunity of absorbing the spirit of the East through the medium of the Bible. . . . The Western literature is doing the same work with us, bringing into our life the elements some of which supplement and some contradict our

tendencies. This is what we need. . . . We seek in your writings not simply what is artistic but what is vivid and forceful. . . . Whatever is broadly human and deeply true can be safely shipped for distant times and remote countries" (Chakravarty 1961, 23–24).

10. Kopf summarizes his thesis in Kopf and Joarder 1977: "On the one side of the encounter were the British Orientalists, shaped by the eighteenth-century values of rationalism, classicism and cosmopolitanism [men like William Carey, who had mastered Sanskrit and Bengali to produce textbooks, articles, and translations used at the College]. . . . On the other side of the encounter were the [Bengali] intelligentsia" (7–8). Kopf bases his dating of the Bengal Renaissance on three events: the 1773 decision of Warren Hastings to turn Calcutta from "a straggling village of mud-houses" to a commercial urban center as capital of British India, the establishment of the College of Fort William in Calcutta in 1800 to educate British civil servants in India "in the languages and cultures of the East," and finally the dissolution of that College in 1835, which Kopf describes as the victory of Macaulayism ("to educate Asiatics in the sciences of the West") over the Orientalists.

11. David Hare came to Calcutta in 1800 at the age of twenty-five as a watch trader and, after giving far more energy in the next sixteen years to discussing and making contacts for the cause of spreading secular education, he sold his watch shop to a friend and used the money to buy pieces of land and set up several schools for boys in 1816–17. From then on, this secular idealist spent all his time, energy, and money on nurturing those schools, among them (and the Hindu College, started in 1817, which became the Calcutta Presidency College in 1855). He personally selected the boys and took care of them, often washing them, feeding them, playing ball with them in the school yard, talking with them after school, and seeing them home if the talking went into the night. He was one of the organizers of the School Society and the School Book Society started in 1817 and 1818 to promote the setting up of schools using modern teaching methods and the writing of textbooks in English and in Bengali for schoolchildren—a significant inversion of the earlier Fort William College textbook initiative for the acculturation of the British civil servants. In all these, he worked closely with almost all the major early figures of the Bengal Renaissance, from Rammohun Roy to Ramtanu Lahiri. When he died of cholera "on a very wet day [June 1, 1841] with cyclonic weather, five thousand Indians followed his hearse. . . . His statue on the lawn of the Presidency College is surely the one monument to a foreigner in the city which even the most fanatic of nationalists would not dream of removing" (Sarkar 1958, 28).

Drinkwater Bethune, after coming to Calcutta to head the Governor-General's Council of Education, played a similar collaborative role in the 1840s and 1850s with Rammohun Roy, Iswarchandra Vidyasagar, Debendranath Thakur, and Shibnath Shastri in the founding of secular schools for girls in Calcutta.

12. The incidence of higher education was more limited among the Bengali Muslims than among the Hindus, partly because of the smaller size of the middle class, both the rural propertied and the urban professional-administrative. The Bengali Muslim awakening (from unquestioning acceptance of religious practices, beliefs, and authority), like its Hindu counterpart, did not show much interest in the rural minirevolts of peasants and weavers, such as the militantly religious Wahabi and Faraezi rebellions (1831–68) led by Titu Mian and Haji Shariatullah of Faridpur. The religious revivalist leadership and sectarian approach of most of the agitations of the mid-eighteenth to the

mid-nineteenth century posed a cultural and attitudinal barrier that few enlightened Bengalis of the time, Hindu or Muslim, felt any desire to overcome, particularly when the militancy was directed at them. The indigo growers' revolt, on the other hand, being directed almost entirely at the English planters and merchants, aroused much greater interest and response among the Bengali intelligentsia. Dinabandhu Mitra's *Nil Darpan*, which portrayed that revolt, was enormously popular and effective.

The religious-sectarian format of most of the late eighteenth- and early nine-teenth-century rebellions also proved to be a major obstacle to their consolidation into one massive peasant movement. That kind of consolidation occurred only in the Tebha-ga movement during the three decades from the 1920s through the 1940s. It inspired and engaged Bengali literary and intellectual efforts as nothing had before, and the move-ment itself in turn received inspiring infusions from those efforts. This phenomenon of mutual inspiration between mass movement and literary creativity reappeared in the 1970s in the context of the Naxalite movement.

13. The sharp increase in the urban underclass in the early decades of this century resulted from a number of causes, some of them linked to the crisis in rural Bengal, especially rack-renting and agricultural stagnation, which had been cumulating for over a hundred years. The depression for the rural and urban artisans came after the turn of the century. The decline of Calcutta as a commercial and industrial center (the locus of commerce and industry having shifted to Bombay) also contributed to the steady growth of the urban underclass in and around Calcutta, which exploded in the 1940s when the famine and the Partition suddenly added millions to its ranks.

14. The Tebhaga movement stood for the division of crops into three parts, one to go to the owner of the land, one to the provider of the labor, and the third to the undertaker of production costs, in Bengal usually the tenant. The traditional fifty-fifty rule had become a sham, because the tenant had to borrow from the landlord to raise the crop, and the loan was recovered from the harvest. In years of poor harvest, the usurious interest-in-kind served to shift the burden of the loss onto the tenant, forcing him into additional debt just to stay alive, ensnaring him deeper into the extraction process. Sharecroppers were more severely exploited in eastern India, where the particular revenue settlement by the British produced absentee landlords, subten-ancy, and layers of land intermediaries, and where the tying of landlease and credit was and still is more common than in northwestern India. The movement was concen-trated in four districts in East Bengal and four in West Bengal. Peasant lives were lost, and their homes and storages set on fire. Peasant women too fought the land-lords' goons and the police with anything from kitchen knives to chili powder. They watched for the police, fought the fires, and provided the link between the fighting men and the movement organizers. Some of the peasant leaders were women, and in recognition of the role of women in the revolt one was sent to the negotiation with the government of Bengal in 1946. For more details on the Tebhaga movement, see Sunil Sen (1982).

The unity that the movement had forged among Bengal's Hindu and Muslim peasantry was shattered in 1947 by the Partition and the riots, which were at least partly caused by political scheming. One immediate benefit of the unity built through the years of common struggle of the poor of both religions, however, was in the form of communities sheltering the members of a religious minority from the killer gangs from outside the community. Among the long-term contributions of the movement, in addition to the politicizing of Bengal's peasantry, one must count the persistence of the sharecroppers' issue in all the demands for land reform and in the tenancy reform attempted so far, especially in West Bengal. Absentee landowning was eventually abolished in the fifties and tenancy reform laws passed in West Bengal in the sixties. In some parts of West Bengal, sharecropping peasants have been able to get registered in recent years so that the laws regulating rent and tenure can be implemented for them. In some areas, the cropsharing arrangement is adjusted to the costsharing. Although the demands of the movement remain unmet in many parts of Bengal, the ongoing lower-key struggle of a politicized peasantry has its roots in the Tebhaga experience.

15. My translation from Bandyopadhyay (1957, 111–15). Manik illustrated the point thus: "If the story is about the peasant wife selling her body, then one must look for the meaning of that in the reality of peasant life. One can't look at it as a crisis of morality, in the sense one would in the case of a middle-class wife. We often remark, 'The poor wife, driven to it by poverty!,' as if she had done it to deserve our pity, as if the idea of having our pity has any place in her life, any meaning in her mind."

16. From an interview given in Bengali to Samik Banerji in 1983.

17. Each one of Rabindranath's hundreds of poems, nearly one hundred short stories, and scores of novels and plays and essays is minutely documented by date, month, and year, and often also by the place where he wrote it. In contrast, Manik Bandyopadhyay almost never wrote down the date on any of his short stories and the only way of tracing their approximate date of writing is to check the issue of the magazines in which they were first published. For this reason, even the published collections of Manik's stories do not attach specific dates to the stories.

18. In his lecture titled "My Life," delivered on his visit to China in 1924, Rabindranath said, "Three currents met about the time I was born. . . . One of these movements was religious, . . . to reopen the channel of spiritual life. . . . There was a second movement of equal importance, the literary revolution which occurred in Bengal about that time, pioneered by Bankimchandra Chatterjee (1823–1894), . . . who lifted from our language the dead weight of ponderous forms. . . . The third movement which started about this time was national, a voice of indignation at the humiliation constantly heaped upon us by those who had the habit of dividing people into good and bad according to what was similar to their life and what was different" (Tagore 1928, 1–3).

19. A spiritualist and an accomplished singer and dancer, Meerabai composed her famous *bhajans* with lines like "I'll rather sing of Giridhar than be a *sati*" and "Meera is going to stick by you, my lord, even if she is rejected by her father, mother, by everybody else, no matter what their rejections bring upon her," which is quoted by Mrinal at the end of her letter.

20. Neo-realism had its effect on the style of painting too, which was profoundly changed from the earlier tradition of legend- and myth-inspired image painting to various forms of contemporary realism, some of which still incorporated mythical subjects.

21. Ashish Chakravorty, publisher of Manik's collected works, in the preface to the second volume (my translation).

22. Her uncle was the filmmaker Ritwik Ghatak, and her first husband, Bijan Bhattacharya, a leading playwright and actor of the Gananatya and a radical journalist.

23. One of the readers of this manuscript remarked on the relation of some of the stories to folklore, "not only in terms of substance but in terms of technique, which amounts to a kind of antilyrical realism which still contains in itself remnants of the lyricism of folk tales." This remark holds very well for Tarashankar's "Witch" and some of Mahasweta's stories.

24. Devi, "Lekha Lekhi" (unpublished essay, 1986). Mahasweta also runs a magazine, *Bortika*, dedicated to the cause of the oppressed communities. She collects accounts of the lives, problems, and experiences of rickshaw pullers, farm laborers, and poor tribals, which she publishes in the magazine with little or no editorial change, consciously minimizing intellectual mediation between the people and their stories. In recent years she has involved herself with a number of grassroots organizations of the tribals and the untouchables, some of which she has been instrumental in starting. When I went to see her in her home in August 1988, she was more interested in talking about the tubewells for drinking water that she was trying to get funded for some of those communities she has been writing about than she was in talking about her storywriting. At one point, a professor of an elite women's college in Calcutta came to ask her to give a lecture, remarking that the students were eager to hear her speak as a woman writer on women's condition. Mahasweta replied that she would like to be regarded as a writer, not a *woman* writer, and that she was not sure whether she should give priority to speaking on women's condition over getting those tubewells installed.

25. The stories by Mahasweta include large amounts of dialogue, with an emphasis on the authenticity of dialect and expression. In some of the stories by Manik and Hasan Azizul also, the dialogue, while more spare than in Mahasweta, is faithful to the dialect and speech of the characters. Rabindranath's practice, however, is quite different (see Sidhanta 1961, 291–92). Rabindranath was against the recommendation made by a committee on educational methods in the schools of Bengal at the beginning of the century that textbooks be translated into the regional dialects of north, east, central, and west Bengal to help peasant children assimilate the knowledge. He regarded it as an attempt to divide the Bengalis. He said that despite the regional differences in dialect in Britain, the British never tried to reflect these in their schoolbooks. Another reason he avoided dialects, he said, was that he would then have to use half a dozen dialects in his stories. He also believed that the use of dialects produces emotional distance between the characters and the reader, constantly reminding the reader that he or she does not live in the same world as they do.

26. Interviews with Hasan Azizul Huq (1988, 34, 36, 41, and 61). The remarks quoted here and in the next paragraph are my translations.

Hasan Azizul regards Rabindranath as the greatest writer in the tradition of humanist idealism, with a superb ability to elevate the human being, distilled from all communal and religious divisions. But then Rabindranath was writing long before the turbulent 1940s (31–32).

27. "Writing as if [society's divisiveness] does not exist, or shying away from it, is certainly not going to remedy it. The remedy involves change in the society, most of all at the level of the acute inequality in wealth distribution that is behind many of the contradictions in our social relations. Supposing that problem were remedied, there would still be the religious or ethnic minorities in each region. There would still be Muslims in West Bengal, Hindus in Bangladesh, Buddhists and Christian tribal com-

munities in both Bengals. Because these are products of history, and one cannot start anything, nor change, by assuming that the slate is clean when it is not" (Huq 1988, 33–34).

28. When Mencher (1980) explored the extent to which a South Indian untouchable community accepted or rejected the definition of themselves formed by others, she found that they regarded the stigmatization as basically a method of, and smokescreen for, economic exploitation, with the help of brutal force.

29. See Wright (1985, chap. 3) on the unequal distribution of organizational assets as a mechanism of class exploitation. Organizational power in the Indian subcontinent is to be understood not just in terms of increasing statism, but also in terms of power derived from religious institutions, the control of which is stratified by class.

30. The concept of sisterhood in terms of the experience and consciousness of black American women has been explored in the works of Elizabeth Fox-Genovese, Phyllis Marynick Palmer, and Bonnie Thornton Dill, among others.

31. Wright (1985, 126–30) notes that agrarian feudalism and patriarchy have in common a personal form of paternalism and domination; although similar in some respects, they should not be equated with class exploitation, which takes place primarily through unequal ownership and control of the economic means of production. Feudalism and patriarchy tend to rely substantially on extraeconomic coercion.

32. Foucault (1980), Scott (1985), Guha (1982–87), Ross (1980).

33. In 1944, during the food riots following the 1943 famine and the sharecroppers' revolt, Manik Bandyopadhyay became a member of the Communist Party of India, which was then actively engaged in the food marches and in the peasant movement. The first one of his four stories in this collection was written well before 1944, the other three afterwards.

REFERENCES

Bandyopadhyay, Manik. *About This Author's Perspective* (*Lekhakera Katha*). Calcutta: New Age Publishers, 1957. (Passages quoted are my translation.)

Chakraborty, Jugantar. "Manik Bandyopadhyay's Literary Works." *Ekshan* (literary periodical in Bengali edited by Nirmalya Acharya and Soumitra Chattopadhyay), no. 2, 1972–73.

Chakravarty, Amiya, ed. *A Tagore Reader.* Boston: Beacon Press (Macmillan Co.), 1961.

————, ed. Introduction to *The Housewarming and Other Selected Writings.* See Rabindranath Tagore 1965.

Chatterjee, Partha. "More on Modes of Power and the Peasantry." In *Selected Subaltern Studies*, edited by Ranajit Guha and Gayatri Chakravorty Spivak. New Delhi: Oxford University Press, 1988.

Chatterji, Suniti Kumar. *The Origin and Development of the Bengali Language.* 2 vols. Calcutta: Calcutta University, 1926.

Chattopadhyay, Gautam, ed. *Bengal: Early Nineteenth Century.* 2 vols. Calcutta: Research India Publications, 1978.

Desai, A. R., ed. *Peasant Struggles in India.* New Delhi: Oxford University Press, 1979.

Devi, Mahasweta. "My Various Writings" ("Lekha Lekhi"). Unpublished article for Frankfurt Book Fair, 1986. (Excerpt my translation.)

Foucault, Michel. *Power/Knowledge: Selected Interviews and Other Writings*. Edited and translated with an afterword by Colin Gordon. Brighton, Sussex: Harvester Press, 1980.

Guha, Ranajit, ed. *Subaltern Studies: Writings on South Asian History and Society*. Volumes 1–5. New Delhi: Oxford University Press, 1982–87.

Gupta, Atulchandra, ed. *Studies in the Bengal Renaissance*. In commemoration of the birth centenary of Bipinchandra Pal. Jadavpur, Calcutta: The National Council of Education, 1958.

Huq, Hasan Azizul. Interviews given in Bengali published in the 1988 issue of *Vignapanparba*, a literary magazine edited by Robin Ghosh in Calcutta.

Joarder, Safiuddin. "The Bengal Renaissance and the Bengali Muslims." In *Reflections on the Bengal Renaissance*. See Kopf and Joarder 1977.

Kopf, David. *British Orientalism and the Bengal Renaissance: The Dynamics of Indian Modernization, 1773–1835*. Berkeley and Los Angeles: University of California Press, 1969.

———. *The Brahmo Samaj and the Shaping of the Modern Indian Mind*. Princeton: Princeton University Press, 1979.

Kopf, David, and Safiuddin Joarder, eds. *Reflections on the Bengal Renaissance*. Seminar on Perspectives of the Bengal Renaissance, held in 1976 at the Institute of Bangladesh Studies, Rajshahi University. Rajshahi: Institute of Bangladesh Studies, 1977.

Kripalani, Krishna. *Tagore: A Life*. New Delhi: Malancha, 1961.

Mencher, Joan. "On Being an Untouchable in India." In *Beyond the Myths of Culture: Essays in Cultural Materialism*. See Ross 1980.

Moore, Barrington, Jr. *The Social Bases of Obedience and Revolt*. New York: M. E. Sharpe, 1978.

Rabindranath Tagore: A Centenary Volume: 1861–1961. New Delhi: Sahitya Akademi Publication, 1961.

Rao, M. S. A. *Social Movements in India*. Vol. 1 (*Peasant and Backward Classes Movements*) and Vol. 2 (*Sectarian, Tribal and Women's Movements*). Delhi: Manohar Publications, 1978, 1979.

Ray, Ratnalekha. *Change in the Bengali Agrarian Society*. Delhi: Manohar Publications, 1980.

Ross, Eric, ed. *Beyond the Myths of Culture: Essays in Cultural Materialism*. New York: Academic Press, 1980.

Roy, Nihar Ranjan. *Bangalir Itihash: Adi Parva*. Vol. 2. Calcutta: West Bengal Illiteracy Eradication Committee, 1980. (First published in Calcutta in 1950.)

Sarkar, Susobhan. "Derozio and Young Bengal." In *Studies in the Bengal Renaissance*. See Gupta 1958.

———. *On the Bengal Renaissance*. Calcutta: Papyrus, 1979.

———. *Prasanga Rabindranath*. Calcutta: Ananda Publishers, 1982. (Lines quoted are my translation.)

Scott, James. *Weapons of the Weak: Everyday Forms of Peasant Resistance*. New Haven: Yale University Press, 1985.

Scott, James, and Benedict Kerkvliet, eds. *Everyday Forms of Peasant Resistance in Southeast Asia*. London: Frank Cass & Co., 1986.

Sen, Sukumar. *History of Bengali Literature*. New Delhi: Sahitya Akademi, 1960.

Sen, Sunil. *Peasant Movements in India: Mid-Nineteenth and Twentieth Centuries.* Calcutta: K. P. Bagchi, 1982.

Shastri, Shibnath. *Ramtanu Lahiri O Tatkaleen Banga Samaj.* Calcutta: Paschim Banga Niraksharata Doorikaran Samiti, 1979. (First published in 1903.)

Sidhanta, Nirmal K. "Rabindranath's Short Stories." In *Rabindranath Tagore* 1961.

Tagore [Thakur], Rabindranath. *The Hungry Stones and Other Stories.* Various translators, including Tagore. London and New York: Macmillan Co., 1916.

———. *Lectures and Addresses.* Edited and translated by Anthony Soares. London: Macmillan Co., 1928.

———. *The Housewarming and Other Selected Writings.* New York: New American Library, Signet Classics Edition, 1965.

Visva-Bharati University. *Rabindra Parichay.* Collection of essays by and on Rabindranath. Calcutta: Visva-Bharati Granthayan Bibhag, 1982.

Wadud, Kazi Abdul. "The Mussalmans of Bengal." In *Studies in the Bengal Renaissance.* See Gupta 1958.

Wright, Erik Olin. *Classes.* Chapters 3, 4, and 7. London: Verso (New Left Books), 1985.

The Living and the Dead

Rabindranath Thakur

1

The young widow Kadambini had stayed on in the extended family of Sharadashankar-babu, her husband's elder brother, who was a small landlord in Ranihat village. In her own family hardly anyone was left to go back to. Here too she was, strictly speaking, without a family, with her husband dead and no child of her own. But she was bound to this little child, the son of her brother-in-law. The child's mother was sick for a long time after he was born, and the widowed Kadambini took care of him. She came to love the baby, her heart almost aching with tenderness for him. With that welling affection, deprived of any other outlet, she enveloped and nurtured the baby for whom she was supposed to be no more than a good caretaker. Loving a child not one's own is perhaps always like this. One is ever so painfully aware of having no socially validated hold, no legal claim. The claim of mere love? One dare not try to make a case for it, for fear of losing even tentative access to the loved one. Maybe one does not even want to try. One simply reaches out, with still more intense ardor, toward this uncertain, unsecured object of a love that is so precious and so certain.

One pouring monsoon night, Kadambini died—quite suddenly, gasping, having showered the little boy with all the pent-up affection of a childless widow. Her heart somehow stopped beating. Everywhere else, except in this acutely loving heart, time went on ticking as before.

To avoid troublesome investigation, the cremation was quickly arranged.

Dated Shravana 1299 (July to August 1892), "Jibita O Mrita" appears in Rabindranath's collection of stories, *Galpaguchha*, vol. 1 (Calcutta: Visva-Bharati Granthayan Bibhag, 1926), 98–107.

Four of the landlord's regular Brahman employees were entrusted with the task. They took the body away, in the little funeral cot of bamboo and rope, for cremation that very night. The cremation ground was quite far from the village. It was an enormous barren ground, with nothing but a pond, a little hut beside it, and a great old banyan tree. Beyond it, on all sides, lay the endless array of fields. The river that at one time flowed this way had long since dried up. To the villagers, the pond, dug in the dried riverbed, represented the unseen sacred river for performing the rituals of cremating the dead.

The four men came there carrying the cot with the body. They went inside the hut, put the cot down, and sat there waiting for the firewood to arrive. Time dragged on so slowly, so wearing out the silently waiting men that finally two of them, Nitai and Gurucharan, went off to investigate the delay in delivering the wood. The other two, Bidhu and Banamali, stayed back guarding the body.

It was one of those enveloping, engulfing nights of the monsoon: pitch dark all around, somber clouds hanging low overhead, not a single star visible in the sky. Inside the dark little hut, the two silent men sat uneasily by the body awaiting cremation. One had packed a match and a candle in one end of his wrapper, but the damp match would not light; and the lantern they had brought had long since gone out.

After some seemingly endless and excruciating silence, one of the waiting men said, "Wish we could at least have a smoke. Forgot to bring the hookah and tobacco in the midst of that rush to get here." The other suggested, "Why don't I run and get some?" "Really!" snapped Bidhu, well aware of Banamali's intention. "And you expect me to stay here alone!"

The conversation stopped there. Minutes seemed like hours, and silently they cursed those supposed to bring the firewood and their two companions who had deserted them on the pretext of finding out about it. Gradually, their foggy suspicion solidified into a conviction that those two were having a nice smoke and chatting somewhere safer than this hut where they were left with the dead body.

Silence. Dreadful silence was all around, except for the ceaseless, unchanging chorus made by the crickets and the frogs at the edge of the pond. The cot seemed to move slightly for a moment, as if the corpse turned on its side. Bidhu and Banamali began to tremble as they muttered the name of Rama, the dispeller of evil. Then, they distinctly heard a sigh inside the hut. Instantly, they shot out and ran in the direction of the village.

A couple of miles down the way, they came upon the other two men coming back with a lighted lantern. They really had been having a leisurely smoke and knew nothing whatsoever of the wood delivery, but nonetheless they assured their frantic companions that wood was on its way; a tree had been felled for the purpose and was being split into logs. They did not believe one word of the account of the two frightened, breathless men and scolded them for abandoning their post.

The four of them quickly walked back to the cremation ground, entered the hut, and found the cot empty. They stood staring at each other. Could it be the jackals? But, then, the sheet that covered the body would not be missing as well. They searched outside the hut and noticed fresh small footprints in the soft mud, footprints much smaller and fewer than their own. They knew that their employer, Sharadashankar, was not naive, not likely to accept a ghost story. So, after much discussion, they decided to report that the cremation had been properly completed.

Toward dawn, when the men in charge of delivering the wood arrived with the supply, they learned from the men about to leave that, because of their delay, they had done the cremation with whatever wood they could find inside the hut. The delivery men neither questioned nor doubted that. A corpse, after all, was not some valuable property likely to be stolen.

2

It is not unknown that life, even when all its apparent signs have disappeared, can linger on, sunk motionless underneath, and in time can start ticking again in the seemingly lifeless body. Kadambini was not really dead. For some reason, her vital signs had stopped for a while.

As she recovered consciousness, she saw only darkness, thick darkness, all around her. It did not feel like her usual sleeping place. She called softly, just once, for her sister-in-law, the mother of the baby in whose room she normally slept. No answer came from the darkness that enveloped her. She sat up terrified, suddenly recalling the last moments before what she had thought was death—the sudden choking pain in the chest. Her sister-in-law was heating milk for the baby on a little stove in a corner of the room. Kadambini had called her, as she collapsed on the bed gasping for breath, "Bring the baby to me, sister. I feel so terrible!"

Then, all was engulfed in blackness, as if a whole pot of ink had suddenly spilled over a written page, instantly deranging and obliterating her entire memory, all the words and letters in the script of her conscious life. She could not quite remember now if she had heard the baby's sweet voice calling her, if she had managed to collect that last token of love to sustain her through the long and unknown journey away from the familiar world of the living.

She now tried hard to think clearly, to understand what might actually have happened to her. Her first thought was that only the realm of Yama could be as still and as dark as this. With nothing to see or hear, nothing to do, the dead would most likely sit there like this forever, awake in the dark. Then, as she felt on her skin the cool damp wind that blew in through the open door and heard the rain-delighted frogs croaking, in a flash, all her memories of the monsoon, all of them since her earliest childhood, came rushing back together, nestling her once again in filial closeness with the earth. But the very next moment, lightning streaked across the black sky, and she caught a glimpse of the pond, the banyan tree, the barren expanse, and the distant rows of trees beyond. She recognized the place. She had come here once with other women, on some sacred occasion, for a dip in the pond. She vividly recalled how she had shuddered at the sight of corpses in this very barren ground, where she was now sitting alone in the dark.

I must get back home, she thought. But if I am not living any more, they will not let me among them! I am now my spirit, my ghost, exiled forever from the world of the living.

She was now convinced of this. How else could she, in the middle of such a night, be sitting here in the cremation ground so far away from the protected interior of the closely guarded household? If she were not already cremated, wouldn't those supposed to burn her dead body be still around? She considered her last conscious moment in the lighted room inside Sharadashankar's house and, right after that, this moment, alone in this dark and desolate cremation ground. She was sure of it: she was now a spirit, scary and ominous for the living. With this conviction, a strange feeling came over her, a feeling of having been cut loose from all the familiar restrictions, all the regulations that rule society. She suddenly felt as if she had acquired powers she had never known before and infinite freedom; she could now go anywhere and do anything she wished. Reeling from this strange new feeling of freedom and power, she got up and walked out across the pitch-dark cremation ground. She walked like a gust of nocturnal wind, without any trace of fear, anxiety, or prudence.

After a while, her feet grew tired from walking, her body weary. All those endless fields, each covered with either flooded paddy or knee-deep bog. With the sky now growing faintly light, a few bird calls came from some clumps of bamboo at the edge of some village that was getting closer. Fear now crept back into her. What was to be her new relationship with the living? As long as she was in the cremation ground, in the open fields, in the enveloping darkness and desolation of the monsoon night, she had felt fearless, as if moving in her own domain. Now, in the approaching daylight, the sight of people's habitat terrified her. Spirits are as afraid of people as people are of spirits, because they live on opposite sides of the river of death.

3

The way Kadambini looked that morning—her clothes splattered with mud, her eyes blazing with strange intensity from the extraordinary thoughts racking her brain through the sleepless night, her wandering alone—would surely have scared the villagers and prompted the urchins to run for hiding places from which to stone her. Luckily, a passing traveler first saw her in her strange condition. He came up to her, asking politely where she was going alone at that hour, whether he could be of any help to her, saying that he could tell she was from a good family. She stared at him, without answering. It seemed so improbable that she could still be in human society and still look like a woman from a respectable family, that on a village path she was looking at a gentleman traveler offering her kind help.

The traveler repeated his offer to escort her to her destination and asked her what address she wanted to reach. His question now started her thinking in practical terms. Going back to her in-laws' house was out of the question, and she had no parental home left. Then she remembered her childhood friend, Jogamaya.

Although they had not seen each other for a long time, almost since childhood, after marriage when they went off to different villages, they often wrote letters to each other, sometimes almost competing in expression of love, each proclaiming a stronger love than the other, each complaining about the other's lack of response, and both convinced that if they were ever to meet again they would not be parted easily. Kadambini finally gave the patiently waiting stranger her childhood friend's address: "The house of Sripaticharan-babu in Nishindapur village." Although the gentleman was going to Calcutta, the village was not far off his way, and he took the trouble to see her there.

The two friends had not met for a very long time. It took them some minutes to recognize each other, until each deciphered in the other's face the faded resemblance to the dearly loved face of childhood. Jogamaya trilled with delight, saying that she had never imagined she would have the luck to see her friend ever again. Then, she expressed her surprise and curiosity about how Kadambini managed to get here, how her in-laws could let her go, alone.

Kadambini remained quiet for a while and finally said, "Please, don't ask me about them. Let me stay in a corner of your home like a maid; I'll do all the work of your household."

"How could you even think of such a thing? Why should you stay here like a maid? You're my dearest, best friend, you're my . . . "

At that point, Jogamaya's husband, Sripati, walked into the room. Kadambini simply gazed at his face, and then she slowly got up and left the room, without making any of the expected gestures of modesty and politeness, like pulling the edge of her sari over her head.

Jogamaya started making excuses on Kadambini's behalf, worried that he might be offended by her strange demeanor. But it took so little explaining, and Sripati so readily approved of his wife's suggestion to have her friend stay with them for a while, that it left Jogamaya vaguely displeased and more than a little uneasy.

Kadambini stayed on with her friend, but she could not really be friendly with her because of her knowledge of the barrier of death between them. With constant, relentless consciousness and doubt of her own identity, she could not be close to her friend. She just watched her and wondered. How far away her friend seemed to be! Always so busy with her husband and her household, with her many responsibilities and attachments, so definitely belonging to the tangible world of existence. While she herself felt like a mere shadow, devoid of content, a part of some unknown and endless nothingness!

Jogamaya also started feeling uncomfortable, puzzled. Women cannot stand enigmas. One can be poetic, one can be philosophical, even chivalrous about an enigmatic person. But one cannot run a busy household with an enigmatic, intriguing presence around all the time. Hence, a woman either refuses to recognize the existence of something that does not make sense to her, or she defines it into something that fits in with her own practical and usable way of thinking. If neither seems possible, then it tends to make her angry. The more insistently perplexing Kadambini's behavior remained, the more it began to annoy Jogamaya. What a nuisance to have to put up with!

There was another problem. Kadambini's fear of herself became even more troublesome in the effect it produced among those around her. The common fear of ghosts makes one afraid of looking behind, because that is the side one cannot watch as well as the other sides and that is where the ghost is most likely to lurk. Kadambini feared her inside, not the outside, and she could not escape herself! On a quiet afternoon, alone in her own room, she would be screaming in cold terror. The sight of her own shadow in the evening within the lamplit room sent shivers down her spine. Her strangely haunted behavior heightened, beyond the usual levels, the fear of ghosts among everyone else in the household. All the maids and servants, and even their mistress, started seeing ghosts more frequently and in many more places than they ever had before.

Late one night, Kadambini came out of her own bedroom, sobbing frantically, to the sleeping couple's bedroom door, begging her friend not to leave her alone. Jogamaya became scared as she became annoyed. She felt like throwing Kadambini out of the house that very moment. The kindly Sripati managed with much effort to calm Kadambini and let her sleep the rest of the night in the room adjoining their bedroom.

The day after that incident, Sripati was summoned to the inner quarter of his house at a rather unusual hour. Jogamaya confronted him with a barrage of rebukes and questions doubting his motive and sense of responsibility.

"What kind of man are you, really? A woman leaves her place in her in-laws' home, installs herself in yours with hardly any reasonable excuse.

It's been over a month, still she mentions nothing of going back, and I don't hear you express the slightest objection! Why don't you explain to me what you have in mind? You men are a strange lot indeed!"

As a matter of fact, men often have an unreasoning bias toward women in general, and for that they get criticized and accused most by women themselves, their own women. Indeed, Sripati's more than justifiable compassion for the helpless, beautiful widow was manifest in his behavior, which belied his protestations and his swearing against anything improper in his mind. He was only concerned, thinking that probably the mistreatment by her in-laws had made the childless widow leave in despair and, as none of her family was alive, he could not possibly refuse her shelter or ask her to go back. Thus, he had refrained from making inquiries and had not felt like troubling Kadambini with questions about this unpleasant subject.

Now that his wife kept hitting in so many ways at this passive area, submerged in ambivalence, of his sense of propriety and male responsibility, he finally realized that simply to have peace at home, he must make contact with Kadambini's in-laws. To find out about the matter, he decided that it would be more effective to go to Ranihat and visit them himself than to send them an unexpected letter.

After Sripati had left on his mission, Jogamaya approached Kadambini with the subject of social impropriety in further prolonging her stay away from her in-laws. "You are my dear friend. But what will people think if you stay here too long?" Kadambini listened and answered, looking gravely at Jogamaya, "What do I have to do with people and what they think about me?" Jogamaya was shocked at this strange answer. She was also annoyed and said matter-of-factly, "We care about society and what people think, even if you don't. How would we justify keeping an unrelated woman away from her lawful home?"

"Where's my lawful home," remarked Kadambini with a kind of sadness that made Jogamaya wonder what the weird woman was talking about. Kadambini continued pondering aloud, "Where is my lawful home? Am I part of this world? You all are busy laughing, crying, loving, each of you engaged in your own business, while I am only a shadow, just looking on. I don't understand why God has left me in the midst of you and your worldly activities. My ominous presence worries you, lest it ruin the joys of your daily life. I too have no notion of how I should behave with people, how I am to relate to them. But because the Almighty created no place for us, we keep hovering about you, even after the vital links are severed."

Kadambini's appearance as she spoke these words curiously impressed the practical Jogamaya. She vaguely understood something of what she was talking about, but not exactly the essence of what she meant. So Jogamaya could bring herself neither to answer her nor to raise the question a second time. She just walked away, heavy with a feeling of anxiety and foreboding.

4

It was pouring when Sripati came back at ten o'clock, very late for a village night during the monsoon. The ceaseless sound of rainfall was boring into one's mind the conviction that the rainy night was there always and was going to stay forever.

To his wife's anxious questions about his investigation, he just said that it was a long story and must wait. He then quietly went about his routine of changing out of travel clothes, eating his supper, and smoking the hookah. Then he went to bed, looking very worried and maintaining complete silence throughout these activities. Jogamaya, trying hard to be patient for so long, while watching with mounting tension his silent routine, immediately joined him in bed and demanded a full account.

He started by saying that she must have made a mistake about the whole thing. She could not help feeling annoyed. A woman hardly ever makes a mistake, and if she ever does, a sensible man should at least not point it out so bluntly, even if he cannot take it on himself.

"What is my mistake?" she demanded curtly.

"The woman you've let in our home is not exactly who you think she is." For Jogamaya, this statement was even more annoying, particularly coming from her husband.

"What sort of reasoning is that? Can't I recognize my childhood friend without your help?"

Sripati tried to explain to her that this involved not the elegance of reasoning, but evidence. The evidence showed beyond a doubt that her friend was dead. Her exasperated answer was that he must have gone to a wrong address, that writing a letter would have been a more efficient method after all. Offended by her disdain for his efficiency, Sripati kept elaborating his evidence, to no avail. Half the night they spent arguing back and forth, debating evidence.

Husband and wife were by now in total agreement about expelling Kadambini from their house, though each had a different reason: Sripati was convinced that the woman was not the person she claimed to be, having cheated his wife into letting her stay on as their guest; and Jogamaya was convinced that she was right all along in suspecting that the woman had run away, dishonoring her family by violating the propriety of her station. Still, they continued arguing, neither willing to accept defeat in the argument. Their voices became louder as they kept arguing, unmindful that the person about whom they argued was in the adjoining room.

Finally, Jogamaya said, "All right. Give me the date on which she supposedly died." She decided that she could disprove his evidence by checking with the date in the last letter she had received from Kadambini. He told her the date; at once both felt faint with consternation, realizing that on the very next day Kadambini had come to their house.

Then their bedroom door was pushed open. The rain-soaked wind blew in and put out the lamp, immediately filling the room with the outside darkness. Kadambini stood inside the room, with the continuous sound of rainfall surrounding her, enveloping her. Grimly she said, "I'm still Kadambini, the childhood friend of yours, even though I exist as dead."

Jogamaya screamed in terror, and Sripati was silent with shock.

Kadambini continued, "But what wrong have I done other than being dead? If I have no place in your world, nor in any other world, then where shall I go? Tell me, where?"

Her voice rose sharply as she repeated her question, and it tore through the rain-filled night, as if trying to wake up her sleepy creator. She left the fainting couple in the dark room and went out to look for her rightful place in the universe.

5

It is hard to imagine how she managed, under the circumstances, to get back to her village. She even managed to keep herself out of sight of anyone in her village. For a whole day she hid, without food, in a ruined, deserted temple on the outskirts of the village. Then, as the monsoon night set in thick and early and as all the villagers hurried back home for shelter from the imminent, nightlong downpour, Kadambini came out of hiding and walked the deserted paths toward the house. At the gate, her heart fluttered. But, as the shrouded woman entered the house, the maids did not quite notice anything out of the ordinary, and the watchman did not think of stopping her. Right then, the rain started, carried along by a strong wind.

The mistress of the house was playing cards with her husband's widowed sister, the chambermaid was in the kitchen, and in his bedroom the baby was sleeping while his fever subsided. Kadambini managed to reach the baby, somehow evading all the others in the large household. We don't know what made her return to him. Perhaps she herself didn't quite know, except that she wanted to see the baby just once more, the very last time before leaving forever. She had given no thought to where she would go, what she would do afterward.

Now, as she stood watching, in the dim light of the oil lamp, the baby sleeping with his little closed fists, she longed to hug him just once more. It also occurred to her that while she had been there to take care of him, his mother, given to parlor games and conversation, never had to bother much about his care. The child must have been deprived of attention while she was gone. As she stood looking at him, the child turned and muttered half asleep, asking for aunt as he always did for water when thirsty at night.

Her heart, warmed once again in the familiar way, melted to find that he hadn't forgotten his aunt! She brought some water from the earthen jug and cradled the baby, who was used to drinking water like this, in her arms, at night. Then, as she gently kissed his face and was about to put him back to bed, he woke up and clung on to her.

"Did you go away to die?" he asked, wide awake.

"Yes, my dear."

"You are back now! Promise me you won't go away to die again."

Before she could reassure him and put him back to bed, trouble started. The maid came in with a bowl of tapioca gruel for the sick child. At the sight of Kadambini, she screamed and fainted, dropping the brass bowl clanging to the floor. At that noise, the mistress of the house dropped her cards, rushed to the room, and stood at the threshold like a wooden figure, unable to say anything or to turn back from what she saw there. All this strange commotion scared the child. He started crying, saying, "You leave now, aunt."

Kadambini had just realized, for the first time since she died, that she was not really dead. The baby, her tenderly aching love for him, and the familiar bedroom were as alive as before. Her supposed death and the long absence had made no difference to these feelings! At the other place, she had clearly felt that her friend's childhood friend was dead. But here, in the baby's room, she was intensely aware that his loving aunt was not dead at all.

Desperately, she now wanted to reassure them. "Why do you fear me so? Look at me closely. See, I am the same as I was before."

The mistress of the house could keep on her feet no longer and fainted. Meanwhile, the master of the house had been informed by his sister of what was going on. He hurried into the room. He held his palms together and fearfully pleaded with Kadambini.

"How can you do this to us, dear sister-in-law! Please, spare the child! You know that he is our family's only heir. Your near ones do not deserve this treatment from you. Ever since you died, the poor child has been sick, pining away, calling for you all the time. Please, let go of this attachment, now that you've left this world! I promise we'll properly perform all the postfuneral rites for your passage to the other world."

Kadambini could not endure any more. Her voice came out strangely shrill: "But I'm not dead! How can I make you believe that I am really not dead? Look! I can show you I'm still alive."

Then she picked up the heavy brass bowl the maid had dropped, and she kept hitting her forehead with it until blood spurted out and streamed down her face.

"Now can you see that I'm not dead yet?" she stopped to ask.

The head of the household stood petrified. The scared child was crying, now calling for his father, and the two women lay fainted on the floor. Kadambini ran out of the room screaming, "I'm not dead! I'm not!"

She ran down the stairs, and she ran all the way into the pond in the backyard. The master of the house, standing in the room upstairs, heard the splash quite clearly through the pervasive sound of rain.

It rained continuously throughout that night and the following morning. There was no sign of letting up even by the afternoon. Kadambini died last night and proved that she was not dead before.

The Punishment

Rabindranath Thakur

1

Dukhiram Rui and Chhidam Rui were brothers. Both worked as hired hands to earn their bare living. On that morning, as they were preparing to leave for work, carrying their sickles, their wives were quarreling and shouting at each other. The entire neighborhood had gotten used to it, as if it were part of the variety of usual noises and sounds that filled their natural environment. Whenever those two voices were heard rising and shrill, the neighbors' response was no more than resigned mutterings of "there they go again!" It was something expected and habitual, not at all exceptional. Nobody was particularly curious any longer about the causes of the vocal fights between the two sisters-in-law, any more than about the cause of sunrise in the east. On that day, none could have imagined that an occurrence of such expected regularity was to end in a strangely twisted tragedy.

The quarreling, of course, affected their husbands somewhat more than their neighbors. But the two brothers managed not to let it become more than a minor nuisance. In any case they had come to accept as inescapable their relentlessly hard life, which was like an uncontrollably rough ride in an old one-horse buggy, its wheels with broken springs rattling endlessly, driven on and on by some incomprehensible ruthless force. The frequent racket at home actually bothered them much less than its rare absence. Then, heavy with the abnormal silence, their home would seem to be crouching fearfully under some imminent blow, some unknown catastrophe about to befall them. That kind of uneasy silence was much more oppressive to them because of the total unpredictability of the outcome.

Dated Shravana 1300 (July to August 1893), "Shashti" appears in Rabindranath's *Galpaguchha*, vol. 1 (Calcutta: Visva-Bharati Granthayan Bibhag, 1926), 182–90.

In the evening of that fateful day, when the brothers returned, worn out and distraught from the day's worse than usual lot, they felt their home almost reverberating with deliberate, sullen silence.

The outside too seemed to be holding its breath. The sky, after one or two sharp midday showers, was still heavy with the dark clouds that hung menacingly low and still. There was no wind at all. They noticed that the weeds and shrubs, nourished by the monsoon, were crowding upon their hut. The smell of damp vegetation rising from them and the dense vapor from the flooded jute fields beyond seemed to have raised an invisible solid wall closing in on them from all sides. The ceaseless chorus of frogs and crickets, rising from the marsh behind the cowshed, seemed to have filled the entire space overhead under the leaden evening sky.

Not very far from there, the rain-swollen river, Padma, looked menacingly somber reflecting on her bosom the dark clouds overhead. Overflowing the banks, she had already started engulfing the crop fields and approaching the village. The ground was washed off several mango and jackfruit trees in the outskirts, their bared roots looking like so many gnarled fingers clawing the air for something to hold on to.

Dukhiram and Chhidam had worked the day at the landlord's estate office quarters. On the silt-raised islands close to the other side of the river, the early-ripened wet-paddy fields waited to be reaped before they would be flooded. Almost all the poor in that part of Bengal at this time of year were engaged in cutting paddy or jute, either in their own little fields or as hired laborers for a fraction of the harvest as part of their wages. But on that day, the Rui brothers had been picked up by the landlord's men and taken away to spend the whole day mending the rotting parts of the fences and the leaking parts of the roof of the landlord's estate office. The pay for this kind of work was worse than for harvest labor, and they had ended up getting even less than their due wages and more than their due insults. They had received some breakfast there but had to go on working in the rain without anything for lunch.

As they came home in the evening, wading back through muddy paths and waterlogged fields, they saw this domestic scene. The younger wife, Chandara, lay on the floor of the porch, her face turned away to the wall, one end of her sari spread under the upper part of her body. Like the rainy, cloudy day, she too had wept much in the afternoon and was now quiet but sulky like the sky. Radha, the older one, sat by the porch wearing a long, grim face. Her little boy of a year and a half, tired from crying, was asleep on his naked back in a corner of the dark porch.

A very hungry Dukhiram curtly asked his wife for the supper of rice. Like a bag of explosives touched by a spark, her shrill voice was instantly pitched sky-high as she answered, "Where's the food to serve you? Did you leave any rice to cook? Did you expect me to go out and find ways to earn it to feed you?"

After the whole day of underpaid labor and insults, and now facing this joyless and foodless home, with his empty stomach churning fiercely, Dukhiram suddenly felt his wife's usual rudeness unbearable. Particularly the indecent sarcasm of her last question. He growled like a tormented tiger, "What did you say!" And, before he could think of what he was doing, he had struck her on the head with the sickle in his hand.

Killed instantly, Radha rolled down by the lap of Chandara. Her clothes soaking with Radha's blood, Chandara screamed, "What have you done!" Chhidam sprang forward to cover her screaming mouth with his hands. Dukhiram dropped his sickle and slouched onto the ground, staring blankly, his hand over his mouth like an idiot. The child woke up scared and began crying.

In the rest of the village, it was perfectly peaceful at that moment. The cowherd boys were coming back with the animals in their charge. Those who had gone to cut the ripe paddy in the raised lands on the other side of the flooding river had already crossed the waters in small groups huddled in tiny boats. Most of them were now back home, with little bundles of the golden paddy on their heads as reward for their day's work.

In the Chakraborty household, "Uncle" Ramlochan sat smoking his hookah totally contented, having returned from mailing a letter at the village post office. Suddenly he remembered that his subtenant, Dukhiram, had promised to pay on that day some back rent he still owed. Deciding that the brothers must be back from work by then, he picked up his umbrella and his scarf and went out.

As the village uncle entered the yard of the Rui home, he felt strange about it. No lamp was lit there yet. He could barely make out some silent figures on the dark porch. From a corner of it, a woman's whimpering was turning into sobbing. The child was frantically crying for his "ma," and Chhidam equally frantically was trying to stop the child from crying out.

The uncle, a little frightened, addressed the dark porch from where he stood in the yard: "Dukhi? Are you there?"

Dukhiram, who was sitting absolutely still like a stone figure, burst out crying like a disconsolate child the moment he heard his name called.

Chhidam quickly stepped down from the porch and came to face the unexpected visitor, who remarked, "Your women have been at it again, right? We heard them shouting through the whole day."

Up to that point, Chhidam had been trying desperately to think up some way to take care of the terrible event. All kinds of ideas were flitting through his head, and he had not yet been able to decide what to do. For the time being, he was thinking of removing the body somewhere later in the night. He had not considered the possibility of an unexpected visitor in the meantime. Now he went totally blank and could think of nothing to hide the situation from the visitor's curiosity. All he could do was to vaguely mumble, "Yes. They had a bad fight today."

The growing curiosity of the gentleman distracted him from the original purpose of his visit. He now approached the porch, asking, "But why does that make Dukhi weep like that?"

Chhidam saw no way out, and, in his terrible panic, he blurted out, "In the fight, my wife struck her older sister-in-law with the cleaver."

Sometimes, the immediate trouble so totally grips one's mind that it blocks out all thoughts of other, even worse, troubles that might follow a certain move. All Chhidam could think of at that moment was how to hide the terrible truth; it did not occur to him that his lie might produce an even more terrible reality. Faced with the suspicious visitor's question, his bewildered head simply had made up a story likely to sound somewhat plausible.

The startled gentleman asked if she was dead. Chhidam said yes, and fell at his feet, begging for his help. The visitor, his curiosity satisfied, was now eager to leave the scene. What a trouble to get involved in on what was to be a peaceful evening! Would he need to kill himself running around to be a witness in a court case of no interest to him?

But Chhidam clung to his feet with all his strength and kept begging him to suggest some way to save his wife. Chhidam had a good reason for behaving this way. The gentleman happened to be the undisputed village expert on the intricacies of court cases. It seemed to work. He thought a little and said, "Well, here is a way out. Run to the police station, and report that when your brother came home hungry and found that his wife had not cooked, he struck her with his sickle. I can guarantee that it will save your wife's neck."

Chhidam now felt his throat drying. He got up from the gentleman's feet and feebly said, "But it is possible to replace a wife, not a brother." He had not reasoned this way at all when he blurted out the first lie, which he did in a frantic rush of panic and confusion. But once he had done that, he unconsciously started rationalizing it, even trying to use it as a kind of consolation for the loss he was implicitly risking.

The village uncle and legal expert agreed that it was a valid point and said, "All right. Then tell them the way it actually happened; you can't save them both." With that, he quickly exited.

Soon, the news spread throughout the village that the young wife of Chhidam, in a quarrel, hit her older sister-in-law in the head with a cleaver and killed her. The next day, the police came to the village: something that was as uncommon and overwhelming an external intrusion as a flashflood.

2

Chhidam saw that he no longer had any choice; he was trapped in what he had said. The lie he had blurted out to the influential Uncle Ramlochan was now established as truth in all the villagers' minds. He simply could not make out what might result if he now said anything contradicting that. It seemed to him that the least damaging thing now would be to stick to his basic account, working it into additional stories toward her defense and attempting to reduce her sentence.

Thinking along this line, he went up to Chandara and asked her to plead guilty. He tried as hard as he could to assure the shocked, terrified girl that he was working out plans to get her off the punishment. But even as he uttered those words of assurance to her, he felt his throat become parched and his face ashen.

Chandara was very young, about eighteen, with a round full face and a small firm body. Her healthy young limbs moved about with such ease and grace that she reminded one of a finely crafted little boat, all smoothly carved and neatly joined together, gliding effortlessly about the water. Nearly everything in the little world around her caught her quick glimpse and amused her. She never missed a chance to chat with other village women, and, on her daily trips to the pond with the water vessel perched at her waist and her sari partly veiling her face, her quick dark eyes always managed to notice every little thing.

Her older sister-in-law was the exact opposite. Disorganized and lackadaisical, she always seemed unable to cope with the obligatory end of her sari over her head, her little boy, and her daily chores. Even when there was not much work to do, she looked harried and starved of rest. Their quarrels usually started with some softly spoken stinger from the younger one, to which she invariably responded with disproportionate loudness and uncontrollable verbal outpourings; these formed the major part of the noisy outbursts the neighbors were used to hearing.

Their husbands too showed an amazingly parallel contrast. Dukhi was large and big-boned but with uncomprehending and unquestioning eyes. He gave the rare impression of a completely harmless yet potentially terrible man, so big and strong physically yet so helpless in his looks and so dependent in his behavior. Young Chhidam's body looked as if it were carefully chiseled out of shiny black stone, without the slightest bulge or dent anywhere. His limbs were so balanced with strength and discipline that whatever he was engaged in doing produced a picture of energy flowing with perfect smoothness—especially when he dove into the river from a carefully chosen high point on its bank, when he plied a boat with the long pole, slowly pushing in and pulling out, or when he climbed up a tall bamboo to cut the part needed for making thin strips. He always had his longish black hair carefully oiled and combed off his forehead and down to his shoulders. Even in his ordinary dressing, there were clear touches of care and decoration. He certainly could not be described as indifferent to his appearance.

Nor was he indifferent to the attractions of the village women, but he had a special fondness for his wife. They had fights and reconciliations, neither quite managing to subdue the other. Each had an acute anxiety about losing the other, and the element of uncertainty intensified their mutual attraction. He thought that the lively, carefree girl could not be trusted too much. She thought that she had to design and use some special binding devices if she was not to lose her fancy husband with his wandering eyes.

For some time prior to the fateful incident, both of them were getting rather worked up thinking about each other along these lines. She watched him occasionally go off for some distant work, returning after a day or two without any credible earning. She responded to this bad sign by acting to arouse his already heightened jealousy. She resorted to taking more frequent trips to the pond and returning home bubbling with some irrelevant account she had just heard about the second son of some particular neighbor, of no significance except to excite his jealousy.

Chhidam felt his days and his nights poisoned. He could not have peace for a moment, he felt restless at work, and he could not concentrate on any of the sporting activities he had always enjoyed. One day he admonished his sister-in-law for not guarding the girl enough. He got a blast of shouting and finger-shaking from her: "Don't ask me to keep an eye on her. That girl moves ahead of a storm. I tell you she's going to get in trouble one of these days." At that point, the girl quietly emerged from the adjoining room, sweetly asking, "What makes you, dear sister, worry so much about me?" This was about to set off one of those quarrels. But instead Chhidam, glowering at her, told her that he would smash her bones if she went out alone to the pond one more time. She replied that her bones would then have peace at long last, promptly picking up the empty water vessel and proceeding to go out. Chhidam caught up with her in one leap, grasped her by the hair, and took her inside. He bolted the door from outside and left. When he came back from work, he found the room empty. She had somehow managed to open the door and run away, as he later found out, to her uncle's home, three villages away. Chhidam then had to go there and plead with her; it was not easy to persuade her to come back home with him. After that, he came to accept his defeat, or at least the impossibility of victory. He came to realize that trying to control his young wife was like trying to hold a fistful of mercury, so amazingly capable of slipping away through invisible chinks between tightly closed fingers.

He stopped trying to control her, but he did not recover his peace of mind. His anxiety-ridden love stayed in him like a lump of acute, persistent pain.

Sometimes he even wished her dead. Grief seemed preferable to this constant, painful anxiety. One cannot feel as jealous of Yama, the god of death, as of mortal men like oneself.

About this time, in the midst of their mutually heightened anguish about each other's noncompliance, the calamity took place.

When a bewildered, panicky Chhidam asked her to take the blame, Chandara froze, her coal-black eyes staring at him, burning him silently. Her whole body and mind searched for some way to shrink away from, and become invisible to, the demon that had suddenly taken the form of her husband. Her soul turned back on him, totally and irrevocably.

While Chhidam was frantically repeating to her the life-saving story that she was to tell the police and the court, she was not listening to a single word. She just sat there, a blankly staring wooden figure.

The older brother had always relied on Chhidam. When told that Chandara was to plead guilty, he only asked what would happen to her then. Once Chhidam told him that he had plans to save her, the big-bodied, distraught Dukhiram was reassured like a little child.

3

The story Chhidam thought he had taught Chandara to tell was that during the quarrel the older sister-in-law had picked up the cleaver and was about to strike her and then, as Chandara struggled to prevent it from striking her, it accidentally hit her attacker. The basic story, complete with appropriate gestures, flourishes, and contingent arguments, was drilled into Chhidam by the legal expert Uncle Ramlochan.

By the time the police started interrogating the villagers, the idea that Chandara had killed her sister-in-law was rooted in their minds. They all gave the same account. When the police asked Chandara, she readily confessed committing the murder.

"Why did you do it?"

"Because I couldn't stand her."

"Was there any provocation from her?"

"None at all."

"Did she try to hit you first?"

"No."

"Did she ever torment you?"

"Of course not."

Everybody was baffled. An agitated Chhidam could control himself no longer and broke in. "But she's not telling the truth! Her sister-in-law first . . ." The police chief shouted roughly at him and stopped him there. To all the systematically repeated questioning, Chandara gave the same account

of killing her sister-in-law, the same flat denial of any provocation or intention of assault from her.

Whoever had seen such stubbornness! Whoever had heard of someone so
totally determined to reach the hangman's noose, so resolutely shaking off all
the outstretched hands trying to hold her back. How terribly she was react-
ing to her hurt feeling, how cruelly she was giving him her terrible message—
"I am leaving you, and, bedecked with all the glory of my flowering youth, I
am going to receive death himself. With him shall I have the final union of
my life."

Then, with her hands cuffed, Chandara left the village. She was no longer
the sprightly young wife, always amused by all its little happenings. She left
along those familiar paths. She went past those very same steps leading down
to the pond, the place of her favorite daily gatherings, past those particular
houses whose inmates were the subject of all that lively gossip. She went past
the village post office and the school building. She walked past the fairground
for the chariot festival and finally through the marketplace. She walked at the
center of the damning procession, under those watching eyes of all the people
she knew, people who until then thought they knew her. She left home forever, bearing the terribly branded mark of misdoing they shuddered even to
think of, followed all the way out of the village by the entire lot of the urchins.
Even without looking, she could see those eyes of women watching, some of
them her close friends, peeking through the veils, standing behind the door
openings and the trees. She could vividly imagine how they cringed with
shame, with contempt, with fear, as they witnessed this unimaginable spectacle of a perfectly ordinary village housewife being taken away by the police
for committing murder.

Before the district magistrate's deputy, Chandara pleaded guilty in the
same calm manner, admitting no provocation whatsoever from the victim.
Chhidam, when he came to the witness stand, wept uncontrollably, pleading
with folded hands, saying that his wife was in fact innocent, and begging to
let him explain. The judge's stern rebuke stopped his crying; and once interrogation proceeded, Chhidam revealed the true events in their true sequence.

The deputy magistrate did not believe his account because the case's only
gentleman witness, Ramlochan Chakraborty, said that he himself was at the
site shortly after the murder had taken place. He said that Chhidam at that
time told him that his wife had killed her sister-in-law and then begged him
for advice about how to save his wife. The gentleman said that he, of course,
had refused to give any such advice. And when Chhidam had pressed him,
"If I tell that my brother, coming home hungry and finding no food from his
wife, struck her in a rage with his sickle, will that save my wife?" Ramlochan
claimed he dutifully warned the illiterate man that lying in court
was the worst of all crimes, and so on. Ramlochan had, of course, composed

the story supposed to save Chandara's life. But when she herself so stubbornly turned her back to it, he decided against risking perjury just to try out
his own cleverness.

The deputy sent the case to the higher court for the final hearing.

In the surrounding world, meanwhile, there was laughing and crying as
usual, and all the regular activities continued—farmers worked in the fields,
people went about their daily chores, pursuing their little or big livelihoods,
and all the buying and selling in the marketplace proceeded as before. As in
all other years at this time, the fresh green stretches of fields laden with
young paddy received, with joy and adoration, the blessing of the ceaseless,
gentle rainfall of the month of Shravana.

The courtroom was in session again; the accused, the police, and the witnesses assembled for their final hearings. In the large courtyard outside, people
waited in groups near the smaller courts dealing with civil cases; all the
groups busily prepared for the hearings on their respective cases. A Calcutta
lawyer was conspicuously present to deal with one case that concerned the
ownership of a marsh behind somebody's kitchen, and the defendant had
assembled no less than forty-nine witnesses. Chhidam was gazing through
the courtroom window at those earnestly preoccupied people. So many people were so anxiously absorbed in matters of minute settlement of disputed
property. Watching them, it did not seem possible that anything else in the
world could be more important. To him it felt like a strange scene in a dream.
He was also listening to the *koels* sweetly trilling from the big banyan tree in
the middle of the courtyard, the only ones there not busy with any kind of
lawsuit.

Chandara made the same statement before the English judge. Further
probings she answered by asking the white man how many more times she
would have to repeat her account. The judge patiently explained to the
blunt-speaking, impatient girl that she must think and speak more carefully,
for the crime to which she was pleading guilty would carry the sentence of
death by hanging.

She answered, "Please, I beg you, saheb, let me have that punishment.
Please do anything you want, except prolong my torment, because I can't
bear it any longer."

When Chhidam was brought to the stand, she turned her face away. The
judge asked her to look at the witness and state her relationship with him.
Covering her face with her hands, she answered that he was her husband.

The judge asked, "Do you think that he does not love you?"

She answered, "Oh, he loves me a whole lot!"

The judge asked, "Don't you love him?"

She answered, "Yes, I love him."

As soon as he was questioned, Chhidam said that it was he who had committed the murder.

"Why did you do it?"

"Because my sister-in-law refused to serve food when I came home hungry."

Dukhiram was brought in next. He staggered to the witness stand and fainted in it. When he recovered, he said, "Saheb, I am the one who murdered my wife."

"What was the reason?"

"I was very hungry and asked for my rice, but my wife didn't give it to me."

The kindly judge, after careful deliberation based on his review of all the evidence from interrogation and from the other witnesses, concluded that the brothers must both be lying, confessing to the murder in order to save the young housewife from the humiliation of being hanged for murder. The woman, on the other hand, had consistently given the same account throughout, from the police's first questioning in the village until this final hearing.

Two lawyers had volunteered and tried everything they could think of in defense of a reduced sentence. But the girl managed to defeat all their efforts.

The day a plump, round-faced girl with comely dark skin left her dolls behind at her parental home to become a wife, who could have thought, on that auspicious occasion, that her life was to end in this manner! Her father was at peace in his deathbed, thinking that he had at least been able to set his only child along the right path in her life.

Before the execution was to take place, a compassionate civil surgeon came to the calmly waiting girl and asked if she wished to see anyone.

"Yes. I wish to see my mother once before I die."

"Your husband has been waiting outside for a long time to see you. Shall I go and ask him in?"

"He can go to hell!"

The Girl in Between

Rabindranath Thakur

1

In Nibaran's way of life, there was no place for anything irregular. Absolutely no role for the unusual, the extraordinary. No room for poetry—tragic, romantic, or any other kind. It never occurred to him that something like poetry may have a place somewhere in life. He lived his thoroughly habitual life without thinking about it, like the way in which one slips one's feet into one's well-worn sandals. He lived his days without even blundering into anything involving wonder or excitement, without ever reflecting on any aspect of his life.

Each morning, he sat by the front door of his house on a little lane in old Calcutta, smoking his hookah with absolute contentment, listening to the accustomed sounds, and watching the accustomed sights. People passed by on their various business; carriages rolled along; the Vaishnav minstrel went singing from door to door for alms; the buyer of old bottles plodded by with his heavy sack, loudly announcing his presence to potential customers. These familiar sights and sounds kept his mind lightly engaged as he enjoyed his morning smoke. Once in a while, when a vendor appeared on the scene with green mangoes or delicate baby catfish, he would get up to bargain and perhaps purchase some; then he would go to the kitchen, at that time the focus of busy activities in the house, to arrange a special variation in the lunch menu.

At a certain fixed hour, he would finally get up, go inside, and proceed to massage his body with mustard oil before taking his bath. Then he would sit

Dated Jaishtha 1300 (May to June 1893), "Madhyabartini" appears in Rabindranath's *Galpaguchha*, vol. 1 (Calcutta: Visva-Bharati Granthayan Bihag, 1926), 164–74.

down for the lunch served to him. After lunch, he would don his office jacket, which at other times hung on the rope strung across one corner of the room, and pause briefly for an after-lunch smoke while chewing a dressed roll of betel leaf. Finally, with a second roll of betel in his mouth, he would go to his office for the rest of the day.

Back from work, he would spend the evening in the front room of the house of his neighbor Ramlochan Ghosh, enjoying a quiet time in solemn spirit in the company of like-minded men. Following that, first he took his dinner and then went to the bedroom to join his wife, Harasundari.

There, before going to sleep, they briefly exchanged opinions and information on such things as the quality of the gifts sent from the groom's side at the wedding of a certain neighbor's son, the disobedience of the new housemaid, and the agreeability of a certain combination of spices for a particular dish that day. No poet had ever thought of writing about such conjugal conversation, but that never bothered Nibaran in any way.

One spring, the set ways of Nibaran's orderly life were disrupted when his wife came down with a severe case of malaria. The fever refused to let up, in spite of heavy doses of quinine. She remained in the grip of the racking fever for twenty, twenty-two, eventually forty-one days. He had to skip going to the office and miss the early evening sessions at his favorite neighbor's all-male front room. His meticulous daily routine was all upset, as he shuttled between the bedroom to check on his sick wife and the porch to smoke anxiously. He worried, changed doctors, tried every home remedy recommended by various well-wishers.

In spite of the concerned disarray of medical treatment, the fever finally let go of her on the forty-second day. However, it left her body so thin and weak that her response to all the loving, anxious queries was very faint and spare, like a signal trying to reach across a vast distance.

It was spring then. In their crowded neighborhood, although the nights are still hot, a fresh breeze from the south and cool moonlight softly make their way into stuffy bedrooms through the tiniest of back windows. Just below Harasundari's bedroom was the neighbor's backyard. It was not pretty, but a few crotons that someone had planted sometime and forgotten about were in bloom among the weeds. A hardy pumpkin vine was steadily climbing up a clumsy prop of dried twigs. Weeds crowded under an old plum tree now covered with blossoms. Part of the decrepit brick wall beside the kitchen at the other end of the yard had crumbled into a pile of rubble, on which the daily dumping of ash from the coal stove had grown into a large rubbish heap.

Looking at this garden from her bed by the window, where she lay absolutely peaceful all day, she received from time to time a flow of joy such as she had never felt before in the healthy years of her life filled with the daily routine of busy trivialities. It was like the glassy transparence that a muddy river achieves in late summer, after the months of heat have nearly reduced it to its sandy bed, so that the light of the morning sun shines through its crystal clear flow and touches the bottom of its heart, the slightest breeze makes its shiver with ecstasy, and the starry sky is reflected on the surface as so many shining points of light like pleasant memories. The joyful fingers of spring lightly touched the delicate strings in the mind of the silently convalescing woman, playing an exquisitely sweet, mysteriously ecstatic music.

At those moments, her husband's routine bedside visits and his mundane "how do you feel?" nearly brought tears of intense happiness to her eyes. Her large eyes shone even larger in her thin, pale face. When she placed those eyes gently, lovingly on his face and held his hand in her thin hand without saying a word, then he too felt touched by an unfamiliar ray of joy coming from somewhere beyond the ordinary.

She spent many days in this manner, quietly lying in her bed, stirred only inside by euphoria. One night, a big round moon was rising behind the shivering leaves of the young banyan tree that had grown from the rubbish heap by the crumbled wall. A nocturnal breeze suddenly flew in and dispelled the evening's still, humid heat. She was silently stroking his hair, when she said to him in a tone that was at once light and grave, "We have no child. I wish you could marry again and have a child."

She had thought about it for a while. In a rare moment of intense joy and overexpanded love, one is convinced that one can do anything, sacrifice everything, no matter how stupid one would normally consider the idea to be. Like the wave rising and crashing on the rock, swollen love seems to long for a big challenge, some great sorrow to dash itself on. In that state of mind, she joyfully decided one day to do for him something extraordinarily magnanimous.

She kept thinking what it could be, searching her mind for an act that would match her intense desire to give out of great love. She did not have wealth, power, intellect. All she had was her life. If only she knew how to make a nice gift of it! Besides, she was not sure if it was valuable enough as a gift. She knew she wanted to give him a baby, milk white and butter soft, but that had remained unrealized so far and seemed to her unrealizable. Then it occurred to her that she could make him the gift of another wife to bear him a child. She wondered why women dreaded it and found it unbearable. If one loved one's husband, how could it be so hard to love his other wife? The thought made her very proud of herself, proud that she could think so clearly and see no inconsistency between loving and sharing the loved one with another woman.

Nibaran laughed it away the first time she mentioned it. He ignored it the second and the third time. His lack of response increased her happiness, but it also heightened her conviction and her determination to make it happen.

The recurrence of her proposal started acting on his mind too, slowly increasing its appeal, slowly covering its preposterousness. When he sat by himself having his morning smoke, his mind viewed with pleasure the picture of a home with children.

One day he himself brought up the subject, with only the reservation that a busy, mature man like him could not possibly spend the amount of energy necessary to bring up a young bride into a responsible wife. She asked him not to worry about that because she herself would do the bringing up. As the childless woman said this, she fondly imagined the face of a child bride, a sweet and shy adolescent torn off her mother's arms. Her heart felt affection, not jealousy.

He, of course, kept stressing his lack of time to spare, his preoccupations, including his own dear wife to look after; he could not waste his time on a childish girl. She assured him each time that she would do all the work that was involved. She even joked, "We'll see then what happens to your work, to your concern for me, and to you, my dear." He did not consider it worth answering in words, but he smiled at her, tapping her cheek in a gesture of loving reprimand.

This, briefly, is the prologue of this story.

2

Then one day Nibaran had his second marriage with a short, plump girl, with teardrops and jewelry dangling from her pierced nose. Her name was Shailabala.

Nibaran thought that the name was rather sweet and that her face was rather lovely. Her looks, her moods, her movements interested him. Curiosity inclined him to observe her closely. However, he could not appear to be interested in her and had to pretend that he could not wait to set aside the girl and get back to the normal sphere of occupations appropriate to his age and his station in life.

The awkward appearance of Nibaran as a serious man bothered with unworthy trivialities bemused Harasundari. Sometimes, she held him back by the hand, "Why do you run away? She's only a little girl, not going to eat you up!"

Nibaran would then appear twice as troubled, saying, "Stop it. I've some urgent work to attend to," and pretend to be helplessly trapped.

Harasundari would then whisper in his ear that he should not completely ignore the poor girl after bringing her to his home. Then she would make him sit, make Shailabala sit on his left side, raise her veil and lift her unwilling face to him, and say to him, "Look at her pretty face, sweet like the full moon."

Sometimes, she would get up abruptly and leave the room, as if she remembered some household work to be finished, leaving the two of them inside, and latch the door from outside. Nibaran knew that two curious eyes must be watching through some hole, and he would feign indifference to the bride and turn away as if to go to sleep; and Shailabala would wrap her veil around tighter and become a bundle in a corner of the bed.

Finally Harasundari gave up trying, disappointed but not unhappy.

When Harasundari gave up, Nibaran gave in to the pull of curiosity, to the power of mystery. If one suddenly finds oneself holding a diamond, one wants to turn it and watch it from its many sides. Here was the mind of an unknown young girl, so much more fascinating. So many different ways in which it could be touched and caressed. So many ways it could be seen, from hiding, face-to-face, and sideways. Sometimes lightly, touching the dangling earring or lifting the veil just a little; sometimes swiftly like lightning; sometimes gazing on with the steadiness of a distant star—so many new, unfamiliar facets of beauty were to be discovered.

Such an experience had never happened to the hero of our story, the head clerk of McMoran Company. He was a mere boy at the time of his first marriage. By the time he attained adulthood, his wife was familiar and his conjugal life habitual. He certainly loved Harasundari, but never before had he consciously felt the influence of erotic love. The insect born and matured inside a ripe mango never had to search for its lovely nectar; it never knew the intense desire to savor its sweetness. Release that insect in a spring garden in bloom and then watch its eagerness: how it keeps hovering around the half-open rosebud; how a bit of the flower's perfume and a bit of its nectar intoxicate it for more, and more!

Nibaran started making his overtures to Shailabala with secret presents of little girlish things, like a china doll, a packet of sweets, a bottle of scent. That was how their intimacy was initiated.

At some point in this process, Harasundari finally discovered them together. Sometime between her endless chores one day, she saw them, through the slightly open door, playing a game of shells. A man of his age so totally absorbed in a girlish game! He had given Harasundari the appearance of leaving for the office after his lunch; instead, he had stolen back to Shailabala's room! What was the need for this little deception? The shock opened up Harasundari's vision as if with the stab of a red hot iron rod, and its heat vaporized her tears before they could flow.

Harasundari thought to herself, "I'm the one who initiated the process of bringing her into this home, of getting them together; and now he acts as if I'm standing between them and blocking their happiness."

Harasundari used to teach Shailabala how to do some of the household chores. One day Nibaran spoke up, "You're working her too hard. She's too young, and not strong enough for housework."

A sharp answer came to her lips; but she did not utter it. She kept silent. After that she never asked the new bride to help in any housework; she herself did all the cooking and all the caretaking. As a result, Shailabala learned to do nothing, no work at all. Harasundari tended her needs like a maid; and Nibaran entertained her like a court jester. She could not learn that working and taking care of others were important parts of life. She did not learn anything about responsibility.

Harasundari silently worked all day like their maid. She felt pride, not self-pity, in this. She did not think of herself as demeaned or reduced because she thought herself capable of taking charge of the household and letting the two of them play like little children.

3

As time went by, however, Harasundari found her strength draining, the strength that once made her feel sure she could give away half of her fully owned love of her husband for the rest of her life. When a full moon night brings a sudden high tide in one's life, overflowing the banks, the mind is easily moved to regard itself as limitless, endlessly capable. At such a moment, one may make oneself a very large promise. Later on, during the long drought of life, the effort involved in keeping that promise becomes a strain beyond human endurance. At a time of sudden abundance, it seems easy to make an extravagant gift with a stroke of the pen. Later on, when one has to pay every painful bit through days of endless poverty for the rest of life, one realizes how little we are, how weak our minds, and how limited our capacities.

Harasundari, at the end of her long illness, was like a pale thin crescent of the new moon. She felt weightless, floating effortlessly over life. At that time, she felt in need of nothing for herself. As her body gained strength and its blood supply increased, her mind was besieged by claimants whose existence she was not aware of before, all shouting at her, "You've written the gift; but we are not about to give up our due."

The day Harasundari for the first time clearly understood her situation, she left her own bedroom and started sleeping in a different part of the house. Their conjugal bed, to which she first came on her wedding night at the age of eight, she left after twenty-seven years. That night, while this married woman blew out the lamp and, with the unbearable weight of her pain, lay awake on her new bed of widowhood, a fancy young man was singing in a house at the other end of the lane. It was a song about a certain flower girl, a song composed in *behaag raga*,* which was accompanied not only by the *tabla*

* The musical mood conveying the pain of separation.

player but also the appreciative "hah-hah" noise from his audience of friends
near the end of each *sam.* *

On that otherwise quiet, moonlit night, the song sounded rather pleasant
in another bedroom, where Nibaran was whispering a certain term of
endearment to the very sleepy Shailabala. The term, *shoi*, he had learned
from reading Bankimchandra's novel, *Chandrasekhar.*† Nibaran had also
tried reading to Shailabala love poems by some modern poets, poems he had
never read before, written by poets he had never heard of before.

This hidden layer of erotic feeling, more like an adolescent's, which had
remained suppressed, suddenly struck rather late in his life, swelled up
incongruously at this utterly inappropriate time. Nobody, not even he himself, was quite prepared for this to happen and make his practical senses and
his organized life come apart. Our poor hero never knew that man's mind
could have such troublesome traits hidden away, such uncontrollable forces
that could wreck all that was rationally organized, disciplined, and clearly
understood in life.

It was a distressing revelation not just to Nibaran. Harasundari too came
to know a new kind of pain that she had never felt before, the desire for the
unattained and the unbearable feeling of deprivation. What her mind now
craved, it had never before wanted. Before she had never even thought of it,
and so she did not notice missing it either. When Nibaran lived his routine
life centered on his office-going, when they had brief conversations at night
about the milkman's bill, the rising prices of things, and matters of their
social duties, there was no trace then of any such internal turmoil. There was
love; but it was without dazzle, without heat; it was like some combustible
material before the spark.

Now it seemed to her as if she was condemned to eternal deprivation from
the experience of success and fulfillment in life. She felt as if her heart had
always been starved, her entire woman's life had remained in total poverty.
She had spent twenty-seven years, the prime of her life, chained like a slave
to the household mill, endlessly occupied with little things needed for running it, the vegetables and spices to be bought and stored and measured out
every day. Now, midway through her life, she found, next to her own mundane conjugal bedroom, a young girl reigning like a queen in the midst of
enormous riches she had unlocked with some key Harasundari did not have.
Woman serves, but she also reigns. How could it become so polarized that
one woman was only a servant and the other only a queen! That took the
pride out of one's service and the happiness out of the other's power.

---

* The terminal point of the *tala* (beats) cycle in the rhythm of a song.
† *Shoi*, literally meaning dearest (female) friend, was the term in which the hero of the novel
addressed the woman of his illicit love, Shaibalini, a name that did not seem too different from
Shailabala in Nibaran's mind.

As a matter of fact, Shailabala too was denied the real felicity of a woman's life. She received such constant loving that she did not have any scope to love back. A river is naturally fulfilled by flowing toward the ocean and merging into it; but if the ocean constantly floods in at the pull of the river, then the river keeps swelling inside inward, which is not a very normal condition for a river. As the world around her delivered love and care to her day and night, Shailabala grew excessively self-indulgent, incapable of loving anyone but herself. She learned that everything and everybody was for her but that she was for nobody. She became egotistical but unsatisfied in her life.

4

It was an intensely rainy day. A day so dark with clouds that doing the chores inside the home had become difficult. Outside, the rain was falling noisily, flooding the backyard of weeds and vines. Along the open drain by the wall, muddy rainwater rushed by, mimicking the sound of a river. Harasundari sat watching by the window in the darkened room, her new solitary bedroom.

Nibaran approached her door, cautiously like a thief, unsure of whether to come in or back off. Harasundari saw him and his hesitation, but she said nothing. Then he quickly walked in, as if his mind was suddenly made up by some desperation, and spoke to her in one breath. "I need some of your jewelry. Perhaps you know that I've quite a few debts. The creditors are giving me trouble. I must mortgage something, but I expect to get it back to you soon."

Harasundari did not answer. Nibaran waited timidly, almost guiltily. After waiting some time, he asked diffidently, "I can't have it today, then?"

Harasundari merely said, "No."

Entering her room was difficult for him; going out immediately after her monosyllabic answer seemed just as difficult. Nibaran stood hesitating, looking at nothing in particular; then he left, saying quite pointlessly, "Then let me try some other source."

Harasundari understood his debt, to whom he wanted to mortgage her jewelry. He must have been worked over by his child bride the night before. She must have taunted this pathetic slave of hers about why she could not wear his older wife's jewelry.

After Nibaran had left, Harasundari got up. She opened her iron safe and took out all her jewelry. Then she called in Shailabala. She dressed the girl in the gold-embroidered Banarasi sari that she had worn at her own wedding, and then she decorated the girl from head to toe with all the jewelry. Finally she carefully combed her hair into a pretty bun. She lighted the lamp to clearly see the result of her work. She saw that the girl's face was sweet, smooth, and plump like a just ripe, juicy, fragrant fruit.

When Shailabala left her room, with all those anklets tinkling at each step,

the sound seemed to echo through Harasundari's veins for a long time. She
said to herself, "Today there can be no comparison between you and me, but
there was a time when I was your age, when I too was in the full bloom of
youth. Why was it that nobody ever let me know it then? I never knew when
that time came to me and when it left me. Look at how she goes, so conscious
of the glory of her youth, of the waves of pride she raises with each step as she
walks!"

When Harasundari had lived her life absorbed with her household,
her jewelry was valuable to her. She could not have parted with it so easily
then, so stupidly in an instant, giving in to a mood of renunciation. Now,
after she had come to know something beyond running her household,
something missing that is bigger than a well-run home, any thought of the
value of the jewelry and concern for the future seemed trite and insignificant.

And what was Shailabala's thought? Glittering all over in the gems and
gold with which Harasundari had adorned her and now happily walking
back to her own bedroom, she did not wonder for one moment how much
Harasundari had just given her with the jewelry. She merely felt confirmed,
once again, in her belief that all wealth, nurturance, and good fortune should
flow in her direction, like a law of nature, because she was Shailabala, because she was the darling of all.

5

Once in a while, we hear about the somnambulist, who walks fearlessly
through dangerous terrain, never pausing to think for a moment while
dreaming in deep sleep. Some fully awake people seem to enter a state of
pseudo-dreaming, and like the true sleepwalker, they walk dangerous paths
without the slightest worry. Only after reaching total disaster do they become really awake.

Our hapless hero, the head clerk of McMoran Company, had become like
that. Shailabala had become a whirlpool at the center of his life, and its
powerful pull kept swallowing all kinds of valuables from near and far. Not
just Nibaran's human integrity, along with his monthly salary, and not just
Harasundari's happiness, along with her best clothes and jewelry, were lost
in that whirlpool. Its pull worked secretly in the cash box of McMoran
Company, and bundles of notes kept vanishing from there in ones and
twos. Nibaran made resolutions to put it back bit by bit out of each of the
next few months' salary. However, each month's salary had the habit of disappearing at the speed of lightning, to the last two-penny bit, barely leaving
a glimpse of its metallic flash.

Finally he was caught. The job had been held by quite a few trusted men
from the family over several generations. The owner of the company was
really fond of him and allowed him two days to put back what he had taken

out over many months. Nibaran was shattered to learn that what he had slowly taken out amounted to twenty-five hundred rupees. He came to Harasundari like a crazed man. "I'm destroyed," he said.

Harasundari turned pale hearing his account of what had happened.

"Please let me have your jewelry," he said.

"But I've given it all to your young wife," she said.

Like an anxious, disconsolate child, Nibaran kept asking, "Why did you give her your jewelry? Who asked you to do such a terrible thing?"

Harasundari did not think it was the time to go into the true answer. She simply said, "That should be quite all right. I didn't throw it into the river."

But he begged Harasundari, with pathetic cowardice, to go by herself and retrieve them from Shailabala, using any pretext that did not reveal that he wanted them and why. Harasundari was now filled with anger, irritation, and contempt. "Is this the time for deception, for pretense, for keeping up appearance? Come right now."

She took him to his young wife's room.

The girl listened but refused to understand or help. Her only reply to all their reasoning and appealing was, "I can't do anything about that."

Had anyone ever told her that she might have to worry about any of life's problems? The rule was that people should take care of their own problems, and all of them should take care of her, making her happy and comfortable. It now seemed extremely unfair to her that there could be an aberration from this undisputed rule.

Nibaran clasped her feet and begged with tears in his eyes. But she would not budge. "I don't care what happens to you. Why should I give up what belongs to me?"

Nibaran realized that the small, pretty, seemingly soft girl was tougher than the iron safe. The sight of her husband's pathetic weakness at a time of desperate crisis made Harasundari cringe with shame and anger. She tried to take the bunch of keys away from the girl, but Shailabala promptly threw it into the pond beyond the wall. Harasundari asked the paralyzed Nibaran to break the lock. Shailabala calmly declared that she would hang herself if he tried that.

Nibaran left, flustered and confused, saying, "I'll try something else."

Within two hours, he came back, after having sold his home, the home that he inherited from his father, for twenty-five hundred rupees.

With much effort, he was spared the handcuffs, but he lost the job. Of all the movable and immovable property he had accumulated over the years, he was left with nothing except his two wives. The young one, who easily tired even in normal times, had now become almost immovable with her pregnancy. The family left the large ancestral home and took shelter in a small and damp rented place down the lane.

6

There was no end to the unhappiness and complaint of the pregnant young wife. She absolutely refused to understand her husband's predicament, that he had no choice. If he was not able to do better, then why did he marry her?

There were now only two rooms in the rented place: one was the bedroom of Shailabala and Nibaran; the other was Harasundari's. Shailabala complained incessantly about having to spend all day and night confined to one room. Nibaran gave her false assurances of finding a better and bigger house soon. Shailabala promptly pointed to the room next to hers, asking why she could not have it too.

Shailabala had never even looked at her neighbors while she lived in the big house. One day they came to pay them a visit in their little place, to express sympathy in their time of trouble. Shailabala locked herself in her room, ignored all requests to come out, and after they had left she ranted, cried, went without food, and became so hysterical that the entire neighborhood knew what was going on and why she was having a tantrum.

This kind of trouble became increasingly frequent as her pregnancy advanced. Eventually she became so ill that it seemed she could lose the baby. Nibaran came to Harasundari, and he begged her to save the girl.

Harasundari nursed her day and night, silently taking all the abuse the girl hurled at her for the slightest fault. Shailabala absolutely refused to have the tapioca gruel the doctor prescribed; instead, with a high temperature, she insisted on having rice with a sour chutney of green mangoes. If she did not get it, she cried and threw terrible temper tantrums. Harasundari tried to calm her down, crooning to her soothing, loving words, like a mother to a distraught child.

Shailabala did not live. After receiving all the love and attention that the world offered her, the young girl's short, incomplete, and useless life came to an end, not only in physical illness, but also in total unhappiness.

7

Nibaran at first broke down with grief. Then, almost at once he realized that he was released from a terrible bondage. Even in his grief, he felt a certain joy of liberation. He suddenly woke up from the nightmare that had gripped his chest, choked his breathing. The moment he realized that the nightmare was over his anxious existence felt very light. The life that was just gone, the lush vine that grew coiling around him, was that his beloved Shailabala? He took a deep breath, and saw that it was the rope with which he was about to hang himself.

And Harasundari? Was she not the true companion through his life? He saw her, and her alone, as the one steady center of all his joys and sorrows, looking after his home, looking over his life throughout its ups and downs.

Yet their separation was total, and there was no way it could be bridged. A small knife, shiny and beautiful, sharp and cruel, had made a painful, complete cut between the left and the right sides of one heart.

Late one night, when the whole city was asleep, a sleepless Nibaran slowly entered Harasundari's bedroom. Silently, he sat on the empty right side of the old bed, and then he lay down there as he did in the earlier years of his life. But this time, he came like a thief to what used to be his eternal, unquestionable right.

Harasundari too did not say a word.

They lay next to each other, as they did in the old days; but between them lay the body of a dead girl. And neither could cross it.

Haimanti

Rabindranath Thakur

The bride's father would have gladly waited some more time, but the groom's father did not want to. The girl's age already exceeded the appropriate prepubescent range, and further delay would have made it hard to cover that up by any means, nice or not-so-nice. Although the girl's age was over what could strictly be considered appropriate, the relative attractiveness of the dowry still weighed somewhat heavier. Hence the wedding was rushed a bit.

I was the bridegroom. It was therefore considered unnecessary to ask for my opinion and give it any thought. I had been dutifully doing what was required of me: studying in college on a scholarship, about to graduate. Hence, both sides of the god of marriage, both wings of the butterfly symbolizing nuptiality,* fluttered with a sense of urgency, ignoring me completely.

In our country, once a man is married, he no longer has, or needs to have, any kind of concern about the marriage. His attitude toward his wife becomes like that of a man-eating tiger's need to have a human, any human. Whatever his condition and age, as soon as he lacks a wife, he has no hesitation, nothing but compulsion, to get another. Only the young men about to graduate from college are plagued by all the anxieties and hesitations about marriage. As the marriage offers arrive, their fathers' gray hair becomes black with the repeated application of dye, while their own black hair starts turning gray with anxiety about what is being arranged for them.

But frankly, I did not feel much anxiety. On the contrary, the idea of

Dated Jaishtha 1321 (May to June 1914), "Haimanti" appears in Rabindranath's *Galpaguchha*, vol. 3 (Calcutta: Visva-Bharati Granthayan Bihag, 1926), 239–49.

* *Prajapati*, meaning both procreator and protector, stands for the both Brahma, the god of creation, and the butterfly, whose image adorns all invitations to weddings in Bengal.

getting married felt like a fresh spring breeze gently, playfully brushing against my mind. All the new leaves and buds in my mind were stirred with curiosity and imagination by its touch. The sensation was very pleasant, though a bit troublesome, for someone with several notebooks to memorize on Burke's treatise on the French Revolution. If I thought there was any danger that what I am about to write might come under the scrutiny of a textbook advisory committee, I would be more cautious in writing it; but, as there is no such danger, I can open up.

What am I really trying to say with this kind of introduction? It is not a fiction that I can keep spinning into a novel. I had no idea that I would begin an account of my life in this manner. I had wanted to release my several years of anguish; I needed a release like the torrential rain that follows the first storm after the long hot summer. But this is not a moral tale with a lesson. I can't write that because I haven't mastered enough Sanskrit grammar to make it grammatically instructive for students. Nor can I write poetry about it because I haven't cultivated my mother language enough to make it bloom forth with the not-so-beautiful material of my life, to express with tragic effect my darkest inner turmoil. I am aware that, ultimately, the deserter in me, the escapist *sannyasi* roaming the cremation grounds alone, laughing wildly at life, has come forward to write this. To ridicule himself. What else could he do! All his tears have dried up. Isn't the scorching heat of Jaishtha really the tearless scream of pain that rises from the heart of that cruelly punished month?

Perhaps I shouldn't use the true name of the person to whom I was married. Not that I fear any future archaeological quarrels over the matter. The ancient copper plaque with her name inscribed is hidden away in my heart. That plaque and the name on it will never be lost. That realm of immortality, where it remains vivid—never dimmed, never covered with dust—is unlikely ever to be visited by any historian.

Let her name be Shishir because it means the dew, which mingles a teardrop with a smile when the first ray of sun shines briefly on it, and because the dew has the story of dawn, about to end with the sunrise and the morning's arrival.

Shishir was only two years younger than I. That was not because my father was against the prepuberty marriage of girls. His father (that is, my grandfather) was a staunch rebel against the tradition, with no belief in any of the established customs and rituals. He had eagerly read and absorbed English liberalism. But my father was a staunch follower of the tradition. Nothing that he did not approve could be found anywhere in either the inner or the outer quarters of our house, within the compound adjoining the house or even near its outermost gate. He too had read much written in English. My grandfather and my father both held rebellious opinions, belonging to the two extreme poles; neither was quite normal or natural. Still, my father let his son be married to a postpubescent girl because the amount anticipated in dowry was large, in proportion to the girl's age. She was her father's only child. My father thought that all her father's money and property would pour into the future of the son-in-law.

My father-in-law, in contrast, didn't have the compulsion to hold any extreme opinion. He was a salaried employee of some prince in the hilly northwestern part of the country. Shishir was a baby when her mother died. He had none of the usual concerns about the age of his daughter increasing with the passage of each year, and he associated with few rigidly traditional people who might have drawn his attention to the worrisome fact.

When Shishir became sixteen, she was a natural sixteen-year-old girl, not a society-manufactured one. Nobody had taught her how to behave in ways considered socially appropriate for her age, and she herself never had bothered to pay attention to the implications of her age.

I was nineteen years old, and in my third year at college, when I was married to Shishir. I did not care if the traditionalists and the reformers fought over whether I should have been married so young, before finishing my studies. I did not care even if they shed blood and killed each other. My attitude was that nineteen might be the right age for passing exams, but it was also the right age for dreaming about marriage and realizing those dreams.

The sunrise finally came upon my daydreaming, with the glimpse of a photograph. I was studying, cramming away, when a female relative, who was in a position to joke with me, placed a picture of Shishir on my books, saying, "Do some real studying now. Go on, break your neck studying this!"

The photograph must have been taken by someone inexperienced in the craft. She was motherless, and no one had tried to do her hair with gold-threaded ribbons and dress her in a fancy, frilly blouse made by the Saha Company of Calcutta. There was no attempt to counterfeit, to create a flattering illusion meant for the finicky eyes on the prospective groom's side. It was a simple face, with simple eyes, and the sari she wore was ordinary. But the whole image glowed with beauty. She was sitting on an ordinary stool, with a striped sheet behind her as a backdrop; a vase of flowers was on the table at her side, and under the curve of the border of the sari, her bare feet rested, without the slightest artifice, on the rug.

The picture came to life at the touch of my mind, as if the fairy-tale maiden in magic sleep was touched with the golden stick. In all my thoughts throughout that day, and the following days, those dark eyes looked on, and those bare feet under the curved border of an ordinary sari occupied my heart like the feet of a goddess on the open lotus.

The pages kept turning in the calendar, the days for auspicious occasions were checked anxiously. Two or three auspicious dates had to be missed, as the girl's father could not get the necessary leave from his job. A long stretch of several inauspicious months was approaching, conspiring to prolong my bachelorhood quite pointlessly into my twentieth year. I was beginning to feel annoyed with my would-be father-in-law and his uncooperative employer.

Finally, the date of the wedding was fixed just before the inauspicious stretch set in the calendar. I still remember every single tune that was played on the *shehnai* that day. Every moment of that day was touched and felt with my whole consciousness. May that nineteenth year of my life live in my mind forever with all its beauty!

The wedding scene hummed with people and activities. In the midst of all the commotion, the girl's soft hand was placed over mine. It felt like the wonder of wonders! My mind kept repeating to itself, "I am receiving her!" I was receiving the most precious, the woman, with all the wonder and mystery about her.

The name of my father-in-law was Gourishankar, the same as the Himalayan peak, near which he lived and worked. Like that mountain, his somber placidity was topped with a quietly brilliant smile, and anyone who knew of the spring of affection hidden behind his quiet exterior must have found it hard to leave his side.

On the eve of leaving for his place of work, my father-in-law called me aside and said, "My dear son, I've known my daughter for seventeen years, and I've known you for a few days. Still, I'm leaving her in your hands. I've no better blessing for you than that you appreciate her, that you recognize the value of the priceless gem that I've given to you."

My parents asked him not to worry. They assured him repeatedly that, although she would have to live away from her father, she would find here in them both a father and a mother.

He smiled, as he took leave of his daughter, "I'll be off now, old girl. This father of yours was your charge all these years. From now on, if any part of him is lost, stolen, or damaged, don't hold me responsible!"

His daughter answered, "No, you won't get away with that. If any part of you is lost or damaged, you have to pay me heavy compensation."

She kept both cautioning him about the various difficulties of his daily living from which she constantly rescued him and reminding him to stay away from the items of food that he craved but was not supposed to have. She held onto his arm, begging him to promise her that he would do as she said. He smiled and said that it was better not to promise, because people simply had to break promises in order to unshackle themselves.

When her father had taken leave of her, she closed the door of her room, and nobody could know what went through her mind in there.

The tearless leave-taking between father and daughter was seen and heard by all the curious women in the inner quarters. They agreed that such lack of expression of emotions was very strange and concluded that perhaps the aberration was due to the years of living among the uncouth upcountry people.*

Banamali-babu, who had acted as the go-between for our marriage, was a friend of my father-in-law, and he also knew our family. He requested my father-in-law to leave his work and come to live near his only daughter. He replied that what he had just given he had given completely, that turning back now would mean even more suffering for him, that there was nothing more treacherous in life than trying to reclaim what one had renounced.

Finally, when he wanted to take leave of me, he sought a place where we could be alone and hesitantly said that his daughter was fond of reading books, and that she also liked to feed people. He said that, as he didn't want my father to be burdened with those expenses, he would like to send me from time to time some money for these things and he hoped that my father would not be offended by it if he came to know of it.

I was baffled by his hesitation because I had never known my father to be upset about any kind of inflow of money. I didn't think he was that ill-tempered! My father-in-law then silently took my hand and put some money in it, looking embarrassed as if he were bribing me. Then, he turned and left quickly, without even waiting for me to perform the customary touching of his feet. From behind, I watched him finally taking out his handkerchief. Silently, I sat there, pondering my realization of the kind of human beings this father and daughter were.

I have seen several of my friends get married. As soon as the chanting of the *mantras* is finished, the wife is swallowed in one gulp. After the consumption is over, even some time after it has reached the stomach and the intestines, the good and the bad aspects of the object consumed may be felt by the consumer. Later on, it may even give the consumer much internal discomfort. But while they are busy consuming, they do not hesitate or pause to think. But I had understood, even at the time the wedding was taking place, that the part of one's wife that one got with the *kanyadan* mantra might be enough for the way most marriages went,† but ninety percent of what could be received remained unattained, if not lost forever. I suspect that most men just marry their wives but do not really receive them, not even realizing that they have received almost nothing of what they could have. Even for their

---

* Bengalis tend to group the varied peoples living in the northern Gangetic plains and in the lower Himalayan foothills and refer to them all as *khottas*, the term used in the original text. This derogatory term, often used by Bengalis, shows both their lack of sensitivity to cultural diversity and considerable chauvinism.
† The Hindu concept of marriage as the unconditional giving away (*dan*) of a virgin daughter (*kanya*), bedecked with fineries and ornaments, and correspondingly the unconditional receiving of her as a gift.

wives, this truth may remain unperceived all their lives. I knew that receiving her was to be the reward of my strivings. She was to be my cherished one, not my property.

I cannot use the name Shishir any more. It was not her real name, and besides she was constant like the sun, not evanescent like the teardrops of a departing dawn. Her real name was Haimanti.*

I saw that although the seventeen-year-old girl was bathed in the light of fresh youth, her mind had not yet awakened from the lap of adolescence. The analogy that came to my mind was that of the first rays of the sun sparkling off the frozen white peak of a mountain before the ice begins to warm and start melting. I knew how immaculate and pure that state of nature could be.

I was worried that I did not know how to win the mind of an educated, grown-up girl. But soon I found out that there was no conflict between the road to the bookstore and the road to her heart. I do not know exactly when the pure white of her mind gradually started changing to colors, when her body and her mind turned toward me with eagerness.

There is another, less beautiful, part of my story. I cannot postpone any longer coming to that part.

Because my father-in-law was employed by a princely family, people speculated wildly about how much money he had saved in the bank. None of the guesses stopped at less than six figures. As a result, Haimanti's treatment in our household was proportional to the estimate of her father's financial situation. She was eager to learn the way our household was run, but my mother kept her from housework, as a show of affection that, I knew, was based purely on her potential financial worth. My mother did not even question the caste of the maid Haimanti had brought with her, lest the answer be hard to swallow; they just did not let her maid into their own rooms.

Things could perhaps have gone on a bit longer like this, helped by greedy illusion, but one day my father's face was darkened and grim; he had just learned from a broker friend of his that, of the fifteen thousand rupees in cash and the five thousand rupees worth of jewelry that my father-in-law gave, all the cash dowry was in fact borrowed, for which he was paying heavily in interest. The hearsay about a six-figure bank account was totally baseless.

Although my father had never talked directly with my father-in-law about the amount of his property, still he concluded, I do not know by what kind of logic, that his in-law had cheated him, that he had cheated him deliberately. Besides, my father had an impression that my father-in-law was something like a chief minister to the prince. Now he inquired and found that he merely

* The word has several pleasant associations. It means one with the beauty of gold (*hema*), a fair complexion with the glow of gold. It also means one belonging to the season of autumn (Hemanta) or reminiscent of the season's beauty, when the paddy is golden ripe, the air holds fulfillment and serenity, and people rejoice in the bounty of nature.

headed the education department, which to my father was the same as being the headmaster of a school, the worst possible position for a gentleman in our society in his opinion. My father's fond hopes were dashed, especially his hope that I would become the prince's chief minister after my father-in-law retired in a few years.

About this time, a number of our village relatives congregated in our Calcutta home, visiting in connection with the Ras festival. After seeing the new bride, they started whispering with each other, and finally, when she had left the room, a distantly related grandmother exclaimed loudly, "The granddaughter-in-law seems to rival me in age!" Another old lady, a relative of similar rank, added that it was no wonder because they had gone out of their way to bring the bride from outside their own society.

My mother emphatically protested, saying that the bride had not yet completed her eleventh year, that the diet of wheat and lentils of the upcountry people made her grow so much for her age.

The grandmothers' verdict was that their eyes were not yet so dim, that the bride's family must have lied about her age.

My mother said, "But we checked her horoscope." She was right. They had indeed checked her horoscope, according to which she was seventeen. The relatives insisted that the horoscope could have been made up.

A big argument about this was going on when Haimanti came in. One of those grandmother-rank ladies immediately asked her how old she was.

My mother signed to her to keep quiet, but she didn't understand what it meant and politely answered that she was seventeen.

My mother snapped at her, saying that she didn't know her age.

"Of course I know that I'm seventeen," said Haimanti.

The old women started elbowing each other in amusement.

My mother was furious at the new bride's stupidity. She said, "You seem to know everything! Your father said that you're eleven."

Haimanti was startled. "My father? He couldn't have said that."

Mother replied, "I'm amazed. The father said one thing to us, and the daughter says that he couldn't have." And she again started signing frantically to get her to stop answering back.

Haimanti got the meaning of the signing this time. In an even stronger voice, she said, "My father could never have said that."

My mother shouted at her, "You dare to call me a liar?"

Haimanti calmly said, "No. I am only saying that my father never tells a lie."

After that, the more my mother became abusive to her, the more the muck oozed out from the little incident to cover everything else in our life.

My mother finally stomped off to my father to report the idiocy and, worse still, the stubbornness of the daughter-in-law.

He sent for Haimanti to chastise her. "What's there to be so proud about not being married until seventeen that you've to go around declaring it with drumbeat? I'm warning you, this kind of behavior won't be tolerated here."

How dramatically my father's voice for his daughter-in-law changed from the sweetened fifth note she had heard until then to the harshly distant bass!

Haima painfully asked, "What should I say if someone asks me my age?"

My father replied, "You don't have to lie about it. Just say that you don't know, that your mother-in-law knows."

Haima's stony silence after hearing his advice on how to avoid lying informed my father that his good advice was totally wasted. It displeased him even more.

Worse than feeling sorry for Haima for her plight, I felt utterly diminished before her. That day I saw the clear, open look in her eyes, the look like the cloudless blue of autumn sky, become dimmed with doubt and anxiety. She looked at me like a frightened doe, probably worried whether I really knew my parents. That day I had bought for her a beautifully bound volume of English poetry. She accepted the book from my hands, and she put it in her lap without opening it.

I took her hand in mine and said, "Haima, don't be angry with me. I'll never insult your truthfulness. You know that I'm bound by your truth."

She said nothing, only smiled sadly. For one whom god has given the ability to smile in that way, talking is unnecessary for expression.

Later on, with my father's financial situation improving, our household became enthusiastic for grandiose worshiping in order to make the kindly glance of divine bounty more permanent. Until then, the new bride had not been recruited for the tasks of the rituals. One day, she was asked to make things ready for the worship.

She said to my mother, "Please tell me what I'm supposed to do."

Her request for help and advice was nothing that could really have shocked anyone because they all knew that she was motherless and had been brought up in a household without such rituals of worship. But the purpose of the assignment was to shame Haima publicly. So all the women put their hands to their cheeks feigning surprise at her request, saying how terrible it was that she did not know. Was she from one of those atheist families? In that case, Laxmi, the goddess of wealth, was about to leave the household.

The event was used as an excuse to say all kinds of things about her father, things that were not supposed to be said so easily. Ever since she had started hearing harsh words, she had always done it in total silence. She had never even shed a tear in front of anybody. On that day, however, tears welled up in her large eyes and fell in big drops. She got up and said, "Do you know that the people where my father lives call him a sage?"

Calling him a sage! There was a round of laughter. Since that day her father was referred to as "your sagely father." My family had learned where the softest spot in her mind was, where she could be hit to hurt the most.

As a matter of fact, my father-in-law avowed nothing as far as religion was concerned. He was neither a Brahmo, nor a Christian, maybe not even an atheist in categorical terms. He had never given much thought to any kind of worshiping. He had tried to give his daughter education and knowledge but never instructed her on anything to do with god and religion. Banamali-babu had once asked him about this gap. He answered: "If I try to teach something that I myself don't understand well, then that would amount to teaching hypocrisy."

Haima had one real fan in our household—my little sister Narani. She had to take a lot of rebuke for loving her brother's wife. From her I learned of the insulting episodes that Haima had to endure inside our household. Not once did I hear of it from Haima herself. She was too embarrassed to talk about it; her embarrassment was not for herself, but for me.

Haima let me read all the letters that she received from her father, short letters full of love and humor. She let me read the letters that she wrote to her father, too. She wanted to share with me her relationship with her father; she felt it to be a natural, vital part of fulfilling our conjugal love. Her letters never contained the slightest hint of complaint or dissatisfaction about her in-laws. It would have meant more trouble if they had. I learned from Narani that Haima's letters were often opened to find out what she might be writing about the household.

The absence of any evidence of misbehavior in her letters did not bring peace to the minds of the higher-ups. Maybe the disappointment hurt them. They were annoyed, and said, "Why does she write so many letters? Her father seems to be everything to her and we are nothing?"

Much unpleasant talk went around, fueling this vague complaint. Utterly disgusted, I told Haima that from now on she need not ask others to mail her letters to her father; she could give them to me to mail on my way to college. She was surprised and asked why. I was ashamed to give the real reason.

Now my family, everybody in the household, started talking about how my head was being taken over by her, that there was no hope of my ever getting the B.A. degree, and that it was not my fault after all.

Obviously not, because the fault was entirely Haima's. Her fault was that she was seventeen, that I loved her, and that nature's way was to make the whole sky play the sweetest flute into every pore of my heart.

I would have dropped the idea of graduating without the slightest hesitation. But for the sake of Haima's well-being, I vowed to pass the exams and pass them well. If it was going to be possible for me to fulfil that vow in my state of ecstasy, there were two reasons: first, and most important, Haima's love had the expansiveness of the sky. It never confined the mind to desire. The air surrounding her love was very wholesome, very healthy. Second, the books I had to study for my exams could very well be read together with Haima.

I geared myself up to prepare for the final examination. One Sunday afternoon, I was sitting in the drawing room, studying Martineau's book on ethics. I was busily plowing my blue pencil through selected passages when I happened to look out, and I saw her at a distance.

To the north of the courtyard adjacent to the room was the staircase to the inner quarters. Along its side, at regular gaps were little windows with iron bars. I saw Haima sitting at one of the windows, sitting very quietly, looking to the west, where a *kanchan* tree in the Malliks' garden was covered with pink bloom.

It hit me, almost startled me. A curtain lifted in my mind, exposing what I did not know was there. Never before had I seen so clearly this depth of her sadness! I could not see very much, only the way she was sitting there. Her hands in her lap, one over the other, her head leaned against the wall, her undone hair twisted around the left shoulder and hanging over her chest. My heart ached with despair.

My own life was so filled with happiness that I had been unobservant of emptiness in others' lives. Now, all of a sudden, I had chanced upon this huge hole of hopelessness, so close to my heart. How was I going to fill it? And with what?

I did not have to give up anything—none of my family, or my habits, nothing really. Haima had left everything to come to live with me. I had never tried to think very clearly about how much she had left behind. Here in our household, she was on a bed of thorns—of humiliation. I have shared that bed of thorns with her. That pain joined us; it did not separate us. But this girl had grown up for seventeen years with so much freedom, freedom outside and inside. I could imagine the unconstrained life environment that made her nature so straight, pure, and forthright. It was a simple environment of uncluttered truth, freedom, and enlightenment. I had not understood till then how totally and cruelly she had been torn away from her own environment. I was incapable of fully understanding how wrenching it must have been for her, because I had never experienced that environment myself.

Haima was dying every moment. Her soul was dying slowly, and her body was wilting away. I could give her everything, but not freedom. Was there any freedom inside me that I could give her? She knew that very well. That was why, sitting at the barred window, she silently communicated with the sky. That was why in the middle of some nights I woke up to find her, not in bed, but on the roof, lying on her back with her hands clasped under her head and looking at the star-filled sky.

I left Martineau and worried about what I could do to help her survive. Ever since childhood I had been extremely hesitant about approaching my father. I had never had the courage; I never tried to ask him for something or negotiate with him. But I could not hold back any more. I pushed away my lifelong inhibition and confronted him with my request: "My wife is in poor health. She needs to be sent to her father's place to stay for a while until she feels a little better."

My father was struck dumb, without the slightest doubt in his mind that it must be Haima who had prompted me to such impertinence. Without bothering to say anything to me, he got up at once, walked to the inner quarters, and asked Haima, "Well, my daughter-in-law, what is the illness that I hear you've got?"

"I have no illness," she answered, surprised.

My father thought her reply was meant to express arrogance.

Being used to seeing her every day, I still had not realized that her health had deteriorated so much that her body was becoming emaciated. One day Banamali-babu came to visit us. He was startled when he saw her. "What is it, Haimi? Why do you look so sickly? Have you been unwell?" Haima said, "No."

About ten days after that, my father-in-law suddenly turned up. Banamali-babu must have written to him about Haima's health.

After the wedding, when it was time to take leave of her father, both had held their tears back. At their reunion, as soon as he came near her and lifted her downcast face, holding up her chin with his fingers, her tears streamed down. She could not stop them flowing. Her father did not say anything; he did not even ask how she was. He read something so terrible in her face that it seemed to shatter him.

Haima led her father by the hand to her room. She had much to ask him about. She noted that her father's health did not look good either. When her father asked her, "Do you want to come with me for a while, old girl?" she eagerly said yes, almost like a starving beggar who has just been made an offer of fresh food.

Her father said, "Very well. Let me make the travel arrangements."

If my father-in-law had not been so preoccupied with worry about his daughter, he would have noticed, the moment he entered the house, that he had lost his initial position here. My father made it quite clear, by hardly talking with him, that his unexpected visit was a nuisance. My father-in-law had carried in his memory the repeated assurance from my father that he could any time take his daughter for a visit with him. He had believed that, and it never occurred to him that these assurances would be so altered.

My father kept smoking his hookah, finally answering my father-in-law's proposal with, "I have no say in this matter; the 'indoor' opinion must be taken into account."

I knew the meaning of saying that the decision belonged to the women-folk. It meant there would be no luck. There was no luck; there was furious indignation instead. What an unjust accusation to say that the girl was not keeping well here!

My father-in-law then went out. He came back with a good doctor to give her a check-up. The doctor said that she needed a change of environment; otherwise, she could suddenly become very sick.

My father laughed at this. "Anyone can suddenly get very sick. What kind of diagnosis is that?"

My father-in-law tried to reason, saying that he was a famous doctor.

My father said, "I have seen many such doctors. Money can buy medical pronouncement and a sickness certificate to suit one's wish."

My father-in-law fell totally silent at this. Haima understood that her father's proposal had been turned down with insult. She became a wooden figure.

I could not take it any more. I went to my father and said that I would then take Haima away for a change of environment.

He roared at me, "How dare you," and so on.

Some of my friends asked me later why I did not do what I had said I would do. All I had to do was just leave with my wife. Why did I not take such an obvious simple step? Why indeed! If I am not to sacrifice my true feelings for what people regard as proper, if I am not to sacrifice my dearest one for the extended family, then what about the ages of social indoctrination running in my blood? What is it there for?

Don't you know that on the day the people of Ayodhya demanded the banishment of Sita, I was among them? Those who sang the glory of that sacrifice, generation after countless generation, I was one of them too. All those authors of articles published in monthly magazines, acclaiming the virtue of abandoning a beloved wife to please the people, I had read them. Had I ever thought that one day I would be writing my own story of the banishment of Sita, writing it with the blood of my heart's arteries?

Once again, it was time for father and daughter to say goodbye to each other. This time, too, both were smiling. With a smile, she scolded him, "Father, if you ever come running like this again, worrying unnecessarily about me, I'll not see you; I'll lock myself in so you can't see me."

Her father said, also with a smile, "In that case, next time I'll have to bring along a drill so I can break in your room to see you."

After that, not once did I see on Haima's face the smile of peace and happiness that she always had before.

I cannot write any more about what happened after that.

I have been hearing that my mother is looking for a more suitable girl this time. Perhaps some day I will no longer be able to resist my mother's entreaties and give in. Even that does not seem impossible after all that has happened. Because, . . . why belabor the point!

Letter from a Wife

Rabindranath Thakur

To your lotus feet,

This day completes nearly fifteen years of our marriage. I have never written to you before today. All this time that I was with you, you have heard many words from me, and I have heard many from you. There was never the gap that is necessary for one to write a letter to someone close.

I am now at the holy place by the Bay of Bengal, on pilgrimage; and you are at work in your office. You have grown attached to Calcutta the way snails are attached to their shells. It has simply adhered to your body and mind. That is why you did not even apply for a leave to come along. Perhaps it was divine intention that I was granted my desire for leave, my need for some distance.

In your joint family, I am known as the second daughter-in-law. All these years I have known myself as no more than that. Today, after fifteen years, as I stand alone by the sea, I know that I have another identity, which is my relationship with the universe and its creator. That gives me the courage to write this letter as myself, not as the second daughter-in-law of your family.

Long before anyone, except perhaps fate, knew of the possibility that my life would become linked with yours, when I was a small child, my brother and I both became ill with typhoid fever. My brother died of it, and I recovered. The women in our neighborhood were unanimous, "Mrinal survived because she's a girl." Yama, as the master robber that he is, always has his eyes out for the more valuable lives.

I am not one to die easily. That is what I want to say in this letter.

Dated Shravana 1321 (July to August 1914), "Streer Patra" appears in Rabindranath's *Galpa-guchha*, vol. 3 (Calcutta: Visva-Bharati Granthayan Bihag, 1926), 213–23.

The day a distant uncle of yours and your friend Nirad came to our house to see me as the potential bride for you, I was only twelve years old. We lived in a remote village, where jackals could be heard howling in daytime. To reach our village from the nearest railway station, they had to travel fifteen miles in a one-horse buggy and then six more miles along village paths carried in a palanquin. Your folks took quite a bit of trouble for that trip. Besides the difficult travel, they had to deal with our local East Bengali cuisine, which your uncle is still fond of recounting as quite a farce.

Your mother was determined, in looking for her second son's bride, to make up for her elder daughter-in-law's lack of beauty. Otherwise, they would not have taken so much trouble to go to our village to see me. We all know that in Bengal nobody ever has to go looking for an enlarged spleen, gastric pain, or bridal proposals—these things come crowding in and are hard to get rid of.

My father's heart palpitated; my mother muttered prayers to the goddess Durga throughout that day of hectic backstage activities and onstage nervousness. They worried and fussed. They were village devotees who were not sure of how to please city deities. The only thing they had in their favor was their daughter's beauty, but they could not count on its value. The girl herself hardly knew the value of her beauty. The value of whatever a girl has in her is decided by what the customer is willing to pay. Perhaps that is why women rarely know what pride and confidence feel like, no matter how talented, intelligent, or beautiful they may be.

The fright and the frantic efforts that gripped the entire household, almost the whole neighborhood, sat on my girl's mind like a huge rock that day. It seemed to me that everything in the world, even the light from the sky, acted like policemen in charge of holding a twelve-year-old village girl up before two pairs of scrutinizing eyes. There was no way to escape, no place to hide.

Then one day, the flutes filled the whole sky with the sweet sadness of the tunes of parting. I left my home and my people in tears, and came to yours. The older women gathered in your house for the occasion checked me carefully for blemishes until they finally had to agree that I was on the whole really beautiful. Their verdict visibly darkened the face of my elder sister-in-law.

Since then I have often wondered why it was necessary for me to have physical beauty in order to be valued. If beauty were something crafted by human hands, like that of the images of goddesses created by the image-makers out of clay from the Ganga, then it should be a matter of credit and appreciation. It seems ironic to me that human beauty, which the Creator makes in a flitting mood of enjoyment, should be priced like a commodity in a religious society such as yours.

It did not take you and your family long to forget that I was endowed with beauty. However, you were constantly reminded and dismayed that I had intelligence. My intelligence was stubborn enough to stay with me after all these years of living within your family, inside your household. My mother did always worry about my intelligence, which she knew to be a troublesome quality for a woman. If one must bend to a multitude of barriers throughout one's life, then the inclination to respect one's own intelligence was, in her common wisdom, bound to cause endless trouble and, ultimately, disaster. There was not much I could do about it, though. If my creator was careless to put more intelligence in my head than a wife in your family should have, then how would I possibly give back the excess? You all rebuked me for having thoughts and views of my own about the matters of my life. Verbal abuse is the only recourse of the logically weak; therefore, I forgive you for endlessly calling me an opinionated and precocious female.

There was a part of me that escaped the watchful eyes of your household. None of you knew that I wrote poems when I was alone. No matter what the quality of the poems I wrote, that was where I was absolutely free to be myself, where the barriers and strictures that go with living in your household could not surround me. You never recognized in these fifteen years the part of me that wrote poetry, perhaps because you did not wish to see in me anything that went beyond my role as your wife and a daughter-in-law of the family.

Of my earliest memories after I came into your urban household, the one that I remember most vividly is the cowshed. It was a small dark room, next to the staircase to the inner quarters. The poor cows had no room to move except in the tiny cement porch, facing that cell, where they stayed tethered most of the day. Because the servants were busy with other morning duties, it was a long time before they could come to put their fodder in the wooden vats in the corner of the walled cement porch. The hungry cows stood by the vats, licking them and trying to chew bits off their edges. I watched, feeling the misery of those two cows and their three calves. Because they were the only familiar things for a village girl in the big city, they were to me like relatives in an unfamiliar land. At first, when I was still a new bride, I secretly used to feed them my breakfast. As I got older, my open care and concern for the creatures prompted some of you to jokingly doubt my genealogy.

Our daughter died almost immediately after she was born. She called me to go along with her, but I lived on. If she had lived, she might have brought me all that is good and true and sublime in this life. From the second daughter-in-law of a wealthy family I would have become a mother. Being a mother is to be related with the whole world, even if she lives all her life inside one household. I suffered the pain involved in becoming a mother, but I could not taste the freedom that comes from actually being a mother.

I still remember the English doctor, who was brought in for my difficult delivery. I remember how shocked and angry he was to see the lack of hygiene in the inner quarters, especially in the room reserved only for child-birth and for mother and child to stay during the "impure" days after birth.

In the front part of your house, there is a well-kept decorative garden; and in the drawing room plenty of expensive furniture. The inner part of the house is like the wrong side of a piece of knitting, full of exposed knots and seams, the side where the lack of care and neatness does not seem to matter. Even the daylight is dimmer there, and air has to sneak in like a thief; the back porch is rarely free of rubbish; and the dirt-filled cracks and gouges in the walls and the floors of the inner rooms have remained there for ages.

The doctor was rightly upset about these; but he was wrong in one respect. He thought that it was a source of constant pain for us. Quite the contrary. Neglect works like ashes; it holds the heat inside and keeps the outside cool to the touch. To those with low self-regard, neglect does not seem unjust, and so it does not cause them pain. That is why women feel ashamed to be upset about the injustice they encounter. If a woman must accept so much injustice in the life ordered for her, then it is perhaps less painful for her to be kept in total neglect; otherwise, she is bound to suffer, and suffer pointlessly, the pain of injustice, if she cannot change the rules governing her life.

Whatever the condition that you kept us in, it rarely occurred to me that there was pain and deprivation in it. When I came close to death at childbirth, it was not fear that I felt. What is so precious in our lives that we have to be afraid of death? The idea of death naturally scares only those who are attached to life with love, nurturance, and privilege. If death really wanted me that day, I would have come off, roots and all, like a chunk of grass land. Bengali women so often talk about wishing to be dead. But what is the point, let alone the glory, in their deaths? It is so easy for us to be dead, and it makes so little difference that we should really be ashamed of merely dying.

My daughter appeared briefly like the evening star, and then she disappeared. I picked up my life of daily chores and caring for the cows and the calves. My life might have rolled on like that to the very end. In that case, I would have had no reason to write you this letter. But something came and stuck in, imperceptible at first, like a tiny wind-borne seed that lodges in a small crevice of a concrete building. It sprouts one day and slowly grows its roots inward, unseen. Eventually, when a leafy stem comes out, the roots have already cracked the concrete wall. In the tightly built order of my daily life, a tiny flake of another life blew in from nowhere; then started the process that finally cracked it open.

My sister-in-law had a little sister, Bindu. When her widowed mother died, she first went to live in the household of her uncle's sons, who soon drove her away by their ill treatment, forcing her to seek shelter with her sister in your household. All of you regarded her as an utter nuisance. Blame my nature, not me, for standing by her when I saw how annoyed you all were by her presence, how unwanted she was made to feel. I imagined myself in her place—having to seek shelter in the home of others in the face of their unwillingness and explicit hostility. If she had no choice but to accept such terrible humiliation, I could not ignore her and pretend that her suffering was insignificant.

I also saw the predicament of my elder sister-in-law. She had let her sister stay out of love and pity. Yet, once she saw her husband's annoyed reaction, she started acting as if the girl were a terrible nuisance she really wanted to be rid of. She could not find the courage to open her heart to her own helpless sister, to make her the slightest gesture of love. She could not be both honest with her feeling and also the obedient wife that she had to be. So she tried to hide her feeling.

The terrible dilemma of my sister-in-law intensified both my sadness and my outrage. Watching her conspicuously arrange for the girl inferior food and clothing and a lot of menial work, in her pathetic effort to make her sister's presence less annoying for the family, filled me with not only sorrow but also shame. She was frantically trying to prove to the family that Bindu was really a good bargain, a servant who worked very hard for the household but cost very little.

My elder sister-in-law was from a family with high social status but no wealth; and she did not have much beauty. Your family let everybody, including her, know all about how your father was begged on hands and knees, how he was manipulated, to make him agree to take her in as his son's wife. She always regarded her marriage as a terrible wrong done to the family, as if she was guilty of cheating her way in. That is why she always, in all matters, shrinks and constricts herself, trying to take up as little space as possible living in this family.

Her exemplary modesty and self-effacement have always been a problem for me. I can never denigrate myself so much in all matters of my life and life around me. If I see something as right, I am unwilling to change my mind for anyone's sake and start calling it wrong. I am sure you have often encountered this highly inconvenient disability of mine, and I am sure it has caused you much irritation.

I rescued Bindu from the place assigned to her, and I brought her into my own room. My sister-in-law loudly complained that I was spoiling a poor girl from a poor family who must get used to deprivation. She acted as if I was creating trouble, but I could feel that she was greatly relieved inside. She knew that from then on the burden of blame would be on me. Moreover, her agony was lessened to see that the love and sympathy she did not dare to give her sister were now being received by her through me. Bindu must have been at least fourteen at the time, although my sister-in-law tried very hard to understate her age. Bindu was poor in her appearance, as you all know, so poor that if she were to fall on a concrete floor and break her head, people would be more concerned with the floor than with her head. With parents dead, she had no one to try to find her a groom. Besides, how many men would have the strength to marry a girl who was neither pretty nor from a wealthy family?

Bindu first came to me fearfully, very hesitantly, as if she were an untouchable before a Brahman. She seemed fearful that the slightest contact with her would cause me great harm. The way she behaved, always avoiding people and contact with their eyes, revealed how truly she believed that she was not supposed to be born and to live in this world. Of the relatives left on her parents' side, her male cousins had denied her even the space they would allow to store junk. Useless rubbish easily sits around here and there in every household because people can forget about it and not see it; however, a useless woman is not just useless but so annoyingly hard to put out of mind that she is not allowed to live even where the garbage is dumped. It would be hard to argue that Bindu's male cousins are very useful in this world. Yet they had no trouble finding a place to live, and, in fact, they are living quite well.

So, when I asked Bindu to come into my room, she was very afraid. Her fear made me sadder. It took me a while and quite a bit of loving effort to make her understand that I was willing to give her a little space to live in my room.

Because my room is not absolutely mine, my attempt proved more difficult than I thought. Within a few days of being with me, she developed some red spots on her skin, perhaps heat rash or something like that. But you all decided that it must be smallpox. You would not have done that to anyone but Bindu. A neighborhood quack was called in to confirm your opinion, but even he said that he could not be so sure before a couple more days. But you were not willing to wait a couple more days. Bindu was about to die of shame for being ill and thus drawing attention. I said that even if it turned out to be pox, I was going to take her to the room kept for deliveries, and nobody would have to do anything for her because I would stay there with her and nurse her. When you all grew red with anger at what I dared to say, when even Bindu's own sister kept saying that she should be sent to the hospital, just about then her red spots disappeared. That seemed to annoy your family even more, and you all said that the pox must have grown in instead of coming out. How could that be possible? Because she happened to be only Bindu.

One benefit of having grown up in neglect is that the body becomes tough in the process. It does not catch illness easily; the most common roads to death seem closed to it. Bindu's illness teased her, but it did nothing serious. However, it also made me see that the hardest task in this world is to shelter the most insignificant person. I realized that the one in greatest need for shelter faces the staunchest barriers to its access.

When Bindu finally got over her fear of being near me, she developed another problem. She began to love me so much that it scared me. Never before had I encountered a love so intense yet so totally unselfish. I had read about such things in some fiction, but even there it was between a man and a woman.

It had been many years since anyone had reminded me that I was beautiful. The beautyless girl became enchanted with my forgotten beauty. Her eyes found endless joy in seeing my face. When I asked why, she said that she saw in my beauty some quality that perhaps nobody else had seen. If I did my own hair, she became sad because she loved to feel my hair and rejoiced in arranging it. I never found any reason to bedeck myself except when invited out or on a special occasion. Now Bindu persuaded me to get nicely dressed every day, which was somewhat distressing to me, but I also found it hard to disappoint the poor girl and shake her out of her silly ecstasy.

In the inner quarters of your house, there is almost no piece of land for any plant to grow. However, at the northern edge of the surrounding wall, right beside the open drain a lowly *gaab* tree has somehow managed to survive. Each year when I see its ugly bare branches suddenly covered with glowing red leaves, then I know that spring has arrived on earth. Inside our household, when I saw the neglected ugly girl's unnourished mind magically touched by love with colors, then I learned that hearts too bloom in the most inhospitable surroundings at the touch of a spring breeze that comes from some unknown heaven, not exactly down the winding lane as in the case of the *gaab* tree.

Though I was often annoyed with the intensity of Bindu's love, still it was her love that somehow made me see myself in a new light, in a way I had never done before. I found myself beautiful as a free human mind, in being my natural self.

The reaction of the entire household to my taking Bindu in persisted as one of unbearable irritation. To you all, it remained unacceptably impertinent and idiosyncratic behavior. Endless complaining and bickering went on about what was seen as confrontation between me and the rest of the family over Bindu. When a piece of my jewelry could not be found, none of you felt ashamed to immediately point the finger at Bindu. When during the Swadeshi movement the police started searching houses for subversive materials, you all said that Bindu must be a paid spy of the police and so keeping her meant inviting a police raid. No proof was needed to accuse her, because she was only Bindu.

The maids in your house refused to do anything for her, and if I ever asked any of them to do anything for her, she herself stiffened up with shame and apprehension. That increased my expenses because I hired a separate maid. All of you were outraged by it. You did not like my giving Bindu some of my saris to wear. You disliked it so much that you stopped giving me the usual cash allowance. When you did that, I started wearing cheap millmade saris and asked the housemaid to stop picking up my dishes after the meals. I myself took my plate and bowls out, fed the calves the unfinished rice, and washed my dishes at the tap where the maids washed the others' dishes. You once saw me doing that, and you were not quite happy. Why it was quite all right for me to be unhappy but absolutely necessary for you not to be unhappy is something that I managed neither to understand nor to accept, even for the sake of my own convenience.

While you were getting angrier, Bindu was growing in age, a natural phenomenon that in her case became another reason for your increasing annoyance with her presence. One thing that still surprises me is why you did not throw her out of the house by force. The only explanation I can think of is that inside you were a little afraid of me. My capacity for independent thinking was something that you could not help respecting a little, even though you disliked it intensely. Unable to get her out by force or other direct means, your family determined to get her out by somehow marrying her off. It managed to find a groom for Bindu. My sister-in-law loudly proclaimed relief about the face of her family line being finally saved. I wanted to know about the groom; and you assured me that he was quite a catch on the whole.

Bindu clung to my feet and wept, asking, "Why marriage for someone like me?" I tried to console her, ease her fears, telling her that I had heard the groom was all right. She asked the question I should have asked too: "If the groom is all right, then what have I got that he would want to marry me?"

The groom's side never sent anyone to see the prospective bride. That provided my sister-in-law with relief from the anxiety of rejection from that side.

Bindu wept day and night, and I watched her terrible pain and despair. Though I had fought for her so far, I did not have the courage to fight to stop her marriage. My strength failed me on that front, only because I worried about what would happen to her if I were to die before her. A pathetic-looking girl of very dark complexion was going to be married off who knows to whom, where, into what kind of family. I tried not to think about it because, when I thought about it, I could not face my terror. Bindu asked me if it was possible for her to die within the five days that were left before her scheduled marriage. I scolded her for saying such a thing, but god knows that if I could have thought of any painless way to bring about Bindu's death, then I too might have found relief, even in grief.

The day before her wedding Bindu finally appealed to her sister and begged her to let her live there, maybe in a corner of the cowshed, and she would do any kind and any amount of work to earn that. Bindu's sister had been crying secretly the last few days. She cried again, but ended up telling her that a woman's life was not worth living without a husband and that she had to go through whatever fate had written for her, something no human being could change.

The fact was that no other way of getting rid of Bindu would appear respectable. Marriage, any kind of marriage, was seen as the only way left to you to throw her out. Nobody cared about what might happen to her after that.

I pleaded that at least the wedding be held in our house, but you said that the groom's family had a special custom of holding the men's marriage ceremony at their place. I interpreted that answer as your family's unwillingness to spend money on someone so worthless to you. So I did not insist. However, I did something without letting you know, though I considered telling my sister-in-law but did not in order not to aggravate her scared state. When helping Bindu get dressed to leave for her wedding, I put some pieces of my jewelry on her in a manner that made them hard for others to detect. Perhaps my sister-in-law detected some, but she appeared not to have seen. Please, forgive her for not telling you what she might have noticed.

Before taking leave of me, Bindu finally embraced me and said, "I am now truly abandoned."

I said to her, "No, Bindu. Whatever happens to you, I'll never abandon you. I'll always stand by you, to the very end."

Three days had gone by since she left.

One of the tenants of your estate had sent a lamb meanwhile. I had saved it from being served for a meal and kept it tethered in the cell that was used for storing coal for the stoves. Each morning I went there to feed it because the servants seemed more keen to eat it than to feed it.

Three days after Bindu's departure, I went into the cell to feed the lamb, and I found her there, crouched in a dark corner. She came to me and wept silently. Her husband, she had discovered, was a madman.

"Are you sure?" I asked her.

"Would I tell you such a terrible lie?" she said. "He's really insane. His father was against this marriage, but the poor man was so terrified of his wife that, unable to stop it, he left home before the wedding and went to Banaras to spend the rest of his life there. The mother insisted on getting a wife for her son."

I sat down right there on the pile of coal. Women have no pity for women. They would say a madman is after all a man, better than a woman. I gathered from Bindu that her husband sometimes appeared normal but sometimes he went totally berserk. He had seemed normal on the evening of the wedding, but the strain of the ceremony and the staying up late brought out his madness the day after. When Bindu was eating rice from a brass plate, he suddenly snatched the plate and threw it away, food and all. The reason soon became clear: he thought Bindu was none other than Rani Rash-moni, and he was furious that the servants had stolen her usual golden plate and served her on one of their old brass plates instead. Bindu was terrified, but she was saved that night by the custom of newlyweds not seeing each other on the second night after the wedding. The following night, when her mother-in-law ordered her into his room, she felt paralyzed with terror. Her mother-in-law was famous for her terrible temper. She could do such terrible things when she got angry that it would be correct to describe her too as mad, except that she was more terrifying because she was not as totally mad as her son. So Bindu did not dare not to go into his room. He was somewhat quiet that night, but Bindu was stiff with fear that any moment something might explode inside his head. Late in the night when he had fallen asleep, she managed to escape. How she ran away that night and how she managed to find her way back to our house is in itself a harrowing story that I need not go into in this letter.

Her account filled me with anger and shame. I told her that such a deceit-ful marriage was no marriage at all. I asked her to stay with me exactly as she did before and assured her that I would not let anybody drag her back into that marriage.

Your unanimous verdict on my report was that Bindu was lying. I said that Bindu never lied. You challenged me: how could I be so sure? I said I was absolutely sure that she was not lying. Then you tried to scare me, saying that if Bindu's in-laws informed the police, it would put your family into trouble. I answered that marriage to a madman without the girl's knowl-edge was something that the court was very likely to nullify. You asked why you would want to be bothered with a court case for her sake and to spend money and effort on her account. I asked you not to worry about spending money; I would sell my own jewelry to meet the expense. You retorted by asking whether I could also deal with the lawyers on my own. I had no ready answer to that, except to slap my forehead in despair.

Soon after, the elder brother of Bindu's husband turned up, making much noise, threatening to inform the police. I did not know whether I stood any chance, but if even a calf had run away from the butcher and come to me, I would not send it back to the butcher even if the police had ordered me. I do not know from what source I found the strength to say, "Let him go to the police station." Having said that, I decided to take Bindu to my bedroom, to lock ourselves in, and just wait there until the row had subsided. I looked for her, but she was gone. While I was arguing with you, all united against her, she had gone out and surrendered herself to her brother-in-law. She had realized that her staying on would involve me in a one-woman battle against the rest of the world; she did not want me to fight so hopeless a battle.

Bindu's unsuccessful attempt to run away only compounded her troubles. When she returned, her mother-in-law harangued her, supported by everybody around. Why did she run away? Was her son going to eat her up? After all, there were plenty of bad husbands. Her son was like the golden moon compared to most of them.

As for my sister-in-law, she had only this to say about the terrible plight of her own sister: "Mad or idiot, one's husband remains one's husband as long as one lives. There's nothing that can be done about sheer bad luck as far as a woman is concerned."

Perhaps she was also recalling, like many others, the oft-quoted legend of wifely devotion, the story of a woman carrying her leprosy-deformed husband to the prostitute he lusted after. It never ceases to amaze me how this story of cowardice of the lowest order can go on being repeated for ages without driving men to disgusted rage. Perhaps the same factor that keeps the story circulating, with approval instead of shame, explains why none of you felt ashamed to get angry with Bindu for running away from her forced marriage to a madman. Instead, you were ashamed of me for fighting on her behalf, for creating a scene out of the pain I felt for her, instead of silently sympathizing. How could a village girl, married into your family for so many years, dare to have her own ideas and use them to dissent? I do have a mind of my own, and I can never stand for a moment the talk of exemplary wifehood.

After this incident, I was quite sure that Bindu would rather die than come back here again. I could not, however, forget the promise I had made her the day she left for her wedding. I had promised that I would never abandon her. Then I thought of my younger brother Sharat, who, as you know, has stayed in college for a few years too many because he spent so much time volunteering for everything—from flood relief in faraway places to neighborhood campaigns for the eradication of plague-carrying rats—that he had little time left to study for passing the exams.

I sent for Sharat. I asked him to find out about Bindu and inform me in person because she would not write to me about her troubles and I would not get the letter even if she wrote. Sharat was so eager to help that he seemed almost disappointed with this minor assignment. He would have found it more challenging if I had asked him to abduct Bindu from her marital prison, even by smashing her mad husband's head if necessary.

While I was talking with Sharat, you came in and asked me if I was planning to cause you and your family more trouble. I said the real cause of all their trouble was my coming to their household as your wife, but that was their own doing, not mine really. You ignored my answer and asked whether I had already brought Bindu back and was hiding her somewhere. I said that, if she did come back, I certainly would hide her somewhere, but you need not worry because she would never come back.

You were really suspicious to see Sharat with me, and nothing I said assured you. I knew that you did not want Sharat to come to your house anyway. You disliked his political work and what not and worried about the police noticing his coming to your house. That is why I never asked him to come and see me; instead of inviting him over for Bhaiphonta,* I sent him my gift through a servant.

One day you told me that Bindu had run away again, for her brother-in-law was there looking for her; but she had not come to me. I no longer knew what I could do to help her. Sharat again did some running around to find out. It did not take him long. He was back that evening with the news that Bindu had gone to her cousins' house; not only had they sent her back immediately, but they were also furious because of the travel money and time they had to spend in doing that.

About that time your aunt came from her village to your house in Calcutta on her way to Puri, the holy place of Jagannath. I decided to go with her. You were all so relieved to see my mind suddenly directed to religion that no one objected at all. My presence in the house had become a constant source of worry about what I might be up to next to become involved in Bindu's lot again.

It was a Sunday, and I was to leave with your aunt on Wednesday. I called for Sharat and asked him somehow to get Bindu on the train to Puri with us. Sharat's face lit up. He asked me not to worry. He was sure he could do it and even joked that he might come along with the three of us to look at the magnificent waves and the temple by the shore.

But Sharat was back that very evening. His face told me that the plan had failed. When I asked him if that was the case, he only nodded.

Fearfully I probed, "Couldn't you persuade her to come along with you?"

"There was no need for that," he said. "There's no need to worry anymore, for last night she killed herself by setting fire to her clothes. Her brother-in-law's son, with whom I had struck up friendship in order to get information, also told me that she had left a letter for you before incinerating herself, but they destroyed the letter."

Finally, Bindu had ceased being a source of trouble; she had ended her own troubles too.

Everybody criticized her action. Everybody talked about how it was becoming a fashion for women to create drama by setting fire to their saris. You are right to say that it is dramatic. But should you not think for a minute why the drama gets enacted only on women's saris and not on men's dhotis?

Poor Bindu was blamed even in her death. As long as she lived, she had been constantly blamed for her lack of beauty and other qualities. When

* The occasion on which married sisters customarily invite their brothers over for a ceremony wishing the brothers long life and prosperity.

killing herself, she had not managed to use a new method, which might have earned her praise from the men of this country. She had annoyed them even by ending her unwanted existence.

My sister-in-law secretly cried for her. But there was relief in her tears, not anger or despair. After all, the pain she had suffered in dying was probably nothing compared to the pain she would have had to endure if she had lived.

I still came to the holy place by the sea. Bindu was no longer the reason, but I needed to leave, to come away.

In all these years in your household, I have never experienced suffering as it is commonly known. Nothing was ever lacking in matters of food and clothing. I cannot find any fault with your character in the usual sense of marital fidelity, whatever your brother's case may be. Perhaps, if you were unfaithful like your brother, I might have turned out obedient like his wife, living mindlessly as the silently suffering devoted wife, blaming fate instead of human failure and weakness. Therefore, this letter is not to accuse you personally, none of you really. That is not the purpose of this letter.

However, I am not coming back to the house at 27 Makhan Barhal Lane. I have seen Bindu's life. I have learned about the place of a woman in the world I know. I do not want that place. I have no need for it any more.

I have also seen that no matter how much oppression, scorn, and neglect you all heaped on Bindu, there was a limit that could not be crossed. The pathetic girl was, after all, bigger than her life of misfortunes. To keep her under your feet all the time, your legs had to be impossibly long. Death is far more powerful. In death, she ceased to be merely a plain, lower-middle-class girl in this society, an orphan unwanted by her cousins, the deceived wife of a mad stranger. She became part of something infinitely bigger than anything she had known in her life.

When, through the broken heart of the girl I loved, I heard the music playing on the flute of death, on the banks of the Yamuna flowing outside my routine life, the pain at first seemed to pierce my heart like a lethal arrow. Then I asked my creator: Why is it that the most insignificant things in life seem to be the hardest obstacles? Why does this walled-in house in an old city lane, no more than a totally insignificant and joyless bubble, work as a terrifying barrier? Why can't I cross the little threshold of this inner quarter, even when I am beckoned by the world that is endlessly rejoicing in the changing beauty of the six seasons? Why, in the midst of all the beauty and freedom in your creation, my soul, also created by you, has to die slowly decaying in a prison of mere bricks and wood? How utterly insignificant our daily life is, how banal its set rules, old habits, the unquestioned notions it is based on, the standard penalties for violations! Why should these miserable chains, this bondage of trivialities, win in the end? Why should the joy and freedom in the universe of your creation be constantly defeated?

The flute of death kept playing inside me: and the masonry walls crumbled; the barbed wire fence of the rules and the punishments for violating the rules dissolved before my eyes. When I saw the banner of life upheld by death, I knew that all the measures for inflicting pain and insult, which the society devised to subdue, were the clamping of fake chains and the cracking of false whips. Then I was no longer afraid; I knew it would take not even an instant to break out of the shell of the second daughter-in-law of your family.

I am not afraid anymore of giving up the life in your house by the narrow lane. I see before me the vast ocean, and above my head the clouds of Asarh gathered to give the rain of life.

All these years you had kept me under the dense cover of habits and customs. For a moment, Bindu saw me through a tiny hole she made in that cover. With her own death, the girl managed to tear it up completely, from end to end. Now, stepping out of it, I see how boundless the glory of my human destiny can be. My creator, who appreciated this aspect of my beauty and intelligence, is watching me from all over the boundless sky. The second daughter-in-law of your family is finally dead.

Do not fear that I am about to kill myself. I am not going to play that old joke on you. Meerabai too was a woman like me, and her chains were by no means light, but she did not seek death in order to live. In her joyfully rebellious songs, she said, "Meera is going to stick by you, my lord, even if she is rejected by her father, mother, by everybody else, no matter what their rejections may bring upon her." To stick by one's truth is to live. I am going to live. I have just started living.

This is from Mrinal—
who is torn off the shelter of your feet

The Witch

Tarashankar Bandyopadhyay

Nobody can recall any more who came up with the name and on what occasion. Its history lies buried in the depths of shared memory; but the name itself is used to this day, and its association of terror and damnation is still overpowering. *The field of killer thirst!* If you stand by its edge on this side and look across the scorched land, with no shadow, no water, stretched to the horizon, the trees of the villages beyond some faint smears along the rim of the hazy sky, your mind becomes strangely disoriented. You feel detached, almost philosophical, as you wonder. If one had to walk through it in the midday of summer, one would surely die of thirst. Its name then seems to be almost reaching for the rank of dreadful glory held by the word *epidemic*.

All day long a pall of dust hovers like smoke between the ground and the sky, the ashen ground like a gigantic burnt-out cremation pyre, the smoldering heat lashing up toward the sky. All that stands across that lifeless expanse is a foot or so of dust, with a few thorn bushes and an occasional dry waterhole.

In the small villages near the edge of the field live poor and illiterate peasants, not trained in reticence about expressing beliefs. They would tell you that in some distant past a gigantic snake used to live there. His poison burnt out everything and killed the source of fertility deep inside the land. In those days, even the birds and insects in flight would be paralyzed in midair and float down like dry leaves into the open mouth of the giant serpent. The snake is not there any more, but the field remains poisoned, barren, accursed. The field of killer thirst! Fate has since added to its envenomed

First published in the periodical *Bedeni* (Calcutta, 1940), "Daini" is reprinted in Tarashankar's collected works, *Tarashankar Rachanabali*, ed. Gajendra Mitra, Sumatha Ghosh, et al., vol. 7 (Calcutta: Mitra & Ghosh Publishers, 1973), 479–93.

sterility yet another evil presence—a pair of eyes, constantly peering across. On the east end of the field, near a cluster of mango trees beside a muddy spring, a witch has been living for the past forty years. A powerful and vicious old witch, the villagers would tell you. Although they avoid her by all means, forty years of watching from a distance have produced a vivid collective picture of her features and her behavior, especially her unblinking gaze cast over the field all these years.

They all know that her hut stands beside the mango grove near the dried spring; it faces the terrible field with a thatched porch in front. There she sits most of the time, very still; her unblinking eyes scan the field of killer thirst. Her daily chores do not take much time. In the morning she cleans the hut and goes out to beg in one village or another. Visiting two or three houses gets her a pound or two of rice, which is all she wants. Fear does the work for her. On the way back, she sells half the rice for salt, oil, and kerosene. Some days she leaves the hut once more to gather twigs and dry dung. Then, for the rest of the long hot day, she sits on her porch, motionless, unblinking, staring at the field. She has been sitting there, staring at the field in the same manner, for the last forty long years.

Nobody really can tell, nobody knows, where she came from. Few, however, doubt the common story that once, a long time ago, while riding a tree across the sky and destroying several villages along the way, she had been charmed by the desolation of the field. She had descended and made it her home. Those of her kind like to stay away from human company, as everybody knows.

It is true that she does not want to see human beings because they seem to rouse her desire to harm. The killer greed seems to raise its head, like a cobra with tongue flicking eagerly. Except for that, she does not think she is unlike any human being.

The sight of her own look makes her shiver. She has an old hand mirror among her few possessions, and whenever she sees her eyes in it she is terrified. Small, narrow eyes, their tawny irises gleaming like sharpened steel. Old wrinkled face, flaxen hair, toothless mouth, but her eyes have the glint of a knife. As she looks at the image, her lips start to tremble in agitation, and she puts the mirror down. Its wood frame is blackened, worn out, but she remembers its shiny reddish color when she first got it. The glass was like the sunlit surface of a very still pond. And on that surface, one face frequently appeared: a clear and bright face with a small forehead fringed with reddish hair, not black hair like everybody else's, a sharp nose under that forehead, and small eyes with pale, almost yellow irises that somehow frightened people. She used to like those eyes, though. She liked the way, when she narrowed them into slits, she could see everything, everything under the sky and up to the sky. Those eyes now make her shudder with fear. Whoever catches their lightning glance is doomed. She still does not understand what goes wrong and how, but each time something terrible does happen.

She can vividly recall the first time it happened. She was at the bottom of the broken steps leading into the pond that faced the crumbling old temple of Shiva. She was alone, absorbed in watching an image swirl and slither in the water. Every time the water grew still, the face of a girl of about ten, a face exactly like hers, appeared smiling at her. Suddenly she heard someone rushing down the steps and saw Haru Sarkar. He dragged her by the hair and flung her down on the old brick steps. His shout still rings in her ears, "Witch! You dared to cast your evil look on my son. I'll kill you."

She still remembers the murderous rage in his face. She remembers how scared she was, how she cried, "Please don't kill me, I beg at your feet."

"If you craved for the mango and puffed rice he was eating, why didn't you ask for some instead of eyeing his, you witch?"

She did crave it. She really did. Her mouth was filled with warm, flowing saliva.

"Bitch! Witch! You made my boy sick, tossing with stomach pain."

To this day, she is puzzled about the link, about how it actually worked. No doubt it worked that way, but how? She wept frantically outside Haru Sarkar's house, as she prayed to god to make the boy well. Then she said to herself, "I take the evil look back. Here, I've taken it back. Be well now." The strangest of strange things was that soon the boy felt better, after throwing up a couple of times, and fell asleep.

Sarkar then asked his wife to give her a mango and some puffed rice. His wife raised the broom at her, "I'll shove stove ash in that witch's mouth. I've always been kind to her, thinking of her as a poor orphan. Whenever she comes, I give her something to eat. In return, she eyes my son's food. Look how she stands there listening about her deed! I always suspected those eyes and never let the children eat in her presence. Today I'd gone to the pond for barely a minute after settling the boy down to his meal. I come back and see her right up beside him! And how she was eyeing his food!"

She couldn't bear to listen any more. She ran, scared and ashamed. That night she did not seek shelter in anyone's porch to sleep. She went back to the abandoned temple at the edge of her village, and the whole night she lay outside its door, crying to the god inside, "God, please take the evil look out of my eyes. Or make me blind."

Her ancient body, motionless like a faded old clay figure, absorbed in remembering, stirs back to life with a deep sigh. She has been sitting so still for so long. Now the lips tremble with agitation. There is no undoing the sins of previous births. No point blaming the gods. Even they cannot undo it, after all.

That night long ago, she decided never to enter any home, always to stay outside and away from the inhabitants. Even as her voice weakened with age, she took care to stay off the doorways she begged at, straining her voice, "Spare some rice for me. May god bless you."

"Who is it? Oh, it's you! Don't cross the threshold."

"No dear, I'll stay out," she would say, but the very next moment something would wake up inside her, wriggling and writhing. It still does, even as she recalls the moment. Lovely smell of frying fish! Must be thick slices of a fresh big carp!

"Hey you, shameless creature! Stop peeping in with your snake eyes."

She is ashamed. They were right. She was peering into the kitchen. Through the narrowed slits, her eyes had indeed seen all that was laid out there. Her mouth was filled with the warm flow from the spring hidden under her tongue.

She stirs again, awkwardly, like a crumbling old clay figure shaking from a bump with something moving. Rusty stiff limbs start moving aimlessly, without coordination. The squatting figure shifts restlessly. The nails of the bony long fingers dig into the clay floor, as the agitated hand presses down. In all this time, with the whole life of thinking about it, she still cannot make out the why and the how of it. Her mind reels with the unbearable frustration of all the futile effort to understand the matter. The whole world seems to reel away from her.

What can she ever do about it? Can anyone tell her? All of a sudden, she lets out a shrill cry, like a wounded beast howling. Furiously shaking her head, tossing the flaxen hair, she sits up bolt straight. Clamping the toothless gums, narrowing the slit eyes, she scans the field like a hawk, panting.

She sees that the field has become extremely hazy today, almost smoky, as it does in the noontime of the driest month, Chaitra. Then she notices something moving inside the haze, something shimmering like a mirage. She looks hard but cannot quite make it out. With a single blow from her mouth she can lift the whole field of dust and scatter it in the sky, to see what it is! No, she does not wish to think of that.

But what is that little solid white thing moving in the haze? A human being? Yes, it must be. She suddenly feels agitated. Would she like to blow away all the dust along with the human being? Something starts rearing its head inside her. Some vague urge, cruel and mischievous, laughing the senselessly gleeful laughter of the crazed. Hee, hee, hee. No, no, no! She clenches her fists in the effort to stifle it, to regain composure. She should not do it because it would make the human being suffocate in the heated dust. She is going to stop looking in that direction. Better sweep the porch once more and gather the fallen leaves and twigs into a pile.

She drags her tired old body, still squatting, sweeping the porch with the broom of palm leaf sticks. Suddenly, the leaves she is sweeping flutter and fly in a spiral. The dust she has gathered up joins the spiral circling her; the dust gets into her eyes, into her mouth, and the dry leaves beat about her body. She hisses like a hairless mangy cat under attack, brandishing the broom. "Go away from me, get out," she keeps hitting at the spiral. The spiral then staggers out of her porch and rushes across the field. The dust rises off the field to join it and forms a moving pillar. Not just one any more! Here, there, large and small. So many crazy, running columns of swirling dust and leaves. One becoming a thousand! The field seems to be dancing wildly. It fills her with a strange, eager, childlike joy. Her bent body stands up as best as it can from squatting, and she starts to circle along with them, the broom held in her raised hand. Then she staggers and feels herself falling, tumbling over, as if the earth has heaved to roll her off in space. She lays for a while where she fell. Then very slowly she crawls back to the porch. Her throat is parched and full of dust.

"Anybody home? Help me, please help me."

The old woman, slumped in a corner of the porch, her body twisted and limp like a rotting branch, raises her head with effort in the direction of the female voice. "Who is it?"

She sees a young woman standing there, her face pale and tired, dust all over her, clasping something carefully to her bosom covered with her sari. She has trudged across the field. Following the old woman's voice, the girl finally spots her. Startled, she becomes more pale and begins to back away, hesitantly saying, "I . . . I only wanted a little water. . . ."

The old woman raises herself, slowly pushing up with her hands, and sees the girl's pale, tired face. "Poor girl! Come in, dear, and sit down."

The girl, still afraid, hesitates and sits cautiously, tentatively on the edge of the porch, saying it is only a little water that she wants. The old woman melts with affection. She goes into the hut, fills the brass pot with water and reaches into the jar of jaggery for a piece to offer her with the water.

"Poor daughter! Why did you go out in the sun in this killer field?"

The girl is still panting a little. Her dry voice quivers and cracks. "My mother is very sick, and I'm on my way to see her. I started before dawn but lost my way near the field. Instead of following the path along its edge, I strayed in the middle of the field—I don't know how."

The old woman sets down the pot of water and the piece of jaggery before the girl. Then she spots, to her consternation, the baby beside the girl, his body limp like steamed greens. Anxiously, she asks the girl to give water to the baby. The girl wets the end of her sari and gently wipes the baby's sweating body.

The old woman sits a little apart from them and silently watches the baby. Must be the firstborn of the healthy young mother. Soft and chubby. Tender and juicy like baby squash. Inside her toothless mouth, the tongue slowly stirs and turns on the hidden spring. The familiar warm flow starts to fill her mouth.

How the baby is sweating! On and on! All the water of his soft little body seems to be draining out, and his eyes are turning red. Is it happening again? What can she do? Why did the girl have to come near her? How she longs to hold the baby, to snuggle his soft body, to press it against her bony dried-up chest! Her wrinkled old skin tingles all over, and her body trembles with excitement. The baby's juice seems to be squeezed out in the sweat, and she finds a taste of the juice in her saliva.

"Oh, no!" She cries out helplessly, "Your baby is getting eaten up by me! Run away with your baby. Run right now!"

At that moment the young mother has both her hands holding up the waterpot, pouring water into her lifted mouth. The pot falls off her hands with a start. She looks at the old woman's agitated slit eyes and asks, "Is this Ramnagar, then? Are you the one . . . ?"

Half uttering something between a sob and a scream, she snatches up her baby and flees like a small bird attacked by the hawk.

How can she help it? She feels like tearing her chest open with her nails, catching hold of that killer greed, and throwing it out. Maybe cutting the tongue off would set her free. Tomorrow, how is she going to go into a village to beg? Nobody would dare to say anything to her face. She knows that; but she will see it in the expression on their silent faces, in their eyes. How is she going to bear that? Little children run away as soon as they see her. Some cry in fear. After today's incident, they will probably faint with terror at the sight of her. She cringes trying to visualize herself on her begging trip into the village tomorrow. This shame had once made her leave her native village in the dead of night long ago.

She was almost a woman then, not the little girl she was the first time. Sabitri, a girl of about her own age in her own caste community, had given birth to a baby boy the night before. Next morning she went to see them. The teenage mother was sitting in the porch with the newborn, taking in the soft sunshine. How beautiful the baby was, how shiny black! Just like today, she had a sudden urge to hug the lovely baby, to cover his soft doughy body with kisses. She had not realized then that it could be anything but a longing to hold and caress the adorable baby.

She remembers how the baby's grandmother suddenly rushed out in consternation and how she scolded the daughter-in-law.

"You stupid low-born! Lost your senses, chatting away with that one. If something happens to my grandson, I'll finish you off."

The poor girl, startled and terrified, picked up the baby to her bosom and ran inside the house; her weak body was shaking and unsteady. As she was standing there quite surprised, the mother-in-law turned to her. Pointing her finger to the gate, she shouted at her, "Out! Out! You with the evil eyes. Just see that awful look!"

She left, shocked and so terribly hurt by the accusation. She might have witchlike eyes, but how could anyone think that she would ever wish to harm the baby of her own dear friend? All day she tossed and turned with pain and bewilderment. She prayed to god: "Reveal your judgment. Give the baby a life of one hundred years, and make them see that I felt only love for the baby."

But before the afternoon was over, it was demonstrated to all that her eager look worked like lethal poison. She soon heard about how her friend's newborn screamed with pain as his body bent back, as if someone unseen was sucking away his lifeblood.

That evening she ran away from her native village in shame and horror, and hid among the bushes in the cremation ground outside it. There she stayed up all night, coughing up over and over again and checking the spit for traces of blood. There was none at first. But she kept probing her throat with her fingers, deeper and deeper, peering hard for red in the watery mucus she managed to bring out of her empty stomach. She wanted concrete evidence. After several attempts there were some red spots and finally quite a bit of fresh blood. That finally convinced her of the terrible, abominable power with which she was cursed.

Later on that dark moonless night, she heard the distant drumbeats coming from the midnight worship of the goddess Tara in Her temple near village Bakul. The destroyer-savior goddess is known all over the area to be alive and extremely powerful. On the pitch-dark fourteenth night of every phase of the waxing moon, the Mother is worshiped with goats sacrificed to the frenzied beating of drums. From her hideout she prayed to the Mother and promised to offer Her blood from her own chest, not goat blood, if She would change her from witch to human being. Her prayer was not answered.

With a deep sigh she jars herself from remembrance. Her mind now wanders in a daze, feeling unbearably hopeless and sad. The thoughts she was absorbed in are floating away like kites suddenly released from tension, their taut strings snapped, floating away, swinging helplessly toward somewhere unknown. Her yellow eyes, their concentration gone, stare vacantly at the field. She sits there looking at the field of killer thirst; the air is dead still over it, and the pale gray pall of dust has obliterated everything from view.

The baby of the thirsty young mother who lost her way in the field has died on the way, soon after she fled from here, even before she crossed over to the villages. The terrible sweating never stopped, as if someone was relentlessly wringing his little body. Who else could have done it? The young mother has wept, hitting her forehead and her chest with her fists, "What have I done? How could I wander off to the witch?"

The villagers gathered around her have shuddered and silently wished death for the killer witch. Shortly after that, several tough young men have ventured in a group to teach her a lesson. The angry old woman has hissed like a snake at them. Why did the girl come near her, and why did she hold all that soft innocent grace before her evil eyes? Overcome with despair, she has shrieked at them at one point. Its sound, so like the shrill shriek of a hawk in the silent heat of the noon sky, has frightened them away. She is still hissing by herself, like an angry snake, working up her poison and swallowing it back.

How can she find relief from the poison she is engorged with? Would she like to laugh wildly? Or shake the dusty field with an angry scream? Maybe she could find relief in crying aloud. How she wants to cry! Beating her chest and tearing her hair, she wants to let off the cry that would crack the earth all across!

She has no need to cook today; she is not hungry. No wonder. She has drunk the juice of a whole baby, in one long invisible draft. The day is over too.

It is the ninth night of the waxing moon. The pale moonlight has made the dusty field look like a vast white bed. Somewhere nearby a nightbird belts out her aria, eagerly, tirelessly: *Chokh ge-lo, chokh ge-lo!* Eyes gone, eyes gone! The mango grove is holding the ceaseless, monotonic orchestra of the crickets chirping away. She listens.

She then hears two people whispering near the muddy spring at the back. Are those boys back to punish her? She tiptoes cautiously to the edge of her hut and peers out. She spots the spirited Bauri girl, deserted by her husband, with the Bauri boy head over heels in love with her. The girl is saying, "I better get back. Someone can come by and see us."

"Sure! They're coming! Nobody comes here even during the day."

"Maybe. But why should I be here with you anyway, knowing that your father is never going to let you marry me?"

So, that is why they have to meet away from their village, in this godforsaken place by the dried spring. She is suddenly overcome with tender shyness, feeling sorry that the lovers have to meet out here and wishing they would meet inside her cottage instead of the dusty spot out there. They need not be embarrassed in the presence of a lonely old woman. What is the boy saying to her now?—"If my parents won't let us marry, we can go to some distant village, marry and set up our home there. You know I can't live without you."

Such taste that boy has! So much in love with that homely girl!

She remembers her own love.

She was then twenty miles away from her village. She was standing in front of a *pan* shop in Bolpur town and looking at the big mirror in the little shop where passersby stopped for a *pan* or a *bidi*. In the mirror was a tall slim girl, about fifteen years of age, with a headful of unoiled reddish hair, a small forehead, a sharp nose, fine lips, and little tawny eyes that were shiny and pretty. She was totally absorbed in her image in the big mirror. That was before she got her own little mirror.

"Hey! Who are you? Where have you come from?" A muscular young man appeared in the mirror asking her. She had reached the town the previous evening. She had walked many miles nonstop since the night she left her village after eating her friend's newborn baby. She did not mind the man, but his way of talking irritated her. She glared at him, unblinking, and snapped, "What's it to you where I'm from?"

"What's it to me? See my fist? Can level you down with one blow."

Gnashing her teeth in anger, she wished to drink his blood. She glanced at his smooth black body that looked like a sculpture in black stone. The spring under her tongue turned on the warm flow. Without answering, she slowly walked off, holding her steel-sharp sidelong stare fixed on him as long as she could see him.

It was almost dusk later on that same day. As soon as the sun had dipped below the horizon, a huge yellow disk of a moon rose. She was watching the moonrise, sitting by the pond near the railway tracks near the end of the town. She was holding one end of her sari gathered into a bag with puffed rice in it, which she was eating while watching for the moonlight to grow milky white. The light was still weaker than the dark. A figure suddenly sprang right in front of her. Startled, she looked hard at it in the dim light. That man again! He stood there, grinning at her. There were dimples in his cheeks. Smiling always dimpled his cheeks.

"Why did you walk away that time without answering?"

"Hear me now. Leave me alone. Go away now. Or I'll scream."

"Scream. See the mud under the water? I'll strangle you and bury you under the mud if you even try to scream."

She was so terrified that she just sat there looking at him blankly.

He suddenly stamped his foot impatiently and shouted, "Come on!"

She started violently, dropping the puffed rice she held in her sari. The man laughed as her puffed rice fell in a gentle shower at her feet. She started crying. The man was embarrassed, but he scolded her, "Don't be such a crybaby. You're a strange girl." His scolding words clearly reflected a touch of affection.

"Are you really going to hit me?" she asked, still crying.

"Of course not. All I asked you was where you're from, and you snarled at me. That's why I've been talking this way." He laughed again.

"My home is far from here, in Patharghata village."

"What's your name, and your caste?"

"My name is Soradhoni. They call me Sora. I'm a Dome."

The man looked very pleased and said, "I'm a Dome too. So why did you run away from home, Sora?"

Tears of another kind came to her eyes. She was silent, wondering how to answer his question about why she ran away.

"Did you have a fight with your folks?"

"No."

"What is it then?"

"I've got no parents, no family, nobody to provide for me. So I came here looking for work to support myself."

"Why are you still unmarried? Hey! Why haven't you married?"

She looked at him, surprised by his question. Who will marry a witch? She shuddered at the terrible idea. Then she felt overcome with a strangely soft shyness.

Even today, after all these years, she feels strangely overwhelmed as she sits in the dark porch recalling that moment. She lowers her head, and her hands needlessly brush the mud floor at her feet, gathering the dust and bits of stone. The continuity of her thought is flustered. The needle has dropped off the thread along which she has been stringing the flowers into a garland.

The mosquitoes! Like bees off a broken hive, they are all over her body. Those two don't seem to be talking any more! Have they left?

Carefully holding on to the clay wall in the dark, she manages to come out and around the porch. They are gone! But they will surely be back tomorrow. No other place is as quiet and deserted as the back of her hut. Nobody else will dare to come here. But those two will because love knows no fear.

What about eating the boy? His fleshy young body! That thing inside her wriggles a little. Horrified, she shakes her head and pushes it back down. No. No. No. She cannot allow that.

She sits swaying absentmindedly for a while. Then she gets up and walks round and round all over the dark porch. This is what she has to do all through the night. She cannot sleep, not after eating a whole baby. How she wishes she could leave this field right now and go far away. They say she can ride a tree across the sky. She wishes she knew how. Then she could just sit on one and fly through the clouds to wherever she wanted. But then she wouldn't be able to listen to the pair of lovers. They'll be back tomorrow.

Hee, hee, hee. They're back. Just him now, sitting quietly, turning his head every now and then in the direction of the girl's path.

She recalls her own sweet appointment with the muscular man. The following evening he was back at the pond by the railway tracks. He sat on the bank, his legs dangling, waiting for her and looking the way she was to come. This time it was she who stood before him; and there was a tiny smile in the corners of her lips.

"So you've come! I've been waiting so long."

The old woman is startled to hear the boy say the very same words to the girl standing before him. She must have a smile in the corners of her lips too.

Her own man had brought some sweets in a packet of leaves. He held it to her, saying, "Yesterday I made you drop your puffed rice. This is for you."

But she could not make her hand reach out and take the sweets. Her witch greed swayed like a snake at the flute of the snake charmer but forgot to strike.

And then? What did he do then? Yes, she remembers that too. These young lovers can't do it; they do not know how to. But this boy is doing the same! He is feeding the girl with his own fingers! The old woman is flooded with joy. She breaks into silent laughter. Her old bony fingers joyfully tap the ground she is now sitting on stooped over.

She stops abruptly. The silent ripple is gone, followed by a sigh. She sits dejectedly, leaning against the tree that is a pole for the roof sloping over the porch.

The next thing he said to her was, "Will you marry me, Sora?"

Sora could not say anything; she could not think of anything. She was so strangely confused. Her ears felt so hot. Her hands and feet were sweaty, almost dripping. He kept on, "Look at me. I work at the factory and make good money. Yet I haven't got a wife because there are few women of my caste around here and women of other castes won't marry an untouchable. Marry me."

She hears the boy beside the spring at the back of her hut saying, "They'll stop us marrying from here in our village. Your folks and mine will raise hell. We better run away, to a far-off village and be happy there."

They are talking softly, yet their words float to her so clearly in this quiet place. She sighs as she remembers her own love, how they forgot the rest of the world and set up home together. He used to shovel coal all day into the machine that looked like a giant barrel. They called it a boiler. He did the hardest work in the factory and got the highest wage.

The beloved girl by the dry spring is now saying, "That's not good enough. I'll go with you only after you give me silver bangles and ten rupees in a knot in my sari. I'm not running away to a strange place with no money in my hands and risk starving there away from home."

Foolish girl! You should be ashamed. Your loud mouth deserves the broom. A strong young man clings to your sari, and you worry about bangles and food. Some day you'll wear on your wrists more than silver bangles, maybe gold-rimmed conchshell bangles. How can you be so stupid?

The boy has fallen silent. The girl says, "What's the matter with you? Didn't you hear what I said? If you have anything to say, better say it soon because I have to leave."

The boy sighs, "What can I say? If I had the money, I'd have given it to you and silver bangles, too, even before you asked for them."

"Well, I'm leaving then."

"Go."

"Don't ask me to come here anymore."

"All right."

The girl walks away, and her white-clad figure recedes and soon merges into the lovely moonlight. Poor boy! Who knows what he is going to do after this. He might renounce life and become a hermit. He might go and hang himself. She shudders thinking about it. Perhaps she could give him her own silver bangles. What about the money? She cannot give ten rupees. She has only twenty in all, but she can give him two or even five out of it. Maybe the girl will accept that. So young! It is their time to be happy, to have their wishes fulfilled. She is going to call the boy and give him her bangles and money. She will be his grandmother, and he her grandson; and she is going to tease him to her heart's content!

Bent over like a hunchback, one hand on the ground for balance, she walks over to him and looks up at him from behind. The boy has not been aware of her coming; he has been sitting still, preoccupied with his sadness.

She smiles as she addresses him, "Hello, beloved. Can you hear me?"

At the sound of her toothless, distorted speech, the boy starts, turns around, and screams in terror. He jumps out and runs for his life.

At once, the old woman also has an unimaginable transformation. Bristling like an angry cat, she hisses at him, "You die. Die. Die." She furiously desires to suck off his body all his blood, flesh, fat, and marrow.

The boy, running away, suddenly screams in pain and drops to the ground. The next moment he gets up and frantically limps away.

The following day, before the morning is over, an entire village is stunned with shock and terror. The killer witch has claimed a Bauri boy. He had gone to the spring in the evening; and, like a tigress attracted by the smell of prey, the witch had approached him in soundless steps. When he realized her presence, he tried to run away, but the witch's arrow struck him down. She cast in his path a sharp piece of bone with her spell in it, and it drove deep in his foot. After they managed to pull it out, there was such terrible bleeding followed by raging fever. His helpless body is bent back like a bow; his head and feet are in the iron grips of someone relentlessly squeezing out the vital juice of his young body.

But how could she help it?

Why did he try to run away? How can anyone expect to run away from her grasp? Even her own man, strong and muscular, who used to grapple with fire every day at work, even he became in the end like a bare fishbone with all the flesh picked away.

They have brought a witch doctor. He says he can cure the boy. She remembers her own man slowly pale and wither away before her eyes. He was ill with a persistent cough and fever. But that could not be the real cause. Why then did he throw up all that blood?

In the hot stillness of noon, she keeps pacing on the porch, round and round, driven insane with agitated anxiety. The field of killer thirst lies inert like a corpse, burning away in the fiery sun. Nothing at all seems to be stirring in the field. Even the wind seems to be holding its breath.

The one whom she loved more than her own life and with whom she was never even the slightest bit angry wilted from her loving look and died drained of all his blood. And this witch doctor thinks he can save the boy from her blasting look, from the merciless draining power of her anger, from her demonic will!

She laughs, an utterly cruel laugh. How her chest is gripped with labored breathing, suffocating her. The pain in her body and her mind makes her want to scream and shatter the tightness in her chest. It is probably the effect of the witch doctor trying to destroy her, riddle her with counterspells. Go on. Do your utmost!

She must run away from here now. After her husband's death, when the people in her neighborhood in Bolpur came to know of her secret, they tormented and persecuted her. She herself had let the secret out. She was friendly with a woman named Shankari in the community of millworkers from Handi caste. One day she had confided to Shankari about her curse.

Since that time she has lived outside communities, at the edge of villages, carefully avoiding people. So many times she has had to move to so many different places. She has to move again to some other place she does not know.

What is that! Suddenly, the sleepy silence of the hot noon is shattered by the sound of heartrending wailing from the village. She listens for a moment. Then she frantically runs inside and bolts her door. When dusk is about to fall, she steps out of her hut, carrying a little bundle, out into the field of killer thirst. She must run away now. She must escape the wrath of the villagers.

The darkness seems to be setting in unusually rapidly and with unusual density. Everything around her is awfully still and silent in the field. She scampers through the windless field, making the unusually passive dust fly only at her heels. After running some distance, she stops and sits on the ground exhausted. She cannot go on any more!

After so many years, she weeps, brokenhearted; she cries aloud for her husband long dead from her own unconscious malevolence. "Where are you, my dearest? I need you, I need you."

Suddenly she notices with horror the northwest corner of the sky, rapidly turning tawny like the irises of her knife-slit eyes.

Swiftly the storm sweeps in, the ferocious *kalbaisakhi* of a hot summer afternoon. All the dust flies from the ground and covers everything from view. In that terrible storm, the old woman disappears completely. A tornado runs its deadly pointed finger across the field of killer thirst, followed by just a few raindrops.

Next morning, the shocked villagers gather near the edge of the field, and they silently look up at a jagged branch of a thorny bush. Hanging there, skewered on the branch, is the old witch. While flying through the sky, she must have been hit by the witch doctor's spell and dropped, like a bird with a broken wing, on the thornbush to die impaled on the sharp branch. The dust under the branch, where the witch's black blood had dripped, has turned into a black lump of clay. The field of killer thirst now appears to them even more terrifying as the witch's blood mixes with the poison of the giant snake from the distant past.

The horizon across from the field is completely obliterated today. From the ground to the sky, it is all dismal gray, smoky, and dusty.

The villagers suddenly notice a few dots in the gray sky. The dots are moving, and they seem to be slowly growing bigger as they descend through the uniform gray.

Vultures—a horde of them—are descending from the sky.

Variation on "The Witch": An Excerpt

Tarashankar Bandyopadhyay

In our village, near the east end of our house there was a large pond with tall palm trees around it. A 45-degree line from the pond toward the northeast would be pointing to the hut of Swarna the witch, Shawna *dain*, as the folks said. It was at the very edge of the village, in a large barren field that lay between two clusters of huts—one the fishermen's and the other the Bauri untouchables'. A large banyan tree stood in the field, and under that tree was the one-room hut of Swarna. There were no more huts after it, only the barren plain of sandy dark dirt that stretched on. Nobody ever went near that edge of the village, except on the way to cremate the dead, stopping by the waterhole in the middle of the barren stretch to do the last rites. The spot was littered with the remains of the mats, mattresses, and pillows used for carrying the dead body and with the clay pots and half-burnt sticks and twigs used for the ritual of touching the mouth of the dead with fire. The big leafy banyan tree stood on the other side of the waterhole. Nobody dared to go near the tree even in daylight, and at night the tree looked like a huge solid presence of dense darkness against the dark sky.

Swarna used to spend her time sitting at her porch, looking at the tree.

At least, that is what we thought she did.

The green paddy fields were at the far end of the barren land, away from her. A witch does not, cannot, tolerate any lush green nearby.

Shawna dain was thin like a stick. She had two full rows of strong teeth and small slits of eyes with pupils the color of catechu. The look in her eyes was strangely fixed, with no emotion, dry like the stones on a dried riverbed.

This excerpt is taken from a narrative sketch on the same theme as the preceding story and is also titled "Daini." First published in the literary magazine *Mouchak* (Calcutta, 1951) and reprinted in *Tarashankar Rachanabali*, vol. 7 (Calcutta: Mitra & Ghosh Publishers, 1973), 503–6.

They said a witch's stare was like that. That stare could see through young plump flesh, the inside of graceful, beautiful human bodies. Those eyes could penetrate young wives' skin, flesh, fat, and bones, searching for the new life forming inside their wombs. The stare would suck dry anything that was growing and lovely. Plump bodies became all skin and bones, golden complexion became scorched, and brides lost their gracious beauty. Not just people. Even a growing plant full of healthy new shoots would suddenly dry up, as the witch's stare sucked away its sap.

In the hot still noon of summer, you heard the shrill cry of the hawk coming from the top of the palm tree. If you listened carefully, you could also hear the witch whining along, singing in her high-pitched nasal voice.

At night, very late at night, if you were anywhere near the witch's hut and if you listened hard, you could hear strange thumping and bumping; the witch made those sounds, restlessly crawling about the dark porch. Those who are cursed by the gods to become witches have to spend all night awake, walking on their chest along the floor, back and forth, back and forth, throughout the whole night.

Who would not be afraid after hearing all this?

Swarna used to sell vegetables for a living. She would buy the vegetables—green plantains, ripe bananas, pumpkins, and leafy greens—from the market seven or eight miles away and sell them in the nearby villages. Not in our village, but we heard that she sold vegetables in other villages. She never crossed the threshold of anyone's house. She could not trust herself—she might harm someone without meaning to! The greed that lurked inside her might at any time start salivating for someone, something. It would not listen to her forbidding! And Swarna would die of shame! She was not the master of the witch that lived inside her; she was its slave; all her life she was to do its bidding. She could not even die without its permission. Swarna would not die until the witch in her managed to find someone else to transfer into.

They said Swarna's aunt was a witch. She lived alone, and when she was dying she sent a message to her relatives. But nobody went near her deathbed. Swarna did not go to see her dying aunt, afraid that the terrible witch power might be transferred to her at the moment of death. She went after the aunt died, thinking that the transference must be over by then, for otherwise she could not have died. She found that many relatives had come by then and divided up the dead woman's belongings to take back home with them; they had all left with their shares. Swarna was a young childless widow. She sat alone in the porch of her dead aunt. Suddenly her aunt's pet cat came meowing to her. It softly brushed against her legs and purred, as if saying to her, "Take me along. You have got nothing from your aunt, and nobody took me." Swarna felt sorry for the cat and brought it back with her.

She fed the cat, she let it sleep beside her, and she took it along wherever she went about in her village.

One day the fishermen's neighborhood was shocked by a terrible thing. A baby boy was sick, his body was bent back, and he cried, wailed almost like a cat, in fact, exactly like a cat. The witch doctor examined the baby and said that it must be the work of a witch. But . . .

"What?"

"The witch seems to be a . . ."

Before he finished the sentence, Swarna's cat came up meowing and sat down purring. "Yes. The cat is the witch."

"Cat witch?"

"Of course. A witch must have passed the power on to it when dying."

Then they all remembered that Swarna's aunt was a witch and the cat had belonged to her. It was the only living creature with her in her last moment. What a terrible thing!

A young man in the crowd that had gathered was so agitated that he picked up a stick and hit the cat in the head. Its head was totally smashed. But the cat did not die. Its tail kept twitching, and its nails slowly scratched the ground.

"Watch out," the witch doctor said. "Nobody should go near it because it is now trying to pass the power on to someone; otherwise, it can't die."

He muttered charms to safeguard himself, carefully picked up the cat by the tail, took it to the edge of the village, and left it there.

Swarna was at home at the time. She heard about what happened. She was terrified. People came by to scold her. Why did she bring the curse into the village?

Later in the afternoon, some boys passing by her home told her how the cat was moaning in terrible agony, still unable to die. They shuddered with horror as they talked about it. Swarna finally went there. She could not keep from going to see her dying cat. The fluffy, milky-white cat was covered with blood and dirt, and its cry was so tortured. Slowly, one step at a time, she came close to it. Very gently, she touched the nose of the dying cat, and the cat died.

Swarna's vision suddenly changed. She could see things she had never seen before. The pregnant goat grazing over there—Swarna could see the two kids inside her! And the banana plant—she was seeing the baby bananas inside the cone of flowers and thinking of the nice curry it would make. Her tongue became moist, alive. God! What was happening to her?

This is the legend of how Swarna became a witch.

She too would have to find a recipient for the power before she could die. Otherwise, she would suffer and suffer like the cat with its smashed head. Death would sit waiting before her, and she would be unable to die. She would beg Death to release her from the agony. Death would reply that she could not be delivered until she had transferred her power to someone.

Because Swarna had no control over the witch lodged in her, she never could, and never would, go inside any home in a village!

Swarna lived there alone for a very long time. When I grew to be a young man, I used to refer to her and address her as aunt Swarna. Sometimes when I passed her hut, I saw her sitting still inside the almost dark hut. Just sitting still. She rarely talked with anyone. If a passerby happened to ask her something, she would answer as briefly as possible and disappear inside her hut.

When I was twenty, or maybe twenty-two, I began to understand how terribly painful the woman's life was. She herself believed she was a witch. If she felt affection for anyone, she would cringe with fear. If someone looked nice in her eyes, she would immediately shut her eyes. If she was attracted to anyone, she dreaded that the witch in her might devour, or maybe it already had devoured, the object of her affection. She believed that her witch power poisoned her love, turned it into a lethal arrow to pierce the heart of anyone she felt any love for.

All the time she prayed to god to free her from the curse, to end her terrible life. When she cried, she frantically wiped the tears off her eyes and shuddered if a drop fell on the ground because witch tears would scorch the kindly bosom of mother earth.

The Unlucky Woman

Manik Bandyopadhyay

1

Kusum felt harried all the time, running her household with a small baby. She found even the baby difficult to manage; he was awake exactly when she had the most housework to do and, unlike her neighbor Susila's baby, would not play by himself if left for a minute in his bed of quilted rag. She had to carry him when doing the work because he would start crying as soon as she put him down. Her family was small, just her husband Tarak and the baby. But however small, it still involved running a household; every little task must still be attended to. She had to get up early in the morning to clean and mop the floor, wash the pots and plates, light the coal stove, feed the baby, and finish cooking the lunch by nine, in time for Tarak to have it before he left for work—not one of these tasks could be left out even for a day.

A small household is only a scaled down version of a large household; each task is smaller in size, but the number of tasks is no fewer. These are only the major chores she did every morning. There were a thousand little things she had to do each morning apart from these, not to mention other major chores in the rest of the day. Take a seemingly small task like fetching a glass of water. One must look around for the invariably misplaced glass, after finding it bring it to the earthen pitcher to pour the water, take the glass of water to the person who wanted it, and wait until the person finishes drinking so that one can at least try to put the glass back in its place. One must go through each step to complete that little task.

First published as "Podakapali," in *Atashi Mami O Anyanya Galpa* [Aunt Atashi and Other Stories] (Calcutta: Gurudas Chattopadhyay and Sons, 1935). Reprinted in Manik's collected works, *Manik Granthabali*, ed. Saroj Mohan Mitra, vol. 3 (Calcutta: Granthalaya, 1969), 397–404.

How can a human being do so much and so many different kinds of work, while carrying a baby much of the time? Somehow Kusum had to do all her housework because they could not afford a servant or a cook. She was not keeping well either, ever since she gave birth. She was having a recurrent fever, for a few days at a time; she still had not recovered from the last bout. She was so run down that many mornings just getting up from bed seemed hard work. Each afternoon she felt sick with acid indigestion; every evening she had a throbbing headache. The headache was the most unbearable of her everyday ailments; her head felt so heavy that it seemed about to roll off her neck. It was so bad that she wished her head was knocked off; that would at least relieve the pain. Everybody has a head, but nobody is given so much trouble by it.

Tarak expressed sympathy and concern. "Let me buy some hair oil for you," he said. "You're losing all your hair."

Kusum knew how expensive hair oil was. How could she use hair oil regularly, when she knew that the cost would cut into something essential like milk for the baby? She did not say that in her casual reply, though.

"Poor me! It's not for lack of hair oil. It's because you don't love your old wife any more."

Tarak was very devoted to his wife. His love for his wife of four years was truly romantic, as if he had crossed seven seas and thirteen rivers, fought terrible obstacles, and passed many hard tests, like the fairy-tale prince, to win his princess only the other day.

She knew that. Take, for example, the fever she came down with a short time ago. It was not a fatal disease, but Tarak behaved as if it were, skipping his meals, his bath, and his sleep, even skipping his office.

Too much of this love and attention was not healthy for Kusum, and she was smothered like a plant that was shaded from the sun all day by the very cloud that kept watering it. She came from an environment of deprivation; she grew up in neglect in her uncle's household, where the evenings were lit only by the clay lamp and expressions of emotion—whether love or lack of love—were limited in frequency and intensity. She felt only discomfort in the face of intense emotional expression. A plant that thrived by a little stream had been transplanted on the bank of a river that kept swelling and flooding over throughout the year!

Kusum had increasingly been talking to herself. She had not gone out of her mind, though, not at the time.

The problem was that when Tarak was around she suffered exposure to excessive emotional expression and when he was away she suffered acute loneliness. In the mornings Tarak tutored a boy in the neighborhood, and then he left for his office for the rest of the day. A Bengali clerk at a Marwari merchant office, he rarely managed to come home before evening. Kusum had to spend the whole day with her mouth shut because she had no one to talk to. The rush of housework slowed around noon and came to a standstill in the early afternoon, but the child always slept through that time of day.

Kusum was not literate enough to be able to read for enjoyment. Once in a while she came upon a magazine and started reading a story, but it took her three days and much effort to finish it. It taxed her patience and brought little enjoyment, especially because the clever twists in the stories written these days are likely to be missed unless one reads at one sitting.

In the lonely confines of the little home, Kusum found her free time no less oppressive than her harried time of work. Even the presence of a pet bird with its undemanding chirpings would have relieved her misery. Tarak often offered to buy her a bird, but Kusum shook her head at his offer, sadly remembering the white cockatoo she once had shortly after their marriage. She said she had her lesson. She was not going to have a pet bird any more only to have to weep from the loss when it died.

Days rolled on for Kusum in this manner, in terrible mental and material poverty, alternating between harried housework and acute loneliness. However, later those days seemed to be the happy days of her life. They ended suddenly one evening when Tarak came home from work with two bottles of hair oil in his two pockets and discomfort in his body. The occasion for such extravagance was the raise of a few rupees in his salary.

"How could you waste two rupees like this!" she complained.

"No, I paid only fourteen annas a bottle."

"Big difference between a rupee and fourteen annas!" she argued. "Why couldn't you buy just one bottle if you felt like doing something after your raise?"

"I may forget to buy another in time. The two bottles will hardly last more than two months," Tarak reasoned in his mild manner.

Kusum was happy. She smiled and wondered, "Finish two bottles of oil in two months! We are not so rich!" Smiling, she said that it was not fair: Tarak had received the raise, but she received the hair oil. He should get some reward, and hence she was going to make *loochi* for dinner that night.

Tarak was feeling really unwell. He had vomited once when he was at the office, and he felt like a fever was coming. Now, at the mention of loochi for dinner, he was nauseous again, but he did not want to dampen Kusum's rare moment of enthusiasm. He did not want to see her lovely smile disappear with concern and apprehension. Besides, he thought, he only felt feverish. The fever had not come yet; maybe it was not going to come after all. Why deprive Kusum of a happy evening making loochi for dinner?

Kusum quickly lighted the coal stove. When she finished kneading the dough for loochi, she called Tarak to come over to the kitchen and help her roll it out. "Come here, *babumashai*, help me make it."

Tarak was sitting on the porch smoking his hookah. He tried to put the unfinished hookah upright on the ground, propped against the wall, but it rolled over, spilling the tobacco and charcoal; the wind at once made the ashen charcoal glow. As he tried to stamp out the charcoal with his sandal, quite a few sparks flew to the other side of the porch, and a few touched his dhoti, instantly making tiny black holes in it. He propped the hookah back up again and, annoyed by the accident, muttered to himself about the unexpected fierceness of the bit of charcoal ember.

Meanwhile Kusum was calling him again and, perhaps wondering about the unusual delay in his response, saying, "You just come here and sit near me, so we can talk. Don't bother about rolling out the dough."

Tarak came to her in the kitchen and said that he did not know how to roll out loochi anyway, but he could fry them if she rolled them.

"You don't have to do either. You just sit here and talk to me. The whole day I don't hear a human voice! Let me listen to you while I cook."

Tarak, however, insisted that he could fry the loochi. Kusum finally put aside her doubts to make room for him by the stove and the *kadai* on it with hot oil. Tarak moved in saying, "Of course I can fry them. Better than you."

But he could not fry the loochi that evening. While sliding the first one in, his finger touched the hot oil, and, while moving the hand with the scalded finger away, he knocked the pot of hot oil off the stove. The hot oil burnt many parts of his body, but most injured was his right leg. Very soon it had a gigantic blister such as she had never seen before. His blisters did not have time to heal because he had a raging fever that night, the kind of fever that the doctors call malignant. Long before his blisters could heal he died.

He died near the end of the night, and it was close to noon by the time she managed to get people to help her take him to the cremation ground. The weather was terrible, with rain and storm since daybreak. She could not manage to procure enough wood for burning a full-sized body on a rainy day. Parts of his body remained without wood when it was laid in the pyre. Because there was no other family member to do it, Kusum had to touch the fire to his mouth and light the pyre.

She remained standing close to the pyre, and when it started burning she moved only a little, just enough to bear the heat from the pyre. She had no tears in her eyes; perhaps they evaporated in the heat. She stood watching closely the huge blisters forming on his body and bursting, releasing steam and hot air, not water like usual blisters.

The world then seemed to be tumbling inside Kusum's head, and the pyre looked as if the sun had suddenly come very close and was burning at arm's length. Just before she fainted, Kusum thought that the blisters forming on his body in the burning pyre were not really blisters, but loochis, flat-rolled rounds of dough puffing up in hot oil.

2

About a month after becoming a widow, Kusum is back in her uncle's village household; she is cooking one evening in its kitchen. She has finished the *dal* and the vegetables and is about to start the pot of rice to cook, when her aunt comes and asks her to prepare loochi for her uncle who is not feeling well enough to have rice on the rainy night. Kusum turns pale with fear and tells her that she would do any work except making loochi. Her aunt is annoyed at how she could refuse to do such a simple thing as making loochi for her feverish uncle and asks if she could at least knead the dough. While silently kneading the dough, Kusum thinks again about the events preceding Tarak's untimely death and blames herself even more than she has done every day during the past one month.

After she fainted in the cremation ground and woke up at home, she could not cry at all. The self-castigation that kept her from crying then now constantly engages her mind in punishing herself. She thinks up all sorts of grounds on which to blame herself.

She knew that it was inauspicious for a married woman if vermillion was brought for her by her husband. Now she is convinced that it must be inauspicious for a married woman to have her hair oil brought by her husband, especially on a Thursday afternoon. She reasons that both vermillion and hair oil are used by married women; and of all the items used in the worship of deities and distributed afterward, the oil-vermillion paste goes only to married women. She is not absolutely certain of her reasoning, though, because she remembers many other times when Tarak had brought hair oil for her but nothing happened to him. However, the idea serves her need to punish herself well enough.

In any case, she does not have the slightest doubt that Tarak's high temperature that night was caused by the pot of hot oil knocked over his feet. She does not believe the doctor's word that it was malignant malaria. She herself had had malaria several times. Malaria does not kill so fast.

She torments herself by also thinking about how she could not arrange for good medical treatment. There was no time for treatment. Everything happened so fast, and she was so overwhelmed by the happenings. The money saved at the post office remained untouched, not one piece of her jewelry was mortgaged, and no expensive physician was consulted for her husband. She became a widow without resisting; she merely fainted out of weakness and heat near the cremation pyre.

Kusum watches the lively fire in the wood-burning stove. In spite of the rain outside, the wood is very dry, as it was stored in a corner of the kitchen. Squatting near the stove, waiting for her aunt to finish frying the loochis, Kusum watches the fire. She is transfixed, mesmerized by the flames. In all the time that she has spent by the fire cooking, she has never before noticed such vibrant color in fire. She had not seen such color in Tarak's funeral pyre either.

She watches the stove fire almost, but not totally, hypnotized because she also smells the *ghee* in which aunt is frying the loochi and senses the sick feeling the smell produces in her whole body to the very inside of her bones. She sits feeling nauseous and sick.

Kusum has become very thin in this one month. There are serious reasons for her not keeping well. In a few months she is going to give birth, and widowhood is not conducive to the health of an expectant mother. Moreover, she does not sleep at night. She stays up through the night in the company of her grief, darkness, her sleeping child, and her odd thoughts. The grief makes her weep, the darkness scares her, the child bothers her from time to time, and the thoughts in her head keep her awake.

Night after night she lies awake with meaningless, weird thoughts like this. She would recall the time she spent staying up in bed talking with Tarak and decide that she ought to spend a lot more time staying awake now grieving for him. As soon as she feels sleepy at night while lying in bed, she has only to recall the scene of Tarak's fair skin becoming covered with blisters and then charred black; sleep at once leaves, not to return during the rest of the night.

Her aunt's elder daughter comes into the kitchen to fetch a bowl and, noticing the roaring fire in the stove, asks why she put in so much wood. "Are you going to finish all the wood to cook one meal?"

She apologizes for being absentminded, pulls out some of the pieces of wood, and sprinkles water on them. The smoke makes her eyes water. She notices how similar the smell of the partly extinguished wood is to the smell of the cremation ground! Tears of grief mingle with tears from her irritated eyes. She weeps so copiously these days that her tears could fill a small bowl. She sits wiping the tears until her eyes are dry.

When she looks up, she sees the beginning of what can become a disaster. The bundle of jute stalks stored for kindling, propped up against the woven bamboo fence of the kitchen, has caught fire at the bottom from sparks off the lighted wood that she took out of the stove and doused a few minutes ago. She makes no effort to extinguish it. In a few minutes, the fence will catch fire and then the straw roof of the kitchen. The top layer of straw on the roof is wet, but that will not be able to stop the fire by the time it reaches up. If the kitchen is on fire, some of the rooms of the main house near the kitchen will catch fire too. Perhaps also the Mukherjee house on the other side of the kitchen. The god of fire just born and growing in the bundle of jute stalks will definitely reenact the burning of Lanka here tonight. She feels strangely excited trying to visualize the potential disaster. A huge cremation pyre will destroy some people tonight! The heat and the light of the blaze will displace the wet darkness of the night. There will be screaming in the air and the beating of chests. A few people will die in the fire tonight.

Kusum watches intently the tongues of flame crawl like snakes up the bundle of jute stalks. The little flames are gradually growing in size with their slow but determined advance toward the straw roof. The kitchen is bound to catch fire.

Even if nobody else dies in the fire, Kusum will. She cannot escape it because she is glued to her plank seat on the floor. Not only has she no intention of moving, but her limbs also lack the power to move; she is paralyzed. If she cannot even reach out and pull the bundle of burning jute stalks away from the kitchen fencing, how can she get out of the kitchen?

Kusum can clearly see herself, trapped under the fallen heap of the burning straw roof, tossing in pain, huge blisters appearing on her skin and releasing steam as they burst, and her body becoming charred. The terror, the horror of her imaginary death gives her a strange kind of pleasure, and she sits there relishing it.

She does not in the slightest doubt that her inability to stop a disaster, although she is capable, is really the judgment of god, who must have taken away the power to move her limbs. She must be a *sati* because otherwise she would not be so unable to save herself from this delayed burning of sati.

She could not kill herself on her own because in her condition suicide would also involve murdering the child growing within her. But if the house catches fire and she dies in it, then it is not suicide, and she will not have to go to hell or explain her action to the god of death. She will go smiling to join Tarak in heaven. People will sing the glory of a woman who did not live more than thirty-five days after her husband's tragic death.

She has thought about her little boy. He is now asleep with her aunt's youngest son and grandchildren. When the house catches fire, they will definitely remove him from there along with the other sleeping children. Her boy will not be killed. He will, of course, suffer a lot, the loss of his mother and maybe minor injuries too. But because that is god's will, there is nothing she can do about it. The god who is now arranging the mother's death will also arrange saving her son; he will survive and live a long life.

By now the fire has reached the middle of the bundle of jute stalks and is burning quite fiercely. When the tied middle of the jute stalks has burned through, the tops of the stalks drop to the floor. The chance of the kitchen being on fire does not appear as strong any more.

The tips of the jute stalks lie on the floor by the stove and burn away. After a few minutes even those are finished burning. Only some ash and a few little jute sticks are left.

Kusum feels terribly frustrated, deeply disappointed, but with the spell broken, she recovers the strength in her limbs.

She picks up the iron spatula used for cooking and stirs the burnt-out remains of her pathetic fantasy. In the little pile of ash, she finds a half-burnt dead cockroach.

A Tale of These Days

Manik Bandyopadhyay

1

The sun had climbed up the sky of Mansukia village and was right over-head at the time. Rampada was about to sit down to a lunch of rice and *shol* fish with chilies that he had cooked. The straw on the roof over the mud walls was rotted. Only the walls and the roof remained; nobody had taken these away in the six months when the hut had been abandoned. Everything else was gone, the bamboo fence, the poles to prop the slope of the thatched roof, the door planks, the bamboo shelf for storage—even the blackened, old earthen cooking pots inside. Without the poles, the roof over the porch in front of the hut had nearly collapsed. Rampada had not bothered to repair it yet. For whom would he bother to do it? He could manage to walk in and out through the side of the porch, lowering his head. With the porch blocked by the falling roof, it was dark inside, but he did not care.

As Rampada sat down to eat the rice and shol fish clumsily cooked by himself, in the porch darkened at noon by the collapsing roof, three women and a young man got off a small boat at Mansukia. One of them was Ram-pada's wife Mukta. The sari covering her head reached over her forehead. The sari edge over Surama's head did not cover even the line of vermillion in the parting of her hair. From this and the different ways they wore the sari and walked and spoke, it was easy to tell that Mukta was a peasant wife and the other two were educated city women, at ease with going out and working away from home, whatever the opinion in the country about their

"Aaj Kal Parshur Galpa" appears in *Uttarkaler Galpa Sangraha*, ed. Pijush Dasgupta (Calcutta: National Book Agency, 1963), 1–19, a collection of stories from Manik's later years, published seven years after his death. This story is set in the aftermath of the Great Bengal Famine of 1943.

work being good or bad. There was not much difference in the quality of what they wore. Mukta's sari was perhaps finer than Surama's and Sadhana's, but she did not have any other of poorer quality or less clean; if she had, she would have worn it for the occasion of coming back home in order to make her arrival less conspicuous.

Her heartbeat was abnormal, and her face was drawn with anxiety. She wished she had come inside a gunny sack so that she would be invisible to the villagers. In that case, it might have been harder for them to see her. But they all knew that she was coming that day, that the city ladies and gentlemen who had rescued Rampada's wife were bringing her back home.

Gagan's *paan bidi* shop in front of a large tree was merely a tiny shed of palm leaves atop four poles. If he had set up the shop closer to the trunk, he would not have needed the shed, as the tree would have served the purpose. A few people sitting at the store were dozing as if worn out by the sheer effort to remain alive. They sat up now. The jaw bones of old Sudas stuck out so much that it was hard to get past them and see how clearly his rib cage showed under the skin of his bare chest. "Ram's wife is back then," he said in a lethargic voice.

"Looks like she is," Nikunja answered absently, as he considered whether to light the half-burnt bidi that he managed to save from the four he had bought the day before for one paisa.

Gokul came out of the tin shade of Ghanashyam's grain warehouse and joined the group in Gagan's store. He was animated after getting a close look at the passing group, by pretending to cross the road in front of them.

Gada's wife had died last year. He was morose. After they had walked away toward the village, he sullenly asked if Ram would take her back.

"If he doesn't, it will be his loss," Gokul remarked excitedly. Working at Ghanashyam's warehouse, which had increased his food intake and so his blood supply, seemed to have given him the urge to differ from the older folks.

Old Sudas dejectedly said, "It'll not be right to take her back."

He did not ask young Gokul to shut up as he would normally have done; he did not make vulgar remarks to denounce the very idea of Mukta being accepted back. He merely said, as if indirectly agreeing with Gokul, "Why did she need to come back?"

Gokul had spoken jokingly, but the impression was real enough for all of them, and the joke did not lighten the evidence.

By the time she left, Mukta had looked like a skeleton draped in dirty rags. Like the others, Sudas too noticed Mukta's sari. He too was aware that there was now flesh between her skin and her bones.

The group that arrived walked along the winding village paths lined by ponds, waterholes with rotting vegetation, clumps of bamboo, and quiet groves of fruit trees. Mukta knew the shortcut to home through the village, but in her effort to avoid the residential areas, she led them through a still shorter route across fields and woods not frequented by people. However, they could not completely escape all neighborhoods and all eyes. The eyes of the affluent watched them indifferently, only a little curious and amused, as they too had heard the rumors. The young women of the peasant homes watched with excitement from behind doors and fences, the sound of their animated whispering quite audible to Mukta. The older women came out to the path to watch them; some of them made sharp and heated comments intended to inflict cuts and burns on Mukta, but some of them watched very silently, perhaps with sympathy, thinking of her dead child and pondering what she must have gone through in all this time.

Giri's mother, the wife of Madhu the blacksmith, confronted them, blocking their way with her bloated body. Madhu had disappeared ten months ago. Giri had disappeared soon after. She shouted angrily at Mukta, "Why have you come back, whore? How dare you come back to the village? I'll chase you with the broom out of the village. Out! Out!"

She panted as her angry and hateful words came out in volleys, like the heat from a furnace. Surama tried to calm her with smiling, soothing words but retreated at the blast of abusive words. It seemed as if Giri's mother was about to attack Mukta, and bite and scratch her. Mukta stood absolutely still. The others exchanged glances, not sure of what to do.

A few men had by that time gathered nearby to watch the goings on. One of them, wearing a *gamchha* around his waist and a dhoti around his head like a turban,* suddenly laughed loudly. Another then said bravo, slapping his thigh in vulgar delight, and clapped.

A little further up the path apart from the bunch of spectators, Gadadhar watched all this, sitting on this end of a cut trunk of palm tree laid across the water channel. Suddenly he called out to Giri's mother loudly, as if calling from a great distance. When she turned her head toward him, he said just as loudly, "Giri has been calling you, Giri's mother. Didn't you hear her?"

Her abusive words stopped abruptly. For a minute she looked baffled and dazed, like a person just awakened from a nightmare. Then she started back, saying, "Really? Giri is calling me? I'm coming Giri, I'm coming!" Suddenly noticing so many people before her, she was embarrassed. She quickly took the torn quilt that was wrapped around her waist over her sari, and, covering her head with the quilt, she walked back to her hut.

Rampada, meanwhile, had finished his meal and was sitting under the jackfruit tree, about to smoke the hookah he had just prepared. Seeing the group with Mukta coming, he put it down against the tree trunk and stood up, letting the hard-earned little lump of tobacco burn away.

When the group came near, he said "Please come in" to the outsiders in a

---

* The odd reversal in the man's dressing, the dhoti on his head instead of around his waist and the gauzy towel around his waist instead of on his shoulder or head, indicates a derangement that matches his odd response.

strained voice, in the voice of someone afraid and helpless, oppressed with doubts and ambivalence. As the three approached him, he offered them an uncertain welcome without looking at them. His eyes were fixed on Mukta, who stopped short and stood, battling her turmoil.

"We wanted your wife to reach you safely. You have been told everything. Her mind is made up. What happened is past and gone, try to forget it and start your life again. We will come back another day and see if things are all right with you."

A sad, unexcited Rampada stood there blinking, scratching his head, swallowing hard a few times, and vaguely telling them that bringing her back did not mean the end of his problem. His thin face was pockmarked, and on his sunken left cheek was a rather long scar. Even the unattractive face showed his mind's agitation, in spite of the message conveyed by his slack dejected manner and his dispirited body.

"Why didn't you go to bring her back yourself, Rampada? You told us that you would."

"That is because of the problem that has come up, *didimoni*."

The problem was that the village society had meanwhile threatened him with trouble if he took her back. It was really a few people like Ghanashyam Das, Kanai Biswas, Nidhu Nandi, Lochan Kumar, Bidhu Ghosh, and Madhu Nandi. Ghanashyam was the social pillar of the area's poor community—the community of peasants, milkmen, blacksmiths, potters, and fishermen. He had summoned Rampada the day before and threatened him. Some of those men were with Ghanashyam at the time. That was the reason Rampada was a little afraid and worried. A little indeed!

The cotton mat they had brought along for sitting in the boat, they now spread under the jackfruit tree. The group sat down and made Rampada sit down too. Mukta then came over and sat on the ground, huddling beside Surama. The sari edge covering her head had receded, and she was looking straight at Rampada, her anxious gaze fixed on his face. He had never before seen his wife look at him in that way.

Rampada's problem was not something that could be ignored, although it consisted of only a self-appointed pillar of society and his lackeys meddling in personal lives. For if they had not been campaigning, most people could not be bothered. A few would at the most have made fun of him for a few days. A few would have avoided him. But nothing more serious would have happened to Rampada. With the terrible things that had happened all around, with so many dead of starvation and sickness, so many families splintered and members lost track of—hardly two of a ten-member family tottering back home from their separate journeys for food—with so many young wives and girls picked up by procurers and traffickers, who would bother? Who would have fussed, in the midst of all this, about whose wife came back home after surviving for a few months by immoral means? It would be like bothering about who was dirtying whose tank at a time after a catastrophic flood.

Few would do that. But if the likes of Ghanashyam went out of their way to stir up trouble by goading the ordinary people, they might manage to do so. It worried them. But Surama calmly said, "Anyway. Do you have any rice for your wife, Rampada?"

"Well . . . What about your lunch?"

"Our lunch is arranged. Why don't you go in with your wife and give her something to eat. Why haven't you put your roof up, Rampada?"

"I will some time."

Surama managed to talk the couple into being together in the hut on this pretext of his having to give her some food. Whatever trouble they were going to get from outside, the couple should have a chance to talk and reach some understanding before they could face it and hope to cope with it. As for the group's midday bath and lunch, they were going to have that at the home of Shankar, another social worker who lived in the village. He should have been there already. They also needed to talk to him about this new problem because he knew more about the village.

Rampada propped up one side of the collapsed roof to let some light in, asking her, "Do you want a bath first?" She said, "You have cooked lunch for me!" "Yes, rice and shol fish with chilies, but it is undersalted."

After eleven months of separation and terrible happenings, the biggest barrier was not knowing what to say to each other, being so much alone with the burden of one's thoughts. Hesitating about saying anything was only natural, but not saying anything was now painful. The thoughts and the terrible memories stirred in Mukta's mind. Her baby boy was seven months old when Rampada went away. What happened to the baby after he left was something that she could tell him and lighten her mind a little. Haltingly, she started: "The baby died after eating food that a baby should not have. After my milk dried up, I fed him gruel of ground rice for some time. Then the rice was finished. I had nothing to give him except the wild greens that I boiled for myself. That's what killed him! What could I do?"

She could not finish the account as dry-eyed as she had intended. Perhaps she could have done that earlier, when her feelings were numbed with starvation. Now that the body was not starving any more, could the feeling of grief be dammed up merely by the unmentionable experience of the last few months? Her voice choked up and eyes brimmed with tears, as she tried to tell him how terribly the baby suffered for two days before it died, how its shriveled body twisted, tormented by stomach pain. She allowed her tears to flow.

"Nobody in the village tried to help you?" he now asked her.

"Das-babu offered to give milk for the baby, food and clothing for me if I obliged him. How would I know then that this was going to happen to me? If I had known, I would have taken his offer. At least the baby would have lived. I was ruined anyway, and I lost the baby."

She wiped her tears and tried to calm herself. She now had to explain her actions to him without tears. She had decided not to plead for his pity with tearful accounts of what drove her out. She was not looking for justice either. She wanted Rampada to decide on his own, to do as he thought right. Calmly she started the account of what happened.

"The baby was dead, and you still were not back. Das-babu was sending Nedi's mother to me every day to find out if I would give in. I didn't have anything to eat for days. Then one night two men came for me. I bit their hands and ran away. I hid in the forest for a few days. Then I was at the end of my wits and went to the town."

"So much help we got from Das-babu!" Rampada remarked, the bitterness of his tone barely revealing the anger he felt. "You go and have a bath now."

Mukta had just sat down to the rice and shol fish, when the voice of Ghanashyam Das was heard outside, summoning Rampada.

Rampada asked her to stay in and eat her food. He went out.

Meanwhile Shankar had come there looking for Surama and her group. Now they could not leave due to the appearance of Ghanashyam with his lackeys, striking the pose of policemen on official duty.

"Is your wife back, Rampada?"

"Yes, sir."

"You took her in?"

"Yes, sir."

"Throw her out right this minute. She has to return with those who brought her back here."

"She is eating right now."

Rampada's response and his manner did not please Ghanashyam and company. The bald Nandi asked Rampada what he was really up to. Rampada cautiously, very mildly, said yes, he was going to have her back.

"What? You are even thinking of keeping her?"

"She is my duly married wife, sir. How can I throw her out?"

2

The event of Mukta returning home did cause a bit of a stir among the peasants and dirt-poor folks of Mansukia. Ghanashyam and company did not allow it to go to sleep, but they too did not hope for anything more than humiliating Rampada socially, publicly. If the landlord was living in the village, then they could try to talk him into some economic sanction against Rampada. Social punishment—apart from chastising Rampada, getting people to avoid him and not talk to him—would do for now to establish formally Ghanashyam's informal social control. Everybody knew that social disapproval would be followed by taunts, abuses, beatings, and setting fire to the home. If they could arrange a public show of people being either against or indifferent to Rampada with nobody strongly in his favor, then the stage would be set for doing those things to Rampada. If nobody would publicly stick up for him, then the things to follow could be carried out by just a few lackeys who enjoyed the sport of tormenting a helpless man.

The times, however, were not very convenient for this age-old method to work out. Almost all the common people were wounded, harassed, feeling socially discarded themselves; their spirits were broken along with their bodies. Each was so preoccupied with getting through the day and wondering what the next day would bring that it was hard these days to work them up to collective conspiracy against one of them. They seemed lacking the time and the desire to get worked up about anything. That was what Ghanashyam's men realized when they went around trying to whip up outrage about Rampada's audacity.

Most people were uninterested; they wanted to talk more about things like the prices of rice and salt and clothing, about the war, and so on. When approached by the big shot's lackeys, they would come to life at the glimmer of hope of getting some favor, some sort of help with making a living, but as soon as the topic of Rampada was raised they would fall back into half daze. They did not get excited about holding a public trial of Rampada to ostracize him. Some ordinary folks the lackeys approached even remarked that they should leave them alone because there were so many such cases at this time and it would be hard for the guardians of social norms to discipline so many offenders. Especially disinterested, or interested only in burying the topic, were both those who had lost contact with a family member who went away from the village leaving them behind and those who had come back after losing some members to starvation and disease in the city. So few families were left intact that the task proved much harder than Ghanashyam and company had anticipated.

The disappointment troubled Ghanashyam. The comment of his employee Gokul added irritation. "You went a bit too far," he said. "You could just have him beaten up by your thugs. Instead, you called a public trial. What are you going to do if someone says things that you don't want to hear? What if someone asks about Dugga?"

"Shut up, bastard." Even as Ghanashyam shouted at his lackey, his hand absently went to his hairy chest and scratched as he worried. But the thought of Rampada's defiance egged him on. He heard how he was going about putting together his broken life, repairing the roof, mending the fence, setting up his household again, even telling villagers that if his life in the village was going to be made miserable he would go away with his wife and live somewhere else. Ghanashyam, having made so much money from the rice trade and now being treated so much better than he used to be, could not let himself be defeated in the eyes of the society by that insignificant Rampada. The very thought was unbearably irritating.

The day before the public trial was to be held in the village, Ghanashyam decided to finish his work in town quickly and return to the village, skipping the visit to Giri. He finished his work by early afternoon, but things did not turn out as well as he thought. He felt a little depressed. He felt like having some *vilaiti* liquor and spending the night with Giri.* He told himself that there was no need to rush back that day because the trial was going to be held in the afternoon of the next day. He ordered Gokul to get a cheap bottle of vilaiti and headed for the place where he kept Giri.

From the wide open door of the place, he had the shock of his life to see Giri inside sitting on the mat with four city ladies. Two of them he had seen before; they had brought Mukta back. With the attack of anxiety, his hand automatically reached under his shirt for the hair on his chest.

He was trying to back away silently, but Giri saw him and jumped up, calling him. Without waiting, she ran to him and grabbed his coat from behind. "Why are you running away? You've things to answer."

"Who are they?"

"That's none of your business," Giri shouted at him, without letting go of his coat, only shifting her grip from its back to its front. She glared at him for a minute with furious eyes, gnashing her teeth. "Haven't you told me repeatedly that my mother is all right? My poor mother?"

"Isn't she?" said Ghanashyam, a mouse in the paws of a cat.

"Is she? Who has gone out of her mind then? Me? Yes, I am going mad! My head is reeling with what I just learned. You, cheater, liar, scum . . . "

Surama's voice intervened from inside, "Giribala, calm down."

Giri restrained the stream of epithets and asked in a lower voice, "Who made my father leave the village to die who knows where by offering him money for going away?"

"They told you that?"

"Is that false?" Giri suddenly started sobbing. "O, my poor father! You gave your life to save your daughter's. And this bitch of your daughter still lives without shame."

Surama's nice voice came from inside again, "Giribala, we didn't say that your father was dead. We haven't been able to trace him yet. Maybe he is still alive somewhere. Why do you assume that he is dead?"

Giri controlled herself but argued back, "It's been ten months since he disappeared without a trace."

The other women inside the room were meanwhile checking around, looking out the window, looking in the back porch. The cement porch was swept clean, but the drain along its side emitted some obscene smell. Even the unwashed dishes gave off the obscene odor of the unwholesome food that was eaten off them. Surama and the other three women then left the place, with-

---

* *Vilaiti* (foreign) or distilled as opposed to *deshi* (native) or undistilled liquor.

out looking at Giri and her man, but addressing her as they left, "So we'll come back in the morning, Giribala. Be ready then."

"Why are they coming back in the morning?" Ghanashyam asked Giri.

"To take me back to the village, to my mother. Come inside now." Giri dragged the unsettled man inside. Pieces of hundreds of tricky plans that made up his mind whirled in his brain under the pressure of apprehension and anxiety. He sat on the mat, lighting a bidi, and said to her, "Why bother to go back to the village? Why don't I instead . . . "

"Stop your instead business. I'm going to take care of my mother and have her treated. You're going to pay the cost of her treatment, no matter what it costs. If you don't, I'm going to make you lose face."

She went through Ghanashyam's pockets and found the packet of cigarettes he had saved. She lit one and sat on the floor smoking, leaning back on one arm. In these few months, the soft sweetness of her face had hardened. Her complexion too had darkened a bit. But her figure had become even more tempting. No wonder, Ghanashyam thought, that he went to such lengths to procure her and against his better senses had not yet been able to let go of her. If she were a Kayastha girl, he would definitely have married her instead of having her installed here. For the last few days he had been thinking of giving her up; he was now regretting not having done it. He would not then have had to get involved with this mess, thanks to those nosy city broads.

She watched him watching her and taunted him for smoking bidis after all the money he had made. Then she sat bolt upright and said, shrewd and sharp, "I heard that you are after Rampada. Trying to get him ostracized by the village? As if you're a saint! You're doing it to stop me from going back to the village. Right? If they don't let Rampada's wife come back, then they won't let me go back either. Isn't that your plan? If they'll ostracize me, then in fear I'll not be able to go back home, ever."

At that point Gokul came with the bottle. Giri's eyes were instantly riveted to it. She licked her lips, and her expression changed to the anguish of the sick, the delirious greed of the addicted for the forbidden. She asked if it was distilled. Gokul nodded. Giri, sitting upright a minute ago and talking sharply, suddenly went slack and numb. "All right. Stay on for the last time. But remember to leave early in the morning."

Ghanashyam, taking a few gulps of the liquor to settle his mind, tried to think. There seemed to be no way out. Threatening, using force, sweet words and bribes, false stories—nothing was going to work with Giri any more. She was no longer the timid, shy, and naive village girl she used to be. She had become frighteningly precocious in a few months.

Gokul was dismissed after he had been given some liquor. He was told to come back early in the morning, to wake up Ghanashyam and accompany him back.

The night advanced, and Giri's drunk speech grew slurred, "What can I do? I've agreed to go back with them in the morning. I'm dying to see my mother, you know. Don't worry. I'll come back here after a few days, once I've made the arrangement for my mother's care. It's all right here if you let me go back home once in a while. Won't you? Don't worry. I promise I'll come back here."

Liquor spilled from the glass in her unsteady hand and wetted her sari. She giggled but got angry too and hurled the glass across the room.

3

The size of the gathering at the public trial of Rampada was not impressive, if one took into account the cluster of five or six villages adjacent to Mansukia. The number of common people available for such an event had declined. Many were sick and bedridden. Some perhaps had thought of coming but then were laid down with malaria fever instead. Many did not come because they did not want to. The gathering of those who came was lifeless, unexcited, sleepy. The bodies were tired and thin; the eyes had blank looks. They did not talk much either. The hum of talking was subdued, as if they thought that the days of liking to talk were over. Ghanashyam recalled, in contrast, the excitement only two or two-and-a-half years ago at a similar trial he had called about the sister of Padmalochan. Common peasant folks had then filled the grounds, waiting with animated curiosity to hear the misdeeds of a married woman being publicly discussed and denounced. Compared to that, this was more like a meeting of peasants called by the government to lecture about what they should do in the present condition of the country.

On the raised porch sat the elders of the community. In their midst sat Ghanashyam, but he sat very quietly and looked worried. The look on his face and the lackluster gathering made the elders feel uncomfortable. In a far corner of the porch sat Shankar on a cane stool. He was not invited. Some could guess the reason for his presence, but most could not comprehend why he was there. In the gathering down below in the yard, Rampada sat in the south corner with a cluster of about seven men, mostly his old friends including Karali and Buno. On the women's side of the gathering, Mukta sat right next to Giri! She had not come to Giri, but Giri had sought her out and purposely sat next to her. The women's side seemed more crowded than the men's side.

Ghanashyam's eyes kept straying toward Giri, though each time he promptly looked away.

There was trouble right at the beginning of the trial. As soon as the bald Nandi started his introduction the way they had planned, Banamali shouted at him from the gathering. A crazy looking man, he stood up in his torn khaki shirt with his unoiled, uncombed hair flying and his face covered with stubbly beard. He shouted, "What trial? Whose trial? Rampada's wife has done no wrong."

Everybody knew that Banamali's wife had been enticed out of their home by the town's Datta-babu, who was her pimp. At first he kept her in the town, but when Banamali went to town looking for her and almost found her, Datta-babu sold her to procurers supplying distant markets. Banamali then lost track of her, although even now he went to town looking for her.

The bald Nandi tried to pacify him by saying, "You see, that's what we're all here to judge, if she did anything wrong or not."

"What?" Banamali became more furious. "She has done nothing wrong, and yet there should be a trial to find out if she has done anything wrong? What you're saying is very wrong, uncle. If any man or woman of the village who has been away for some time has to face a trial after coming back, then it is going to be a problem for most of us."

Karali, one of the men Rampada sat with, spoke without getting up, "He's right. She was starving in the village, and her husband was away. So she went to town to live by earning. She's done nothing wrong."

Another man quietly remarked without looking up, "Nobody came forward to help her with food at the time when she was starving here."

Kanai, who had left the village with his whole family but had returned with only his wife and his eldest son's wife, having lost his three sons and two daughters in strange places, stood up to speak. They were used to hearing him say that the three of them survived only because life clung to them the way it clings to the *koi* fish even as the fish is scaled and gutted. He was trembling, and there was extreme agitation in his face and his eyes. His words came out all confused and incoherent, "That she has come back alive and well shows that god is still there. God won't have saved her, though. She had to die first in order to be saved and come back. Still it shows that god is there."

Nobody laughed. The topic of god at this trial, like the uninvited appearance of Shankar, produced a curious feeling in many of them.

After this the people gathered there sat silently wondering for some time. Even those who were against the likes of Mukta returning to their village homes sat quietly. Only the women's side was stirred with animated tension, with constant whispering back and forth.

Finally, from the raised porch Bhuban tried to restart the trial by saying, "The point is that if she went away to live by honest work, she would have done that . . ."

Suddenly Giri straightened up, stuck her head forward and shouted at the top of her voice, "Of course, she lived by honest work there. I know because we worked together. We worked as part-time maids washing and cleaning. We did the work of making puffed rice for a store. Which burnt-faced bloke here says that we did not earn our food by honest work? Which one? Speak up so we can hear."

Almost everybody knew that what Giri claimed was not true. Some had seen Mukta in the town's brothel area. But nobody said a word. They were amazed, electrified by the transformation of Giri whom they remembered as the shy young girl of a few months back. However, they got over the surprise as they thought about it. Nothing really continued to surprise them for very long these days. Nobody said anything. Only the bald Nandi made another attempt by saying, "But many have seen with their own eyes. Phani here said that he himself saw . . ." He could not finish because the middle-aged, short-statured Phani quickly got up and protested, "No, no. I never said any such thing. Why should I?"

Finally Ghanashyam opened his mouth. Even though the gathering was silent, except for the whispers on the women's side, he gestured with both hands raised like a leader trying to quiet a noisy crowd and said, "Let's try to forget it, brothers. These days we can't take offense at every deviation. I suggest that because questions have been raised, Rampada's wife should do a repentance ritual, and the matter will rest."

Banamali hissed at him, "What repentance ritual, when she's done no wrong?"

Giri strained to make her voice as shrill as possible, "Do I also have to do a repentance ritual? Come on, answer me."

With this anticlimax, the meeting ended in disorder, as people got up to walk away or turned to other matters. One woman came to Mukta and looked at her face through the tears that blurred her vision, and kissed Mukta on the cheek. Some women looked sideways at Mukta's face while passing by her. Shankar got up and left the way he came in, without a word to anybody. He caught up with Banamali, who was walking away alone, and said, "Will you take her back if we manage to find her?" Banamali was surprised at his question. "If I won't take her back, then why am I looking for her everywhere?"

Shankar was about to say something in answer, but he stopped himself and thought. Not everybody who survived physically managed to survive mentally, to pick up the pieces of their cruelly broken lives. Very few were in a fit condition either to be brought back or be brought back to.

What was the use of telling Banamali of that problem? If the famine and epidemic caused the moral death of his wife, not unlike the hundreds of thousands of dear ones lost to physical death, then what good would it do to tell him about the tragic state of his wife? Maybe she was not dead, but the person who used to be his wife was dead. Shankar was not sure if the disease of her mind was so advanced that it was beyond recovery, or if it could still recover with treatment and enable her to come back as the wife Banamali was looking for. He had to first find out about that before telling Banamali anything.

"Let me try and see if I can find her," Shankar said, and moved by some deep sympathy, he suddenly grasped Banamali's hand in the way he liked to grasp a close friend's hand in college.

Mansukia was plunged in darkness with the onset of the evening, except for the light of a quarter moon in the sky. The path under the *bael* tree used to be avoided at night for fear of ghosts up in the tree only two years back. These days the people of Mansukia could not be bothered with something as trivial as ghosts. Two persons were standing and talking right under the tree.

Giri was talking to Ghanashyam, "If only you hadn't created this whole thing, if only you ignored it—"

"Didn't you see and hear the things at the meeting? Don't you have eyes and ears? Would it have made any difference if I said one thing or another? I just wanted to sniff the wind to take care of my situation."

Giri's home was near the bael tree. She was not afraid in the thick darkness under the tree, but, as she stepped away from it, she was startled to see a figure by the wayside sitting on the palm tree trunk laid across the channel near her home. Her heart beat like a hammer as if she had seen a ghost.

"Who are you sitting there?"

"It is me, Giri. It's only me."

"Oh. What are you doing here so late in the night?"

"I was watching you and wondering if Giri will feel like staying on here, after taking the trouble to come back to the village."

"What do you think?"

"No. She won't like it here. You will not stay on, Giri. If you and I were married, if we had a baby like Mukta had, if we had lived together for some years, then perhaps. . . . No, Giri. You will not stay."

Giri did not quite see when the man had got up and walked away to the other side of the channel, without waiting to hear Giri's sharp answer. She grimaced with contempt in the uncertain direction he went in the dim moonlight. Next moment she grimaced again with a stab of pain, as if from a wound hidden somewhere in her chest. Then she walked home.

Giri's mother was lying in bed, covered with the same torn quilt.

Giri called to her, "Ma! I'm back, Ma."

Giri's mother sat up startled. She looked at Giri's face, and then she said with disappointment and irritation, before she lay down again, "Who are you? Whoever you are, you didn't have to startle me by calling like that."

The Old Woman

Manik Bandyopadhyay

1

It is a very important day for the old woman. It is the wedding day of her eldest great-grandson, her son's son's son, not a small triumph for her. The home, full of family and relatives, is humming with the busy activities one expects on a wedding day. She is not doing anything, and they are busily going about without paying much attention to her, the way the busy activities in a king's palace go about without involving the king. That is how it seems to her.

She thinks she is present, directly or indirectly, in everything that is going on in the house on this occasion, just as she feels she is present in all the daily activities, the collective life of the household. For sixty years she has been there, the roots and branches of her existence alive with other lives so totally accustomed to her presence that they are oblivious to it. She is like the big old tree on the west side of the big room in the house; its branches are full of birds busily chirping throughout the day, and it can be heard creaking with the wind in the dead of night.

The old woman sits in her usual corner of the porch with her many torn quilts of rag and the bundle that she uses as a pillow. The joints are all rusty, the spine is bent forward, the hair flaxen, the skin loose and wrinkled, the mouth toothless, the cheeks sunken, and the eyes dim with cataract. Seems so very old. But when she walks slowly with the help of a stick, one can see, if one looks closely, that there is strength in the skin-covered bones of her hand. When she shouts, one can tell that there is strength in her lungs. Most of the time, however, she spends lying down or sitting in her corner, talk-

"Boodi" appears in *Uttarkaler Galpa Sangraha*, ed. Pijush Dasgupta (Calcutta: National Book Agency, 1963), 42–46.

ing to herself. From there sometimes she criticizes, at the top of her voice, the small lapses in running the household. She puts in her mouth ground-roasted tobacco leaves. From time to time she breaks into her strange sounding laughter for reasons nobody knows.

The wives of her sons and of her grandsons mutter "There she goes again" when these strange doings make her presence felt. The younger wives remark in low voices. They do so not out of respect for her, because she pretends not to hear even when she does and because it does not matter even if they know that she hears them. They do so for fear of offending their mothers-in-law and the daughters of the house, who would not like big talk in mouths that should be modest.

Nanda, the groom, has got his hair cut specially for the occasion by Nitai the barber. Nitai has charged eight annas, though he should not have because his son was going with the groom's party as the little groom and would get gifts. It has given the people in the house reason to speak ill of Nitai.

The old woman calls the great-grandson to her, "Nanda, come here. Come here, you boy with the fancy haircut. I've a question for you. Getting ready to get married nicely! But are you sure the girl is a virgin?"

Nanda's mother hears it and complains to her sister-in-law, "What an awful thing to say even as a joke!" Then she wonders aloud, "Maybe she has a point. It is a grown-up girl, after all."

"But she belongs to a good family."

"Good families often have bad things inside. Why did they wait for so long that the girl has grown up?"

Nanda squats in front of the old woman and jokes back, "If she is not a virgin, then she is old like you."

She smiles a big toothless smile, "Search the world and see if you can find a virgin like me. I hardly slept with your great-grandfather. He died on the wedding night. I was so scared to hear him breathe so hard! I was so scared that I ran out of the room crying. The people in the house came running to me, asking 'What's the matter?' What's the matter, except with the writing on my forehead! By that time he was dead."

She breaks into her cackle. But her great-grandson does not laugh. His face darkens with a cloud of doubt and suspicion. "Maybe she is not! One is never sure of it with a grown girl!"

"Hey, you stupid monkey! How can you say such a thing? Didn't you choose her to be your wife?"

"Yes. I chose her, but . . ."

"What a stupid boy! Don't you know that a virgin can never become bad? Look at me. My husband died on the night of the wedding. As time passed, so many tried to make me become bad, but I did not. I swear by your father's head that I did not become bad. A girl goes for the bad thing only after she tastes it, not as long as she's a virgin."

The argument may be strange, but the boy's face brightens up.

"Are you sure what you just said is true?"

"Of course, it is true."

The people in the busy household notice Nanda squatting in front of the old woman and the two of them talking to each other in low voice; and once in a while they hear a loud cackle and a youthful laugh break out together.

2

Menaka has been weeping and lamenting all day, "Where can I go? I've no one to go back to!"

Nobody in the family liked Nanda's bride. Not only was she a grown girl, but also, because she had no parents and was married off by her uncle's family, they could not get back at the shrewd uncle for not giving all of the promised dowry. On top of that, Nanda had chosen her, married her against the wishes of the family, and after marriage he worshiped her without bothering about the family's feelings about it. Families never cease to be angry about the son's disobedience in marriage. Because they couldn't take it out on their earning son, their minds stayed poisoned against his wife.

On top of all of those faults of hers, Nanda died within a year of his marriage. As soon as the rainy season was over, even before the mud in the yard started drying, Nanda had started getting ready to take his wife on a trip. No wife of this family ever went on a trip alone with her husband!

Who would keep a woman with so many faults and so much ill luck?

They wrote to Menaka's uncle asking him to take her back, but the letter was not even answered. So they have decided to take Menaka to the door of her uncle's home, leave her there, and be done with it.

Menaka does not want to go. She fears not just the beatings and the burning with hot objects there, which she is used to, but she knows that her uncle would not let her in.

That is why she sits crying all day, "Where shall I go?"

The old woman calls her to her corner of the porch, "Hey, girl! Come over here. I have something to tell you."

Menaka goes to her. The old woman scolds her, "Why are you crying like a baby? A strong young woman like you?"

"Because they are throwing me out," she says sobbing.

"Who is throwing you out? You will go merely because they want to throw you out? This is your husband's home. How can they throw you out if you refuse to leave?"

Menaka listens. The old woman goes on, "Look at me. Could they throw me out? I spent less than one night with my husband. After he died on the wedding night, they all said, 'Throw out that unlucky wife.' They said that I ate my husband as soon as I got him to myself. 'Out! Out!' they said.

They said everything they could. Did I leave? Could anybody make me leave? I bit the ground that the home stood on and hung on. And you? You slept with your husband for almost a whole year; you lived in this house as a wife of the family. You will leave only because they want you to? Just hang on. Bite the ground this home stands on and hang on."

Menaka's eyes light up. She squats in front of the old woman.

The family members notice Menaka and the old woman engrossed in talking, whispering to each other, about who knows what!

A Female Problem
at a Low Level

Manik Bandyopadhyay

1

The girl's name is Durga. She is the daughter of the factory mechanic Noton. Noton has another daughter, an infant that has started crawling on the dirty, damp porch of his hut. The infant girl crawling on the porch sometimes falls off, onto the still more damp yard, and screams. Noton's love for his children can be measured and understood only in relation to life in the slum. Like the usual parental love in the slum, it is weak in some ways and strong in other ways, sort of blunt and practical, hard and soft at the same time. Parental love and concern here are not all-pervasive affection, but they are roused with astounding force and swiftness as soon as the matter at hand is considered serious, and the consequence of neglect perceived as disastrous.

Durga's sudden growth caught the eyes of men in and around the slum and produced a matching growth in Noton's protective paternal instinct. Although he could prevent the infant's falling off the low porch, he did not manage to spend the time and effort. He did not bother because the consequence was mere temporary pain with eventual learning and toughening for the infant, necessary preparation for her hard life ahead. If the consequence was going to be broken bones or skull, then he would certainly not have remained indifferent to its occurrence.

For example, Noton had suddenly become extremely concerned about the safety of his elder daughter Durga. As Durga's entire body, her chest, back, and waist, was rapidly transformed into the shape of fresh youth, like a banana plant with the coming of rain after the dry summer heat, terrible

"Nichu Chokkhe Ekti Meyeli Samasya" appears in *Uttarkaler Galpa Sangraha*, ed. Pijush Dasgupta (Calcutta: National Book Agency, 1963), 335–42.

dangers suddenly waited on her. Noton at once became preoccupied with protecting her.

For a young girl living in the slum, the path is very narrow between virtue and sin, between surviving and being destroyed. And the delicious physical and mental state of a pubescent slum girl is very, very brief. The high tide of youth, brimming overnight, stays for a very short period before it is all gone and she is reduced to a skeleton by the terrible struggle to survive every single day. It is not like female beauty in the *babu* families, where, nurtured with food, leisure, beauty sleep, bottles of tonic, amusement, laughter, cinema, and theater, its duration is stretched into the thirties. In slum homes, perpetually deprived and starving, beauty and youth is purely an act of nature, a brief bounty designed to be the raw material for making unmarried girls pregnant. Then it is gone, and the rest of the female life is having to pay, on and on, dragging the burden left behind by the havoc that the brief bloom brought.

The ugliest greed of men, including the gentlemen, the *malik babus*, is drawn to this lawless world of loot and plunder, all of them waiting to seize and plunder the arrival of youth in the slum girl's body and mind. That is why Noton became fiercely protective of the suddenly youthful girl. He beat up Durga's mother for sending her to work in her place as a maid just one day when she was down with fever. He promptly betrothed her to Binod, a young factory worker. Durga's mother was also concerned for the daughter but not as fiercely as the father, perhaps because she no longer felt strongly for anything at all. She did not want her daughter to lose her head and be ruined, but she saw no great harm in some minor compromise of innocence under the circumstances. She did not see what great good would come of slum parents fighting at all costs to protect the daughter's purity.

In his fierce determination to protect his daughter's fresh youth, in his sudden discovery of a magnificent flower blooming in his own dismal home, Noton almost became a reformed man. He gave up drinking and the drunken brawls; he was eager to return home as soon as his workday at the factory was over. In the process of protecting his daughter, he also became close to her and discovered the good nature of the suddenly beautiful girl.

Slum life has no cover of privacy at all. Parents can stay awake all night guarding their daughter, but they cannot shelter her from the preying eyes and the predators, except by virtually imprisoning her. Usually, that itself becomes another source of danger. The girl, used only to neglect and deprivation all her life, suddenly senses the presence of powerful desire eagerly waiting for her outside. The sudden surge in her value in a world that has ignored and neglected her until then makes her lose her head and her sense of reality.

Durga is an exception to this. Her innate sensibility prompts and enables her not to lose her head. She has looked at the reaction of the small world around her; she has sensed the tension, the currents suddenly generated by her physical change; she knows that she herself is the pivot that will resolve the tension surrounding her one way or another. Even in the unaccustomed, heady pleasure of being youthful and attractive, she likes to keep in mind that she herself must be the one in charge, the one to steer her own life and decide the battle over her. She has regarded her father's efforts as no more than helpful in maintaining her proprietorship over herself.

Durga dutifully does her work, takes care of her father. She regards Sukhlal the contractor's eager looks and flashing rupees with indifferent eyes and unresponsive silence. She sneers at the offers proposed through the old procuress Matangini, offers to keep her like a queen the rest of her life made by someone or other going crazy for her according to Matangini's description. With a knowing smile, she brushes off the casual attempts of still others to please her.

Her living conditions are harsh, to say the least. The food they can buy from the ration shop rarely fills the stomachs, the sari is too torn and short to cover the body well, and not a single wish for anything beyond the absolute necessity has ever been met; the dark muggy interior of their windowless room seems to turn the prickly heat into permanent skin disorder, the father works in the factory, and the mother cleans and washes all day for the babu households to earn no more than a beggar does. Yet the harsh living conditions do not take away her appreciation of life, the self-contained pride she feels about her transient bloom, her sweet metamorphosis.

2

One day Noton is injured by machinery in the factory and becomes semi-permanently confined to his rope cot at home. The company avoids paying him compensation by fabricating proof that he was drunk when operating the machine and hence responsible for his own injury. The company pays him a few rupees for the initial medical treatment, emphasizing its compassion, not obligation, as the motive. There is some agitation about it at first, but soon it is overwhelmed by the noise connected with the formation of a competing union of the factory workers.

It seems increasingly doubtful if Noton will ever be able to leave his bed and even then if he will find work again. So Durga's mother's earning from cleaning and washing in the babu households becomes the main source of living for the family. She has already been doing two such part-time jobs; now she takes a third. Although she takes Durga along to help with the work, her limbs feel numb with exhaustion, especially since she is in an advanced stage of pregnancy. Soon she will be unable to keep up with the work and will get sacked. Bitter with anxiety and strain, she takes it out on Durga. "Get your hands moving, bitch! Becoming fat sitting around at home and eating.

Don't you know how to move your hands? Trying to get away with washing a couple of plates and carrying a bucket of water. Thinking only of when she can go back home to cook for her father and feed him."

Durga works faster but angrily replies, "How dare you say such things when I do half your work!" For a moment her eyes fill with tears.

They have to buy each day's rice and flour by taking a rupee or two in advance from the wage due at the end of the month. Because part-time washing-and-cleaning women change jobs and have a high turnover, even if only because the jobs have no security and pathetic wages, the babus have devised a clever way to punish their inconvenient mobility. They do not pay the month's wages entirely; instead, they hold some back so that, if the maid leaves without plenty of notice and the women of the house have to wash the dishes, they can at least relish the revenge of depriving the maid of a part of her earned wage. Durga's and her mother's struggles to buy the day's meal with their daily labor is made harder by this strategy of advance revenge on the poor.

Noton's face has become covered with unshaven beard; his eyes have sunk into holes under the forehead. His voice is drowsy, but his eyes glower with frustration and anger. "Why do the two of you work for the same jobs for the same pay? Durga, you take up two households to work by yourself."

"How can Ma do three houses alone?"

"Take one house then. Take up the Mitra house. Their work is light."

"The Mitra house? Let Ma take that, and I'll take one of Ma's houses."

They both know that won't work. Mitra-babu wants Durga, not her mother. Not so long ago one day, Noton beat up her mother for sending Durga alone to work in her place. Now he knowingly, deceitfully prods Durga to take up work by herself at the Mitra house. Helplessly confined to bed, the hope of getting back to work receding, and the specter of starvation replacing what earlier seemed like a few days of fasting, how many can remain steadfast in their resolution, the promise they made to themselves?

To Durga, life starts feeling bitter as she watches the horizon cloud with the terrible doubts rising in her mind. The doubts arise not merely because Noton is disabled, not even because Ma is going to give birth in a short while, which will threaten their tenuous living and push her to the brink. A slum girl and daughter of a laborer cannot mentally depend on her father or brother, like the daughters of the babu families who even as grown women see individual disaster in any family mishap. She is used to fending for herself, relying on her own wits. But now her wits seem to be failing her, and the perspective she kept in mind is clouded. The aggravations in her family would have been only a matter of anxiety for her, terrible but manageable, had they not been compounded by the strike now going on in Binod's factory and the layoff of strikers. Faced with the terrible coincidence of Binod's troubles and her parents' troubles, she realizes that she has reached the last step of the escape ladder in her perspective. She must now jump one way or another.

One evening, when she has no work to do because there is no food to cook, no reason to light the stove, Durga tries to collect her thoughts sitting by herself in a corner of the room and going through the trinkets that were Binod's presents to her—useless things like a comb, a bead necklace, sequined glass bangles, artificial flowers for the hair bun, useless for the hunger churning in the stomach. The pain of starvation is not lessened one bit by emotional fulfilment.

Her mother is moaning in another corner of the room with the baby girl in her lap. Noton is in his bed, cursing and hurling filthy words at them, two able-bodied women who have lived off his labor for so long and are now unable to provide a few handfuls of rice for a few days. The store near the road has its radio on at top volume, but nearer to their hut someone is playing a flute at shrill pitch and off tune.

Durga has not clearly heard what her mother just said, something referring to his parents. Noton raises himself to a half-sitting position and hurls at her the only object he finds within reach, the used clay bowl that her mother got from one of the houses and which served as Noton's spittoon. It hits the baby in the head and smashes on the floor. The baby bleeds and screams.

Durga gets up to leave.

"Where are you going this late in the night?" her mother asks.

"To hell," she answers.

Noton hopefully says, "Let her go, if she wants to. Don't stop her."

She finds Binod too lying in his rope cot and moaning. He has been beaten up by the police while picketing at the factory gate. Durga by then is so filled with anger, sorrow, and anxiety that she is almost trembling and in no mind to listen to any more moaning from anybody.

"Listen," she says, "I want your final answer right this minute."

Binod knows what she is talking about, what final answer. He had an argument with her a few days back. He knows from Durga's agitated face. He suddenly feels very helpless and weak, watching her thin pale face and flustered condition.

"Do you want me, or do you want the strike?"

"What is the matter now?"

"Nothing. I want to know your final answer before I go my way."

Binod silently thinks for a minute, then says, "I want you, Durga."

"Then go to Sukhlal right now and tell him that you agree to the terms of hiring. Borrow money from him and buy some food. I haven't eaten the whole day. Nobody in my family has eaten today."

"I'll do it. You go home. I'll come soon with food." Binod is resigned.

Durga, still breathing hard with agitation and the suppressed tears, now notices the condition of the man. He is bruised all over.

"What happened to you?"

"What else? Beatings at the picket line." Binod's voice too is suddenly angry and agitated. "You go back home. I'll be there soon."

She does not leave, but stands silently watching him and thinking.

Then she asks him what will happen if he compromises by himself. He does not answer her question; he just stares at the dark corner of the hut.

Durga still does not move. She stands there rethinking the whole situation, going through her premises, reexamining her options. While her mind fiercely searches for alternatives, her body stands still, her head cocked to one side. She questions in her mind what good would come of breaking the man's spirit, his rather brave struggle against the terrible odds. What interest will that serve?

Finally, she comes to a conclusion different from the one she came in with. If somehow she can manage things on her own for a little longer, if she can hold on for some more time, then she will survive, the man will still be there, unbroken, and their joint future will still hold some hope.

"Don't do anything tonight." Her voice is no longer agitated. "I'll come back tomorrow, and we'll think about it more carefully. All right?"

"What are you going to eat tonight, then?"

"We'll manage. Mother will go to ask for an advance from her wage."

Taking leave of Binod, Durga slowly, deliberately walks towards the shack of Sukhlal the contractor, who stared at her even yesterday and flashed ten-rupee notes!

What else can one do, she argues to herself, except fight for survival? The survival of oneself, one's loved ones, and the hopes that really matter.

Paddy Seeds

Mahasweta Devi

1

To the north of Kuruda and Hesadi, the twin villages of outcastes and tribals, the bare soil, sunbaked and bone-dry, becomes wavy. No grass grows there even after the rains. A few solitary cactuses stand like cobras with raised hoods. In the middle of this vast, undulating, burned-out stretch is a little green patch, hull shaped, hardly an acre in size. It leaps into the range of vision only when one stands atop one of the high crests of the wavy brown landscape. There is something almost spectral about that flourish of lush green.

Even more unexpected, apparition-like, is the little straw-roofed platform perched on four posts in the middle of that green patch surrounded by arid stretches of brown earth. This kind of shed is set up for watching over crops at night, but the green plants standing there are only thorny sisal and wild weeds with fibrous leaves like pineapple tops, unlikely to attract even the hungriest herbivore.

Soon after darkness sets in, the most unreal, almost ghostly, appearance is that of a man approaching in long brisk strides from the direction of Kuruda. As the figure comes closer, one can make out that he is a wizened old man, covered with wrinkled leathery skin, clad only in a loincloth, from one side of which hangs a pouch made of patched old quilt. He has a stick with which he strikes the green weeds randomly, absentmindedly, as he walks to the watch-post. He climbs up the wobbly crude ladder made from branches. He strikes

"Bichhan" appears in Mahasweta's *Nairhite Megh* [Clouds in the Southwestern Sky] (Calcutta: Karuna Prakashani, 1979), 132–63.

the flintstones to light a *bidi* and sits in the shed smoking for a while. Some time after it gets quite dark, he unrolls his mat and lies down, seemingly to sleep. From a high crest of the wavy brown land, he can be seen every evening going through the same routine.

Every evening, back in Kuruda village, Dulan Ganju's old wife can be heard grumbling and complaining, loudly and at length, about the man. Nobody can say she has no right to, for the man out there is Dulan Ganju. Their two sons, the daughters-in-law, and the grandchildren do not like this nightly repetition of futile shouting, but there is nothing they can do to make her stop. They know that if they were to say anything, she would turn her steam to blast them. The old woman, known simply as Dhatua's mother, is famous in the area for her powerful voice and quarreling skills. Her skills are valued in the community, and she is respectfully invited to help out in crucial verbal battles. She would arrive in the arena and launch right into her strategy of abusing seven generations of the antagonist's ancestry, in descending order of succession. The antagonist usually beats retreat by the time she comes to the great-grandfather.

She inspires their respect and awe. Earlier during the Emergency rule,* when trouble broke out in the nearby town, the police came to the village looking for some fugitives they were pursuing. Dhatua's mother managed to have the police leave in no time, spraying them with her fiery language. One fugitive was actually hiding in the loft of her cowshed. "Come on, you corpse-eaters, search my home to your hearts' content!" she had invited the police in her shrill voice. "All you can find in the village now are the old and the children. Want to round them up? Go on, do it!" she challenged them at the top of her voice. Her shouting was so unbearable that they left convinced that the village was safe from agitators.

After the police had left, she turned to blast the fugitive lad. "When are you going to be able to use your brain, Rotoni? Even an old she-goat holds more intelligence. It's not bad that you got the moneylender in the leg with a pick axe. It would have been better if you could get him in the neck and rid us of the curse. But don't you know you're supposed to hide in the forest? Whoever heard of such an idiot, coming back to the village? Go away now, and hide in the forest!"

Dhatua and his brother Latua know that they can never gather enough courage to ask her to stop the futile complaining about Father's strange behavior. It would only refuel her: "So Father is now the beloved of his sons, and Mother is the useless old she-goat! What do they know of his real nature? . . . Mother does!"

* From the last week of June 1975 to February 1977, when most civil liberties were suspended.

Pledged in marriage at four, she came to live with him at fourteen. She knows every quirk and twist of the man's mind—the man who guards his estate of weeds out in the wilderness alone all night. "If he gets bitten by a snake or eaten by a tiger, who will become a widow? Who will then manage things so the family can survive? Dhatua and Latua? Have they got his wits, to use a bit of uncultivated land to bring supplies of seed paddy year after year? To get free fertilizer from the government to sell in the market for cash? To get loan installments every other year for the purchase of a bullock by showing them the plow-bullock of his neighbor Pahan?"

The sons would keep quiet, listening to Mother all worked up, taking quick puffs from her hookah. Finally she would lie down with her closing complaint: "You never will appreciate me until I'm dead!"

The daughters-in-law whisper words of relief to their husbands at the passing of yet another evening. Their mother would then be lamenting softly, addressing the darkness: "Some day he's going to meet his end out there alone, and I won't even be able to be by his side. . . . "

The sons do think that staying out night after night guarding a patch of weeds is strange behavior. But then, they never count their father among ordinary people. He has always been complex, dark-natured, inscrutable. The hereditary occupation of the Ganju caste is skinning dead cattle. Once, he poisoned several buffaloes that belonged to Lachman Singh, the ruthless Rajput landlord and moneylender, the owner of ten guns. He did it right in Tamadi, where the landlord lives, then sold the skin in the market. Lachman Singh naturally suspected only Daitari Singh, his cousin and rival landlord, of such a daring act. The feud between the two families that followed from the incident has not subsided yet, but their father remained untouched, proof enough that he is unlike the others of his community. His mind is always so busy working on tricks for survival that he never has time to talk to his sons or even his grandson.

Mother does not measure any less than him. Her spare old body of sturdy bones holds such capacity for hard labor, courage, and stubbornness—and anger—that she too is regarded by them as beyond the common measuring rod for humans.

They rarely see their parents talking close together. But whenever Father is about to undertake something big, he asks Mother to sit by him on the porch. He lights the hookah for her and says, "Come over, Dhatua's mother, let's have one of your brainwaves! Everybody in the village takes your advice; even the police are scared of you." She answers his invitation in her usual loud voice but without the sharp angry edge: "What is it churning inside that head this time? Going to trick or cheat someone?" These loud preliminaries are followed by a long conference in lowered voices. It occurs about once a year or so.

The rest of the time, he hardly ever speaks to her directly, and she complains about it, muttering to herself but within his hearing: "I don't know why I stay here instead of going back to my parents!" With a sly smile, Father addresses the air, "Yes! What a big house your father's got in his village!" She has none of her family left. She knows she has no place to go, and, of course, she doesn't want to go away. She just says so to make him break his silence, to let him make some such sly remark.

Dhatua and Latua can do nothing about their parents being so strange—just as there is nothing to be done about the hill being on the west and the Kuruda river flowing its own way. Sanichari is right when she says, "Both your parents are crazy, but your father is insane. Why else would he go on guarding that land ever since he got it and not bother to plant anything on it?"

There is a saying that what falls into your lap is worth only fourteen annas, if its value would otherwise have been sixteen. The piece of land fell in Dulan's lap, though it is not worth even fourteen annas. It used to be part of Lachman Singh's far-flung property. A few years ago, Bhoodan workers came to the area,* and they went making their rounds among the landlords with their lofty plea. Sanichari was quick to size them up, saying that they were the crazies from the babu class;† they thought they were going to make the landlords repent and say what a shame it was that they had so much land and others none at all and give away their land. Sanichari said she would know when that was going to happen because she would then find herself seated in a chair drinking buttermilk and cooking rice for two meals a day. She had not, however, considered one thing, that the landlords might enjoy showing off to others of their class. Most of them owned a hundred acres or two of crop land that regularly yielded rice, wheat, maize, pulses, and peanuts. Some of them did give away bits of uncultivable, barren, and stony wasteland from their estates; these gifts did not diminish their wealth in any way and yet produced so many other gains.

Come to think of it, this business of giving land served many purposes at the same time. The Bhoodan leaders and workers were becoming the laughingstock of the nation. It saved their face. They could now go and talk about the mission accomplished, of "changing the hearts of Rajput and Kayastha landlord moneylenders in the Kuruda belt." It demonstrated that

* The Bhoodan movement was started by Vinoba Bhave, based on the Gandhian idea of wealth redistribution by means of moral persuasion rather than through class struggle or state intervention. Bhoodan workers try to persuade landlords to give away some of their land, announcing the amounts donated in different areas to arouse a kind of contest for goodwill.
† *Babu* stands for an urban, educated gentleman, as distinct from a landlord.

Sarvodaya was still alive and potent.* They could next move on to the bandit-infested area of Madhya Pradesh, to change the bandits' hearts. Their vocation was to bring repentance to the hearts of bandits and land-lords. But that was not all that these little gifts of land did. The landlords also got rid of their barren plots and in return staked out the lifelong allegiance of the favored recipients. And above all these gains was the pleasure of knowing oneself as compassionate, delectable like the taste of the white spheres of sweet *rasagollas* to top off a perfect meal.

That was when Dulan Ganju got the plot of land. He was rather reluctant to accept it, but then the mighty Lachman Singh glowered at him saying, "See how the stupid lowly behave! Today I'm giving it because I'm overcome with goodness. I may not feel this way tomorrow!"

"You are our father-and-mother, *huzur*," Dulan promptly supplicated.

"Keep that in mind," Lachman Singh said. "The plot is under a slope. Rainwater washes over it. You can grow anything in it."

It is true that rainwater washes down there, leaving a reddish sediment, but it is surrounded by long stretches of barren earth and rocks. Who would haul over that distance all the things necessary for cultivating it? If it had been worth the trouble, would the owner have left it unused?

Dulan had gone to Lachman Singh that day to borrow some money, and he came back as the owner of a piece of land. The villagers had no doubt that it was one of those tricky whims of the rich. Too many buttery *parathas* obviously had overheated his brain. Tomorrow, he would forget all about this land gift business.

"But suppose he doesn't forget," Dulan argued.

They reminded him that in the Arah and Chhapra areas, where some landlords did this kind of thing to the applause of Bhoodan workers, those who got the land soon either sold it to the moneylender or mortgaged it back to the landlord for a loan. Dulan would end up doing the same. The landlord would get the land back at a profit.

"But why would he bother to do that?" Dulan argued. The landlord was only too happy to be rid of it, with fame and goodwill as an added bonus.

Dulan would have kept arguing in this fashion, but his neighbor Pahan shut him up.† They had enough problems to worry about. Dulan's problem

---

* *Sarvodaya* translates as the uplifting of all. This Gandhian concept of social activism advocates bringing about equality and justice through moral pressure. Sarvodaya workers involved in the Bhoodan movement are relatively more active and prominent in north-central India. Apart from Bhoodan, they have also been involved in several other campaigns: agitation for banning cow slaughter, rehabilitation of the bandits in Madhya Pradesh by persuading them to surrender to law, and more recently the ecological protection movements.

† Pahan (from *pradhan* or chief) is the tribal priest. Mahasweta pointed out to me that in a village of tribals and outcastes in Bihar, like the one here, the groups generally coexist in neighborly harmony, aware of, but not really divided by, the differences in their customs and rituals.

of being saddled with this bizarre gift of land was trivial by comparison. Dulan grumbled at this lack of interest.

His wife remarked that at the back of his skeptical arguments, his mind was busy planning how to put the land to work for profit—"Could anybody ever guess the workings of his mind?" Dulan retorted, "Profit from that land? Don't make me laugh."

The next day, Sanichari came over and listened to the account. She thought carefully, then said, "Why not? Listen, Dhatua's mother. Once he gets the land, Dhatua's father should go down to Tohri, to the *Biddi* office.* The government will give him seed and a cash loan to cultivate the land!" Dulan smiled with pleasure as he listened. His eyes took on a dreamy far-away look. In the fairy tales, the wish-cow always gives milk without ever calving. Not even Dulan's crooked mind had grasped until then how the piece of barren land could help him feed his family.

One day the land did come to Dulan in the form of legal paper. For him and his family, the world was confined to his hut in the Ganju neighborhood of the village, the two little rooms and a porch, in a corner of which the old couple slept. Destitute people like him usually become broken, feeble in mind and spirit. Blue-blooded landlords and creditors rule everywhere and everything they can see. Then there is Hanuman Misra in Tahad, the priest, also a powerful and influential man in the area. Living under the constant tyranny of the landed upper castes, it would have been only natural for Dulan to lose his spine. But his urge to survive remained stubborn, and it drove him to manipulate and scheme, to milk every situation in some way. Because he always had to live by tricking and fooling his powerful adversaries, he figured out all the twists and turns of contingency, and he knew them as if they were all written in codes on his thumbnail.

Dhatua's mother was her sarcastic self when Dulan got the papers for the land. "A big plot of fertile land he's got! Dhatua, ask your father to build a granary! And Latua, remember that your father's become a real landowner!" Despite the sarcasm, she waited with curiosity, like all the other villagers, watching Dulan for what he might be up to next.

The villagers regarded Dulan's single-handed, crafty battle with the powerful with awe and a touch of admiration. They all knew what really happened with the buffaloes of Lachman Singh, but nobody let out a word. Every time he goes to the house of Daitari Singh to sell a pumpkin, he manages to get paid twice, by the mother and then by the wife. At the time of Chhat festival,† when a bullock cart loaded with offerings of fruits and vegetables from Lachman Singh's house travels ceremoniously to the bank of

* Block development (B.D.) office.
† Chhat festival is usually observed in north-central India to mark the winter solstice. Offerings to the sun are taken to a river and placed in the water.

Kuruda river, Dulan solicitously walks alongside, loudly shooing nonexistent birds while transferring some of the contents of the cart to his tattered clothes. He never shares any of these goodies with the villagers. Yet they support him and admire him because he manages to do what they cannot.

2

After he formally got the land, Dulan went to Lachman Singh, bowed to touch his knees, and said, "*Malik parwar!* You've so generously given me the land, but what a pity that I can't make use of it, merely because I can't expect to get any help from the Biddi office!"

"Why? The B.D. office is supposed to supply you everything to till it."

"They won't, huzur, because we are of low caste."

"Of course, you're of low caste. You people have a tendency to forget that and have to be kicked to be reminded how to behave. But to refuse to help the one I've given land to? That is something the B.D. officer won't dare to do."

"But, malik, I've heard those Kayastha officers speak ill of you.* They say that Rajputs like you, sir, are uncouth and ignorant, always staying glued to the radio and using the left hand to hold the glass of water or the cup of tea while drinking."

"That's disgusting! That's outrageous!"

"I saw them with my own eyes, malik, and I heard them saying so."

"All right, I'll have the application written out for you."

Lachman Singh took pride in his education and had a lawyer on his payroll. The lawyer wrote a strong application in chaste Hindi about Dulan's right to receive annual supplies of seed and fertilizer and an installment loan to buy a plow-bullock. The block development officer was located in the town of Tohri, not quite within Lachman Singh's domain. But he knew better than to risk his one and only head. The subdivisional officer had specifically instructed him to avoid confrontation with Lachman Singh and Hanuman Misra. So, when Dulan came to him with the letter, he complied immediately. Very politely, he explained to the illiterate man in loincloth that he would get everything—the seed, the fertilizer, and part of the loan to buy a bullock right away, the rest of it later, upon showing the bullock.

Dulan came back and remarked to Pahan that the rules the government made showed that it knew nothing about how things worked in reality. "Whoever heard of anyone selling a bullock on installment? Lend me your plow-bullock, so I can show it and get the rest of my loan."

He managed to use Pahan's bullock to get a bullock loan every other year. He would go to the officer with his woeful tale of how the bullock died soon

---

* The Kayasthas are regarded as urbane and polished, compared to the Rajput landlords with their feudal lifestyle.

after he bought it with the earlier loan. From his trips to Tohri he would bring back the loan money, the money from selling the fertilizer in the market on his way, and the bundle of seed paddy on his head.

He brought the seed paddy for food. It was not easy to get edible rice out of seed paddy, but he managed to. The first time, his wife asked him, "How much land have you got that you brought so much seed paddy?"

"That land can't be measured. It's endless."

"What do you mean?"

"I mean our stomachs. Who can measure our hunger? The empty space in our stomachs keeps expanding! You're crazy if you think I'm going to plant it in that barren patch over there."

"What are you going to do with the seed then?"

"You're going to parboil it, dry it, husk it, and then cook the rice."

"Eat seed paddy? Do you want to die?"

"Think of all the things we didn't die from. The rats we ate during famines . . . If we die from eating seed paddy, we'll at least know that we had a meal of rice before dying. We'll go straight to heaven."

After tasting the rice from the seed paddy, his wife realized that she had never tasted anything more delicious in her life. She went around the village, proudly telling folks about this newfound food source. Was there any other married woman in the village who could claim that her man was so clever that he fed his family rice out of government-supplied seeds?

The villagers were on the whole pleased about it. The government never did a thing for them, the B.D. officer never bothered to help them, and their boys could never get into the government school. Gun-toting Lachman Singh or his cousin made them harvest their crops for a daily wage of four annas and a meal.

Tension was lately growing on that issue, especially because in the neighboring village the Dusads and the Ganjus and the Dhobis were getting a wage of eight annas a day. They were at least getting their rice along with being kicked. The laborers from this village were asking for a four-anna raise. The subdivisional officer and the police knew that their demand was reasonable; yet as soon as it built up into an agitation, they would come to round up the laborers, leaving Lachman and Daitari Singh alone. It was obvious to them that the government belonged to Lachman Singh, to Daitari, and to Hanuman Misra. If the man who could fool such a government happened to be Dulan Ganju, they couldn't but admire him.

Like the *Kamadhenu*,* the plot of cropless land kept yielding for Dulan a

---

* According to the mythology, Suravi, the original Kamadhenu, was among the fourteen treasures (*ratnas*) that were yielded by the oceans at the time of *Samudra-manthan* (the churning of the oceans by gods and demons). However, in the course of time, Kamadhenu became, like the wish-cow, part of much folklore and fairy tales.

hundred rupees or so a year. He was still spending nights at home, sleeping by the side of Dhatua's mother, on the bamboo bunk in one corner of the porch. Dhatua's mother had asthma and a chronic cough. The goat stayed tethered for the night under the bunk. The two sons with their wives and children slept in the two rooms, beside the store of grains and firewood and the clay pots and pans. The money from the land, of course, did not see them through the year. When it ran out, the father and the sons worked for daily wages, went in the forest digging for roots, and worked as coolies in the town of Tohri. Like everybody else in their community, they would also steal from the venerable Misra's vast orchard.

3

In the midst of their routine life turned up Karan Dusad of village Ta-madi, a bright and courageous man. He used to live on daily wages from his labor for Lachman Singh. Then he fought against the landlord over the wage rate and was jailed. In the big prison at Hazaribagh, he came in contact with political prisoners from all over Bihar, so many of them from the urban, educated babu class! They did not look down upon him for being a Dusad; instead, they respected him for being a fighter. They listened to him with amazement about how a couple of hundred dirt-poor peasants had turned around and confronted their bottomless exploitation, all by themselves, without any organization to lead them, and had set fire to Lachman Singh's field of ripe wheat. They had explained to Karan why his people's fight was indeed the most needed kind because "it was shaped by the concrete needs of the people and motivated by specific, actual reasons." "To fight standing right where one stands, at the point where one is rooted is the right way," they said to him.

The men who said those things were often tortured. From time to time, they went on a fast to protest the treatment at the prison. The jailers would then beat them even more; some were beaten to death. Even then, they kept expressing their admiration for the battle of Karan and his people, kept calling him a fighter and telling him that he had done the right thing and should never forget to fight back.

His jail experience produced a major unsettling in the layers of Karan's mind, shifted its bedrocks. He was no longer someone who thought of fighting only when he was pushed so hard against the wall that he was being crushed and had no choice. The Karan who came back from prison was now talking about "the situation being right for revolt." "If we have to face the landlord's guns and be jailed for refusing to be exploited, why should we wait until he makes things unbearable? We'll band together and prepare in advance. We'll inform him of our demand and ask that the police be present at the time of harvesting. Our demand could not be more modest. We know that tribals and untouchables like us can't expect to get a really good wage in a backward region like this. We'll demand that he pay eight annas a day to each man, woman, and child. He pays four annas now. Our struggle is only for four more annas. It's our 'battle for twenty-five *paisa.*'"

As soon as Dulan heard about this, he sent for Karan to come and see him in Kuruda. Dulan, always wary, took him to his plot in the middle of the brown wilderness to talk privately. Karan Dusad was a small thin man, past middle age, but his new personality bore the marks of his two years with the political prisoners in Hazaribagh jail.

"Everything about this caste thing is false," he said. "The Brahmans and the big shots made it all up, this untouchables thing."

He unsettled and scared Dulan by starting off with such a statement. But it was only for a moment, and Dulan did not let it show. He was a shrewd man, and he simply avoided getting involved in Karan's remark.

"That's what the educated city folks say. Now think carefully of what is relevant. Lachman Singh, the B.D.O., the S.D.O. and the police chief are drinking buddies.* You should first go to the Department of Tribal Affairs and the Harijan Sewa Sangha.† Inform them of your plans of action, and take them along when you go to petition the police and the S.D.O."

"Why? Are we weak? Are we lacking in willpower?"

"Very weak, Karan. When the time comes, the officials will flock to Lachman Singh's side. They'll look away if he fires guns. They'll arrest us if one of us raises a stick. Go to Madanlalji of the Harijan Sewa Sangha. He is a good man, a respected man. Everybody knows him. Have him with you all along if you must go about this plan of yours."

Karan saw Dulan's point and took the advice. The source of Madanlal's power was the vote pool that he controlled and delivered at election time. Therefore, the S.D.O. and the police chief, when they came to know of what was going on, hurried to confer secretly with Lachman Singh first and then they politely agreed to the appeal Madanlal brought.

The harvesting, transporting, and storing of the maize were over. Everything had gone amazingly peacefully. Everybody got eight annas a day. Karan became a hero. What had sounded like a daydream became a reality.

Then suddenly one day, Lachman Singh sent for Dulan. "Make sure to be in the plot tomorrow evening," he said. "And if anybody comes to know about this appointment, you'll become a corpse."

When the tomorrow became today, the S.D.O. left for the headquarters in Ranchi, and the police chief went to Burudiha on a mission to catch some bandits. Before the afternoon was over, in the red glow of the setting sun,

---

* Block development officer and subdivisional officer.
† Translates as Untouchables' Welfare Association, a nongovernmental organization.

Lachman Singh with his Rajput clan attacked the cluster of Dusad homes in Tamadi and set it on fire. People burned. Huts were razed to the ground.

In the pale light of the rising moon, an unearthly picture emerged like a silent movie before the eyes of the waiting Dulan. It was Lachman Singh on his horse. Two more horses were teamed up, and the plank across their backs bore bodies. They were followed by ten of Lachman's men.

The bodies were those of Karan and his meek brother Bulaki. At the silent command of Lachman Singh's gunpoint, Dulan buried them in his land. Fearfully, with his head bent, he kept shoveling to make a large enough hole. Lachman Singh stood on the high edge of the plot, chewing *paan* and watching. When it was all done, he hissed at Dulan, "Ever say a word about it and you'll join Karan Dusad. The jackals and wolves can dig up the bodies. Tomorrow you're going to set up a watchpost and spend every night here. The fire is on. Karan started it. He forgot that Rajput blood flows in my veins. From now on, there will be bodies to be buried here."

Dulan nodded meekly and said, "Whatever you order, huzur."

The next day, the police arrived and made a lot of commotion. They came up with the report that Karan wasn't there at the time of the incident. The newspaper reporters did not manage to write up another sensational "true story of atrocity on Harijans." Nobody said anything against Lachman Singh. One of his henchmen was imprisoned for arson, and the files were closed. Some time later the government offered token financial help to the homeless families for rebuilding their huts.

From that day, Dulan started spending nights in his land in the middle of the wilderness. It was at first thought of as one of his whims, and his sons tried to dissuade him. He became stone deaf to all their pleas and reasoning. To questions of what the matter was with him, he silently stared with blood-shot eyes. Pressed further, he would furiously raise his head and shake his bony fist, "Shut up, Dhatua! Or I'll break your head."

A massive detonation had taken place inside Dulan's mind, setting off landslides in the heaving layers of his consciousness. Things were that simple for the Lachman Singhs of this world? He had always known that human death, like human birth, was bound by time-honored customs and rules. But Lachman Singh had demonstrated how dispensable those rules and customs were, how easily they could be violated. Two dead bodies were thrown on horseback, right in front of all the Dusads of Tamadi, and taken away with the utmost defiance. Lachman knew he did not need to hide the removal of the bodies. Those who witnessed it could not open their mouths. They had read the warrant in his silent glare: whoever talks is dead too. It was not the first time and would not be the last. From time to time, with the flames and the screams of the massacred leaping into the sky, the lowly untouchable must be made to realize that it meant nothing at all that the government had passed laws and appointed officers to enforce them and that the Constitution held declarations. They must not forget that the Rajputs remain Rajputs, the Brahmans remain Brahmans, and all the Dusads, Ganjus, Chamars, and Dhobis remain under their feet. In some places, a few Rajputs or Brahmans or Kayasthas, and more than a few Bhumihars or Jadavs or Kurmis, may be as poor as the untouchables. Sometimes they may be even poorer. But they are not thrown into the fire so readily, with such impunity. The god of fire must have to this day remained partial to the meat of the untouchable, ever since the time of the burning of the Khandava forest,* which gave him the taste for roasted flesh of the dark-skinned dwellers of the forest.

The episode produced a crisis in Dulan's tricky mind. Before this, his cunning and deception operated at the surface level, tricks for day-to-day survival. Now, he was constantly hiding inside his mind two dead bodies. The bodies started to decompose. Under the ground, Karan and Bulaki grew lighter as they lost their flesh, but their bodies in Dulan's mind grew heavier as time passed. Dulan became more silent than before, pale with the burden he was carrying day and night. If he ever unlocked his mouth, the Dusad area of Kuruda too would go up in flames, with ashes flying and the smell of burning flesh in the wind.

Days went by. People's minds unconsciously began to push aside the disappearance of Karan and his brother Bulaki. Meanwhile, railway tracks were laid from Tohri to Burudiha on one side and to Phuljhar on the other. The police and the S.D.O. were given special powers, in selected areas, to investigate and bring to justice the cases of atrocity against tribals and untouchables. In Dhai, a village of outcastes and tribals, the village council received money to dig a tubewell. The region slowly limped along toward the modern age.

The power of Lachman Singh remained undiminished. He still paid no more than forty paisa in daily wages to his farm laborers, ignoring the government regulations. However, he offered a golden cobra to adorn the head of Shiva in the temple of Hanuman Misra. He bought a scooter for the B.D.O. and a transistor radio for the police chief. He also took over the quarter of an acre owned by Karan and Bulaki on account of their old debt to him, which was unpaid when they had disappeared. All parties concerned were happy.

4

Then suddenly, there come both a government circular about farm laborers' wages and a new subdivisional officer with a history of being accused of leftist sympathies. Because the administration wanted to put him in a situa-

---

* *Khandava-Dahana*. In the Mahabharata, the consumption of too much clarified butter in too many *yagnas* held by the kings gave *Agni*, the god of fire, indigestion. To cure it, He consumed vegetables and meat: the Khandava forest with its human inhabitants, offered by the Pandavas.

tion that would justify his dismissal, he is transferred to Tohri barely six weeks before the harvest is to begin. His transfer order is written with impeccable logic. The tribals and untouchables are the peasants and laborers in the Tohri region, it says, and the landlords, the rich farmers, and the moneylenders are all upper-caste. The most important problem of the region is the deep-seated distrust of the farm laborers toward the landlords. Thus, there has been no agricultural growth, and the per capita income has not risen. Income, consumption, health, education, and social consciousness— everything has remained backward, subnormal as a result. The area needs an enlightened and compassionate officer.

The S.D.O. reads the real meaning of the words in his transfer order—he is being handed the end of his career. Before moving, he sees his father-in-law and says to him, "You win, finally. See if that bank job is still open. With my degree in agro-economics, I might get it. Otherwise, if I stay for long where they are sending me, your only daughter is bound to be a widow soon." Having arranged for another job, the officer arrives fearless, filled with energy. He starts his campaign among the farm laborers, assuring them of their right to a daily wage of five rupees and eighty paisa, fourteen times what they have been getting. He also informs the landowners about the wage regulation and his intention to see it implemented.

Lachman Singh's land and the laborers who work on his land are spread throughout many villages in the area, not just Tamadi and Kuruda. The collective thoughts of the laborers are expressed by young Asrafi, the son of the headman of Burudiha village. "We haven't forgotten what happened to Karan, even though three long years have passed. But this S.D.O. seems to be a genuinely good man. Why then should we harvest for forty paisa and a meal? Just imagine. Five rupees and eighty paisa! That's our due. Skip the meal, just add five rupees to the forty paisa we get. That's what we want."

Dulan, just as he had done with Karan, calls Asrafi over and patiently tries to deter him. "Look, Karan too got things started so confidently. But the only result was the Dusad neighborhood of Tamadi got burnt down."

"Where is Karan? And Bulaki?"

"Who knows?"

"They're dead."

"Why do you say that?"

"They were killed and thrown in some ravine in the forest."

"I don't know about that, but whatever you try to do now, you must have the district magistrate support each of your steps."

"We'll do that."

"Make sure he'll protect you against the aftermath. Last time you got the wages, but after that you were set on fire."

The pattern of peasant struggle is always stamped by the special charac- teristics of the region. Lachman's final offer is two rupees plus tiffin.

"Just give us the legal minimum wage, malik."

"Should I?" Lachman Singh's eyes turn mellow with compassion as he speaks. "Let me think it over," he says. "You too should think it over. Even an ass knows that the legal wage should be paid. But do you know what the problem is? You're talking about what the S.D.O. told you. Tell him that no other big landlord in the area is paying the legal wage. Makkhan Singh, Daitari Singh, Ramlagan Singh, Hujuri Prasad Mahato—not one of them. Why should I be the only one to take the beating?"

With a timid yet stubborn smile, Asrafi replies, "You talk of taking the beating, malik? You own the flour mill. Your house can be seen from far away. How can anyone give you a beating?"

Lachman sees defiance in the smile but calmly explains: "This two-rupee wage that I'm offering is the most I'll do to take the government into account. It treats us like criminals just for owning more land. All of you who own small amounts of land get government help and subsidies. I gave some of my land to Dulan. The idiot doesn't even farm it. Yet he gets seed paddy every year. The beast actually *eats* the seeds! Let him! But do we get any free supply? We have to buy everything—seed, fertilizer, medicine to kill pests in the crops—everything. When you go to see the S.D.O., tell him about my problem too."

Asrafi, back from Lachman, comes to caution Dulan: "Be careful, uncle. The bastard knows that you don't till the land and don't harvest anything." He makes the corpses buried in Dulan's mind feel heavier. Lachman Singh has forbidden him to farm the land for a few years. Sadly, and now very worried about Asrafi, Dulan says, "Don't ever believe anything he says or appears to be, my boy. Your father was the one to perform the rites when my Dhatua and Latua were born."*

"You worry too much, uncle."

Asrafi keeps shuttling between the S.D.O. and Lachman Singh. Dulan becomes more and more depressed. Driven insane by the foreknowledge of disaster, he takes to screaming at his sons: "Sons of the lowly remain lowly! Look at you, living on what the poor old father wangles to bring home using that useless land. Any other young men would have gone to the nearest coal mine to work. What are you waiting in this place for?"

Dhatua raises his serene fawnlike eyes to his father and says with wonder in his voice, "We're going to get a much higher wage this time, father." Dulan doesn't know what more to say. He goes down to the B.D.O. in Tohri and asks for more supplies to raise a second crop this time.

The officer probably has managed to get to the bottom of this curious matter of Dulan taking seeds for land that he does not cultivate. He has

* Asrafi is a Hajam, with the hereditary occupation of barber. The barber's service is a necessary part of the rituals connected with birth, wedding, and death in the Hindu society.

joined Lachman Singh and Dulan in the secret game. So he says, "Yes, of course," smiling his toothy, cunning smile.

Dulan notices a very tall papaya tree in the yard of the officer's home. He has never before seen such a big one in this area. "How did that papaya tree grow so tall?" he asks. "Do you know, babu?"

The officer smiles with satisfaction as he explains: "That patch used to be part of my office yard. They used to bury there all the rabid dogs shot in summertime. The fertilizer from rotting flesh and bones made the tree grow so big."

"Is that supposed to make good fertilizer?"

"Excellent fertilizer. Haven't you ever noticed how bushy the flowering plants grow on the coffinless shallow graves of the poor Muslims?"

Strangely, this information seems to lighten the dead weight in Dulan's mind. When returning in the scorching midday, he goes straight to his plot to check. It is true! So, Karan and Bulaki are now in those unusually bushy thorn shrubs! Tears come to his eyes. Karan, you died, and yet you are living in these. But these thorny leaves are of no use to anyone, not even to feed buffaloes and goats. You got killed fighting for our food. Why couldn't you become wheat or corn or millet? Why not at least china grass? We could at least eat porridge made of the grass seeds.

Feeling unbearably depressed, he decides not to go home, but sets off for Tamadi to see Lachman Singh. Finding nobody around in his vegetable garden in the back of the house, he quickly pulls out some fence posts and wire to make a large opening on the pasture side and drives in a few buffaloes to feast on the luscious vegetables. Then he goes around to enter by the front gate and meekly appeals to Lachman Singh.

"Please write me a certificate, malik, so that I can get admitted to the hospital. I've got a terrible cough and chest pain."

"Later. I'll write you a chit after the harvest is over."

"Very well, huzur."

The dead bodies under Dulan's chest become very heavy again. He walks home deep in thought, digging and turning the layers of his mind. He asks Karan and Bulaki to move over and give him some space to think. After the harvest is over! Does that mean others are coming to give Karan and Bulaki company?

The harvesting of paddy begins. It seems to go on forever. After much negotiation, the daily rate is set at two rupees and fifty paisa plus tiffin. Lachman Singh himself, on horseback, is supervising the work. The police come to take formal note that the harvest is proceeding peacefully. The laborers get their wages on the seventh day. The S.D.O., with a sigh of relief, leaves the area, as do the police.

The storm breaks on the eighth day, when Lachman Singh brings in outside laborers to cut the rest of his paddy. Asrafi and his people are faced with a desperate threat. Bristling with fear and anger, they go to Lachman Singh. "You can't do this," they say.

"Who says I can't? Watch me, you bastards."

"But you agreed . . ."

"I let you cut some of the harvest. I paid your wages. Now the game is over!"

Watching the tense, angry faces of Asrafi and his people, the outside laborers put down their sickles and huddle in one place. Then shots are heard. The outside laborers are running away. Soon they are gone. More shots are heard.

How many are killed? Accounts differ. Dulan and his people count eleven. Seven according to Lachman and the police. Asrafi's father becomes sonless because Asrafi and Mohar are there no more. Wailings can be heard from many huts. When the S.D.O. comes back to the village, the parents and children and wives of the killed and the missing cry at his feet. The officer's face is stony grim. He gives them his word to take Lachman Singh to court. He talks to the reporters and shows them around. Lachman Singh is asked not to leave his home until the officer receives the warrant for his arrest.

In the beautiful moonlit night, sweetly cooled by the breeze, Lachman Singh again appears in the view of Dulan as he sits in his watchpost. He is accompanied by four of the great four-legged animals, bearing four dead humans. This time, Lachman's lackeys join Dulan in digging the grave, to make the pit deep enough. The soil has been softened by the monsoon rain and the autumn dew. The four bodies are dropped in. The weight of the dead in Dulan's mind multiplies overnight.

Dulan behaves even more strangely than before. He keeps going to the B.D. office, demanding more seeds and more loans for plow-bullock. Then, within a month, he seems pacified at the sight of some more aloe and lantana plants lushly arching up. The unbelievably green and healthy thorn bushes, greeted each morning by the sun, thrive as silent evidence for the murder of untouchable laborers in a remote neglected area somewhere in southeast Bihar in the days of the Emergency.

Lachman Singh is acquitted, not guilty. The S.D.O. is demoted for inciting farm laborers and disturbing the traditionally harmonious relations between landlords and laborers in the area. At the temple of Hanuman Misra, Lachman Singh and the other landlord moneylenders hold *puja* with wild fanfare, announcing to offer to the reigning god Shiva one hundred and eight of his favorite *bilva* leaves, all made of silver. They also use the occasion to announce that from now on only those bastards and bitches could come to cut the harvest who would do it for a wage of one rupee and no tiffin. Otherwise, outside labor would be arranged to do it. Terror reigns under the cover of the Emergency rule. The hoodlums working for the Congress party have become contractors procuring outside laborers. The game is going to be more exciting. Each laborer would have to pay the contractor four annas out of his daily wage, even if he is not one of the contractor's laborers. The toughs promise to control the harvesting at gunpoint. Let anyone make any kind of noise, and they would douse him with petrol and set him on fire. They will, once and for all, end the troublemaking tendency of the area.

Dulan wanders about listlessly, bearing the leaden load on his chest. He looks at the faces of Dhatua and Latua and thinks of running away with them. But where could he go? Where in his homeland of southeast Bihar will Dulan Ganju be safe? Where will he face no usurpers like Lachman Singh?*

On the day of Holi,† he cannot concentrate even to listen to the revelers' afternoon singing. Suddenly, however, he hears the joyous noise silenced with the sound of an incredible song. Dhatua, tipsy on *mahua*,‡ is singing with his eyes closed, to the beat of his little drum:

> Where did Karan go? And where's Bulaki now?
> Why does no one have their news?
> They're lost in the police books.
> Where's Asrafi Hajam? Where's his brother Mohar?
> Where are Mahuban and Paras?
> Why does no one have their news?
> They're lost in the police books.
> Because they fought the battle of twenty-five paisa.
> Asrafi fought for five rupees and forty paisa.
> Bulaki and Mohar followed their big brothers.
> Mahuban knew how to make the liquor of mahua.
> Paras knew how to dance on the day of Holi.
> They're all lost in the police books.

The song is over, but everybody remains silent. The color of Holi turns ash grey. The drunken lightheartedness is gone. Dulan stands up. "Who made that song?" he asks.

"I did, father."

Dulan sobs and begs his son, "Forget that song. Or you too will join the lost ones in the police books."

Dulan walks away toward his plot and goes to the lush green weeds in the middle. Very gently, he whispers to them: "Now you're a song. Could you hear it? A song that my son Dhatua made. You've become a song. Not rice,

---

* Usurpers in two senses: the moneylender increases his power as the landlord by foreclosing (usurping) the lands of his debtors; and the Rajput landlord moneylender is an ethnic outsider in Bihar, usurping the lands of the area's native peasants.
† Holi is the spring festival, celebrating the love of Radha and Krishna. Gender and caste divisions are set aside as people smear each other with brightly colored powder and squirt colored water at each other. Holi stands for laughter, playful irreverence, singing, dancing, and drinking.
‡ Liquor from flowers of the *mahua* tree, common in the forests in eastern India.

not even china grass, but only a song. Now please get off my chest; I can't
carry you any more."

The shiny green leaves of the full-bodied aloe bushes and the bunches of
lantana flowers, all drenched in the light of the full moon of Holi, wave and
roll like a bunch of children giggling at hearing something very funny. Dulan
feels beating inside his chest a terrible fear for Dhatua. When he climbs up
the post, he hears Dhatua's song again, faintly floating in with the breeze.
Now they are all singing it together. But they are not lost in the police books,
Dulan knows, although he can never tell anyone. Lachman Singh's paw is
poised over him with its pointed claws bared.

One day the Emergency rule ends. One day the "Sun of India's Freedom"
leaves the seat of power just to watch the fun,* and after a bit of rest, starts
running to get back into the seat. Lachman Singh's vast crops once again
grow ripe for harvest. After two years of drought and damaged crops, the soil
has poured out her bounties to harvest. All across to the horizon, one can see
rows and rows of the watchposts that have been put up in the paddy fields.
Swarms of birds are busy day and night feeding among the ripe paddy.

The man who had been the Congress worker, the goon, and the labor
contractor two years earlier has now dropped his first two credentials and
reappeared just as the labor contractor. He has with him four lackeys, all
dressed like him in polyester clothes and dark glasses. Speaking in the style
of the movie star Amitabh Bacchan, he informs Lachman Singh: "Your
monopoly is over. Breaking strikes, contracting labor, managing the harvest,
everything is now going to be in the hands of professionals. I am the *mercenary*
supplier of this *service* to the landlords in this part of Bihar. Even if you don't
want me, I'm still your supplier. So pay up the advance of five thousand
rupees for my services."

"Five thousand rupees?"

"Very well. Pay the laborers the legal wage then."

"No. I didn't mean that."

"You make eighty thousand rupees extra by not paying the legal wage, yet
you're saying you can't part with five thousand of it?"

"All right then."

"Agreed. Just give me the names of the villages where your laborers live
and their names. Are there any likely troublemakers among them?"

"Not this time."

* During the Emergency rule, the opposition parties and political dissent in general faced
severe repression. Slogans upholding the ruling party appeared prominently painted on walls
and signboards all over West Bengal and Bihar, where the opposition parties were strong. A
common slogan in Bengali depicted the prime minister Indira Gandhi as the "Rising Sun of
India's Freedom," her likeness painted on a background with the rising sun and the national
flag.

"Good. Now I must go and contract my services to Makkhan Singh and Ramlagan Singh. I'll be back at the right time. There's another thing. Pay them a wage of one rupee and four annas because I'll keep the four annas."

"But I was going to pay a rupee each."

"A rupee and four annas, I said. My name is Amarnath Misra, and I don't like to use too many words."

"Are you related to the Misraji of Tahad?"

"I'm his nephew. He gave me the capital to start this business."

The harvesting is arranged in this manner. Hanuman Misra later tells Lachman Singh, "Yes, he's my nephew. When I bought all my sons surface coal mines, I offered to buy him one too. But he wouldn't do that messy kind of work. He's such a resourceful boy. His services are in great demand from election candidates and from factory owners trying to break strikes. He procures labor for the surface collieries too. Very resourceful young man! Keeps three wives in three towns and he built a house for each. He was much appreciated by the earlier government. None of my sons turned out to be as resourceful as my nephew!"

Lachman Singh is a ruthless Rajput and used to being the absolute ruler in his domain. But even he realizes that if the self-appointed mercenary can routinely impose his paid service, then he too must accept it as a reality, in order not to risk being made a fool of before Makkhan and Ramlagan Singh.

The harvesting of paddy begins but not with outside laborers. Dhatua and his people are doing it themselves, for a rupee and four annas a day plus a tiffin of cornmeal with salt and chili. Dhatua's mother packs some pickle of wild plums for her sons to go with the cornmeal.

Dulan sits in his post, as if waiting for something, while the cutting of the sheaves of paddy goes on. The women sing as they cut. Across the distance, their singing comes floating to him like a lullaby, but it does not make Dulan sleepy. A tune plays in his head, but with different words:

Who has taken away Dulan's sleep?
In the police books he's lost his sleep.

In the afternoons he goes home and waits until Dhatua and Latua return from work. Then he comes back to his plot to spend the night. Dulan spends sleepless nights, just sitting there, looking at the weeds. Nourished by the soil softened with the washed down rainwater and the autumn dew, the aloes have grown bold and brazen, and the lantanas have burst into loads of flowers.

The expected trouble materializes on the pay day. Amarnath returns to claim his cut from the wage. Lachman Singh is not compliant: "I made no agreement with you about how you collect your share of the wage. You'll have to settle it with them. But don't beat up or kill anyone."

"Settle with them? How many of them?" Amarnath laughs like a hyena. "Why don't you pay me out of their wages before you pay them?"

The one who objects the most is Dhatua, Dulan's gentle older son. He is the reason Lachman Singh is reluctant to get involved in this wage discounting. Lachman Singh knows how to silence the lowly poor with his gun, but he does not want to kill this one. Dulan is necessary to him.

"You expect me to negotiate with the dogs?" says Amarnath. "You hand me my cut of the wage. Five hundred laborers for fifteen days. My four-anna share adds up to eighteen hundred and seventy-five rupees."

"No, huzur! We aren't giving it," Dhatua shouts desperately.

Lachman Singh sighs at the thought that he will have to pick up the gun again and repeat the pattern. After he had disposed of Karan, Asrafi came along; and after he had disposed of Asrafi, here comes Dhatua.

"How can you expect us to go home with fifteen rupees for fifteen days of work? You owe us eighteen rupees and twelve annas. Don't you remember that's what you offered? Haven't we worked for you all these days, even with our pay postponed?"

"Watch your words, Dhatua!"

Lachman Singh pays Amarnath off. Then he asks Dhatua to shut up and leave, taking the others with him.

Karan was good at voicing demands. Asrafi was defiant. Dhatua never thought he would have the courage to stand up against paying Amarnath out of their wages. After they leave, he asks the rest of them to go home. He wants to see to the end of the matter before going home. He goes back to Lachman Singh and tells him that unless they are paid the remaining twenty-five paisa of their due wage, they'll stop cutting the harvest from the next day. The better fields of paddy are still to be cut. They're not going to do it, and they're not going to let anybody else do it. Lachman Singh is furious, but he has to hide from Dhatua the fact that Amarnath Misra twisted his arm in front of them. He takes to euphemism: "Dhatua, don't forget that I let you go this time only because the *police* came to collect the *tax*."

"Why? Are you afraid of the police?"

Dhatua leaves, but his parting comment sets Lachman Singh on fire. But, because Dhatua is Dulan's son and because Dulan is helping Lachman Singh with something that must remain unknown, he decides to spare the lowborn lot just this one time and give them a chance to come around.

The next day the laborers come to the field together and pick up their sickles, but they don't start the work. Lachman Singh hisses with anger and frustration. Amarnath, the mercenary, is not available; he has gone to follow up his service to Makkhan Singh and Ramlagan Singh. Outside laborers cannot be found instantly. Hours go by without any work in the tense sit-down strike. As the afternoon sun begins to fade, Lachman Singh finally gives his attendants the directions. Don't shoot if scaring will do the work, he tells them.

Lachman Singh and his attendants then trot their horses through the ripe paddy. After watching movies about the bandits of the Chambal valley, they've taken to wearing olive green uniforms. They approach the laborers on horseback. The laborers stand up and wait, watchful.

"Listen carefully, you bastards and bitches!"

"*You* are the bastard!" someone shouts.

The guns are immediately raised on that side. On this side, they dive swiftly into the field of standing paddy and become invisible. Verbal missiles are exchanged for some time. Then the predictable gunshot is heard. Swarms of birds, hidden from view eating paddy, fly up into the sky. Inside the field, someone's voice sounds gurgling with blood. Then the sharp sickles and knives strike the horses' legs and keep hitting. The animals run away with their riders. The laborers now come out and run too. Latua and Param run toward Tohri for the police station.

The wait at home is excruciating for Dulan. Very late, long past the evening, Latua finally comes home, alone. "Where's Dhatua?" Dulan cries.

"Didn't he come home? I went to the police station."

"Where's Dhatua?"

"We called the police. Remember the good S.D.O., father? He's back now. He's coming with the police."

"Dhatua!"

Why do the corpses nested deep inside him seem to be stirring? Are they making room for someone? Who is it? Dulan knows who and gets up to go out in the night.

"Where are you going?"

"To the land."

"The boy isn't back, and you're leaving! Are you mad or a monster?"

"Shut up!"

He runs toward his plot, with Dhatua's song playing in his head.

Where did Karan go? And where's Bulaki?
They're lost in the police books.

Gentle fawn eyes. The mole on his arm. Don't be lost. Not you, Dhatua. Dhatua must be alive. He must.

Dulan finds Lachman Singh already in his plot with a man. The man's face and eyes are bloodied. Lachman is hitting him. He kicks the man; the man falls to the ground. Two men, but three horses. Why?

Lachman Singh comes to Dulan.

"Is that you, Dulan?"

"Where's my Dhatua?"

"Such a pity, Dulan. The beast fired against my order not to."

He kicks the man again, shouts at him, "Trigger-happy hoodlum!"

"But where's my Dhatua?"

"Buried in your land."

"Who killed him?"

"This beast."

"Him?"

"Yes. But don't let anybody know. If you do, you'll have no wife, son, daughters-in-law, or grandsons. Not one of them will escape. You can come and have as much money as you want. Latua went to call the police. I'll buy off the police. That's not the point. I let Latua get away with it only because he is your son. Do you know that? I haven't used a single bullet from my gun today. I could have stopped Latua with one bullet. I didn't."

They leave. Seven familiar, dear ones are buried inside this little piece of land! Dulan's head reels at the monstrous trick played on him. He slumps and rolls down the slope through the thorn bushes. When he comes to a stop, he is scraped and bruised all over.

This time, the investigation does not end the way it usually does. The S.D.O. steps in. Lachman Singh's lackey, the one who fired the shot, and Amarnath get prison sentences.

Dhatua never comes home.

5

Dulan broods for days, before he decides to go totally insane; after the first rain of summer, he gets desperately busy uprooting the dense growth of thorn bushes in his plot.

"Where's he gone to? At noontime?" his wife asks Latua's wife.

She says that she saw him leave with a sickle and a weeder.

"Why didn't you stop him?"

"Am I supposed to talk to my father-in-law?"

Forgetting her grief, Dulan's wife runs frantically to the plot. She stands on its bank, calling him, "Have you gone mad that you're clearing the jungle at this time of day?"

"Go home!"

"How can I go home?"

"Go home, I said!"

Dulan's wife leaves crying and goes to Pahan. Pahan comes with her to the plot and tries to soothe him. "Dhatua will be back, Dulan. Don't let the anxiety unhinge you. You know that the heat is bad for you."

"Go back home, Pahan. Is your son missing, or mine?"

"Yours."

"Is this piece of land yours, or mine?"

"Yours."

"Well, then? I don't care if I've gone mad or not. I must deal with this bloody land."

"Then let Latua help you with it."

"No. I want to do it all by myself."

Pahan remembers that, although Dulan never cared much for the work of cultivation, he had a knack for it and could do it well when he wanted to. He says to Dulan's wife, "Come, let's go home. Let him do as he feels. From now on, you will have to make the trips to Tohri."

Dulan's wife goes to Tohri with Latua, again and again, to ask about Dhatua at the police station.

Dulan clears the jungle of weeds for several days. Then he prepares the soil. Then he brings the seeds and announces to his wife, "The seeds are not going to be used for cooking rice this time. I'll plant them."

"In that plot?"

"Yes."

As he scatters the seeds in the soil, he mutters like a chant: "I'll not leave you as thorn bushes any more. I'll turn you into paddy. Dhatua, I'll make you all grow into paddy!"

When the seedlings come up, the villagers throng to his land to look at them. The seedlings are so healthy and thick! They beat even those on the fertilized fields of Lachman Singh, Makkhan Singh, and Ramlagan Singh!

"It's because the land was fallow for so long, and this is the first planting," someone tries to explain.

It annoys Dulan. He asks them to leave. He wants to do it all by himself— till the land, plant the seeds, and watch the green beauty of the growing seedlings, all by himself, with no one around. He spends all his time there. Pahan comes and tells him that Lachman Singh would die of jealousy if he could see Dulan's seedlings.

"Who?" asks Dulan, in a strangely disinterested voice.

"Lachman Singh."

"Where is he?"

"He's waiting it out in Gaya, at his in-laws' place."

"I see!" says Dulan.

His paddy plants grow up tall and robust. Then they burst forth into ears of paddy, loads of them. They become ripe. Then Dulan reveals the peak of his madness; he refuses to harvest his paddy.

"Not harvest the paddy? You worked the whole monsoon digging outlets to drain the excess water. You stayed out there for days and nights. I nearly killed myself going back and forth bringing you food and water. Now you say that you're not going to harvest it?"

"Yes. And I want all of you to stay away from the plot. I've work to do there now."

"What kind of work? To sit there forever?"

"Yes. To sit there."

The reason for his sitting there and waiting finally arrives. Lachman Singh returns for the harvest. He has heard about Dulan raising paddy on his plot. A whole year has gone by since the murder of Dhatua. Lachman is back in form. He's himself again.

Lachman Singh comes to Dulan. Dulan knew he would. He had no doubt at all that Lachman Singh would come to him.

"Dulan!"

"Yes, malik parwar!"

"Get up and come here at once."

"How come you're alone, malik?"

"Cut out your small talk. What's going on here?"

"What do you mean?"

"Why is there paddy on this land?"

"I grew it."

"What was my order?"

"You tell me, malik parwar. What was your order?"

"You son of a bitch! Were you supposed to grow paddy? The jungle of weeds was to stay . . ."

Lachman Singh is on horseback. Dulan, standing below him, suddenly grabs Lachman Singh's leg and pulls with all his strength. Lachman Singh falls off the horse, and his gun is thrown out of his hand. The gun is in Dulan's hand now. Before Lachman Singh realizes the situation, the gun's butt hits his head. He screams with pain. The butt hits his collarbone, making the crack of one hard thing against another.

"You son of a bitch! You beast!" Lachman Singh, to his horror, finds himself crying before Dulan, even as he shouts angrily. His tears are tears of pain and fear he has never known before. He, Lachman Singh, down on the ground, and Dulan Ganju standing over him? He reaches for Dulan's leg and at once groans with pain. Dulan has smashed his hand with a rock. He knows that his right hand is going to be useless for a long time.

"You beast! Son of a bitch!"

"What was our understanding, malik? I was not to till the land. Why? Because you were to bury the bodies here, and I was to be their custodian. Why do I have to be that? Because, otherwise, you'll burn our village and kill my entire family. I know that very well. But, malik, there are seven young men lying here! How can I have only thorn bushes and weeds on their graves? That's why I've planted rice. They all say I'm crazy, and now I really have gone mad. Today, I won't let you leave this place, malik. I won't let you go to have your harvest cut again. I'll never let you shoot again and set fire to huts and people. You've harvested enough, malik!"

"You think the police will let you get away with this?"

"Maybe they won't. And your people? Maybe they'll hit us back and kill us. When haven't they done so, malik? When have the police not beaten us? If they attack us again, and if we have to die, maybe we'll die. Everybody has to die some time. Did Dhatua ever die before?"

Lachman Singh, now realizing for the first time his total helplessness, feels the cold fear of death. Even in the grip of the fear of death, however, a Rajput in this part of the country can never beg for mercy from an untouchable. And, even if a Rajput could beg an untouchable for life, the untouchable may not grant it. Dulan cannot now.

Lachman Singh gathers all his strength to get up, to scream, to pick up a stone.

"Such a shame, malik, that you have to die at the hands of a Ganju!"

He pounds Lachman Singh's head with a rock. He keeps pounding. Lachman Singh was skilled at murder. He knew the value of bullets, and he was never moved inside by the act of killing. In Dulan's situation, he would have killed with a single bullet. Dulan is not a skilled murderer, and rocks have no value, and this act of killing is for him the culmination of a very long and hard battle inside his mind. So, he goes on pounding Lachman Singh with the rock, long after he is dead.

Finally, when he feels no more need to pound Lachman Singh, Dulan gets up. He has to take care of the rest of the work, one thing at a time. He takes the horse by the rein and strikes its rump with the stick to make it run. Let it go anywhere it wants to. Then he ties a rope around Lachman Singh and his gun and pulls him across the long stretch to a ravine. He rolls the body into the ravine and rolls rocks after it. Many, many rocks. A gleeful laugh rises inside him. So, malik parwar, now you've become just like one of the Oraons and the Mundas,* those you so despise! Your own funeral is burial under stones in a ravine!

The dry rocky, gritty ground is unlikely to carry any mark, but the spot where they struggled needs tidying up. Dulan breaks a leafy branch of a lantana growing by the bank of his land and sweeps the spot. Then he climbs up into the shed to sleep for the rest of the night.

The search for Lachman Singh goes on in earnest for a few days. Because he rarely consulted anyone about his moves, he had told none about going to see Dulan, particularly because his business with Dulan had to be kept

---

* Although tribal communities, like the Oraon and the Munda, have been virtually incorporated into the Hindu hierarchy as Shudra laborers, and although they are not very different from the untouchables in socioeconomic level, the tribals and the untouchables differ in rituals and religious practices. Tribals traditionally bury their dead in a chosen common ground and mark the grave with a rock; the untouchables customarily cremate their dead. In being killed by an untouchable and buried like a tribal, the high-caste Lachman Singh is doubly disgraced. Dulan's gleeful remark signifies, in Mahasweta's interpretation, his satisfaction in avenging their common oppressor.

secret. Those of his lackeys who knew about the business naturally kept quiet. Because the master himself seems to have disappeared and his horse was found wandering alone in Daitari Singh's paddy field, what is to be gained by probing? Lachman Singh's servant said that the master left for his usual afternoon ride following his usual snack of milk and crystal sugar. How would he know where the master had gone?

Nobody suspects anything, until it strikes everybody that the hyenas have been making quite a racket. For five days and nights, the pack of scavengers has howled, smelling flesh under the pile of rocks, and with great persistence has managed to remove some rocks and eat the corpse's face. The crafty way of hiding the body, in addition to the presence of the horse in the particular paddy field, point suspiciously to Daitari Singh. Lachman Singh's son pursues the suspicion and, given the practices of their clan feud, Daitari suffers harassment for a while. The police close the case for lack of evidence. Daitari Singh and Lachman Singh's son carry on their ancient quarrel. Neither side suspects Dulan. Quite naturally, nobody could imagine why Dulan would have anything to do with the death of Lachman Singh.

While on one side the investigation and search for Lachman Singh proceeds, on the other side a new Dulan comes back from the watchpost of his plot. A serene Dulan, at peace with himself. He talks to Pahan about something, as a result of which the villagers of Kuruda collect one afternoon in Pahan's yard. Dulan starts by telling them that he knows he has never given them anything. Everybody is surprised by his tone and his words. He continues: "You all praised my paddy. When I did not harvest it, you all said that I was mad. You said I was mad earlier too when I toiled over that land. You were quite right to call a madman mad. Will you now grant this madman one request?"

"Please tell us!"

They all feel a kind of lightness, a relief, after Lachman Singh's death. They do not want to worry—not yet—about whether Lachman Singh's son will step into his father's shoes.

"Let my paddy be the seeds for your fields. Use my paddy as seeds."

"You're giving it away to us?"

"Yes. Cut them and take what you need to plant on your land. How the seeds grew so well and why I wish to share them with you, that is a very long story . . ."

"You must have used good fertilizer."

"Yes. Very costly fertilizer," says Dulan, his voice drifting like a kite in the air detached from its string.

He clears his throat, to finish his announcement, "I want you to come to harvest and distribute my paddy seeds. Let me have some too. I'll plant them again, and again, for all of us to use."

They assure him that when it is ready, they'll come to his land and cut the seed paddy for everyone to share. Holding their promise to his chest like a treasure, Dulan then returns to his plot. His mind feels astonishingly light today. He stands on the bank and watches the paddy.

The golden paddy is overflowing with bounty and grace, nourished with the flesh and bones of Karan, Asrafi, Bulaki, Mohar, Paras, Mahuban, and Dhatua. It looks so glorious, Dulan thinks, because it is going to become seeds, the promise of life's regeneration. He slowly goes up in the watchpost. A tune plays through his mind. The refrain of the song keeps coming back, like a naughty, disobedient child. Dhatua once composed it and sang it on a Holi afternoon, as the revelers fell into silence to listen, and then they all joined to sing it again with him.

"Dhatua . . ." Dulan's voice quivers as he repeats his son's name. "Dhatua, I've now turned you into seeds for us to plant and grow over and over again."

Dhowli

Mahasweta Devi

1

The bus starts from Ranchi city in early afternoon and reaches Tahad around eight in the evening. The bus stop is in front of the grocery shop, also the only tea shop, both run by Parashnath, next to the post office. The *shop-cum-teastall*, the post office, and the bus stop form the downtown for the cluster of villages. The passengers get off here and walk the rest of their way home. This is where the unpaved wide road ends; so also ends the outside world with which Tahad is connected by this once-a-day rickety bus run by the Rohatgi company. The Punjabi company runs a brisk fleet of forty buses connecting the business centers in Bihar, twenty going up the highways and twenty coming down along the three routes connecting Ranchi with Patna, Hazaribagh, and Ramgarh. For dirt-poor, remote places like Tahad or Palani, they have a few dilapidated buses running off and on. On the three market days each week, the bus is filled by tribal villagers out to buy and sell. On other days, the bus is almost empty and runs irregularly to cut the company's loss. During the months of monsoon the bus does not come up the unpaved road, and the villages then remain cut off from the outside world.

This year, the rains seemed to be coming early, at the very start of June.

Dhowli was waiting at the bus stop, standing very still, her back to the shop, facing away from the shop's light, the only light there. Parashnath closed his shop when it seemed to him that the bus was not likely to come. He asked Dhowli if she should not be going home now. Dhowli neither answered nor looked at him. She just kept standing. Old Parashnath muttered,

"Dhowli" appears in Mahasweta's *Nairhite Megh* (Calcutta: Karuna Prakashani, 1979), 164–94.

worried, as he left for his home at the back of the shop. His wife was sitting there alone, smoking and thinking. Parashnath told her about the girl waiting again for the bus so late in the evening.

"She'll be finished if she keeps up this way."

"If the landlord comes to know what she's been doing . . . "

"That'll be her end. How long has it been since the Misra boy left?"

"Nearly four months now."

"What does she think? An untouchable, Dusad girl can make a Brahman give her home and food?"

"God only knows. But she's not going to be able to hold off for long."

"What makes you think so?"

"The contractor, and the gang of coolies."

"Yes. She doesn't have much of a chance. Such a young girl! Going back and forth alone in the dark night. What for? Isn't she afraid?"

"The wolf was out last night."

Dhowli had also heard that the wolf was out, but she forgot about it. The unbearable pain just under her chest made her forget everything else. The pain would stay there and then move down her body, as it was now. Dhowli did not know what to do; she could not think of anything.

Dhowli walked back home in the dark. To the shack dimly lit by the smoky oil lamp; their bed on the bamboo bunk; three goats tethered under the bunk. Her mother, lying in the bunk, saw her come in but said nothing. Dhowli tilted the water pot to see if there was any water. She drank some, closed the door, blew out the lamp, and lay down beside her mother. Tears silently flowed from her eyes, tears of hopeless pain. Her mother listened to her crying; she knew why the tears flowed. Later in the night, she said, "We're going to be driven out of the village. You're young. What'll happen to me? Where shall I go?"

"You'll stay here."

"And you? You'll leave?"

"If I have to."

"Where will you go?"

"To death's door."

"It's not so easy! At nineteen, there are obstacles to death's door."

"Not for me."

"Have you been to Sanichari?"

"No!" Dhowli shouted, "I'll not get rid of the baby."

"Will you then go to the Misra house? Tell them that, because their son is the father, they should help to bring up the child carrying their blood?"

"Who is going to believe me? It would have been different if he were here now, if he came back."

"How? He would have looked after you?"

"He promised to."

"They always say such things. You're not the first Dusad girl who has been used by the Misra menfolk. Have they left untouched any young girl of the Dusads, the Dhobis, the Ganjus of the village?"

"He's not like the others."

"No! He knows very well what is expected of a Brahman's son in this situation. He knows what to do, but he's not doing it."

"He's in love with me."

"In love with you? Is that why he has stayed away in Dhanbad for four months, not even coming to visit his own folks?"

"He doesn't come because he's afraid of his parents."

"You're thinking of love. Here I lost my job of tending their goats. The wolf got one of the kids. They accused me of stealing it."

"What has that got to do with me?"

"They did it to punish you, to show that they're annoyed."

"Throw me out, then."

"I will. Go to sleep now."

"How can you say you'll throw me out? Who do you have but me?"

At this point, mother and daughter started arguing, as they did almost every night these days. This time they were interrupted by the watchman's voice from outside. "Dhowli's mother! All day we hear you shout. Do we have to hear you shout in the night, too? There are other Dusads in the neighborhood. They all know that days are for shouting and nights for sleeping. You're the only one who doesn't respect this simple rule."

"Shut up, and go away. I'll be quiet now."

"What's the problem anyway? Is some coolie trying to get in?"

"It's your home that the coolies try to get in."

"Ram! Ram! Don't even say such a thing!"

The watchman walked away. Mother muttered what was on her mind, "I know the custom here. Everybody is waiting, watching to see if the Misra boy supports you after the baby is born. If he doesn't, they'll come to eat pieces off you."

"It's all your fault. Why did you bring me back to you when my husband died? Why didn't you leave me there, to whatever was to happen?"

"Did they want to keep you? Didn't you insist on coming with me?"

"Because his elder brother would have taken my virtue there."

"And the Misra boy has not here!"

The sarcasm felt like a stab. Dhowli said nothing. Her eyelids were dry inside from crying. She pulled the dry lids down over her tired eyes.

But she could not fall asleep. She had not been able to sleep since the day the Misra boy left, taking the early morning bus, running away like a thief. She knew that she could fall asleep forever with the poison for killing maize insects. But she could not die before seeing that betrayer once more face to face, eye to eye.

Betrayer? No. He left Tahad because his parents made him. They came down so hard on their dearly loved youngest boy; Hanuman Misra of Buru-diha threatened them. He wouldn't have left Dhowli unless he was really scared, he who cried like a baby to Dhowli just talking about the possibility that he might be sent away. It still hurt to remember how he wept.

Her mother wanted her to get the medicine from Sanichari to remove the "thorn" from her womb. How could she think of it as a thorn, when it came from their love? It was not like the children of Jhalo, the Ganju wife, and Kundan, the elder Misra son; it was not one of those products of greed and ruthless power.

Dhowli used to sweep their yard. She never lifted her eyes at the young Brahman she knew was always gazing at her. At noon, while tending the goats in the forest, Dhowli was once bathing in the stream when a small leafy branch fell beside her. She looked up and saw the Misra boy. He had followed her. He did not laugh; he did not leer at her; he did nothing she could be ashamed of. He only asked her why she never even looked at him when he was going out of his mind for her.

"Please, *deota*,* don't say such things!"

"What deota! Don't you know that I'm really your slave?"

"I don't want to hear such things."

Dhowli was afraid and turned to leave. Then he said, "You'll have to hear the truth some time, even if you don't want to now."

The young Misra left her with those words, words that still make the breeze waft in her mind, the leaves rustle, and the stream murmur. She stood there after he left. She lingered on, feeling something like a terrible fear beating in her chest. Fear of the unthinkable. The young Misra was so fair, his hair softly curled, and his face so lovely. Anyone could tell from his looks that he was of noble birth. And what was Dhowli? Only a Dusad girl, a widow, with a life of deprivation as far back as she could remember.

When her father died and there was no other man in the family, Kundan took away the lease of land from her mother. Her mother went to them and promised to pay the rent, whatever rent they wanted; she would have the land tilled by her Dusad kinsmen, for, if they wouldn't lease her the land, the two of them would starve to death. Kundan refused. Dhowli's mother then fell at the feet of Kundan's mother, "Please save me and my daughter from starving."

Kundan's mother pleaded with her son, "As long as her husband was alive, he tilled that land and gave us free labor whenever we wanted. Now that he is dead, we can't let her starve."

"Nothing I can do. I've already leased that plot to Jhuman Dusad."

* Lord; deity.

"Let them tend the goats then and clean our garden and yards. We'll give them some money and millet."

She depended on their pity for the gruel at the end of the day. And a son of theirs had just said those words to her. Why? Dhowli knew that her timid eyes, her slender waist, and her budding breasts were her enemies, only to bring her trouble and ruin her. So, she had always kept herself covered as well as she could with her cheap, short sari, and she never looked up when working in their yard, not even at the loads of fruit ripening on the trees. She picked up only the guavas and the custard apples that birds and bats had partly eaten and dropped underneath. Even those she showed to Kundan's mother for permission before bringing them home.

That day, after she came back from the forest, Dhowli scrubbed their brass plate till it gleamed like gold. When her mother was away, she looked at her face in it. A widow was not supposed to see her face in the mirror any more, nor wear the shellac bangles, the vermillion between the brows, the nickel anklets. She saw that her face was beautiful, but a beautiful face was useless for a widow because she could never marry again. She would never even be invited to sing the song "Sita is on her way to her in-laws' place" at another girl's wedding, nor to paint with colored paste flowers, leaves, and birds on the doors and the walls of any celebrating house. Someone like her had just heard the landlord's young son proclaim love, that he was a slave to her. Fear nestled under her chest like some terrible discomfort.

Dhowli told her mother, "You'll sweep the gardens of the Misras, and I would only tend the goats."

"Why?" "Because, you know, Ma, how the leaves fly when you try to sweep them into a pile. I can't cope with the wind scattering them about."

"Did anyone say anything to you?"

"Who can say what to me, Ma?"

"Don't go far into the forest with the goats. A wolf or a hyena is about."

"Don't worry, Ma. Am I that careless?"

She thought a lot, while tending the goats alone in the woods. She thought about everything she could remember from her childhood—going to the fair, perched on her father's shoulders; spending the day looking at all the shops with their expensive things, and then coming home happy with a paisa worth of sesame candy. Of her marital home, all she remembered were the two rooms, the days of work at the farm of the moneylender to whom they were indebted, and her mother-in-law making the gruel at the end of the day, for the men to eat first before the women ate what was left over.

About her wedding she could not recall much because she must have been very small at the time. She was sent to live with her husband when her body blossomed. Her father had to take a large loan from the Misras for her wedding and sending off, and he had to pay back the loan with his labor until he died. She remembered nothing nice about her husband. He used to beat her. He died of a fever. After he died, her mother-in-law asked her to stay on,

"You have to work at your mother's place too in order to eat. Do the same here."

Dhowli knew that much: she could spend the rest of her life there, working all day, clad in the widow's borderless sari, coarse and short, working every day from sunrise to sunset either on the creditor's threshing floor or as some farmer's laborer or leveling the layer of brick pieces with a mallet making some road or other, and then falling asleep by the side of her mother-in-law after eating whatever there was to eat. But then her husband's elder brother came there and started eyeing her. Her mother-in-law then turned against her and Dhowli left. Her only regret was that she had to leave before she could watch the *nautanki* one more time.* The nautanki performers used to come to the village, hired by the moneylender.

After she returned to Tahad, she did not let herself near any Dusad boy. What good could come of it? The same routine of backbreaking work, with kids in your lap, kids following you around, no food, nothing. Dhowli had no desire for that kind of life, the only kind of life for a Dusad girl.

It was so much better to be alone, alone in the woods, with time to think one's own thoughts. She tended the goats, and once in a while she lay down on the end of her sari spread on the forest floor. She was never afraid of the wolf or the hyena. They fear people just as people fear them. The forest felt so peaceful that the constant discomfort and fear she had after hearing the Misra boy speak so strangely to her was slowly going away. She was at peace again.

Then one evening, when coming back from the fair at Jhujhar, she somehow lost the group of women she came with. She knew that the procurers came to the village fairs to catch just such stray girls. So she was walking back as fast as she could. The Misra boy caught up with her.

"Didn't you hear me calling?"

"Why did you call?"

"Don't you know why?"

"No. Please don't say such things to me. I'm a poor Dusad widow, and you are the landlord. Please don't make fun of me."

"But I'm in love with you."

"No, deota. Don't mistake it for love. You are a young Brahman man. You'll marry a bride proper for you. Please stop this."

"But it's you I love. Don't you know what love is?"

"No, I don't. I know that there can be bastards between the landlord and a Ganju or Dusad girl. That happens all the time. But not love."

"But I can't think of anyone but you."

"Please don't play your games with a helpless poor girl."

---

* *Nautanki* is a form of vaudeville, with wild and earthy songs and dances, common in north Indian villages.

"I'm not playing games."

"You'll leave after you tire of the game, and what will become of me? Am I to be like Jhalo? No, deota, not that."

"What if I don't let you go?"

"What good is my saying anything? I'll have to accept it. You landlord people, you take whatever pleases you. If you want to take my honor, take it then. Let me be through with it."

"No, no. Don't say that, Dhowli. Forgive me." The Misra boy ran away from her. She came home, totally amazed by his behavior.

Soon after that, when she heard that the Misra boy was not well, that he seemed to have lost interest in life, she was moved and worried. She knew that the Misra boy could have had her any time he wanted. All the Misra men do that, and there is not a thing that the Dhowlis of the world can do to stop it. But why such strange behavior?

She felt overwhelmed. Then the women at the well surrounded her, "Fate is now all smiles on the poor widow!"

"How can fate ever smile on a widow?"

"The landlord's young son is going out of his mind for you!"

"A pack of lies!"

"Everybody knows it's true. The word is around."

"Don't bother me with gossip."

Dhowli left with the water, resolutely denying it, but she was agitated, and she went to the woods with the goats. What would she do now? The whole village was talking about something that had never happened before. Why did the boy lose his mind like that? Now nobody was going to leave her alone.

She avoided going anywhere near the Misra estate. She heard from her mother that the boy was still unwell and they had to call a doctor from Valatod. She wondered if her mother knew what the women at the well knew. She suggested that they go away from the village, to Valatod maybe, and work at road construction, to which her mother just said, "I'm not out of my mind."

Then one day she heard that the Misra boy had recovered, that they were looking for a beautiful bride for him. They hadn't looked particularly for beauty in Kundan's bride; but for this one they were after beauty.

Dhowli had felt relieved, but she had also felt a twinge of pain and simultaneously a joy of victory at the thought that a mere Dusad girl drove a Brahman's son so out of his mind.

Relieved and peaceful again, she went to the woods and had a cooling dip in the stream. Afterward, she dried half of the sari she was wearing by spreading it on a sun-heated stone, and then wrapped it around her upper body. She decided that she would buy another sari next time her mother got paid for their work. It always made her mother angry to see her in a half-wet sari: "Are you a widow or a marketplace whore, that you're showing your body?"

Suddenly, the Misra boy appeared there.

"I don't want to marry a girl of their choice. It's you I want, Dhowli," he told her in earnest.

The forest in the early afternoon is primitive, gentle, and comforting. The Misra boy's voice was imploring, his eyes full of pain and despair. Dhowli was unguarded in mind and body. She gave in.

For two months since that day, she lived as if in a strange dream. The forest was their meeting place, and the time the early afternoon. Both lost caution and sense, one nineteen and the other twenty-three. Every day, Dhowli worried about what was going to happen next.

"You're going to be married off soon."

"With you."

"Don't joke with me, deota."

"I'm not joking. I don't believe in caste. And Tahad is not the only place in the world to live. Besides, our marriage will be all right by the government rules."

"Don't say such things. If you talk defiant, what will Misraji order? They will then drive me away from the village."

"It's not going to be so easy. There are government laws against it."

"The laws are not for people like us."

"You don't know anything."

In the solitude of the forest, the Misra boy was dauntless, telling her of his plans, and his words seemed to mingle with all the myths associated with the old forest, taking on an enchanting and dreamlike quality. The days thus went by. But not for very long. Dhowli found out that she was pregnant. Strangely, the Misra boy was happy about that. He said, "I'm illiterate, just like you. I don't want anything to do with managing all this farmland and orchard and the estate. We'll go to Valatod, and then from there to Dhanbad, and on to Patna. We'll start a shop there and live from it."

But the day Hanuman Misra came to Tahad to settle the matter, the Misra boy could say none of those things to him. Kundan fretted and said that he was going to kill both mother and daughter and dispose of their bodies overnight.

"No, don't do that," Misraji said. "Clean the inside of the house, and the outside will clean itself."

"I want to kill them."

"That's because you're stupid."

"That bitch of her mother said that the wolf took one of the goats. How did she get three goats in her shack? Didn't she have two before?"

"The idiot talks about goats! Your wife has got more sense. I can talk with her, not you. Kill them, but not directly. Starve them. Take away the job. What your silly brother got himself into has affected the prestige of all of us.

We must restore our position first. What does it matter if you have one goat less? Listen to me, the first thing you should do now is move him away from here."

The young Misra said that he would not leave the village.

"If you don't, your dead body will. You've brought shame to our family by your stupidity."

The Misra boy in desperation appealed to his mother, "Ma, please! Dhowli is carrying my baby."

"Nothing unusual about it, my boy," she consoled him. "Men of this family have had children by Dusad and Ganju girls. Kundan has three by Jhalo. It's only the heat of your age, my boy."

"What'll happen to Dhowli then?"

"She'll be punished for daring to do what she did. She'll pay. She and her mother will starve to death."

"But it's not her fault, Mother."

"The fault is always the woman's. She caused trouble in a Brahman land-lord's home. That equals a crime."

"Mother, you love me, don't you?"

"You're my youngest child."

"Then touch me and swear. I'll listen to you if you'll see that she doesn't starve. Promise."

"I promise," she said hesitantly.

"Also promise me that nobody humiliates her or throws her out."

"I'll try."

"If you don't keep these words, then you know, Mother, that I can be stubborn. I may not be able to stand up to the big Misra. But if you don't keep the promises, then I'll never come to this village, never marry."

"No, no. I'll feed the Dusad girl; I'll look after her."

Dhowli was aware of what was going on, what was in store for her now. She never even thought of protesting. This was not the first time that a Dusad girl had been used by the Brahman landlord's son. According to the village society, all the blame goes to Dhowli. But, because of the love aspect of this case, she was now an outcaste to her own people, in her own commu-nity. She had not encouraged any boy of her own caste. That was no fault. If the Misra boy had taken her by force, then she would not have been faulted either; the Dusad community would not have abandoned her for that. There are quite a few children by Brahman men growing up among the Dusads. Her crime, something nobody was prepared to forgive, was that she gave herself to him of her own accord, out of love. All the Dusad-Ganju boys, the coolies, and the labor contractors were now watching how things would set-tle. If the Misras would support her and the child with a regular supply of corn or money or a job, then they would leave her alone because they did not want to annoy the Misras if they wanted to live in their domain. If not, then they would turn her, a widow with no one but an old mother and a baby, into a prostitute for all of them to use.

Dhowli knew what was going through every mind, and she was numb with fear and sorrow. The woods looked horrible to her, the trees looked like ghoulish guards, and even the rocks seemed to be watching her. She waited for him by the stream. Days passed, but he failed to appear there. When Dhowli was about to give up, he came. Dhowli read her death sentence in his grim face. She cried without a word, her face on his chest. He cried too, his face buried in her hair, her hair smelling of the soap and the scented oil he had given her. He had given her two saris too, but Dhowli never wore them because their printed material was forbidden for a widow.

The Misra boy was filled with hopelessness. All he could say was, "Dhowli, why were you born a Dusad?"

"Spare me the endearments! I can't stand them anymore."

"Listen to me. Don't cry yet."

"Don't I have to cry the rest of my life?"

"I have to leave the village now. I agreed to their conditions for now."

"Why did you tell me those words of love?"

"I'm still telling you."

"Why, master? Your Dhowli is dead now. Don't make fun of a corpse."

"Don't be silly. Listen to me." He made Dhowli sit on a rock. He held her face in his hands and lifted it to his. Then he said to her, "I must stay away for a month, and I'll do so quietly. But I told them that I won't be forced into a marriage, and they agreed not to try."

"They will forget that soon."

"No. Listen, I'll be back as soon as the month is over. I'm not sure where they'll send me or what I'll do in this one month. But I'll manage something for us. I'm not educated, and I don't want a salaried job. And I'm not going to ask my brother for a share of the farmland and orchards. I'll start a shop, and I'll use this time to do it. I need some time away from them to do it, you see?"

"What am I to do?"

"You will stay right in the village."

"What shall we live on? Your brother accused my mother of stealing and sacked her."

"My mother has promised me that she'll supply you with food, and here. . . ," he took out five ten-rupee notes, put them in one end of Dhowli's sari, tied a knot around it, and tucked it in her waist. "Try to stay calm for one month."

Misrilal took leave of her.

Dhowli came back from the forest and told her mother. The two of them put the money in a little can and buried it under their mud floor.

Two days after he had left, Dhowli's mother went to the Misra matriarch and silently stood before her. Silently she got up, brought a kilo of millet and poured it in the outstretched sari of Dhowli's mother, conspicuously avoiding her touch while doing it. Glumly she asked her to come back after three days. After three days, the quantity of grain was reduced to half a kilo. When she next returned after the specified three days, the lady grimly informed her that after the last time she was there, they couldn't find a brass bowl.

"No, lady. Not me . . ."

"My elder son has asked me not to let you inside the house any more. Next time you should stand at the gate and call someone."

Dhowli's mother had to swallow the accusation because it came from a Brahman lady. Next time she was told at the gate that the lady was away, gone to Burudiha to see Hanuman Misra.

Dhowli's mother came home boiling with anger and beat up Dhowli. Dhowli took the beating quietly. When her mother stopped beating, she brought the cleaver and asked her to use it instead because her old hands tired and ached easily and as it was sharpened recently, she would not have to bother to beat her again. Mother and daughter then held each other and cried. When they were through crying, her mother asked her to go to Sanichari and get some medicine to get rid of the thorn in her womb.

"I can't do that."

"Listen to me. He is not going to come back for you. He was just in a rebellious mood toward the family. He may have good intentions; maybe he wasn't lying when he promised to come back. But he won't be able to do it."

"Then I'd rather poison myself."

Mother sat down, pondering a few minutes what her daughter had just said; then, sighing, she got up, as if she had just remembered something. "I'm going to the forest contractor; he once asked if I could cook for him."

"Do you want me to go?"

"No. I'll go. I'm past the age to worry about gossip. Even if he doesn't pay money, he'll give me some food. I'll bring it home."

"Go then, before the job is gone."

"And you remember to tend the goats."

This arrangement kept them going a little longer. Dhowli's mother did not find the cook's job, but she was taken as the cook's helper, and she brought home the bread or rice she managed to get.

Their own folks watched how mother and daughter managed to live—what they did and what they didn't do. The coolies working under the forest contractor also watched them. They had cash from their daily wages for lugging lumber. They had refrained from falling on her so far only because they were not sure if she was going to become the favored woman of Kundan's little brother. They had not given up, though, and watched the goings on. They did not mind the wait; the contract for cutting logs and splitting lumber was to continue for a while, and she was worth waiting for. As a matter of fact, her attraction increased in their minds with the scandal of a Brahman boy falling in love with her.

One month was long over. It was four months now. It had become a ritual with Dhowli to go to the bus stop, stand silently waiting for the bus to come up, and return home disappointed. On this night Dhowli thought of the whole thing, all over again, and then she placed her hand on her abdomen. She felt the baby move a little. Misrilal had said, "If it is a boy, we'll name him Murari." But Misrilal and his words of love now felt like a receding illusion, a fading dream.

2

In late autumn Dhowli gives birth to a son. Sanichari delivers the baby. She cuts the umbilical cord with care and remarks that the baby is so fair because it has Dhowli's complexion. Dhowli's mother had asked Sanichari earlier to make sure she would be infertile after this baby. Sanichari gives her the medicine, telling her that it will make her feel better soon.

Afterward she sits down to talk with Dhowli's mother, who is worried that the medicine is going to kill her or make her a permanent invalid. Sanichari assures her with the account of her success with the medicine in the case of Kundan's wife.

"What are you going to do now?"

"Whatever god has willed for us."

"The Misra boy is going to be married soon."

"Quiet. Don't let Dhowli hear of it now."

"What will you do after that?"

"Whatever is in store for us will happen."

"Pebbles will start falling at your door at night."

"I know."

"After getting him married, they're going to make the couple live in Dhanbad. They've set up a cycle store there for him."

"I told Dhowli this was going to happen."

"As I've already told you, if the landlord doesn't undertake to support her and the baby, I'll try and get the forest overseer for her."

"We'll think about that later."

Because of Sanichari's Manthara-like cunning, and because she is indispensable for her knowledge of medicinal herbs and roots, not even the Misras dare to ignore her or snub her. Seeing Dhowli give birth, delivering her baby, has touched something in Sanichari's heart. She starts building support in Dhowli's favor. When she visits the Misra mother to treat her rheumatic pain, Sanichari tells her that she just delivered Dhowli's baby boy.

"So what?" says the lady.

"His face is exactly like your boy's."

"Nobody tells me such a lie."

"Don't be silly. Everybody knows that your boy was in love with Dhowli. Your men sow their seeds in our women. It is common, but how often does it become such a problem that Hanuman Misra himself has to come to solve it?"

"Because you raised the matter, let me ask you for something . . ."

"What is it?"

"Can you remove them from the village?"

"Remove them where?"

"I don't care where. The problem is that the girl my boy is going to be married to is not exactly a little girl, and the family has a lot of prestige. If they come to know of this, it will make them very annoyed."

"If you pay enough, they'll leave the village."

"How much?"

"A thousand rupees."

"Let me talk to my elder son."

"You have ruined your reputation in the village by failing to look after them and feed them. Your husband and your elder son made Ganju women pregnant, but they never failed to support them afterward. You have always been generous. How come you turned away from your usual *Bhagwati* role this time?"

"It's because Dhowli's mother stole the brass jug . . ."

"Stop giving false excuses."

The Misra matriarch has to let Sanichari get away with telling her so many unpleasant words so bluntly only because she is her secret supplier of the medicine for holding onto her old husband, who is addicted to a certain washerwoman. She cuts short the exchange and asks Sanichari's advice about what could be done now.

"Do something. You can help her if you want to."

"Let me talk to my elder son."

Her elder son, Kundan, dismisses her worries. He is not going to let that troublesome girl manipulate them—a baby today, and customers at her home tomorrow. He is going to fix it all. His brother will get married in Dhanbad and stay there. The matriarch is reassured by her manly son, and she promptly forgets the nagging worry.

But the patriarch Hanuman Misra absolutely refuses to solve the problem that way. "The boy will come here with the new bride, as is the custom, and later on they will go together to Dhanbad. Why can't he come to his home, his own village? For fear of a Dusad girl? What can she do?"

Dhowli, like everybody else, hears about the verdict. She stays home with the baby in her lap, trying to think about what they are going to live on. Mother's odd jobs are getting more scarce, uncertain, and now she depends on her with the baby. They could sell the goats one at a time, but how long would that feed them? What would they do after that?

Misrilal. Just recalling his name makes her mind go limp even now. All those caresses, those sweet words of love were lies? They could not be. There are fantastic associations with the woods and the spring. The ferocious constable Makkhan Singh once saw a fairy bathing in the stream on a moonlit night; he really saw it because he lost his mind from that night. A Ganju girl named Jhulni was in love with her husband's younger brother, and when chastised by the Panchayat, the two of them went into the woods and ate poisonous seeds to die together. Dhowli knew Jhulni and the boy. These were true events—they happened—and yet sound like mythical stories. Their love was true too, and yet it feels so unreal now! In that same forest, beside that stream, a Brahman youth once called a Dusad girl his little bird, his one and only bride-for-ever. Didn't they once lie on the carpet of fallen red flowers and become one body and soul? Once when the Dusad girl got a thorn in her foot, didn't the Brahman youth gently pick it out and kiss the spot of blood under her foot? It is now hard to believe that these things ever happened. They now seem like made up stories. All that seems real is the baby sleeping in her lap and the constant worry about food.

Misrilal has not kept the promise he made her. He can't. There's nothing that Dhowli can say or do about it. What now? When he comes back to the village after his wedding, will he be moved to pity on seeing his boy? Will he give a bit of land to help his child live? The Misra men have done that many times. But Dhowli's mind says, "No, he won't." What will she do then? Will she end up opening her door at night when the pebbles strike? For a few coins from one, some corn or a sari from another? Is that how she must live?

Dhowli's mind says, "No! Never that way!"

Tomorrow, how is she going to go to the well to fetch water? All the girls will be talking about the wedding and the preparations for the groom's party. When a Brahman landlord groom's party comes back after the wedding, even the Dusad girls sing and dance, from a little distance though; and they collect sweets and coins and chickpea flour. Is she going to join them in singing for the reward?

Sanichari, on her way back from the Misra house, after giving the boys' mother a piece of her mind, stops to talk to the fellows in the Dusad neighborhood and tries to put some sense in their heads.

"The poor girl is ruined and unjustly abandoned by the Brahman boy, and even you, her own folks, turn your backs on her. Have you thought about how she is to live?"

"Nobody ruined Dhowli. She fell in love with him. And don't expect us to forget that she turned down the boys from her own caste. So we don't feel involved with her problems; we don't care whether things go well or bad for her. Let her do what she can, however she manages it."

"What choices do you think she has now?"

"Let's see if her Brahman lover supports her and looks after her..."

Misrilal does nothing at all. He arrives, all decorated, at the head of the groom's party back from his wedding. Only in Dhowli's home is no lamp lit that evening. All the Dusads, Ganjus, Dhobis, and Tolis get sweets, country liquor, chickpea flour, even new clothes. All agree that such lavish gift giving has never happened at any other wedding in the area.

Dhowli waits by the side of the spring next day. She waits all evening. Misrilal does not come. Coming back from there, Dhowli stops at Sanichari's place and breaks down. Sanichari informs her that Misrilal was angry when he heard that she and her mother had refused the help his mother offered. "Is that what he told you?"

"Yes."

"Then go and ask him to come and see me. Otherwise, I'm going there with the baby to see his bride, even though I know his brother will kill me for it."

Misrilal does come to see her. He has no words; his eyes are confused. Dhowli reads in his face the power her presence still has on his mind. It makes her happy in a way that also makes her suddenly bold enough to speak up.

"Did you tell Sanichari that we refused your mother's handouts?"

"That's what my mother told me."

"I spit on her lies. Your mother gave us two kilos of millet in all, over a period of ten days. After that she called my mother a thief and turned her away."

"I didn't know that."

"Why did you destroy me like this?"

"I loved..."

"I spit on your love. If you had raped me, then I would have received a tenth of an acre as compensation. You are not a man. Your brother is. He gave Jhalo babies, but he also gave her a home and a farm of her own. And you? What have you done?"

"What I've done I was forced to do. I did not do it of my own wish."

"So you follow others' wishes in marrying, in starting your shop, and you follow your own wish only when it comes to destroying the poor and helpless. Do you know that because of you even my own people are now against me?"

"I'll give you...."

"What? Money? Make sure it's enough to bring up your son."

"I'll send you regularly from my income from the store."

"But your words are all lies, worthless lies."

"For now..."

"How much?"

He brings out a hundred rupees. Dhowli takes it, ties it in a knot in her sari, and goes on, "With a hundred rupees these days one can't live for long even in Tahad. Because you've ruined me anyway, I'll go to Dhanbad and drop your boy on your lap if I don't get a regular supply."

"I have to accept whatever you say."

"You ruined my life, turned it to ashes, and you can't even hear the hard truth? Is it being rich that makes one so tender-skinned?"

Dhowli comes back, still raging inside. She asks her mother to go to Valatod and make arrangements for her to stay with her aunt there. Her mother is struck by her anger, her belligerence. "If I must sell my body, I'll do it there, not here."

"Why? Does it bring more money there?"

"How should I know?"

On the next day Misrilal leaves with his new wife. When they set into the bus and look at the villagers gathered at the bus stop, his brother-in-law points to Dhowli, "Who's that girl?"

"Which one?"

"The one with a baby in her arms."

"Just a Dusad girl."

"I've never seen such a beautiful Dusad girl."

"Maybe. I never noticed her before."

3

It turns out that Dhowli's aunt in Valatod does not want her. The sum of hundred rupees that Misrilal gave her is now down to nine. He never sent any message or any more money, although later on other stories came up about the money, that he once sent twenty rupees through the bus driver who kept it himself, and so on. Meanwhile, one of the three goats of Dhowli's mother is stolen, and eventually they have to sell the other two for very little, as is always the case when the seller is so hard pressed.

Dhowli senses that the village, the Misra family, the gang of contract coolies are all watching her with increasing interest, closing in on her. They have been watching her boy grow up on gruel and her old mother spend all day in the forest looking for roots and tubers. They have also seen Sanichari going to their hut once in a while, with roasted corn bundled in the fold of her sari. From this they conclude that the Misra boy has finally washed his hands of Dhowli.

Then one night, a well-aimed clod of earth strikes her door. Dhowli shouts, "Whoever you are, you should know that I keep a knife beside me." Someone outside whistles and walks away.

The tap-tap continues; little clods are thrown at her door in the night. Dhowli keeps silent. If it persists, she shouts, "Go home to your mother and to your sister."

Her mother mutters something about how long she would be able to fend them off.

"As long as I can."

"You may have the strength to keep going, but I don't."

"I don't have any more strength either, Ma."

"What are you going to do then?"

"Shall we go to the city and try to live by begging?"

"You think men will see you as a beggar? They'll be after your body."

"I don't have the looks and the body anymore, mother."

"Then why do the clods keep falling at our door every night?"

"It's because they know how desperate I am with the baby."

"I can't take it any more. If it weren't for you and your baby, I would have moved in with Sanichari long ago."

"I'm going to find some job tomorrow. I'll earn by weeding the fields."

"There are many others weeding fields all day long. How much does it bring them?"

"I'll try for some other work then."

Dhowli goes in the morning to Parashnath's shop and begs him to give her some job, maybe sweeping his shop, to keep her from starving.

Parashnath offers her some millet but says that he would not hire her because he cannot afford to incur the wrath of the older Misra.

Dhowli takes the millet from him and sits under the tree to think how many days they can live on it, even if she makes a thin gruel. Kundan Misra is out to kill her, starve her, as punishment for turning his brother's head.

Dhowli's mother does not say anything about the pathetic amount of millet that she brought home, but when offered the gruel, she puts down her bowl untouched and says, "Why don't you and your boy eat this. I'll go away and find something on my own."

"You don't want it?"

"If you can't find something to keep alive, better kill yourself."

"You're right. I'll kill myself."

Next day she goes to the stream, thinking all the way of drowning herself. Once she is dead, then her own kinspeople will at least look after her mother. And the baby? As long as her mother is able to live, she will try to bring up the baby.

But she does not meet her death. On the way, a man in a printed *lungi* and shirt catches up with her. He is a coolie supervisor and a coolie himself. He grabs her hand, and asks, "Where is your knife?"

Dhowli looks at his eyes. She feels very little fear and says firmly, "Let go of my hand." The man lets go of her hand.

"Are you the one who throws clods at my door in the night?"

The man says yes and gestures to indicate why.

Dhowli thinks for a minute. Then she says, "All right. I'll open the door.

But you must bring money and corn with you. I am not selling on credit."

Dhowli comes back home and asks her mother to take the baby to Sanichari's place to sleep from that night on. To her question, she simply informs her that she is going to open the door when the lump of earth strikes. Seeing that her mother is about to cry, Dhowli impatiently, sternly asks her not to raise a row and to come back home before sunrise.

Then she takes out one of the two printed saris that Misrilal gave her. She borrows some oil from Sanichari to oil her hair; she takes a bath and combs her hair into a plait. She is not sure if there is anything else involved in preparing for the customer of one's body.

When a pebble hits the door, she opens it. The man has brought corn, lentils, salt, and one rupee. Dhowli pays him back, with her body, to the very last penny. As the man takes leave, she reminds him that she will let him in as long as he brings the price. When he asks her not to let anybody else in, she says that whoever will pay can come; her only rule is that she will not sell on credit.

Many are willing to pay; she opens the door to many. Dhowli and her mother start having two full meals a day and wearing saris that are not old rags. After the customer leaves, Dhowli sleeps well, better than she has for a long time. She never knew it would be so easy to sell one's body, without any emotion, for corn and millet and salt. If she had known, they could have had full meals much earlier; the baby could have been better fed and cared for. It now seems to her that she has been very stupid in the past.

Kundan has been watching Dhowli carrying on. He knows that by figuring out the means of survival, Dhowli has defeated his revenge, outwitted his plan to kill them indirectly. The Dusad girl's nonchalance bothers Kundan; her new self-assured attractiveness gnaws at his mind. One day, seeing her draw water from the well with the other women, he asks Sanichari if they are going to drink the water touched by Dhowli. It turns out to be a wrong move, given Sanichari's well-known candor and forthrightness.

"That's none of your business, master. And why should we mind the water she touches? Our people now accept what she has to do."

"Why?"

"Why not? What wrong has she done?"

"She has become a prostitute."

"Your brother forced her to become a prostitute. How would your brother's son have lived if she did not? Everybody seems to be happy now, including your friend and business partner the contractor. His coolies no longer have to stray very far for the fun."

"Better watch what you say when you talk to me."

"I don't have to. Your mother and your wife would have been nowhere but for Sanichari here."

Kundan may make wrong moves, but he knows when to retreat. Every family in the village, rich or poor, needs Sanichari. Nobody can do without her help with the medicinal herbs.

Kundan then takes a trip to Dhanbad to work on his brother.

"Better give her money or land. It's your cowardice that now brings the business of selling flesh to the village, right under our nose."

Misrilal's face becomes ashen. "What do you mean?"

Kundan is wild with joy at having hit the spot. His brother is still in love with the whore, and he has managed to hit him right there. What a coward! No pride in his superiority as a Brahman. A man is not a man unless he behaves like one. In his place, Kundan would not have abandoned his favored kept woman at the order of Hanuman Misra. Kundan must prod his unmanly brother into becoming a man. He must be taught how to keep the untouchables under foot, sometimes acting kindly but always forcefully like a man. Otherwise, it is too large an empire for Kundan to control all by himself—so much farm land and orchards, so many illegitimate children and so many fertile untouchable women, so huge a moneylending business. Kundan must bring his soft, defaulting brother up to manhood, cure his weakness, so that he can help Kundan with the job. He goes for the kill.

"Don't you know? I mean the Dusad girl you fell in love with. I spit on it! She became the mother of a son by making a Brahman fall for her. And now the entrance that was once used by a lion is being used by the pigs and the sewer rats."

"I don't believe you. She can't do it."

"She is doing it. She is making us Brahmans the laughingstock."

"No!"

"Yes. I say yes a hundred times. You're not a man! Just a scared worm! You couldn't stand up to Hanumanji and tell him that you wanted her as your kept woman. I've kept Jhalo. Didn't Hanumanji forbid me to give her a place to live? Did I obey? I spit on your love. Lovelorn for a Dusad girl! A man takes what he wants and keeps things ordered to his wish, everything from his *paijars** to the Panchayat. You're no man. You made people spit at the Brahmans."

"I won't believe it until I see it with my own eyes. If it's false, . . ."

Kundan smiles a sly victorious smile and says, "Then you'll kill me? Good! Didn't I get you the license for a gun?"

Soon after that, Misrilal comes to Tahad, tormented by anger and the venom his brother injected in him. Because Dhowli no longer goes to the bus stop, she does not know that he has come.

As soon as the evening sets in, he throws a pebble at her door. It is a

---

* Sandals.

changed Dhowli who opens the door—she is wearing a red sari and green bangles, and her oiled hair is in a plait down her back.

She turns pale at first but recovers almost immediately and invites him coldly, "Does the landlord want to come in?"

Misrilal enters without a word. He sees the new lantern, the bed of clean *shataranji** and pillows on the bunk, the sack of millet, and the can of oil under the bunk.

"You've become a *randi*?"

"Yes, I have."

"Why?"

"Because you ran away after having your fun, and your brother took away our food. How else can I live? How can I bring up your son?"

"Why didn't you kill yourself?"

"At first I wanted to do that. Then I thought, why should I die? You'll marry, run your shop, go to the cinema with your wife, and I'll be the one to die? Why?"

"I'll kill you then."

"Go ahead."

"No Brahman's son is to live on the filthy handouts of the untouchables! How dare you! I'll kill you."

"You can't because you're not a man."

"Don't say that, Dhowli. My brother said that. But don't you say I'm not a man. I'll show you that I'm a man and a Brahman."

Within a few days, Misrilal with the help of Kundan and Hanumanji calls the Panchayat. Without asking anyone in the Panchayat, Hanumanji orders that Dhowli must leave the village; she cannot be allowed to do business in the village. She has to go to Ranchi and get herself registered as a prostitute there. If she does not, her hut will be set on fire to kill her along with her mother and her child. As long as the Brahmans live in the village, as long as Shiva and Narain are worshiped in their homes, such impudent sinning is not going to be tolerated in the village.

When Dhowli protests, "Why didn't the Brahman help me with money to bring up his son," Hanuman Misra shouts, "Shut up, whore!" and throws his sandal at her. Misrilal joins in, "Now at last you know that I am a man and a Brahman."

The Dusads, the Ganjus, and the Dhobis at the meeting do not raise any objection. They only ask how Dhowli is going to be able to go to Ranchi. Kundan answers that his contractor is going to take her there. She has to leave the next morning, no later.

* Flatweave cotton rug.

Early in the following morning Dhowli, a bundle in her hand, boards the bus with the contractor. She is not crying. Her mother, with the baby in her arms, cries standing beside the bus. The baby holds out his hands to Dhowli. She tells her mother to keep some *gur* for him for the night, to put a bit of it in his mouth if he cries.

Dhowli's mother now sobs aloud. "It would have been less terrible if you stayed with your husband's brother."

A faint smile, perhaps of pity, appears on Dhowli's lips, hearing her mother say that. In that case, she would have been a whore individually, only in her private life. Now she is going to be a whore by occupation. She is going to be one of many whores, a member of a part of society. Isn't the society more powerful than the individual? Those who run the society, the very powerful—by making her a public whore—have made her a part of the society. Her mother is not going to understand this. So she smiles and says, "Don't forget to keep some gur by the bed, mother. And keep the lamp lit, so he will not be scared in the dark."

Even the driver of the bus of the Rohatgi company cannot bear to look at Dhowli. He sounds the horn and starts the bus. Dhowli does not look back to see her mother and her child for fear that it will also make her see the brass trident atop the temple of the Misras.

Kundan's contractor cannot look at her when asking her to make herself comfortable because Ranchi is a long way from there.

The bus starts speeding, and her village recedes.

The sun rises, and Dhowli watches the sky, blue as in other days, and the trees, as green as ever. She feels hurt, wounded by nature's indifference to her plight. Tears finally run from her eyes with the pain of this new injury. She never expected that the sky and the greens would be so impervious on the day of turning Dhowli into a public whore. Nothing in nature seems to be at all moved by the monstrosity of what is done to her. Has nature then accepted the disgracing of the Dhowlis as a matter of course? Has nature too gotten used to the Dhowlis being branded as whores and forced to leave home? Or is it that even the earth and the sky and the trees, the nature that was not made by the Misras, have now become their private property?

The Funeral Wailer

Mahasweta Devi

1

Sanichari, an old Ganju woman,* had spent her life in endless poverty, like most of the other Ganju and Dusad villagers in Tahad. Her mother-in-law used to say that her life was bound to be full of misfortune because she was born on a Saturday. When she was a young wife, she could not answer because she was not supposed to. One of her regrets is that she had not managed to answer before her mother-in-law was dead. Too late now. Still, she sometimes mutters the answer to herself, "You were born on a Monday. Has your life been more fortunate? Have any of the Somris,† Budhuas, Mungris, or Bisris fared any better?"

Sanichari did not cry for her mother-in-law when she died. The old woman's two sons were in jail at the time, along with all the able-bodied male Ganjus and Dusads in Tahad, the doing of Ramabatar Singh, their *malik-mahajan* at the time.‡ Furious that some of his stored wheat was stolen

"Rudali" appears in Mahasweta's *Nairhite Megh* (Calcutta: Karuna Prakashani, 1979), 195–237.

* Because there is a Sanichari in many villages, and perhaps more than one in a village, the Sanichari in the different stories by Mahasweta may not be the same person. Sanichari in both "Dhowli" and "The Witch-Hunt" is an herbal medicine woman. Sanichari in this story and in "Paddy Seeds" is probably the same individual in two different stages of her life. Sanichari in this story is in an earlier stage, in the process of weathering the personal misfortunes before she becomes a public personality ready to fight for others. Dulan of "Paddy Seeds" is in this story too, before the tragic events that changed his life.

† Unlike the Sanskritic names with deep meanings or the names of gods and goddesses and the characters in the *puranas* that are adopted by the upper-caste affluent, the tribals and the untouchables in the area usually name their children by the day of the week they were born: Somri (female born on Monday), Bisri (female born on Thursday), Mungri (female born on Tuesday), Budhua (male born on Wednesday), Sanichari (female born on Saturday), and so on.

‡ Landlord-moneylender.

and he could not catch the thief, he had them all thrown in jail. That was when Sanichari's mother-in-law died, sick with dropsy and crying for food in her bed soiled with her own excrement. She died on a rainy night. Sanichari and her sister-in-law had to work throughout the night in order to take the dead body out of the hut before the night was over; they had to go from door to door begging other villagers to help them cremate the body before morning so that they would not have to pay for the repentance rites for keeping the body home overnight. They had no means to pay, not even a basketful of wheat. That night Sanichari was so frantic doing all this that she had no time to cry for her mother-in-law. Even if she had time, though, she would not have cried much for the old woman who had given her trouble to the very end.

The old woman hated being alone when she was alive. Apparently, she hated being alone when dead. Within three years, Sanichari's sister-in-law and brother-in-law were dead. At the time when they died, Ramabatar Singh was throwing many Dusads and Ganjus out of the village. Sanichari and her husband could not mourn their deaths because they were scared of drawing the landlord's attention and because they were preoccupied with scraping together the money to cremate them and do the *sraddha*. They managed that only because the other poor in their village understood their predicament and were happy with sour curd, *gur*, and coarse parched rice full of husks. They even sympathized with their not crying and worried for them, saying to each other that three deaths in the family within three years were making their unreleased tears become like heavy stones inside. Actually, Sanichari was relieved inside; there were now two fewer mouths to feed from the hard-earned gleanings from their landlord-employer's empty fields after harvesting.

However, she did not think she would be unable to cry after the death of her own husband. With her luck, that too came to be. Her son Budhua was about six years old then. Energized with the dream of bringing her household to some order, Sanichari worked day and night for the landlord, splitting wood and cutting grass for fodder and helping her husband harvest the landlord's crops for a wage. They had just managed to build a hut on the tiny plot that her husband's father had left for his elder son, a plot her husband inherited after his brother's death. Sanichari had just finished drawing the decorative designs on the walls of their hut. Her husband was going to fence the yard and grow chilies and eggplants; she was going to get a heifer to raise by working for the landlord's wife. Her husband proposed that they go to Tohri to the Shiva temple, to pay homage for the divine kindness and also see the Baisakhi fair held on the holy occasion. They had a saving of seven rupees for the expenses of the visit and the worship.

The Shivaratri fair was full of people. The nobility were pouring milk from big containers on the Shivalinga. The milk collected in large tanks smelling of sour milk, with hordes of flies hovering over it. People paid the attending *panda* a rupee for a clay cup of the milk from the god's bath. Many died from drinking that milk, including Budhua's father. British government workers came and took away the vomiting and diarrheal people and put them in tents set up in the hospital compound. There were five tents for the sixty to seventy stricken people, and there was barbed wire around the tents. Sanichari waited with her son on the other side of the barbed wire. They were told about the deaths but were not allowed to go near the dead. The government workers burnt the bodies and dragged away the living gathered on the outside of the barbed wire to give them cholera vaccinations. She and Budhua cried from the pain of the injection. Crying with the pain in her arm, Sanichari did the rites of widowhood. In the shallow water of Kuruda river, she washed off her home-made vermillion, broke the shellac bangles she had bought at the fair, and took the dip. The panda of the Shiva temple said that they should offer the *pinda* for the dead man's soul before going back because he had died there. Even offering a pinda of sand and water from Budhua's hands cost her a rupee and a quarter for the panda to solemnize it.

When they came back to their village, the priest of Ramabatar's temple was in a rage, saying that Budhua was no Ramachandra in exile and his father was no Dasarath that a pinda of sand and water would do. When she said that she was asked to do it by the priest there, he said that a Tohri priest would not know the rules for the people of Tahad, that she had insulted their own priest by doing what she did. To pacify the priest, she had to do a proper sraddha, for which she had to take out a twenty-rupee loan from Ramabatar by thumbprinting a contract to pay back fifty rupees by working for five years without wage. After the sraddha, she had to work so hard day and night just to keep them from starving that she had no time to cry for Budhua's father.

One day while weeding Ramabatar's field under the burning summer sun, she put down the trowel and went to sit under the *pipul* tree, telling the other laborers that she was going to let out some of the pent-up crying for Budhua's father. When Dulan Ganju asked why on that day, she said that she was thinking of how the others would be going home after work with their wages and she would go home with the handful of ground corn that she got for a snack. "Why not cry about just that? Why drag in Budhua's father?" Dulan had asked.

He and Sanichari then talked about how long it had been since her husband died. A whole year had gone by. How the preoccupation with hunger made one lose track of time! Dulan advised her to work slower: "Why are you weeding the bastard's field with all your strength? You should do as I do; work slowly and at least prolong getting the handful of corn for snack even if you get no wage like the others." Talking with Dulan, Sanichari was once again distracted from crying for her husband.

Time passed; but Sanichari's debt to Ramabatar Singh did not go away.

It would perhaps never have gone away but for a fortuitous coincidence. She was at the time taking care of a black male calf that Asrafi's mother left with her before going on a trip to Gaya. Ramabatar's uncle was then on his deathbed, and her black calf was brought in and its tail put in the dying man's hand to help him cross the Baitarani river to enter Yama's domain. Sanichari noticed that many relatives were gathered inside, attending the death of Ramabatar's uncle. She was suddenly hit with an idea. From outside she begged Ramabatar loudly, so that his relatives and kinsmen gathered there could hear, to cancel the rest of her debt, now that poor Sanichari had been able to render him such a vital service.

For Ramabatar the death of his uncle meant adding some ten more acres of good land to his wealth. Whether prompted by happiness about the windfall or by an urge to show off to the gathered relatives, Ramabatar was suddenly generous and granted Sanichari debt relief. Later on, he was criticized by the other landlord-moneylenders for his foolish act, which they claimed was the reason why the untouchables were becoming more insolent. It was not the amount of the debt that mattered, they said; the money involved was worth less than the dust of their shoes. The debt served to make the poor work for them, the way the yoke made the bullocks work. Ramabatar, misty-eyed, would then tell them how he was in a mood of renunciation after the death of his uncle.

Ramabatar, however, compensated for his momentary lapse by making Sanichari and other Ganjus pay for the musicians at the wedding of his son Lachman.

Time passed, unnoticed in the daily battle against hunger. Budhua grew up and took up the yoke of poverty like his father. Married in childhood by custom, his wife came to live with them when she came of age. Budhua's son was born. His wife had a demonic appetite. She became fat and big from her trips to the marketplace, where she managed to get food to eat from all sorts of people she mixed with. Budhua, on the other hand, grew thinner by the day, carrying sacks of wheat for Lachman Singh. He caught the wasting fever and cough of tuberculosis. The fever came every night, he coughed up blood, and there were dark shadows under his eyes. Watching him waste away before her eyes, Sanichari felt the cruel hot air of the funeral pyre blow in her mind day and night. She knew that her dream of building a life around Budhua would never come true. Perhaps her fond dream of sitting in the sun on winter mornings with her grandchild and eating chickpea flour and gur with him from the same bowl, while her son and daughter-in-law earned a living, was too ambitious compared to her other little dreams, like making her shellac bangles last for a year or buying a wooden comb. Perhaps that was why Budhua was dying bit by bit.

She blamed her dream. For the sake of Budhua, she could not blame Budhua's unseemly healthy wife. She could not get angry with the mother of her grandson. Budhua understood everything; he understood how his mother felt and begged her not to be angry with his selfish wife. With a sad smile on his wan face he said that he knew all about his wife stealing money out of the marketing to buy herself things to eat, but he understood that she did it because of her appetite, not because she was bad. When Sanichari mentioned the bad things people said about her behavior, Budhua only said that he was not bothered by it because he did not expect her to understand the pain and sorrow that he and his mother had shared, how much they had gone through to build their little life. How would his wife know of that?

His voice choked with a bout of coughing. Sanichari rubbed his chest and said that she no longer prayed for him to get well because if god was there he would have allotted death to a mother before her son. Ever so reasonable Budhua said that it was better this way because his son would be able to live if his mother lived. Sanichari slapped her forehead in despair and got up saying that she was more keen on her son's life than on his son's life.

Budhua's vegetable garden lit up the yard, glowing with healthy vegetable plants, produced with much care and hard work, using good seeds he got from Lachman Singh's garden and manure he picked up. The vegetable garden was part of his effort to fill the stomach of his young healthy wife. She had wanted to go to work in Lachman Singh's fields, arguing that there was not enough food and she wanted to work to feed herself better. Budhua stalled her by saying that he would help her do whatever she wanted to after the child was born. Meanwhile he labored alone to produce food for her in their yard. Day after day he spaded the soil, brought water from the river in buckets slung from a shoulder pole, and gathered dry thorn bush for the fence around it. Sanichari admired the vegetable patch, telling him how much his father had wanted to make a kitchen garden just like that.

Within a month and a half of the birth of her child, Budhua's wife started badgering him to be allowed to go to work. He said, "Yes, you'll go to work, but not in the landlord's field. You can go to the market on Wednesdays to sell vegetables. Young wives don't come back home once they start working in the landlord's field."

"Where do they go?"

"First they go to nice rooms, and then they go to live in the whore colony. I'll kill you if I hear any more about it."

So Budhua's wife went to the market on market days to sell vegetables. When Sanichari said that she could have gone instead, he said that it was better this way because all the time that he and his mother went to work in the fields his wife never did any housework, sweeping, cooking, or fetching water. She did not like doing housework.

Mother and son both knew that his healthy wife was not going to be devoted to her sickly husband, nor was she going to be attached to their poor home built on the labor of love. Sanichari once took her aside and begged her to behave properly at least as long as he lived, which would not be long as anyone could tell from the dark shadows under his eyes.

His wife seemed to have respected that request. She stayed exactly as long as Budhua lived. When the baby was six months old, Budhua's condition deteriorated. It was so bad one day that Sanichari asked his wife to stay with him and ran over a mile to the *ayurvedic* doctor's house for another medicine because the usual medicine was not helping any more, although she knew very well that he was beyond the reach of any medicine. When she recalled it later, she could not imagine how she ran all the way without slowing for a breath. The *vaid* was not home, he was gone to the market. As soon as he came back, she frantically begged for a stronger medicine. The vaid was irritated by what he called the impatience of the *chhotalok* and remarked that if her son was in such bad condition, why had he just seen Budhua's wife going toward the market.

When Sanichari came back from the vaid's place, Budhua was dead, his wife gone, and the baby was crying alone inside their hut.

His wife did not return. Sanichari, with the baby in her arms, worked nonstop to arrange for his cremation and evade the truth about his wife's absence. Again, she had no time to cry, even for her own dead son. Afterward, when she had a moment from work, she would just sit stunned and then lie down with her eyes closed.

She had not imagined her life without Budhua. As far back as she could remember, it seemed that he was always beside her, the quiet, sympathetic son of a mother buffeted by the blows of misfortune and endless struggle. Even when he was a small boy, he helped her in his quiet ways, cleaning the hut, fetching water from the river, and washing the corn or wheat they had gleaned, while she labored on the landlord's field. Later on, after he became ill, caring for him became the most important part of her life, making hot water for him to drink at night when the coughing was bad and rubbing the dream-ordained ointment on his chest. Now she felt totally lost without him, even as she was working hard for his baby, Haroa.

The baby constantly cried because Sanichari could not provide him with milk. One day Dulan's wife, mother of Dhatua and Latua, came to her rescue. She picked up Haroa and said that Dhatua's wife, who just had a baby, was going to breastfeed Haroa along with her own baby. She also said that while they took care of Haroa, Sanichari could go and earn something with which to bring up the baby. She could work on rail line repair because Dhatua's father had gotten a subcontract for a part of the job requiring some twenty laborers.

Thus, with the help and concern of another poor Ganju family, Haroa survived, and Sanichari earned something to help bring him up. The days that she went to work with Dulan, his wife gave *roti* and pickles for her as well as for Dulan, so that Sanichari would not have to cook. Sanichari later returned the wheat flour that went into all those rotis, but that did not fully repay her debt to Dulan and his family. They were not the only ones who stood by her in that terrible time. Parbhu Ganju offered to move her hut into his yard so she would not have to live so alone. Natua Dusad sold her vegetables in the market for her.

Not the least important of their help was that nobody mentioned anything about Budhua's wife becoming a *randi*. But Sanichari knew about it. Her son's wife had gone with one of the medicine men in the market who sold four kinds of medicines for a rupee. He had promised to feed her *poori-kachauri* every day and take her to cities like Gaya and Bhagalpur, to the cinema, the circus, and the *nautanki*.

Sanichari remembered what Moti's mother long ago told Sanichari's mother while grinding her corn in her mother's grindstone. The landlord had offered to keep Moti, but her mother refused. Later when Moti ran away with the contractor in rail line construction, her mother regretted that she had not said yes to the landlord's offer. At least she would have been able to see her daughter's face.

Sanichari did not feel that way at all. She was glad that Budhua's wife had left with some gypsy medicine man instead of staying in the village as the landlord's favorite woman, to the mortification of Sanichari and Haroa working like slaves in the landlord's field. Besides, Sanichari knew from her experience that her community would have shunned her in that case; they certainly would not have sympathized with her. She could live hungry, but she could not possibly live without their moral support and sympathy.

Slowly Sanichari felt normal again, and she did her best to bring up Haroa. The old and the middle-aged in their community used to tell Haroa never to hurt his grandmother who had suffered so much for so long. Haroa would listen silently as if to a legend about a very familiar person.

2

When Haroa became fourteen, Sanichari took him to Lachman Singh, the young malik-mahajan. The times had changed; so had the landlord-moneylender. Ramabatar Singh used to kick and beat up the poor and low-born with his shoe to keep them in line, but when he was in a good mood he sometimes chatted with them. Lachman Singh kept his distance from them and hired musclemen for the job of keeping them in line.

Sanichari took Haroa to Lachman Singh and asked for a job for the boy. Lachman Singh, perhaps in a good mood at the time, hired Haroa for his shop in the marketplace, to haul goods and clean up, for two rupees a month and meals. Sanichari thanked him and came home to get Haroa ready for the job. She made him a talisman with the *prasad* she brought from Mohanlal the priest. She cautioned Haroa about keeping a safe distance from the cattle, taking care not to get kicked by a buffalo, and never listening to the bad people in the market. Haroa said, "Yes, grandma."

The first few months Haroa worked and was a good boy, handing her the monthly two rupees and bringing her part of his meal of chickpea flour and gur. Then one month he had no money for her because he had bought a colored vest. The next month he bought a plastic mouth organ. Sanichari scolded him, and, when Lachman himself told her that Haroa spent a lot of time with the magicians, she beat him up as hard as she could. She warned him that she would rather cut off his legs and feed him with her earnings than let him take the wrong path. Haroa was a good boy again for a few months. Then one day he did not come home, and she learned that he had run away with the magician's party.

She said, "Let him go," but she kept searching for him from one market-place to another, from one fair to another. She did not cry for her grandson, as if it was only natural that something terrible would happen and her life with him would end, too. But she kept looking for him.

On one of her trips looking for Haroa, when she had given up hope of finding him, she bumped into Bikhni, her childhood playmate. Bikhni, who had a big bundle on her shoulder, had accidentally pushed Sanichari. Sanichari shouted at her, she shouted back, and a shouting fight was about to take place. At that moment Sanichari was actually eager for a fight to lighten her frustration, just as Dhatua's mother sometimes quarreled with the crows to keep her mind and tongue sharp. A good fight cleaned the mind and pumped blood through the body like gunshots. As soon as they saw each other's face, they stopped short, recognizing each other at so unexpected a meeting after uncounted years. They discovered that they lived in nearby villages, within half a day's walk from each other; they had not even known that in all these years.

The two old women, long-separated childhood friends, then sat under a *pipul* tree, each cautiously eyeing the other and concluding that life had not been kinder to her friend. Neither had any ornament except arm tattoos and pieces of cork in the distended holes of their pierced ears. The hair of both was unoiled and uncombed. They lighted a bidi each and asked about each other's family. Sanichari told Bikhni, briefly but without hiding the essentials, about Haroa and herself. Bikhni listened, wondering if love and compassion were gone from the world or if it was only their luck. Bikhni told about herself and her only son after three daughters, the son whom she brought up single-handedly since his father's death when he was a child. She got him married and, on the occasion of his marriage, fed the whole village curd, parched rice, and gur with money she borrowed. Now while the moneylender was about to take away her home, her son was preparing to leave her and go to his in-laws' place to live there. She spat when saying the "in-laws' place" and explained that his father-in-law had no son and the sons-in-law stayed with him like purchased men. She wanted to repay the loan by selling the four cows that she had reared herself from calves, but her son took the cows and kept them at his in-laws' place. Disgusted, she had brought her two goats to the marketplace and just sold them for twenty rupees, which she was carrying in the fold of cloth at her waist. She told Sanichari that she was going away somewhere, maybe to a large railway station where she could live on begging, because her only son was no better than dead to her.

Sanichari listened to her troubles, sighed, and invited Bikhni to come and stay with her. Her hut was so empty with its two rooms that she and Budhua had built, each room with its sleeping bunk, and Budhua's vegetable garden in the yard still yielding something to cook.

"What shall I do when my twenty rupees run out?"

"We'll see then. We won't spend your money. Sanichari still earns something, even if it is never enough for a full meal."

Bikhni agreed to come with her. Before they started back from the market, she thought of something and asked Sanichari if water was very scarce in her village. Sanichari said there was the river and the *panchayati* well, though its water tasted bitter. Bikhni asked her to wait for a minute, went into the market, and came back with a packet of lice medicine to be applied mixed with kerosene and washed off: "Even the lice seem to bite more when the mind is on fire."

Sanichari brought Bikhni along to live with her. During the walk back, only once did Bikhni express regret about leaving her own home, "My little granddaughter will cry at night; she slept with me in my bed."

Sanichari said, "For a few days maybe. Then she will get used to it."

Bikhni liked Sanichari's home so much that she immediately got to work, sprinkling water on the floor and sweeping it. They did not need to light the stove that night because Bikhni had with her the roti and pickles she brought for the road. Bikhni went out to see the river and came back carrying some water.

Bikhni loved to do housework. Within a few days, she had put a fresh coating of dung and mud on the floor and porch of the hut, washed her own and Sanichari's clothes with soda and hard soap, put the rag quilts and mats out in the sun. In her own home lately, she had been doing less and less housework because she resented losing control over the household to her daughter-in-law, who then said that her mother-in-law was lazy, not knowing that she shunned work because she was sad and offended. The habit of organizing the household is addictive; it does not die easily. It could make even the unfortunate old Bikhni start dreaming again. Organizing Sanichari's household got hold of Bikhni, and she never stopped to wonder how long she was going to be in it. One day she started spading the vegetable patch in the yard, saying that a little care would make it yield more.

The lice medicine eradicated the creatures sheltered in Sanichari's hair too. After a long night's sleep she realized that for so long she had been unable to sleep from lice bite, not from the pain of mind; no matter how sad one felt, sleep overcame one's work-worn body.

They lived like that for a while, Sanichari working as a field hand and Bikhni working at home, and Bikhni's money slowly dwindled. One day they realized that Bikhni's money was almost finished. That same day Dulan's small calf was taken by the wolf. While everybody was worked up about catching the wolf, the news came that Bhairab Singh, another landlord in the area, had been murdered by someone or several people. His body was found in one of his fields, a field over which a legal dispute had been going on for many years, which would now be promoted to a criminal case. Most agreed that Bhairab's eldest son must be the murderer, because he was unhappy and worried about his father's fondness for the sons by his second marriage. Bhairab's eldest son threatened to charge his step-brothers with the murder of his father. They threatened to charge him for the murder of their father and sought the help of Lachman Singh.

Lachman Singh agreed to intervene, perhaps because the piece of land interested him too. He made a dramatic appearance at the crowded scene near the dead body. He lamented loudly with such pathos in his voice that it amounted to public chastisement of all the sons of Bhairab Singh, "Such terrible misfortune, uncle, that a king like you is lying dead in the field instead of in your own home! You lacked nothing, uncle!"

Then he addressed the sons, "How can you call yourselves his worthy sons? How does it matter who killed him? Oh-ho, uncle! As long as you lived, the lower castes never thought of raising their heads. No Dusad or Ganju ever thought of sending their children to the government school for fear of you! Who will now look after everything?" He continued his speech, "Our duty now is to do the funeral rites befitting the honor and status of uncle! Take his body home. We can't let his body be taken to Tohri and cut up in the morgue. Uncle has died the death of a hero! But is the way he died what he deserved? We can't let it be. People will talk. We must perform the rites and the cremation with pomp and splendor. Place uncle's decorated body in an expensive bed and invite all our Rajput kinsmen for the occasion."

Lachman Singh then took Bhairab Singh's sons aside and scolded them for putting their quarrels above the interest of their clan. He compared his uncle's death to the fall of Indra and said that, because the rival clans of Daitari Singh and Makkhan Singh were looking for ways to give them trouble, they must try to suppress their quarrels now.

Sanichari had gone to see Lachman Singh for a loan or maybe a job for Bikhni. But because the landlord was busy with other things, she came back from her fruitless trip and decided to seek Dulan's advice. With Bikhni she went to see Dulan, the man known in her community for his twisted tem-

perament and incredibly sharp mind. Dulan listened to her account and
remarked that they were not using an obvious way in which they could
earn money. "What way?" Sanichari asked.

"The ways don't come to you, Budhua's mother! They come to the
landlord-moneylender, but not to the Dusads and the Ganjus. They have to
make the ways. How much did you say your friend brought?"

"Twenty rupees. Eighteen we've spent on food."

"If I were you, I would have seen Mahabirji speak to me in dream before
the money ran out."

"What do you mean, Latua's father?"

"Don't you understand? Before the money ran out, I'd have gone to the
Kuruda river and picked out a nice-looking stone from its bed. I'd have
smeared it with oil and vermillion. Then I'd have claimed that I dreamed
that Mahabirji was embodied in it."

"But I never dream."

"Once you found Mahabirji, the dream would have come along in his tail.
Then I would have sat in the market of Tohri and collected money from
devotees. But everyone here knows you. It wouldn't have worked with you.
Your friend is new here. It would have worked if she tried."

"Don't like playing tricks with gods. Even as it is, Mahabirji's followers
don't leave a fruit or vegetable in my yard."

"That's not playing tricks. If you think it is a trick, then it is. If you don't,
then it isn't. You have a sinner's mind if you think it's a trick."

"What on earth are you saying?"

"I'll explain. For example, Lachman's rheumatic mother gave me ten
rupees to bring some divine oil from Chas. I did not even go to Chas; I just
took some oil from my home to her after a couple of days. Yesterday she
massaged it on, and this morning I saw her with pitcher in hand, walking to
the pea field to shit. It worked because my mind was clean. With the right
attitude, Ganga water flows in a piece of wood. Listen, Budhua's mother, the
highest god is one's stomach. For the stomach, doing anything is right. Ramji
Maharaj said so." (Dulan's wife remarked that every time the old man stole
a pumpkin from the landlord's farm he said Ramji Maharaj approved.)

Bikhni interceded, asking for concrete advice on what they could do now,
two old women absolutely at the end of their means. Dulan said they could
try to cash in on the death of Bhairab Singh of Barohi village.

"How?"

"When someone dies in our homes, the near ones cry. In rich homes,
mother kills son, and son kills mother for money. When there is a death, the
near ones are too busy taking possession of the safe to cry for the dead.
Anyway, our landlord has advised them to hold a spectacular funeral. They
want *rudalis* to cry near the dead body. They brought two women for the job,
perhaps they were Bhairab Singh's women some time in the past, now like

old crows, but they are no good for the job. You two can go and cry near the body, go with the cremation procession and cry all the way, and you get paid in money and rice. Go again to cry on the day of *kiriya* and get food and cloth.''

Sanichari was outraged. "What are you saying? Don't you know that I can't cry? I never even cried for the dead in my family. Don't you know that my tears are burnt out?''

Dulan was not moved. He firmly said, "I'm not asking you to shed for Bhairab Singh the tears you could not shed for Budhua. I'm talking about crying as work, for earning money and food. You'll see, you can do it just the same way you can cut the wheat and carry the loads.''

"Why would they hire us?''

"Because Dulan has been asked to find good rudalis to match the prestige of Bhairab Singh. In the old days, Bhairab's father and Ramabatar used to look after their kept women, so when they died the women came and cried on their own. Now, Lachman and the likes of him squash their randis underfoot just as much as their laborers. So they don't get genuine rudalis any more; they must hire them. Bastards! The worst bastard is that Gambhir Singh: he took care of the daughter by his kept woman as long as she lived; as soon as she dies he asks the daughter to fend for herself, saying 'let the randi's daughter become a randi.' The poor girl is now in the *randipatti* of Tohri, a five-rupee randi working as a five-paisa randi. By the way, your daughter-in-law is there, too, reduced to a five-paisa randi.''

"Who wants to hear about her?''

"Remember to wear borderless black saris for the work.''

Dulan took them along. Bikhni was grateful and said that this kind of job once in a while and some farm labor or stone breaking for roads would do nicely for two stomachs.

Bhairab Singh's account keeper knew Dulan through Lachman Singh. The accountant was preoccupied with how to include in the list of articles to be purchased for the kiriya two shovels, a clothes rack, and two brass bowls that he needed for his own home. He said, "Three rupees each," as soon as he saw the two black-clad women. But Dulan was quick to bargain. "No less than five rupees for a rudali for the dead maharaj. Lachmanji told me that two hundred rupees are allowed for the rudali expense, as much as ten to twenty rupees each if needed. These two will do such a great job, you'll want to pay even more.''

The account keeper sighed, wondering how on earth Dulan came to know the amount allotted for the rudali expense, and agreed to pay five rupees each. But Dulan bargained for rice with the money and a good-sized snack right away because good wailing was not possible on an empty stomach. The account keeper sighed again but he had no choice. Bhairab Singh's first wife ordered a big snack of gur and parched rice for the rudalis, saying that her son's father had not left them poor.

While eating, Sanichari thought that perhaps all her tears were saved up
for the time when she would have to fill her stomach by crying.

The two marketplace randis who were wailing before did not pay much
attention to the two village women at first. But when Sanichari and Bikhni
started their act, their voices were so high-pitched and the words of praise for
Bhairab Singh so well-arranged that they had to beat retreat. At the end of
the day's wailing, the two old women took leave with five rupees and two and
a half kilos of rice each. They were asked to come back on the day of kiriya.
On the day of kiriya, their work was paid with cloth and cooked food including sweets, which they took home. Dulan fretted about the bastard accountant who sat on two hundred rupees allotted for rudalis and got away with
paying no more than twenty. But Sanichari was more accepting of such
stealing in high places.

Dulan told her to ask Bikhni to find out, from her trips to the marketplace,
if anyone was sick or dying in the landlord and moneylender families, because
most large stores belonged to them. He also told her to promise to her subsequent clients more wailers if needed. When Sanichari asked how she was
going to get more, he said that they could mobilize the large number of
whores in the marketplace of Tohri. Sanichari was shocked at the suggestion,
but Bikhni said that she did not mind going there to get additional wailers.

Dulan liked her attitude and remarked that not always did so many
women of their community become whores merely to feed themselves. The
real culprits were the Rajput landlords and moneylenders; they brought all
the bad things to their society. The remark made them think of what they
all had heard, of the times before the Rajputs came there and took over their
lands and their lives. Dulan recounted the history, in his own words, of
how the ruthless Rajputs came to rule this land of tribal and untouchable
communities.

The ancestors of these Rajput landlords were once part of the army of a
branch of the house of the king of Nagpur. About two hundred years back,
when the Kol tribals revolted against the many kinds of extortion by the
Hindu rulers, the king turned his foreign Rajput army loose on the native
tribals. Even after the Kol revolt was suppressed, the Rajput soldiers' aggres-
sive impulse was not quelled. They went on killing innocent Kols and burning even the peaceful villages. That forced Harda and Donka Munda to call
on their people to sharpen their spears again, and another Kol revolt was
imminent. The king then sent his uncontrollable Rajput officers to the
sparsely populated Tahad area. He told the seven officers to come down here
and take possession of as much land as could be covered by throwing the
sword in the course of one day and to live off the land. They threw their
swords from sunrise until sunset and took possession. That was how they
came to be the all-powerful landlords in this area. From one century to the
next, the amount of land in their possession has increased, although now they

increase their land, not by throwing swords through the air, but by throwing bullets at people and flaming torches at clusters of huts.

The landlords in the area today are related by ancestry, and, though there is now rivalry and competition among them, they are similar in their interests, attitudes, wealth, and oppressiveness. The homes of the tribals and the untouchables are all close to the ground—mud huts with worn potsherd roofs. The big houses of the landlords tower over their modest habitations. No landlord in the area has to buy anything except salt, kerosene, and postcards. They all own elephants, horses, buffaloes, mistresses and kept women, illegitimate children, venereal disease, and the attitude that land belongs to the gun holder. They all have deities worshiped in their family temples. The deities help them, as large tracts of land are held in the service of the family deity and hence out of reach of taxes and land reform.

Dulan was careful not to leave out the minor individual differences between the landlords, like the six toes of Daitari Singh, the stuffed tiger in Nathuni Singh's house, a mixing of milkman caste blood in Banwari Singh's wife.

He ended his account of the origins of Rajput landlord rule in their lives and the process of turning outcaste women into marketplace prostitutes by reminding Sanichari and Bikhni that they should mobilize the prostitutes as rudalis. It will help the landlords to compete for prestige in each other's eyes, and it will help the prostitutes feed themselves. "I've shown you the line; you make a career of it now."

The two women nodded in agreement. In their hard lives, getting the daily gruel and salt meant doing backbreaking work. The wealthy spent obscene amounts of money on the dead just to show off. Transferring some of that money to those like Sanichari was not at all a bad thing.

Sanichari and Bikhni took to their line of work with enthusiasm. Bikhni, from a different village and at her age, adapted well to the life of working as a laborer in the landlord's fields and working as a rudali for the landlord's dead. She became a part of this village. In her spare time she went to the marketplace or to the shops at the bus stop to collect information about who was dying in which malik family. Upon hearing of a potential client, they would wash the borderless black saris, put them on, pack some ground roasted peas and wheat to eat on the way, and set off for some malik house or other. They rehearsed the expressions and the bargaining strategies. They would directly approach the account keeper or rent collector of a landlord family and make their sales pitch. "The wailing will be so fantastic that it will drown even the *Rama-nam* chants. We will charge five rupees and rice. On the day of kiriya we want cloth and cooked food. Don't bargain, because we won't lower the rate. If you wish, we can bring more rudalis to be paid at the same rate."

Their clients generally had no choice but to accept their terms. After seeing or hearing about their performance at Bhairab Singh's funeral, all the rich families wanted them. They were professional. The landlord's accountant or estate manager knew that, being professionals themselves at manipulating the wages of laborers and the compound interest for peasant debtors, so professional that with a ten-rupee monthly salary they managed to acquire their own farms, their cattle, and often more than one wife. They knew that wailing for the unrelated unloved dead was professional work. In large cities affluent prostitutes vied for this profession, but Tohri was not a city, so the accountants did not have much choice.

Sanichari would then proceed to quote prices for additional features of the service: "That is the rate for just crying. If you want writhing on the ground while crying, then the rate is five rupees and a half. If you want us to beat our chests on the way to cremation and fling ourselves on the dust of the cremation ground and cry, that will cost six rupees. We prefer the sari at the kiriya to be borderless black." With maliks she would add her rehearsed touch: "That's our rate. But because you're a king, who, of course, has made the goddess Laxmi a captive in his house, you wouldn't even notice any difference to your wealth if you give us some lentils and oil with the rice, but Sanichari will sing your praise everywhere she goes."

Their business was going on very well. Ever since Bhairab Singh's funeral, it had become a status symbol to get these wailers. Soon the Lala shopowners and the Sahu moneylenders also started wanting their services. After Gokul Lala's father died, he asked Sanichari to come every day through the day of kiriya; he gave them food for that service, saying that giving to rudalis meant earning virtue. The cloth Gokul gave them was also better quality, unlike what the landlord-moneylenders gave. Bikhni sold the cloth in the market for cash.

Dulan was pleased to hear about the new custom started by Gokul Lala and advised the women to visit their future clients daily through the kiriya day. They're bound to give something to the black-clad rudali because not giving would earn them a bad name from those gathered. Sanichari was not so sure. She had seen Gangadhar Singh substitute hydrogenated oil for clarified butter to anoint the dead body of his uncle. She had seen them never shed a single tear for a dead father or brother. Dulan reminded her that if the relatives themselves cried for their dead, then she would be out of work.

Dulan then told them that Nathuni Singh's mother was about to die, and they were wanted there. He told them why this one was going to be a juicy client. "His mother was the only child of Parakram Singh, the ruthless landlord. As a child, I saw him tie his old tenant, Hathiram Mahato, to his horse's leg because of some unpaid rent and set the horse on the run, killing poor Hathiram in the process. Nathuni's mother owns all the property she inherited from her father. She has been suffering from the wasting fever for a long time; she coughs up fresh blood. Nathuni has done nothing to treat his mother; no doctor, no vaid, no injections, nothing. He has set up a separate shed for her in the yard and put her there with a black goat tied to her cot. None of the family goes in there. A Dusad woman is hired to clean up her excrement, and a *dai* to sleep nearby at night. She is still alive, and he is busy getting sandalwood and *sal* wood for her cremation, to promote his *maan*, his prestige among his peers. He has not spent a single rupee for her treatment, but he is going to spend thirty thousand rupees for her cremation and kiriya. In this cold winter, he has taken away her cotton stuffed quilt and given her a rag-stitched quilt so that she will die quicker. This one is going to be a big client; start going there from now. Be sure to visit his house every day through the day of kiriya. He'll pay whatever you want because he doesn't want to look smaller than Gokul Lala."

The cold of Magh soon killed Nathuni's mother. Sanichari and Bikhni went there every day, and they learned a lot about that family, about Nathuni's three wives.

On their daily visits, Nathuni's first wife reluctantly gave them flour and gur, while loudly remarking how silly it was to spend so much on the funeral of a mother who died merely of old age. Nathuni's second wife was the only offspring of a very rich landlord. Nathuni was rich because his father married the only daughter of a rich landlord. He wanted to do the same. Unfortunately for Nathuni, while his first and third wives were not jealous, his second wife was. She hated his cowives and looked down upon her husband's household as poor compared to her father's. The real reason for her anger was that she had only daughters but the cowives had sons. At the remark of the first wife, she smiled contemptuously and said that spending thirty thousand rupees on kiriya was nothing. She would show what spending meant when the time came for her father to pass away. The first wife replied that she would have to do that in order to compensate for her aunt having a mixture of barber blood. The second wife said that was a lie, and moreover everybody knew that the first wife's widowed sister lived with her dead husband's brother. A major quarrel broke out at this point.

The second wife of Nathuni must be virtuous because god seemed to have listened to her words. Soon after the death of Nathuni's mother, her father was on his deathbed with smallpox, and she sent for Sanichari. She at once gave Sanichari a rupee in tip and said that Nathuni's mother, who died on the inauspicious Tuesday, must be tugging at her father.

Sanichari assumed an air of innocence and said that she was told such beliefs prevailed only among the illiterate lower castes. That was why Sanichari and her folks took the government vaccination as well as worshiped the deity of the disease. Nathuni's second wife said that government vaccination was like cow's blood and quickly changed the topic. She asked Sanichari to bring to her father's place twenty randis as rudalis in addition to Bikhni and herself.

She promised to outdo the payments they had received at Nathuni's mother's funeral; she was going to give them lentils, oil, potatoes, salt, and gur with the rice, and she was willing to pay them more money if the wailing was good enough. Sanichari offered the special features: she and her company would not only wail but also roll on the ground and bang their heads until blood came out—the whole works. Nathuni's wife promised ten rupees each. Money was no consideration, she said, because her purpose was to shame her husband and his other wives. "The cremation and the kiriya have to match what my father is going to leave me. He drank his milk off a silver tumbler, kept women in his youth and in his old age too, never touched anything but 'foreign' liquor. After my mother died, he didn't remarry, thinking that the new wife might mistreat me."

Sanichari wanted an advance payment for the marketplace randis. Nathuni's second wife did not hesitate to pay even the advance.

Thus the funeral of Mohar Singh, Nathuni's second wife's father, became the stuff of legend in more ways than one. The prestige from overspending at the funeral became more coveted among the maliks. The demand for Sanichari's wailing service increased. The priests, who got the lion's share of any spending on any funeral, were now getting more because of the competition. The maliks recovered their overspending from the hides of the Dusad and Ganju and Kol peasants and debtors.

3

When Sanichari told Dulan about what Nathuni's wife had agreed to pay and her request for additional wailers, Dulan smiled his sly smile and said that Sanichari should now form a union of wailing whores, like the union of laborers in the coal mines, and that she should become its president. Sanichari was aghast. But Bikhni readily offered to go to Tohri on market day and recruit prostitutes for the job. She said that the whores were not a caste apart; they were only women whom the landlords and creditors had used and discarded. To back up Bikhni's point, Dulan told Sanichari about the latest misdeed of Gambhir Singh of Nawagarh, "the one who went around the Diwali fair on his elephant."

Gambhir Singh doted on his kept woman Motia. He used to have Motia's daughter Gulbadan bounce on his lap with her anklet-wearing feet when she was little. After Motia died, he said he was going to get Gulbadan nicely married. But Dulan had just seen Gulbadan crying and going toward Tohri, barely three months after Motia's death. She said that her father had turned her out of his house. When Dulan asked why, she said that she merely complained about the trouble his nephew was giving her for refusing to be his mistress. Her father got angry, called her a randi's daughter, and asked her to obey his nephew or else get out and fend for herself. Gulbadan said that she would rather be a marketplace randi than a randi for her father's nephew.

Gulbadan's turn of luck made Sanichari sad, though all that she said was: "Such a beauty! Sure to be picked up by some rich merchant."

Bikhni came back from her trip to the prostitute area of Tohri and reported to Sanichari that they were all keen to work as wailers. Sanichari, for the first time, wanted to know about the prostitutes—how they lived, how they looked. Bikhni told her that they were a sad lot, all those four-anna whores, prematurely aged, still having to stand at the door, smoky oil lamp in hand and kohl in their sunken eyes. Bikhni told her that she saw Budhua's wife there; she had been there for the last ten years; she looked older than Sanichari; she asked Bikhni about her son Haroa.

"What did you tell her?"

"What could I tell her? Why should I? I didn't speak to her."

"You did the right thing."

That evening Sanichari thought about her daughter-in-law, for the first time in many years. While eating gourd curry and lumpy wheat bread, she recalled the big appetite of hers. The year she left home, when Budhua died, was the year a herd of elephants came up on the rail lines and knocked over a standing locomotive engine. The tree in the yard now bearing the sour mangoes was only a seedling that year. Ten years she had been living in Tohri, as a whore! Lucky for Haroa that he ran away before finding out about his mother.

After the meal, when she sat smoking with Bikhni, she was still thinking of her daughter-in-law and finally spoke out, "Perhaps she didn't know that I wouldn't have turned her out after Budhua's death. Did she seem to be very poor, in very bad condition?"

"Very bad," Bikhni said, and Sanichari fell silent again.

Soon Mohar Singh died. His funeral was an unprecedented spectacle. The marketplace whores who came to wail took leave of Sanichari and Bikhni gratefully, respectfully requesting them to send word any time they wanted them again. Bikhni sold the cloth, the bamboo umbrella, and the paper-thin brass bowl they got for their work, and with that money she bought a whole sackful of insect-eaten corn she was going to turn into flour.

As time went by, funeral wailing became for the two women a part of their regular work life of mixed occupations. They did a couple of wailings a year, bought their provisions and had their bellies full for a while. The rest of the year, like everybody else, they worked as field hands with half-empty bellies; when that work was not available, they weeded the landlord's fields and collected roots to eat from the forest.

Bikhni stayed on, to the surprise of everyone, without leaving even once to see her son. She raised a crop of chilies in Sanichari's yard, sold it in the market, and decided to grow garlic next, as it fetched a better price.

Their reputation as wailers grew; their clients all agreed that their price was high but they did a good job. They really banged their heads and rolled in the dust, they did not fake it, and the way they sang the praise of the deceased made even his near ones momentarily forget that he was a scoundrel and feel as if he were an angel strayed from heaven into earth.

Things went on smoothly, except for the occasional disappointment of the recovery of some malik who had seemed about to die. Business was slack for two years. Nathuni's first wife's brother was about to die of dropsy, but came back well from hospital. Their own village landlord Lachman's stepmother was brought back from certain death with rheumatic fever by some outside vaid.

Sanichari was worried about this kind of setback to her new business. From the viewpoint of his sideline business, the barber Parashnath was worried too. He thought it was immoral to keep sick old people alive with medicine; it got in the way of the life's design in which deaths and births were supposed to go hand in hand. Sanichari sighed and said that it affected her worse than him: "They need your services at births, weddings, and deaths. Think of my plight." Bikhni did not give up: "It was not time for them to die. So they didn't. They will when the time is up." Dulan did not think much of such temporary setbacks. He remarked that Sanichari was worried only because she had been eating better on account of it. He joked by giving the example of Lachman's stepmother, who would cry when they made money with a bumper crop, thinking that the next crop might not be as good.

The following year, luck did take a good turn for Sanichari's funeral wailing. One day Bikhni came home with the "good news" that Gambhir Singh was about to die with the same coughing fever Nathuni's mother died of some years ago. His nephew, who was going to inherit the property because Gambhir Singh had no son, had promptly set up a shack in the yard and put him in it with a black goat, declaring that because tuberculosis was Shiva's disease to treat it would be an insult to the Lord. Bikhni had heard it from Parashnath the barber, the most reliable source of information on the circumstances of deaths, births, and marriages. She had also learned that Gambhir Singh, unhappy about the black goat and the shack, had not only ordered his lawyer to make sure that his nephew spent one lakh rupees on a truly spectacular kiriya after his death but had also started holding *pujas* and *yagnas* while he was still alive, declaring that he was going to make sure that no money would be left for the scoundrel.

So, a big job was coming up for them. Meanwhile, Bikhni said that she was going away for only a few days to Ranchi. Why? She had happened to see her husband's nephew in the marketplace. He wanted her to come to his daughter's wedding. At first she did not think of going, but then it occurred to her that her son might come to the wedding, too. If she went, then she might be able to see him without suffering the indignity of going to his in-laws' place or appearing weak-willed. She promised Sanichari that she would be back in four days, well in time for Gambhir Singh's funeral, and asked her to keep track of the goings on there.

Sanichari walked with her the three miles to the bus stop, put her in the bus, and advised her to sit on the bus floor for two rupees instead of in a seat for eight rupees. Walking back alone, she pondered on how extraordinary the bus trip to Ranchi city must be for her friend, who had never used any other means of transportation except her own legs, and hence never been anywhere beyond walkable distance. It also seemed unusual that her nephew-in-law should be living in a big city like Ranchi.

Everybody told Sanichari how lucky it was in her relentlessly unlucky life to find Bikhni, her childhood friend and such a hardworking old woman who was now taking care of Sanichari's household. They reflected on the unforeseeable, inscrutable turns of fate, on how the bark from an unrelated distant tree could come to adhere to another tree.

Sanichari felt lonely in her home without Bikhni. She went out to collect firewood from the forest the way Bikhni did. Bikhni always came home carrying something that she collected for home use: a few twigs, a rope she found on the way, a lump of cowdung, anything that could be useful in running the household. Sanichari was baffled by Bikhni's assiduous housekeeping at her age, when she was left with practically no home or family of her own.

A few days went by. Gambhir Singh's condition deteriorated as expected. Sanichari went there one day to talk to the account keeper. She learnt that although they declared that he had tuberculosis he was really dying of venereal disease. The sins he had committed with endless women throughout his life were now rotting his flesh away. That was why Gambhir Singh was holding so many pujas and yagnas, in the hope of divine mercy to ease his pain.

The account keeper said that the malik was planning to die in the period of the waxing moon. Sanichari asked why. The account keeper said with authority that he could then go straight to heaven and would not have to visit hell first as Yudhisthira, who died in the period of the waning moon, had to. Sanichari did not know much about the puranic characters, but she had no doubt about their greatness, thanks to the calendar portraits of the holy characters modeled on the film stars who acted the roles. Puzzled by the accountant's answer, she said, "But malik-parwar is not Yudhisthira." The accountant patiently explained to the illiterate woman that virtue and sin all depended on the point of view. Bad people would call malik a sinner, saying that he had robbed when he was a young man at the time his father was the landlord and the British were the rulers, that he had killed at least a thousand citizens of independent India, set fire to many Dusad homes, and taken the honor of many women. But malik himself did not think he was a sinner. Hence he had called the astrologers to find out what was the sin that earned him the terrible disease. Sanichari's curiosity was aroused. She asked if they had found out his sin. The accountant said that the only sin they could find was that malik had once hit a pregnant cow with a stick when he was a little boy.

The accountant assured her that malik would die exactly when he wanted to because he had always gotten exactly what he wanted. The accountant also approved of malik's plan to squander his money on his own death because the nephew was not fit to inherit the property. Why not, Sanichari asked. Because, the accountant said, the nephew kept a Muslim woman; the women that the uncle had, no matter how many, were Hindus after all. He told Sanichari that he was going to leave the job once the kiriya was over, but before he left he was going to make sure that the expenditure on his malik's funeral was enough to make people forget the stories about Mohar Singh's cremation and kiriya. He wanted Sanichari to back up his plans by rendering truly spectacular wailing. Sanichari said that she certainly would do her best.

Six days were gone since Bikhni had left saying she would be back in four days. She was not back. To relieve her anxiety, Sanichari ground some corn in the grinding stone, sunned the bed and the rag quilts, and then went out to do her turn of compulsory labor for the repair of the Panchayat's shed. When she returned home carrying a bunch of twigs, she found a barefoot stranger with shaved head waiting for her. She asked him if he was Bikhni's husband's nephew. He said yes. Sanichari knew why he had come. She felt shattered, but with the stoicism acquired from a whole life of bearing losses, deaths, and oppression, she asked him to sit down and then sat down herself. She was silent for a while before asking when Bikhni died. Four days ago, he said. The day, she counted on her fingertips, she was at the place of Gambhir Singh. What did she die of? Her asthma became worse and complicated with a chest cold she had from drinking a glass of iced *sharbat* on the hot trip to Ranchi. Sanichari recalled that Bikhni as a little girl had always craved things like cold colorful sharbat, candied fruit, and spicy digestive lozenges. He brought in a good doctor, who tried medicines and injections, but she did not live. Sanichari had treated Bikhni's asthma differently. She would beat a few cockroaches with the broom, catch them, boil them, have her take a bit of that extract, and Bikhni would breathe normally again. Was she at least able to see her son there? No, because her son did not come to the wedding.

After the man had taken leave, Sanichari sat alone for a long time trying to assess her feelings. What was it that she was feeling? Was it sorrow or was it fear? She felt fear, not just sorrow, with which she was very familiar. She tried to understand why she was so scared this time. Was it because Bikhni's death was a setback for her wailing job? Was she afraid that she would become poorer now, her subsistence more insecure? Or was she afraid because she was growing old? In their life, the old always worked, and it would be better to be able to work to the last day. For them, the only alternative to being old and working was being old and debilitated. Her own aunt became like a bundle; they set her out in the sun before leaving for work each day; one day they came back and found her dead and stiff exactly where they had left her. Sanichari did not want to die like that. She also knew that no one died of sorrow; if one did, she would have been dead by now. Even after the worst grief, people would take a bath, eat the meals, drive away the goat nibbling at the chilies, and do everything in order. People died only when they had nothing to eat. If Sanichari had survived all those losses, she would survive that of Bikhni, too. She felt very sad, but she was not going to cry. Shedding tears without getting money, cloth, and food in exchange seemed to her a foolish luxury.

She got up and went to talk to Dulan. Dulan immediately saw the seriousness of the matter. "Look, Budhua's mother, you know that it is not right to give up one's own land. For you, this wailing job is like your own land. You can't let go of it. This funeral wailing is no passing craze. They are downright serious about their prestige, so serious that they're fighting over it, even dying for it. Look at Gambhir Singh. He knows that he can be cured with allopathic medicine, but he is not even trying to be cured because he is obsessed with how to jack up his position after death; he is thinking only of the splendor of his funeral."

"I don't care to know about their honor and their stupid rivalries."

"After Budhua's father died, didn't you take up the work that he used to do in the malik's field? In the same way you must take up the part that Bikhni did before she died. You must go to the randipatti in Tohri yourself now. You must bring as many of them as you can for the wailing. Otherwise, that money is going to be pocketed by Gambhir Singh's accountant or nephew."

"But I can't go there, because . . ."

"Because Budhua's wife is there? Doesn't she qualify as a discarded randi who now lives as a four-anna whore? Call her too."

"Her too?"

"Of course. Doesn't she have to eat? If a bit of the malik-mahajans' money flows to the marketplace randis, then it's not a bad thing. So many of them were once personal randis of the malik-mahajans and then got kicked out by them to end up in the filthy market."

Sanichari had never given much thought to how all the marketplace whores came to be where they were. But she had been thinking of two of them, Budhua's wife who left home because she could not get used to living on a half-empty stomach and Gulbadan who had regarded Gambhir Singh's nephew as her brother, but whom Gambhir Singh and his nephew had never regarded as more than a randi. She agreed to do as Dulan suggested. Dulan reassured her that in their lives the calculation of virtue and sin could never be made without reference to their hunger. No one would think ill of her if she helped the prostitutes merely to fill their hungry stomachs.

Gambhir Singh of Nawagarh finally died after seventeen days.

When his breathing became spasmodic, Sanichari put on her borderless black sari and set out for Tohri. She did not feel embarrassed to ask people for directions to the randipatti. She kept telling herself that the most important criterion distinguishing virtue from sin was whether it helped put food in hungry stomachs. As soon as she reached the cluster of shacks of whores, she started calling the names she had heard from Bikhni.

"Rupa, Budhni, Somri, Gangu, where are you? Come here! You've got a job to do."

They came crowding around her. They were surprised that Sanichari herself had come. She explained that Bikhni was dead, but that she was going to carry on. She looked around the crowd and spotted a distantly familiar face in the back.

"Is that Budhua's wife? Come closer, *bahu*. Gulbadan, you too come along with me. Gambhir Singh is dying. Cry for him, and take money for crying. Nothing to be embarrassed about. Don't miss your chance to rub salt in their face and take whatever revenge you can. Let's go now. Each will get five rupees and rice, and clothing on the day of the kiriya."

There was excitement and scrambling around her. The younger whores came up to her and asked what about them. Sanichari said that they could come too. Because they would have to do this work anyway when they became older, they had better be trained by her while she lived. Everybody was curiously happy and excited. They brought a cane stool for Sanichari to sit. They brought her tea and bidis. Then they all started with her for Nawagarh.

Gambhir Singh's nephew and all the others assembled there were stunned to see the battalion arrive with Sanichari. The account keeper hissed at her, "Brought the entire randitoli along? Nearly a hundred of them!"

"Why not?" she asked loudly for all to hear. "Didn't the malik want the wailing at his funeral to be so spectacular that it would become a legend? How can a legend be made with some ten wailers? Get out of our way now; let us start our work. The malik now belongs to us."

Gambhir Singh's swollen corpse gave off the smell of decomposed sores. It was now surrounded by Sanichari's flock, wailing and hitting their heads. Tears came to the account keeper's eyes as he realized that nothing was going to be left for him because they would have to be paid twice as much for hitting their heads while wailing. He and the nephew helplessly looked on.

Gulbadan looked up for a moment, dry-eyed from her wailing and head banging. She winked at the nephew and sneered viciously.

Next moment she listened carefully to the lead voice of Sanichari and rejoined the chorus.

Strange Children

Mahasweta Devi

1

The place is called Lohri. It is located at the meeting point of three districts of Bihar—Ranchi, Sarguja, and Palamau—although officially it is part of Ranchi. It does not look like any other area in the region, not like any earthly place at all. The entire place looks like a burnt out valley; it looks as if the temperature is extremely high just beneath the surface. The trees are all stunted, the riverbed dry like a cremation ground, the villages shrouded in dust and smoky heat. The soil has a strange, dark copper color. Even in this region of reddish soil, one never comes across such dark brownish red earth. It is a lifeless sort of red, the color of dried blood.

The relief officer was being briefed during his overnight stop before the last leg of his journey to the godforsaken place called Lohri. He was known as an honest and compassionate public servant. He had been carefully selected for the task and variously forewarned that the place where he was going on the special assignment was rather difficult. He was being told so once again. "The inhabitants don't have any honest way of living."

"What do you mean?"

"They don't cultivate, for one thing."

"Why not? Haven't they got any land?"

The man talking with him was the block development officer inside his bungalow. The outside was not cooled yet. Later in the night, the watchman of the bungalow was going to make his bed on a rope cot outside in the compound. Nobody here sleeps indoors, as it becomes hotter at night.

The relief officer was on loan from the food department for just three

"Shishu" appears in Mahasweta's *Nairhite Megh* (Calcutta: Karuna Prakashani, 1979), 94–112.

months to handle this assignment. Never had he seen such a lifeless, discon-
certing place. His first glimpse of the people coming to collect the relief
supplies was far from pleasant. They were almost naked, emaciated creatures, bellies swollen with worms and sick spleen. He had always had an
image of tribal men playing flutes and tribal women, with flowers in their
oiled black hair, dancing to the tune. Somehow, he had always visualized
them singing and running in the hills.

When he left the jeep at the foot of a hill, having to walk toward one of the
villages above, he realized that running up the hill must be close to impossible. He was out of breath walking. He had always thought that singing had
a very important role in tribal life. Now he could hear them singing in the
distance. It was monotonous and whiny, like the wailing of a lonely old
witch. He was terribly disappointed. His images of tribal life had been drawn
from the movies, particularly Hindi movies. If this was their song, then how
would their mourning wail sound? He was disturbed and uncomfortable with
his first taste of the place.

"Why do they do that awful singing all the time?"

"Because they're primitive people. Whatever goes wrong is to them the
work of evil spirits. They're singing to drive the spirits away."

The block development officer caught the relief officer's slight unease at
the mention of the word *spirits*. He smiled and asked if he was afraid.

"Certainly not."

"Even this drought and famine are to them due to the curse of spirits.
. . . It's a terrible place. Any decent place would have a Hindu community
and a temple of Mahabirji with a holy banner flying atop. No such thing
here. I'm dying to be transferred. Any place but this!"

"Where exactly am I supposed to go tomorrow?"

"Lohri. The people there are the weirdest of the lot. If you gave them land,
they would sell it to the moneylender. Then they would glare at you and
sullenly complain, 'Where's water? Where's seed? Where's the plow, and
the buffalo? How can we cultivate without those?' But even if you gave them
those things, they would sell everything to the moneylender and then argue
back, 'What are we supposed to eat until the crop is ready? We'd borrowed
to eat. We have to repay the loan with the land.'"

"How long do I have to stay there?"

"You'll set up the relief camp. You must stay until the camp is in running
order. I'll send help with you. Don't worry, and don't be afraid."

"What's there to be afraid of?"

"Thieves."

"Thieves?"

"Yes. Every time the relief supplies are sent up there, some small children
come in the dead of night and steal them. A sack or two at a time. Rice, milo,
gur, anything they can find."

"Small children?"

"Yes. Isn't it strange? Nobody manages to catch them. Some have seen them. Once I saw them myself. I even had the gun with me at the time, but . . ."

"You keep a gun with you?"

"I have a license for a gun. As I said, Lohri is a really wicked place. About ten years back, or maybe twelve, there was a massacre. A lot of trouble. The whole place really heated up. A village was burned down by the police."

The block development officer said that it had happened before he started on his present job. He paused and asked the relief officer if he had heard the legend about Lohri. The relief officer had heard no such thing, and he did not care to hear it now. He had come to the terrible place, leaving behind the lights and attractions of Ranchi, only because he had been assigned. He did not answer. The block development officer proceeded to tell him anyway.

"The people who live here, I mean over there, are the Agariyas; they were once blacksmiths. According to the legend, the Agariyas are descendants of subterranean demons. Their occupation was to dig up iron from underground and forge ironware in furnaces in their workshops. They used to eat fire, bathe in a river of fire, and Lohri was their city. Their king's name was Logundi. The demons let only the Agariyas, and nobody else, enter underground to collect the iron ore. King Logundi was one of twelve brothers. They shared one wife."

"Sounds juicier than Draupadi," remarked the relief officer.

"Their king Logundi became too proud, believing that he was stronger than the Sun. The Sun then turned the full blast of his glare to Lohri. It burnt the king, it burnt his eleven brothers, it burnt their city of Lohri, everything. The wife was in a different village at the time, and she survived. Driven by the scorching heat all around her, she ran to a milkman's place and cooled inside the vat of buttermilk. There, under a little tree, she later gave birth to a son who was named Jwalamukhi. When Jwalamukhi became a young man, he challenged the Sun to wrestle with him. The ground where they wrestled in Lohri was completely burned by their heat. After the fight, Jwalamukhi cursed the Sun that he would be unable to unite with his moon-wife, except during the full moon. The Sun cursed Jwalamukhi that the wealth the Agariyas had accumulated through their work as blacksmiths would turn to ashes and blow away. The Agariyas have remained poor ever since. This is the legend, a primitive one, as you can see."

"Of course, it's all primitive."

"The Agariyas thus behave so strangely even to this day. They've lost their traditional occupation as blacksmiths, and they're hard to start in farm work. They believe that they're in a state of impurity. That's why the iron-demon does not give them iron, the coal-demon does not give them coal, and the fire-demon does not grant them the right kind of fire. They still believe that their day will come again."

"Tell me about the trouble and the massacre you mentioned before."

"About twelve or fourteen years ago, the government of India sent a team to explore for iron ore in Lohri. The people of a village called Kuva were the most troublesome of the Agariyas. They said that because their three demon gods lived inside the hill they could not let anyone explore there. Why should two Punjabi officers and a Madrasi geologist back out because of some story of demon gods? They went ahead and blasted the hill.

"Then the Agariyas from Kuva village came in the night and butchered them. After that, they escaped into the forest and just disappeared."

"Disappeared?"

"Yes. Just imagine, Mr. Singh, they vanished in the forest and were lost forever. As if they had metamorphosed into something else! Nobody has seen them since. One hundred to one hundred and fifty people simply vanished!"

"That's unbelievable."

"That's the strange thing I'm talking about. They vanished without a trace. Without a clue."

"Didn't the government investigate?"

"They did. They combed the forest, as thoroughly as a Brahman widow picks old rice clean of mites. But they couldn't find a single one of them."

"Was any other action taken?"

"The government carried on the search for one whole month. Except for Kuva village, nobody was missing from any other village. The investigation showed nobody else involved in the crime. When the investigation was over and the villagers could not be found, the police burned down Kuva village, poured salt over its soil, and left. To teach the other Agariya villages a lesson, the police did a few things to their people, beating them up and confiscating their things."

"No news of those missing people to this day?"

"No news whatsoever."

"Where could they have gone?"

"The forest has so many caves and hills, you know."

"Why do you take a gun when you go to Lohri?"

"The place scares me. So many people missing! Who knows where they're hiding, to jump on you from who knows where?"

"Is that the only reason?"

"No."

"What is it?"

"Every time the relief supplies are sent there, some get stolen. It used to be four or five sacks. In the last few years, a bit less, about two or three sacks get stolen. Besides, the place itself is really nasty. Who knows what's there in the soil? Nothing grows in it. Once my nephew tried to grow some crops, but nothing came of it. The soil grows no rice, no wheat, no maize, no millet, nothing. The plowshare can't enter the soil, as if it's all iron right underneath. It's a cursed land. One look is enough to remove any doubt."

"Has the stealing continued?"

"Yes. They reported that some strange-looking small children came in the dead of night to steal. Naturally, I thought that relief supplies were stolen as usual by those in charge of the distribution. They steal and sell in the market, and the government can never catch them. As you know, no matter if it's summer or winter, they send blankets and clothes along with the food in relief supplies. What will these primitive people do with woolen blankets and clothes and sugar? They will sell them for a few matchboxes, flashlights, or hand mirrors. Knowing that, the relief distributors sell it themselves. There's nothing unusual about it."

"But it's wrong."

"Such wrong things go on all the time. Don't you remember the relief supplies released from Calcutta at the time of the Bangladesh war? Clothes, blankets, shoes, stoves, pots, and pans donated from all over the world. Didn't they turn up in the markets of Ranchi, and didn't we buy them?"

"That's true."

"Anyway. I assumed that they stole themselves and made up the story about some children stealing. Once I went myself with twenty thousand rupees worth of relief supplies. I even took some armed guards along. The relief camp was going to be set up at Lohri for people to come from all the villages for their rations. The night was very dark, black like hair, and it was very hot. I was sleeping outside. Suddenly I woke up to a strange sound. I got up and saw these little people, must be children, running away with a sack of food."

"What did you do then?"

"I fired in the air. What could I do? I couldn't shoot children. They got away. They were naked, only children! How could I shoot them? But . . ."

The block development officer frowned and stared into the dark for some time. The darkness was very thick and hot, like some melting and dripping substance, smothering absolutely everything, plugging all the cracks and holes that might let in any light. The air was so thick with dust and heat rising from the ground that it dimmed the light of the stars in the sky. The new moon was to rise very late that night.

The block development officer resumed, overcoming whatever it was that made him hesitate. "I've told nobody else. You're a trustworthy man; your uncle is a state minister. What I'm going to tell you, I've told nobody else. I'm telling you only to prepare you."

"What is it?"

"You know, Mr. Singh, the place has such bad associations. All these things about demons, spirits, ghosts, and what not. I distinctly saw that the children running away with a sack were not like human children."

"What do you mean?"

"Their limbs were somehow different from ours. Abnormal."

"Different in what ways?"

"I can't quite describe it. They had unusually long hair for children, and they sniggered strangely at me as they ran away!"

"Now I am scared."

"Don't be. It's to tell you this that I've stayed on tonight instead of leaving for Tahad as I had planned. Your uncle is a state minister, and your life is my responsibility. Here, I've got Mahabirji's *prasad* for you. Keep it in your pocket. No fear can touch you as long as it is with you."

"But I don't have a gun."

"That should be all right. You'll have attendants with you."

"What about an armed guard, at least a policeman. . . ?"

"It's too late to get any now. You're leaving tomorrow. All right. I'll try to send a policeman with those going to join you in a few days."

"Shall we have dinner now because we have to start early tomorrow?"

"Would you like to have a bath first?"

The relief officer took a bath with the cool water freshly drawn from the well. Then, his uncle being a state minister, he found at the table the best quality rice for dinner. Fresh peas in the fried rice, meat, pickles, and dark-brown syrupy *gulabjamuns* to end the meal with.

His bed was ready outside in a cot, the ground under and around it cooled by sprinkling water.

But sleep seemed to elude him. The image of a boy wrestling with the sun. A hill, with gods dwelling inside. The sudden flash of axes in the dark of night. Murdered bodies lying around. The image of a Brahman widow sitting all day long, peering and picking through old rice for mites. The police picking through the forest for fugitives. The relief camp. Children, not quite human, running away with stolen sacks of rice. Rows of images marched through his brain. When he felt heat on his face, he realized that he had been asleep the whole time. The sun was on his face.

2

The relief officer started off that morning. Supplies and camping equipment went in the truck. The block development officer left for Tahad.

Very soon the road gave way to a dirt track. The vehicles could go through because it was summer. It must be impossible during monsoon. They passed a relief center opened by missionaries at the mission house. Groups of people were going there. They were all black, thin, and silent!

The jeep driver, watching them, spat out the window and remarked, "They're inhuman! As soon as there's a drought, they leave their babies at the mission door. . . . The white missionaries turn them into Christians, ruining our religious tradition. But these people are wicked too. They become Christians but go on worshiping their spirits and demons."

"Don't the missionaries know about it?"

"They know. Still, they give them medicine and nurse them. The rosy-cheeked white women hold the babies of those animals in their laps and kiss their faces. . . . Just listen to them singing. Would any normal people anywhere sing like that at this time of the day?"

Their singing, that infernally slow wailing, came in waves from the surrounding hills and forests, and hit them sitting inside the moving jeep.

"Why are they singing?"

"They're strange! Those who still can walk go to pick up the relief. Those who can't, the very old, sit in a circle and sing like that. They sing on and on, until they die. When the singing starts in one village, the old women about to die in another village send the young to the relief camp and then sit down to start their own singing."

The relief officer felt as if he were drowning. He thought of the city of Ranchi—the lights, the taxis, the motor cars. The sparkling life was flowing on there, but he was going to a bizarre place where subhuman children sniggered and ran away with relief supplies. There was nothing to see along the way but dusty hills and dull stretches of forest that held old women, who, faced with the prospect of death, didn't even try to live but just sat around in a circle and wailed their chorus for death.

"Have many of them died already?"

"Many. Look at all those vultures and kites flying above. Some are even eaten alive by the vultures! It's a really weird place."

"How far is it to Lohri?"

"We are entering it. See the strange copper color everywhere, on the ground, on the hills, in the trees! That's Lohri. There's poison in its soil."

A cluster of hills could be seen further off. The driver said that was where the relief camp was going to be set up. After some silence, the driver said, "There's something I want to tell you, sir. Please don't take offense. We don't know what's there in Lohri, but we feel scared when we're there. We'll drink, if you don't mind, and we'll stay close to the camp. We're too scared otherwise, after Bahadur went out of his mind with fear."

"Who's Bahadur?"

"The earlier driver. Didn't the officer *saab* tell you about him?"

"No."

"He should have."

"What happened to Bahadur?"

"Nobody still knows exactly what. Those who were with him said that they were all deep asleep that night. Suddenly they heard Bahadur shouting "Thief! Thief!" Then they saw him run after somebody and disappear in the pitch dark. Those who went looking for him ran right back when they heard a strange laughter somewhere out in the dark. Next morning, they found Bahadur lying unconscious. His consciousness returned but not his senses."

"What happened to him after that?"

"He became raving mad. He still is, in the lunatic asylum at Ranchi. Here, we're at our destination."

The camp site had already been cleared. The tax collector of the area was there. He emerged from a shack and asked the relief officer to have some tea. He said that he had got some water stocked for him if he wanted to bathe, water that had to be hauled from a place half a mile away.

"From that tank?" asked the driver.

"Yes, from that one," said the collector.

At the puzzled look of the relief officer, the tax collector explained, "During the Kuva incident, the hill was dynamited. The blast made a crater in the hillside. Water collects in it during the monsoon and serves as our water supply for the rest of the year."

After they finished having tea, the tax collector put up the tent and stacked the relief supplies, carefully counting the number of sacks.

"Don't worry about what I'm doing," he said to the relief officer. "I do it every time. I even have the list of names of the villages to be covered. Distribute relief from ten to four, and the day's work is over."

"How many are expected to come in a day?"

"A thousand, two thousand. Don't know exactly how many will come this time."

"There will be a medical unit this time. They'll need a tent. Set one up for them."

"Very well. But how come? No medical unit ever came along before."

"This Janata government wasn't in office before either, and a special relief officer didn't come here before to take charge."

The tax collector thought, "Son of a pig!" But he said, "As you wish, sir."

"Those who have come from the Sardoha mission will also work with us."

"Them too?"

"Yes. Because they've got nurses and a doctor."

"Very well, sir."

"We need people to bring water, to keep the camp clean, to clean the pots and pans for cooking the relief food. Pick up ten young men from the villages to be hired. Take down their names. They'll work here, have their meals here, and get a rupee a day."

"They always work for just the meals, sir."

"Are you here to instruct me or to follow my instruction? I'm going to run the camp. But you'll have to come once a day."

"For how long is the camp going to remain open?"

"A month, for now. This one is in my charge. There's going to be a camp every twenty miles. And one more thing. I'll sleep close to the tent with the food storage because it's my personal responsibility."

"That, of course, is the right thing to do. However, I would not stay with the stores even for a hundred rupees."

"Why not?"

"There's stealing at night. Those who come to steal are not human."

"Ignore those tales. College students are coming to work as volunteers. They are going to deliver the relief supplies for those who can't come. Tell the people in the villages that their old folks need not sing the death song."

The tax collector was amazed, speechless. Every year he stole the relief supplies and enriched himself. He was utterly dishonest. But he was also very efficient. He immediately picked ten Agariya youths from the villages and hired them for cleaning and servicing the camp.

Next day, with the help of the two watchmen, he laid out the day's relief supplies under the tree. Only dry foodstuff was to be distributed the first day. From the next day on, there would be *khichri* for everybody and milk for the children.

He told the relief officer that the Agariya youths would be staying there at nights beside the storage tent, guarding it.

"None of us wants to be near it at night. It's not right to let you sleep there alone. So, that's what I arranged."

The relief officer felt his suppressed anxiety diminish. The camp was started promptly and very systematically. Khichri was cooked and distributed from the following day. The medics gave shots against cholera and typhoid. The camp site was buzzing with activity.

People were coming from distant villages. From afar little lights could be seen moving toward the camp even after darkness fell. Because of the scorching heat during the day, many found it easier to walk to it in the evening, in groups, carrying lighted torches of oil-dipped rags.

After a few days, even the tax collector complimented the officer, saying that with his highly efficient relief work he had brought hope to the minds of even those hopeless primitive people. Earlier, the old folks knew they were bound to die and sat singing. Now the singing had stopped. He made a suggestion: "There seems to be no need to send supplies to the villages. Because the relief distribution is going on so well this time, why not ask the able-bodied villagers to them bring the old folks along on their backs?"

"No, no. Hunger makes people unkind. Anyone they don't bring would then die. Besides, how are they going to carry the old all the way here? They're too weak. Some of them even die on the way coming here."

The relief officer became extremely involved with this work, with earning credit as an efficient administrator. The place, with its look of dusty burnt clay, its forests of stunted gray-brown leafless trees, the savage reddish hills, all seemed less terrifying now. Its starving destitute people soon assumed top priority in his mind. The young medics left after finishing the vaccination. He promised to help even the doctors and nurses from the mission. Although the regulation allowed for only cholera and typhoid vaccines, he got around that to procure from Ranchi supplies of antibiotics, salve for sores, baby food, even packets of nutri-nugget.

3

The ten Agariya youths remain clustered around him all the time, unwilling only to accompany him to the tank in the blasted hill for his bath after the busy day because they are forbidden to go to it. They take him instead to the hidden spring in the Lohri river, their own water source. There, while bathing in the cool water, he listens to them tell him in their words the legend of the fight between the Sun and Jwalamukhi. Jwalamukhi, an Agariya youth, is their hero, even though because of him they are now poor. Yet the power of his curse prevents the Sun from uniting with his wife except on the full moon. The Agariyas are suffering because the three demon-gods of iron, coal, and fire have withheld their blessings. It takes him well past evening to come back from the bathing trip in the company of the youths.

Lying down for the night in his rope cot in front of the storage tent, he does a lot of thinking. He is convinced that to cover up their own excessive stealing the people in charge had spread that story of child-shaped spirits stealing relief supplies. He starts wondering about how the condition of the Agariyas of Lohri could be improved. An honest and compassionate man is certainly needed, someone who could rehabilitate them in farming. He must write an official note about it as soon as he is back in Ranchi. It is not enough to keep these people barely alive by sending them relief year after year. He falls asleep with these thoughts. He sleeps without anxiety. The Agariya youths are also sleeping near the tent. They have addressed him as *deota*; to him, that feels like winning a trophy. These people, notorious for their unwillingness to trust anyone outside their community, have addressed him as deota. That certainly is a victory for an honest, well-meaning official.

But the ten Agariya youths do not sleep. They stay awake, alert, listening hard. The camp is much bigger this time, with many more people, much more noise. Is that why they are not hearing what they are trying to hear?

Then one night they hear the expected footsteps, several pairs of feet approaching in the cautious manner of pack-hunting animals. There is a muffled whistle, answered by another whistle. They get up and untie some ropes of the tent. Then there are activities, quick and silent. The youths lift the flap at the tent's entrance. The new moon is rising after midnight. Several pairs of small hands remove a sack of rice and a sack of milo.

At that moment the relief officer wakes up. He sits up with his flashlight and finds the Agariya youths gone. Quickly he goes to the other side of the tent and finds the youths tying the tent back to the stakes. Why? Why is the tent's flap lifted? Puzzled and hurt at the betrayal of his trust, he looks at their faces. Strange, unfamiliar faces, even though they are the very same youths. The desperate question in his eyes communicates nothing to them, produces no response in their eyes. With gleeful laughs of victory, the youths instantly take off in the direction of the forest. The officer runs into the tent to check the grain sacks and finds two of them gone. He comes out and runs after them.

He can hear some tiny footsteps in the dark ahead of him. Through the gaps in the forest, he manages to spot the sacks quickly moving away. They are humans, not spirits. From the height at which the sacks are moving, he concludes that the thieves are very short, perhaps children.

These people collect the relief and then send their eight- and ten-year-olds to steal the relief supplies! So much for the government reports saying that the Agariyas never steal, never lie, never commit crimes. He has been so keen to do good for them. The youths have addressed him as deota. It was all deceit? Suddenly he feels as if he has been tricked, robbed, and left destitute! He becomes angry, and the blood rushes to his head. He is a good and honest man, who never takes bribes, and he has sympathy for the tribals. He has tried to prove true to all the reasons for his selection for this job. He has dedicated himself to the work. He has even thought about a solution to their problems, more lasting than merely sending relief to keep them alive a year at a time. Is this how they return kindness? By sending children to steal the relief supplies? He is going to catch them and see to the end of this business of stealing.

Stubbornly he keeps chasing the sound of those fleeing through the forest. They keep running too. The forest becomes thin, giving way to dried up wild grass. Beyond that he sees a huge treeless area, which must be where Jwala-mukhi wrestled with the Sun. The children put the sacks down when they reach that spot.

They must be exhausted, the relief officer thinks. He approaches them. They are standing around the sacks in a ferocious manner, the way beasts of prey crouch when getting ready to pounce. They are silent and still, watching him. In the faint light of the new moon, he can make out only their shapes and the postures, not their features and other details.

Suddenly, they move toward him, and he notices that there are not only boys but also girls. Claws of fear such as he has never known before sink into his chest. They fan out and surround him as they approach him. Then they stop moving. Why?

They watch him, and he watches them. The circle draws a bit closer and stops again. He looks over his shoulders and sees that he is encircled. He cannot easily break away. But why should he run? These are only children. Spirits never steal rice and milo.

He remembers the remarks he had heard. "The land here is cursed." "We'll drink at night; otherwise we're too scared."

He tries to calm his wildly beating heart, but it does not seem to obey him.

They come closer. Cold terror grips him. Why don't they speak? Why do they approach him so silently? Their bodies are more clearly visible now. But what is he seeing? Why are they naked? Why is their hair grown so long?

Why do the little boys have white hair? Why do the little girls have dried leathery breasts hanging from their chests? Why is that one coming forward to him, the one with completely white hair?

"Stay away from me!" The words come out flat as his scream remains soundless.

The white-haired one has come close to show him something. He is showing him his genitalia: wrinkled, dried up, hanging like a dead object.

They are adults! No sound comes out of his mouth, but the realization explodes inside his brain, devastating it like Hiroshima and Nagasaki.

The old man sees that he has understood. He sniggers, a strange inhuman chuckle. The chuckle spreads around. They jump around him and bend over, laughing hysterically. Some do somersaults, flying through the air. Others crouch, ready to spring. What can the officer do now?

"We aren't children. We're the Agariyas of Kuva. Ku-va! Have you heard of it?"

"No! No! No!" The officer wants to cover his eyes, but his hands do not obey him, or perhaps his shattered brain fails to convey his wish to his hands. "Keep the prasad of Mahabirji in your pocket. No harm can touch you as long as you have it."

"Ever since we cut up your folks to save the honor of our gods inside the hill, we've been hiding in the forest. So many soldiers, so many policemen came to catch us. They couldn't!"

The old man sniggers. Ghoulish chuckles go around.

"A few of us have lived with the help of the Agariya villagers. The rest of us died off without food, having to hide in the forest for so long."

The circle gets tighter. They come closer.

"Don't come near me!"

"Why shouldn't we? You've so many sacks of rice there, so many sacks of milo, and you came after us for just a couple of sacks. Because you've come, take a good look. Come, all of you, let him have a good look."

The men show him their genitals, the women their withered breasts. The old man is now very close to him. They all come closer. Their genitalia touch him, from all sides. They feel dry and repulsive, like cast-off snakeskin.

"We're down to just these fourteen. Our bodies have shrunk. The men can't do anything with it except piss. The women can't get pregnant. That's why we steal food. We must eat to grow bigger again. Don't you agree? . . . The Agariya villagers help us with it. The massacre of Kuva! We're like this because of the massacre of Kuva."

The officer repeats to himself that what he is seeing cannot be true. If it is true, then everything else is false: the Copernican system, science, the twentieth century, the Independence of India, the five-year plans, all that he has known to be true. He keeps saying, "No! No! No!"

"What use is saying no? Saying no doesn't make it untrue. How did we get these things? Can't you tell from these that we aren't children?"

They snigger with the joy of revenge. Again they go around him, running and jumping and laughing. From time to time, they rub their genitals against him, to remind him that they too are adult Indians.

How pathetic the new moon looks up there! How weak is the light she sheds on the burned-out empty field of battle between the Sun and Jwala-mukhi, the field in which a handful of child-sized adults are now wildly rejoicing in their revenge. The thrill of decapitating the enemy with blows of axes. Retaliation.

Retaliation against what?

His shadow cast across their dancing little figures tells him what. It is against his five feet and nine inches of height, against the normal growth of his body.

Arguments in self-defense race through his head. He wants to say: "Why should I be the target of your vengeance? I'm only an ordinary Indian. The size of my body is much less than those of the Americans, the Canadians, or the Russians. I've never even seen many of the nutritious things they eat. Never have I eaten much more than the number of calories that is an absolute minimum according to the World Health Organization."

But the arguments do not manage to find his voice. He just stands there, under the pale moon, helplessly listening to their weird laughter and suffering the rubbing of their genitalia. It seems to him that the body of an average Indian, what he has always considered to be puny and short, is the most heinous crime against human civilization, and that he is to blame personally for the hideously stunted forms of these once-proud adults. He stands accused of the crime on behalf of all the others.

He turns his thoughts deliberately to condemn himself to death. Then he lifts his head to the moon and opens his mouth. With the dancing and the laughing and the unbearable rubbing going on about him, he decides that he must scream and go out of his mind. If he is to escape this predicament, he must let out a howl like a mad dog, shrill enough to tear the vast field and become totally insane. But how is it that his brain is disobeying him? Why is it failing to carry out the sentence that he has passed on himself? Why can't his brain make his voice scream, produce any sound at all?

In sheer frustration, the relief officer starts to weep.

The Witch-Hunt

Mahasweta Devi

1

Chaitra, the last month of the past year, brought no spring rain at all. It was now two months into the summer heat of the new year, two endlessly burning months. Finally the month of Asarh came, but not heavy with rain-bearing clouds as in other years. Clouds kept drifting in and out without bringing any rain at all.

The Oraon woman named Budhni was almost philosophically pessimistic. She sounded satisfied in her grim conviction when saying that it was going to be much worse than a drought; it was going to turn into a famine.

The women were trying to fill their vessels by scooping water from the shallow bed that the Kuruda river had been reduced to. Sanichari tried to back up Budhni's pessimism with evidence. She saw inauspicious signs all around, like too many vultures and hawks circling in the sky.

Moti optimistically said that this time the government would not let the people die in a famine. They were going to prepare ahead and make arrangements for distributing gruel.

"Where did you hear that?" Budhni asked.

Moti's husband was just back from the town. He had seen relief being set up at Tohri. They would all dig earth for road building and receive a daily wage and gruel and milo.

"Why wait then till famine enters the village?" Budhni rhetorically asked. "We'll leave beforehand. Let famine be in the village all alone."

Nobody thought much of Budhni's remark at the time, but very soon it assumed a new meaning to them. They agreed that saying "let famine be in

"Daini" appears in Mahasweta's *Nairhite Megh* (Calcutta: Karuna Prakashani, 1979), 238–96.

the village all alone" amounted to inviting it. Kuruda had now caught the attention of the evil, the inauspicious. A vulture had snatched those words from the air and delivered them to the witch.

There were indications that the witch must be seeking to lodge in somewhere there. The strange things that had been happening during this drought could only be due to the presence of the witch in the vicinity. Babies died mysteriously, their necks going limp as they vomited after drinking the soybean milk supplied at the relief center. Cows and buffaloes were dying. Crows flying in treetops would suddenly tumble, swirling through the air dead. Such strange things could only be acts of the witch.

There was no way of knowing beforehand who would be possessed by the witch, whose body the witch would enter. A man or a woman with whom you might have lived all your life could suddenly turn into a demon or a witch. However, you could tell if a witch was around because strange things would happen—things that no one had yet seen with one's own eyes but everyone had heard about happening, mostly in some other village but close enough.

They heard that in Murhai when a Ganju hag struck flintstone to light her bidi, blood came out of the flintstone instead of fire. Somewhere else, a newborn baby was reported to be walking the village path, after it had come out of the birthing shack all by itself, kicking out of the way the clay bowl of live embers placed at the door. In a Munda graveyard, the dead were found sitting up and singing, having pushed aside their burial stones.

The Munda chief of village Tura one day announced that his daughter had simply vanished in the air while returning home from Tahad after work.

Panic spread through the string of villages of tribals and untouchables as they heard stories of such terrible happenings. Finally, they all got together and went to see Hanuman Misra in Tahad. He is the Brahman priest of the temple of Shiva and the preeminent man in the area. Misraji listened to them, and then he sat in a fasting meditation while they waited. When he emerged from the meditation, he told them that the deity had granted him a vision in the form of a terrible figure. It was the figure of a dreadful female, dark and completely naked, flying atop a blood-red cloud and saying "I'm the famine." From the almanac he had figured out that she was indeed the witch. They would have to find her and drive her away. If she were hit and bled, or if she were burned, then even more terrible things might happen.

He said that the witch was roaming in the vicinity of their villages, villages of Oraon and Munda tribes, villages of Ganju and Dusad untouchables, villages like Kuruda, Hesadi, and Murhai.

The reason for this, Hanuman Misra said, was that the people of those villages were terrible sinners. He elaborated to them the evidence of their sins and the many forms in which they were being punished. Why was it that at the times of the Naxalite troubles, the J.P. movement* and the Emergency, the police harassed their villages and left alone the villages of the upper castes? Because all the Ganjus, Dusads, Dhobis, Oraons, and Mundas were terrible sinners, the last two the worst sinners of all. One day they would worship their primitive spirits, another day the mission's Jesus, and still another day the Hindu's deities. Because they were so inconsistent and indiscriminate in their worship, they got no protection from any of the gods in the bad times of drought and famine or police harassment.

"Terrible sinners! Why else should they be the only ones to die whenever the rains are too little or too much? They've no shame about living on hand-outs. Lazy shirkers, always complaining about lack of employment."

Habitations of sinners attract the evil. Witches too. They would remain in mortal danger until they found the witch and drove her away.

2

With this pronouncement, Hanuman Misra lets loose in their daily life an enormous, ghastly shape of terror, its body and face invisible. The unknown terror takes hold of them, drains them, poisons their minds, sickens their bodies. It drives them to suspect each other, to doubt even the well-known behavior of their familiar and loved ones.

Sodan Ganju of Murhai wakes up in the middle of one night and follows his mother when she gets up to urinate. She goes outside of the hut as usual to the corner of the yard and comes back. But after she has closed the door, it suddenly seems to Sodan that the one returning to the straw bed is not his mother. Hysterical with terror, he runs out screaming and calling the neighbors. The neighbors come and light the lamp to make sure that his mother's feet touch the ground and her body casts a proper shadow. In the presence of all, a small slit is made in her finger to check if the blood runs red or black.

The old woman is cleared after the tests, but it leaves her brokenhearted about being suspected as a witch by her own son. She leaves home and goes to sit terminally by the site of Haram deity, determined to fast to death. But as soon as she dozes off in the haze of fast, she senses that Sodan is about to be caught by the witch. She wakes up shouting, "Don't go with it, Sodan! It's the witch!" Frantically she goes looking for Sodan and finds him chasing a female porcupine. She manages to save him by throwing a stone at his foot, crippling him for life. The witch in porcupine's form runs away disappointed.

Every husband, father, brother, or son is asked to keep constant watch on the women in his family. Watch for her shadow on the ground, see if a crow is flying along over her head when she is coming back from relieving herself in

---

* The reference is to a grassroots protest movement in Bihar in the mid-seventies, inspired by the famous Gandhian socialist leader Jayprakash Narain.

the field, check if the woman bolting the door, back in from the yard in the middle of the night, is the same one who went out. Having to constantly suspect everybody is nerve-racking. Mistakes and accidents are inevitable.

During every famine, Daitar Dusad of Hesadi leaves his mother, with a tin can, at the bus station. He has done it this time too. Every time she lives by begging there and sleeping under the banyan tree near the cement terrace on which the bus cleaners sleep on the hot nights. Every time they get used to her constant talking in her sleep. This time, after the first night, they refuse to let her stay. She has been heard calling and coaxing at dead of night who knows which demon: "Come on, come on now!"

Daitari's old mother fails to see the seriousness of the matter and explains with her toothless smile that she was only calling their black cow in her dream. The stupid cow was refusing to go in the cowshed. Her explanation only confirms their suspicion. Dream, black cow, the color black itself, the way she was calling it. All the evidence points against her. The bus cleaners ask her to clear out or else they are going to stone her.

Trying to walk the three miles back home, she dies on the way. Owing to the greedy jackals, Daitari is spared even the funeral cost. Soon everybody is convinced that she has been eaten by the witch, not jackals.

Human nerves are not made to tolerate the constant pressure of unknown, unspecific terror. If to the unknown terror of the witch is added the known terror of an approaching famine, the stress is too much to bear.

Of the many relief organizers gathered in the area—the government officers, the mission workers, the swamis of religious charity—not one has failed to notice the unusually savage look and wariness in the eyes and the faces of these people. Their eyeballs are constantly moving with fierce intensity, as if desperately searching for something. It is very strange, quite unlike those workers' earlier experience with the famine-stricken tribals and untouchables. Their past experience tells them that the tribals in the area do not have feelings. At the onset of famine, they leave their babies at the mission door. After a village catches fire and burns down, they are reluctant to return and rebuild. You ask them why. They say that the babies would at least live in the mission. They say that they do not care to return after a fire because their homes are made only of mud and leaves and they have nothing valuable except an iron pot and the knife they carry at their waist.

Relief organizers have always noticed the change during famine in these, even normally unfeeling, people. They become utterly possessed by some extreme indifference. It seems impossible to cross the walls raised in their eyes and their faces, to rouse any normal human interest and curiosity. The lady social workers have tried toy rattles to amuse the skeletal children in the arms of skeletal mothers, but their glazed eyes look on with merciless indifference. This time, however, their eyes and expressions are strangely alive, very alert and restless, like those of predatory animals.

There are other, even more disquieting reports coming from the village social workers. For example, usually the village dogs drive away any outside mangy dogs that trespass; but now the village people are stoning them savagely. Even in the terrible heat, they are sleeping with fires, and the menfolk are taking turns watching at night. Every year vaccinations are given along with the relief supplies. Every year they take the shots from the female doctors, missionaries, and medical students; this time they have refused the needle from these outside women. A certain rich elderly woman, out to do charity work, was on the way to Tohri in a station wagon fitted with loudspeakers playing Krishna consciousness songs. When she and the white woman accompanying her stopped at one village for water, they were not only refused water but also hit by flying stones. Shocked, they have announced that such people in whose minds no human love was aroused by Krishna in the form of the famine must be destined by the lord to starve to death. They have turned away from Tohri and gone back to Patna with all the money, rice, milk powder, and medicines that they had meant to give away.

The social workers are gravely concerned at such incidents. They have sensed that some terror, some apprehension is transmitting like electric current from village to village, strangely changing the people's attitudes. They are worried about this crisis no less than about the drought.

Everyone seems worried. The rumor is around that Hanuman Misra has offered to perform a *yagna* for seven days, with a quintal of clarified butter, and pray for lessening the animal side of these people's minds and strengthening the divine side. The white man who runs the Krishna Chaitanya Ashram has offered to donate the needed clarified butter, on condition that the chanting for Shiva while pouring the butter in the fire will be done in low voice so as not to interfere with the songs to Lord Krishna to be played on the loudspeaker in the station wagon outside. Hanuman Misra has not yet taken the offer. Not because of the Krishna songs, for after all Shiva and Krishna are different manifestations of the same, but because the clarified butter is made from the milk of Australian cows. Shiva, a quick-tempered god, may become angry because Australia is outside his rule. He is, of course, the Lord of the universe, but Australia was not discovered when he became Lord. For this reason Hanuman Misra is hesitant about going ahead with the yagna using the ghee offered.

The white man who offered the ghee has come to the area after hearing about the witch scare, and he has requested Misraji to see to it that the witch is not killed. If he can get hold of a genuine Indian witch, he will take her to his country. He agrees with Misra that in order to spot the witch, it is necessary to start by suspecting everybody. He says that it may even be necessary to suspect oneself. Misraji likes his point.

Next time they come to him, he admonishes them, "Have you wretched people thought of something? Lot of times you move alone in the forest, the hills, or the fields. Has it occurred to you to check on yourself, check if your shadow is where it should be and if a crow or a vulture or a kite is not circling over you?"

Suspect yourself, watch yourself. The order is too exacting, too deranging for people endangered in so many ways and terrified. On top of it all is the ruling that they must find the witch, but they must not kill her, only chase her away.

Their bewilderment is voiced by the chief of Kuruda village. "I don't understand. We never had this kind of witch before. Last time when Sanichari's aunt was found to be the witch, . . ."

He stops short, catching the cunning glint in the eyes of his listeners. They had stoned the old woman to death, and, because the hyenas had a hearty meal throughout the night, the police had been unable to find any evidence for arresting them.

. He skips to his point, "Why are things different this time?"

Sanichari says skeptically, "Who knows? Misraji has planted such fear in our minds!"

Everything seems to be different about the drought this time. The relief supplies arrive and depart. Still the clouds do not come together to make rain; they drift about separated from each other. The paddy seedlings look lifeless, their leaves wilted like the tongues of pregnant women. The other day, the wife of Bisra Ganju has given birth to a son with a tooth in his mouth. Jackals, wolves, and hyenas roam the village paths in broad day-light.

Maybe the cataclysm is coming this time, the *Sengel-da* once again! Maybe the skies will rain fire and burn everything out, and the gods will reclaim the earth to create her anew.

Pahan, the chief, holds this discussion in the morning. The same night his wife wakes up hearing him weeping and calling for someone, "Come here! Come back!"

"Whom are you calling?"

"My shadow! When I went out to piss, it went with me. I come back and it's no more with me!"

"You don't have your shadow?"

"No. Perhaps I've become the witch!"

As the priest of the tribal village, Pahan is their direct link with their gods. He knows that, but that knowledge does not save him from being swallowed by fear. His wife has stronger nerves. She quickly lights both the kerosene lamps and reassures him: "Look. There's your shadow. You know it is impossible for the witch to possess the priest." But she knows that the chief's confidence is shaken. How else could he in the middle of the night suspect himself of being the witch?

Soon after this, Budhni Oraon, out in the forest collecting wood, sees the reflection of a hairy arm in the river. Is she turning into a witch? She drops her bundle of twigs and kneels by the shallow water, checking with acute concentration her own transformation. When she sees another hairy arm, she frantically screams, "I'm the witch!" That startles even the hungry bear, which jumps over her and flees, making her realize that she was about to be attacked by the bear. She runs toward the village, forgetting all about her bundle of wood.

One day Bisra Dusad of Burudiha village suddenly kills his black heifer, his only material wealth. It seemed to be a normal calf all the time, but when Bisra was drunk on *mahua* it would become a young woman and beckon him. Death of a heifer is a disaster for someone in Bisra Dusad's situation. For several days he sits silently with bloodshot eyes in the empty cowshed. When he realizes that he is ruined without the cow, which was going to calve and give him both milk and money to repay the loan he took to buy her, and that he would now have to borrow more in order to live, he hangs himself with the calf's rope from the beam of the cowshed. Before doing it at night, he has spent the day mending the roof of his hut, bought a spin top for his boy, and told his wife that killing the poor cow was a terrible mistake. She has felt relieved thinking that he might be recovering from the shock.

Bisra Dusad was the best exorciser in the area; they all depended on him for cures. He was also a water diviner—always knew where to dig for water. The death of someone as indispensable to the people of these deprived remote villages is a grave threat to their social structure. Their need for him may have brought him neither affluence nor relief from debt, but he had their respect. People like Bisra Dusad have always known poverty and hardship, as constant and inevitable as the air and the sky. He never felt any personal resentment about being poor and deprived, as they all are—all Dusads, Ganjus, Oraons, Mundas—"comrades" in poverty.

The chief calls a meeting and says, "Bisra's death has been caused by fear. If tomorrow we lose Vurai Lohar the way we've lost Bisra today, how are we to have our metal tools repaired? If the day after tomorrow Bharat dies, who is going to do our carpentry? You must find the witch. I'll fast and pray for the end of our fear and our danger."

The village social workers, when they find out about the seriousness of the witch scare, inform the officer of the Tribal Welfare Commission. The officer informs the police because killing an old man or woman as a witch must be treated as a crime. His official duty obligates the officer to report it. But he is scared stiff after doing it, and he pays Hanuman Misra fifty-one rupees for a talisman for personal protection against the witch.

The police chief says that there has been no murder yet in the witch-hunt, but he would do nothing even if there is one. As a government officer, he would take action about the murder of an untouchable by the Brahmans or the Rajputs. But if the untouchables and the tribals kill one of their own as a witch, he would simply take leave and stay away from the scene. Governments come and go, but witches are always there. Why risk catching the evil eye?

Thoughts and events thus endlessly chase each other, turning this way and that inside the maze of fear, the *bhul-bhulaiya* that anyone can get in but no one can get out of.

Then suddenly one night, terrible noises are heard from the direction of Murhai village; the lights from flaming torches leap against the dark night, and a terrible scream rends the sky. They have found the witch!

3

Murhai has a long-standing association with witches. The villagers are mostly of Dusad and Ganju castes, as in so many other villages in the area. Anyone thinking that there is just one dividing line with high castes on one side and low castes on the other is oversimplifying. The caste hierarchy is like a box inside a box inside still another box, as in an Arabian nights tale. You dig for a worm, and you end up with a dinosaur. That Hanuman Misra would not let Bhola Ganju come near his well is something that is understood without question even by Bhola Ganju. Bhola Ganju, however, is lower in the hierarchy than Bharat Dusad, and Bharat and Bhola both rank higher than Ramrik Dhobi, even though they are all outcastes as far as the upper castes are concerned. Such fine gradations appear quite ridiculous to the Oraon and Munda tribals. They do not understand the caste system. Bhola, Ramrik, and everybody else regard them as ignorant for their inability to see these distinctions and why they matter. Almost all the villages in the area have some Oraon or Munda neighborhood. The remarkable thing is that the authority of Pahan, the chief and priest of Oraon or Munda community, is accepted even by the nontribal outcaste communities of Dusads and Dhobis.

Murhai village chronically suffers from drought, starvation, famine, bonded labor, bloodsucking moneylenders—the whole range of nature-made and man-made troubles. When there is some respite from these troubles, the villagers fight with each other about caste matters, their lives then endlessly hectic from alternating between the waging and the settling of disputes.

Each village in the area has its special characteristic. Hesadi is known for its disobedient self-willed women, the Oraons of Kuruda are known as shirkers, the men of Burudu as vile-tempered, and Murhai is known for harboring a witch or a demon once every ten or fifteen years. Strange things happen then. One's cow or buffalo is mysteriously stricken; another's sleeping wife is called out at dead of night and bitten by the witch in the form of a puppydog; or all their grain sacks are chewed through by the witch as a diabolically clever rat.

Once, following the Shivaratri festival, babies died with convulsion and vomiting. The government doctor said that it was the milk they had fed the children, milk sitting for a day in the dirty tank, where it had drained after being poured on the Shivalinga in Misraji's temple. They had said nothing in the presence of the doctor. But, after burying his three-year-old daughter, Ramrik washerman called together some of his kin. They whispered in the dark and went to the hut of Mahuri, the old washerwoman. She had brought the milk in pails slung on a shoulder pole; they had offered that milk to the deity; Ramrik's baby had some of it afterward. They set fire to Mahuri's hut. When old, wrinkled Mahuri staggered out half-burned, they chased her out of the village. Scared and blinded by pain from the burns, Mahuri stumbled on a rock and died. Ramrik and his cousin are still in jail, sentenced for assault with intent to kill.

Some ten years before that incident, the widow of Roto Munda became a witch. Luckily for her, they did not have to kill her. She became human again as soon as they cut her nose and bled her.

From all these incidents, the people in the area are convinced that Murhai is a favorite place for witches. It is such an unlucky place that when the wind blows through the clumps of pampas grass in the barren tract beside the village, it always sounds like voices moaning and wailing.

Again it is in Murhai that the witch is first spotted—owing to the illicit love between Parsad, Ramrik washerman's son, and Mani, the widowed sister of Baram Ganju the cattle skinner. Luckless love in a luckless place. The rules of caste relation restrict the scope for illicit love. Still, it does occasionally take hold and put the hapless victims through the grinder. Parsad and Mani had known each other since they were children. Parsad's wife is Mani's friend, and Mani's dead husband was known to Parsad. Cousins by village relation, they fall in love dancing at the Karam festival. For a few days their eyes look for each other. They seek out ways to have their paths cross, one returning from the market, the other from the forest carrying wood. Soon they get caught.

Parsad's wife comes to shout at Mani, then goes home to sit and cry. Baram loudly vows to kill his sister if she carries on and then goes to buy the kerosene on ration. Parsad's mother is shrewd and experienced. She visits the Baram home, discreetly smokes their hookah for some time, and says that it is useless to get too upset about it. Her daughter-in-law, thin like a stick, cannot satisfy her young and virile son. Mani is a healthy childless widow. How can Parsad help it? They have to control the matter at their end; they have to control Mani.

The village leaders summon both parties to chastise them. First they address the lovers' guardians, in a tone both tired and solemn, "For the last few years the police have been harassing us, turning our life topsy-turvy, even though we have done nothing to deserve it. On top of it, we are threatened by the droughts and the prospect of famine. Now there is the witch. Who knows if the witch is not behind this infatuation? We can't afford to be troubled by this problem now. You better control them. No more of this nonsense. Or we'll straighten them out with public beating."

Some years ago they would have reacted far more vehemently, right-eously. They have lived with the hardship of moneylenders' extortion, droughts, and hunger as far back as they can remember. But this new thing of police harassment they are not used to, and it has broken their spirit, upset their life. The elders do not find the energy to be worked up about exercising social control and penalizing deviance such as this affair. Besides, they need every young man and woman. They cannot afford to expel Parsad and Mani from the village the way they would have done in earlier times.

The eldest of the leaders finally clears his throat and addresses the lovers. "Parsad! Mani! You know how upset our life is, the problems we're plagued with. We're half dead already. Don't add more blows. We don't want to expel you. Where can you go? What will you live on? And what about Parsad's wife and child? How would they manage?"

Parsad and Mani had come to the meeting expecting to be expelled, at least physically punished. The unexpected kindness brings instant repen-tance. They prostrate before the elders and vow to behave like brother and sister.

But love is an incurable disease. For a few days Mani remains very guarded. Baram notices her effort at proper behavior, and says, "After we bring home the harvest, I'll get you married again. Your brother-in-law has grown into a young man; he is keen to marry you."

The stab of pain, instead of consolation, that Mani feels at her brother's kind plan suddenly makes her realize how much she loves Parsad. Knowing that he means well, she doesn't want to hurt him. Sadly she says, "We'll see. Let's worry about the harvest."

"Harvest! With hardly any water."

"The rain will come."

"How can it rain? The clouds wander. They don't gather together."

The shared anxiety about the fate of their crop suddenly brings brother and sister very close. Baram remembers how harried he was with work when his father died leaving him with an old mother and a lazy wife. Mani has been so useful ever since she came back after her husband's death. She helps with the harvest, milling grain, and marketing. Brother and sister have worked hard to put the household in order.

Quietly, he asks her to try to forget Parsad. She says that she will try. He says that it's not right to break your neighbor's marriage. She agrees to all he says and brings his attention back to work. "Do the roof soon. It's full of holes, won't hold up when the rain comes."

"Do we have all the rope we need?"

"We have some. Pick up from Vura the two bundles he borrowed."

Talking about doing the roof, both at once remember Parsad, his skills in thatching roof. He can tie and knit the leaves so well that the roof does not need mending for years. With a sigh Mani picks up the sickle and sets out for the forest to cut leaves for the roof.

Parsad sees her going to the forest. Soon he takes to joining her there. They know that what they are doing is no good for them; it will have no good ending. Yet their despair seems to drive them into each other's arms. On a bed of leaves in the forest, they become one, without hope, with the knowledge that it will not last; they have to go home holding back the tears.

They both see the witch in the forest, at dusk. They see an ugly dark young woman, naked. Sitting on a stone in the middle of the riverbed and eating the raw meat off a bird that lives on the edge of the water. Spotting the two of them, she stands up swaying, bares her teeth and howls ferociously. The howl is like the bellowing of a buffalo being branded with hot iron. The moneylender Golbadan owns one thousand buffaloes; each is branded so that it cannot be stolen and sold in the town market.

Realizing that it is the witch, Parsad and Mani take off for the village, forgetting to be careful not to reveal their secret meeting place.

The chief beats the drum to signal danger. Everyone realizes that this drumbeat is about the witch because at this time it can't be flood in the river, fire in the village, or wild elephants rampaging through fields of ripe grain. They all come running to him.

Witch! . . . Where? . . . On the riverbed. . . . Eating tatui birds raw! . . . What shall we do? . . . Drive it away. . . . Why? . . . What else can we do? . . . Kill it. . . . No!

"No!" shouts the agitated Pahan. He is not a Hindu, and he does not agree with Hanuman Misra's ruling. But he knows he has no choice. Hanuman Misra is so powerful, so rich, with so much clout with the police, the government officers, the landlords, and the moneylenders, that Pahan cannot go against his order and must abandon the ancient custom of burning a witch.

He hits the drum as he says "No!" But his hands are trembling. "Things are different this time! Have we seen the weather this terrible before? The witch this time is different too!"

Baram and Parsad forget their quarrel and look at each other, "But others ruin and kill us! Why can't we kill the witch?"

"Shut up, Parsad. Are you to obey me, or am I to obey you?"

"Of course, we'll obey you. You're the chief. But . . ."

"What?"

"When the priest in Tahad lectured us that we're sinners, we said nothing. But we aren't the only ones who might have sinned."

"Are you saying that I have sinned?"

Sanichari was intently listening to the exchange, her hands busy picking lice off her hair. She now speaks up firmly, "Why are you misunderstanding us, chief? If you made any slip in the worship it is something between you and the gods, not between you and us. Are we now to debate our sins or do something about the witch?"

Pahan sees that he must prove his leadership or the doubts will grow in his people's minds. He orders the men to come along, the women to go home and bolt their doors, and Parsad to lead the advance group.

"Why him?" Mani objects, forgetting propriety.

"He saw the witch. He has to show the way."

Daylight is almost gone. Pahan lights a fire and chants with folded hands. The men, young and old, all light their torches in that fire and fill the folds of their loincloth with stones. Pahan runs in a circle with the fire, rubs some earth on his chest and forehead, raises his hands to the sky praying at the top of his voice, asking Haramdeo for the power to drive the witch away.

Then he holds his breath and listens for the deity's answer. Perhaps his god hears him and saves his face through an owl. Scared by his loud chant, it screeches and flies out of its hole in the *neem* tree. Because owls do not go out during the meeting of afternoon and evening, Pahan looks pleased with it as a clear sign that the deity has heard his prayer.

They make their battle formation and run to the forest, shouting chants as they run. They enter the forest. Pahan, running with them, cautions them about the torches—be careful that the dry forest does not catch fire, or the forest officer will fine and jail them. Parsad feels like setting fire to the forest, getting into a fight with the police and the forest officer. He feels challenged, fearless. The witch-hunt has filled him with courage. It is not always that he can run like this. He decides to run away with Mani before this excitement of running dies down in his blood. He must act before his courage weakens.

"Look!" he shouts.

They stop all at once and lift up their torches. The flames cast moving reflections in the dark water of Kuruda, swirling like black snakes coiling and uncoiling among the big stones scattered across its bed. On one stone stands a dark naked female; her deformed body is not clearly visible, her face smeared with blood and bits of feather. She raises her hand when she sees them, with a bird's wing in the hand.

"There's the witch!" they all shout at once.

Her eyes seem to light up with expectation. She sways and laughs silently.

"It's laughing!"

Pahan lurches forward, his body withered, but his eyes turned savage with fear. All eyes become killer eyes, wild and desperate. Pahan shouts, "In the name of Haramdeo and all the spirits, we'll drive you away!"

Now the witch's eyes also turn savage. Raising her hands, shaking her hair, she howls. Again it sounds like the bellowing of a buffalo being branded.

"Hit it with stones!" Stones fly at her. "Be careful not to spill its blood! If its blood touches the ground, hundreds of witches will be born of it!"

She too picks up a stone and throws it at them. It hits Pahan in the head, and blood streams down his cheek. "We have to hit it, or it will hit us more!" Stones fly. The men shout frantically and pelt stones at her.

Suddenly she screams. It tears through their collective shouting and rises to the sky, as she steps off the stone onto the riverbed and runs toward the other side of the river.

From this side they keep pelting stones at her until her terrible howl of pain moves away. Pahan listens and says that it is going toward village Hesadi. At least they themselves are saved. He wipes the blood off his face, his eyes shining with the excitement of victory against evil.

"No one sleeps tonight. You'll drink and dance throughout the night."

"And tomorrow?"

"Tomorrow I'll worship."

Pahan chants Haramdeo's name and runs, taking them back to their village. The scream of the witch recedes in the east, toward the abandoned burial ground. Ghosts and spirits haunt it at this time. The witch will like it.

By the time they reach the trickle of the river flowing by the edge of their village, they all seem to be drooping, falling back into the feeling of helplessness. The witch-hunt energized them like tired but hungry wolves on the scent of prey. Now that the excitement of aggression and fear is over, they feel empty and scared. They become diffident, silent, thoughtless. Pahan senses the change of mood. He knows that the soft alluvium of their minds can be turned granite-hard only by involving them in collective efforts like the witch-hunt; but it becomes soft again when witches are gone. Pahan feels deep compassion for these suffering, neglected, and soft people, forgetting that he is one of them, feeling as if he is their patron. He talks to them with affection.

"Don't be afraid. I can't see your faces in the dark, but your voices and your breath tell of fear."

"Is the witch really gone?"

"Yes. My head doesn't bleed any more. Pain has left my body."

"Then it must be gone!"

"Yes, it's gone. You can tell from the freshness in the air."

As they walk to the village, their bodies feel light and free of care. A young man says that now they will get fish in the river. The witch must have been hiding all the fish. Pahan affirms the optimism.

"We'll have rains; the crops will grow. Witches hold back the clouds; they make our crops wilt and the porcupines caught in our traps disappear."

"Are we going to worship?"

"Yes, tomorrow we will."

"And tonight?"

"Tonight you drink and dance. Baram, bring your drum for the singing."

"Shall I dress pot-bellied like the moneylender for the dance?"

"No. This isn't Holi time, to put on a silly costume."

"What about the drink?"

"The brewer Nimchand owes me some on account of the propitiation I did for him."

Baram suggests that rather than risk going out to the brewery near Hesadi, he will supply what he happens to have at home. With the help of the brewer's servant, Baram has in fact stolen ten bottles from the brewer's stock. It was not easy smuggling it out inside piles of straw. He was going to sell it in the market and split the money with the brewer's servant. The night's events have made him generous.

A fire is lit in Pahan's yard. Because he is not familiar with the idea of driving away the witch instead of killing it, he feels fearful about what might happen during the rest of the night. He has called the all-night party in order to have everybody awake and together. Baram brings out his ten bottles of distilled liquor. It is not just impulsive generosity. It is an opportunity to gain status in the eyes of his kin. His kin follow up as best as they can to gain status in the eyes of others and supply the liquor they have stored in clay pots at home. Sanichari leads the women in with snacks of roasted rice and corn, onions and chilies. She appeals to Pahan to be invited to the party. They don't want to be alone at home, and besides they're supplying the snacks. Pahan smiles at their ploy and asks them to join the vigil and drink.

Drinks. Food. Beats of the drum. The songs and the singing along. The vigil feels like a festival. They have not had one for a long time in their own village. The intoxication dissolves the prison of anxiety they have been living in ever since Hanuman Misra's pronouncement.

When all are a bit drunk, carried away by music and laughing with old Sanichari's comically erotic dance, Parsad and Mani look at each other. He signs to her, and separately they edge away from the party, to meet at the back of Pahan's house. He holds her hand, and she puts herself in his hands. Together they start running in the dark, in the direction of the little town Tohri, their gateway to the outside world. From there they can catch a ride in a lumber truck going to a big town like Ranchi or Dhanbad.

Pahan's wife sees them leave but says nothing at the time. Parsad's wife treats her with contempt for being childless, refusing to take from her hand the offerings she distributes as the priest's wife. She now gets her revenge by keeping quiet about Parsad and Mani running away. Next day, of course, she tells. They talk about it and conclude that those who see the witch first must find it the most difficult to resist the lure of committing improper acts; thus, the elopement of Parsad and Mani assumes a deeper meaning in their minds by becoming linked with the witch-hunt.

4

A slick American magazine carries a story with pictures on "the witch of Kuruda river." Many read it. Many others would have liked to read it, but the magazine costs twelve rupees per issue and sells out fast even at that price because reading it is considered necessary for modern education. Even the

ultranationalist politicos who campaign against the use of English language in our schools and colleges grab a copy of the magazine, read it while
traveling from one meeting to the next, and, if caught in the act, say that they
have to know the minds of the country's enemies in order to fight them. The
publishers of such popular magazines in English are not even aware that they
are regarded by the "meeting-busy" babus as the enemy of the country. The
babus' thought process must be either too complex or too simple for ordinary
mortals: they fight to eliminate the English language in public schools and
yet send their own children to English-medium private schools; they aid the
exploitation and extinction of artisans, even as they loudly extol "folk art"
and swoon over the handicrafts sold in posh stores in Calcutta.

The story behind how "the witch of Kuruda" reached an international
magazine is tortuous. The writer is a white man in Patna, a Krishna devotee,
the one who offered Hanuman Misra one quintal of ghee of Australian origin.
His name is now Peter Bharati. He has been in India for a very long time, in
various forms. Once he was known as a bohemian student in Santiniketan,
roaming its sal groves singing Tagore songs. He went home and reemerged
on the Nepal-India border as a historian, but actually drawing maps of the
border regions. He went back again and returned as a geologist specialized in
mountains, but actually staying in Calcutta. This was in the mid-seventies,
the time of the Emergency rule. He went around taking pictures of the beggars, the slogans on the walls, the overflowing garbage bins, and the sacrificial goats tethered at the Kali temple. He became quite famous for his acts
of conspicuous naivete. He danced with the *sannyasis* during the Chadak festival and joined the milkmen going to the Tarakeswar temple carrying buckets slung on shoulder poles. Perhaps due to exhaustion from doing so many
things, one day he fainted in front of a group of reporters and photographers
gathered at the Grand Hotel for some occasion. When he came to, he was yet
another man. He told the curious gathering that he had a vision of a giant-
sized sage who asked him to roam no more in search of himself and who then
opened his mouth wide for Peter to see himself in his successive incarnations
in India. He also spotted in the sage's mouth a picture of the railway station
of Patna, from which he figured that Patna must be the place where he was
destined to be in the present incarnation.

That is how he came to Patna. Then Krishna smiled upon him, and things
looked up. He became a disciple of Swami Ananda Bharati, who named him
Peter Bharati, put him in charge of the ashram, and left for the Himalayas in
his private jet. Peter runs the ashram, with its hordes of Indian and foreign
devotees, a fleet of station wagons, and unlimited money. Rich people come
to see his holy highness and hand him fat checks with tears of gratitude in
their eyes. Everybody knows about the different episodes of his life in India,
and prominent among the visitors are the alumni of Visva-Bharati, nostalgic
about the sal groves, and hippies from Nepal. Peaceful music from hidden
stereo speakers soothes visitors' minds.

Peter Bharati first learned about the witch scare from Hanuman Misra. He expressed interest, and, given the Indian gods' indulgence for him, he kept receiving information—not on his own, but through Sharan Mathur whom he met in Tohri.

Mathur is a schoolteacher in Tohri and the son-in-law of the chief reporter of a daily newspaper in Patna. He takes pride in writing and uses his contact with the paper to publish articles from time to time, which have made him a well-known figure in the town. The son of a rich lumber contractor, he is surprisingly honest, hardworking, and intellectually active. He has been collecting data to write a history of the Kol tribal revolt in the region. This labor of love may sometime become his doctoral dissertation. While doing his field work, he has come to know the villages along the Kuruda river. Peter Bharati offers him five thousand rupees to investigate the witch story from beginning to end. Mathur tells him that he does not want to do it for money; his family is quite rich, and he has become a teacher against his father's wish. What does he want then? Mathur says that he is going to investigate it anyway because he knows the area and is suspicious of the witch scare. He could send him a report provided his name appears in print as the joint author when the story is published. Peter Bharati agrees.

In the magazine story, Mathur's name is not mentioned anywhere. The report is written in the name of a Kurt Mueller. Mathur's agreement was with Peter Bharati. Kurt Mueller, whoever he is, is not obliged to acknowledge Mathur. While Mathur's report was a chronological account of the events, the published story follows its own sweet will. Things are rearranged, and the witch scare in Kuruda is amazingly linked with witch-hunts in medieval Europe and the Nazi persecution of Jews and communists. The story is accompanied by pictures. An ashram devotee named Eileen Bharati in black paint is photographed as the witch. Mathur is speechless at the picture of a black-painted Western woman eating a fried chicken leg, captioned as the witch eating a bird raw. He also learns that there is going to be a movie based on the story, with Eileen as the leading lady. It is going to be shot in Arizona, which has a similar landscape. The movie will also have the distinction of having whites play Indian characters and Indians play white characters.

Mathur shakes his head in disbelief. He has been diligently following the twists and turns of the witch story in real life, with the help of his bicycle. Hesadi is the village he visits most often.

It is in Hesadi that the witch makes her next appearance.

At the early stage of the scare, the people of Hesadi hysterically watched and suspected. They followed all the rules and rituals and kept vigil. For a while they constantly checked their own and each other's shadows; pregnant and menstruating women lived under watchful eyes; animals with a black coat were stoned; the priest stayed awake and staked the village with flowers

from worship and blood from a sacrificed chicken. When the witch was spotted in Murhai, they felt relief in being able to drop the burden of having to
constantly suspect themselves and each other.

Every village in the area has a woman named Sanichari. Sanichari of
Hesadi is a hardworking woman. She has to be. Her son and daughter-in-law
died leaving her with their little boy who is now seven, too small to do any
kind of work. So she has utilized every opportunity to make herself indispensable in the lives of the village people. She is the midwife, the postnatal herb-
alist, and the pediatrician for the villagers. Everybody trusts her knowledge
of herbs and her skills. Bhagat, the shopkeeper, was not one of her faithfuls at
first. But when his wife had three stillbirths in a row, he had to seek her help.
After many oil massages and rituals of protection, Sanichari finally managed
to have his wife deliver a healthy baby. Since then she has received from the
Bhagat household regular supplies of corn and millet, now the main source of
subsistence for herself and her grandchild.

Sanichari and the Pahan of Hesadi one day exchange doubts about the
witch near the road to the bus junction, seven miles away from their village.
She and a few other women have gone there to sell grass to the milkmen.
Seeing Pahan on the way that day, she stops and puts down her load of grass,
asking the others to go ahead as she must have a word with Pahan. Pahan
hands Sanichari a bidi and lights one himself. They have the same thing on
their minds. If the witch has moved near Hesadi, as they say, why is there no
sign of increased witch activity? It is supposed to be in Jilad's field, yet laughter of ghosts and spirits is not heard from there. There are even some clouds
and drizzle. Things do not quite fit.

Pahan smokes his bidi and listens. Halfway through, he puts it out, saves
the unburnt half, frowns, and talks about his doubts. Even if spilling witch
blood would produce more witches, why aren't they to burn the witch this
time? Sanichari touches the tiny burn scar on her cheek as she listens.

"Remember when we were both little?"

"Yes, you always whined 'I'm hungry.'"

"You always cried 'I'm still hungry.' The same words always. Our children said it; our grandchildren will say it. But I'm not talking about that."

Sanichari fingers her scar and talks about when Pahan's uncle was
declared a he-witch. His hut was set on fire to burn him. A spark from the fire
touched her on the cheek. After he was burnt, the crops were saved, the fish
came back to the river, and the drought left.

"Why should it be different now? I wonder . . ."

Pahan slowly and deliberately lights the half-burnt bidi, and goes on,
"Don't tell anyone, but I suspect the whole thing. The Brahman in Tahad is
no well-wisher of ours. If he sees our homes burn, he will throw kerosene at
the fire instead of water. Forever telling us how lowly we are, lower than the
dust of his shoes. I think he planted the scare. There's no witch!"

"What about the big to-do in Murhai?"

"Who can be sure what they saw in the dark? Could be a bear."

"There's no witch then!"

"That's what I suspect. The air feels nice, the forests seem to be safe, Budhna's sick boy has just recovered. What kind of witch would fail to poison the air, scare the forest creatures, and take a sick child's life?"

"You're the priest. It's for you to know the answer."

Pahan reminds her again not to tell anyone yet.

Sanichari leaves, perplexed and worried, but soon she starts thinking in practical terms. Pahan must know what he is saying. If there's no witch, then she need not be afraid to go to Jilad's field.

She instantly sees in her mind the barren field with huge stones and boulders standing on it, the ancient burial ground of the Oraons. Long ago, before the Hindus had settled in the area, they put those stones over the shallow graves of their dead. Now they burn their dead, burying only occasionally, and the rock burial ground is not used much. Along the rocks' edges and crevices grow the plants and herbs she uses as medicine, to treat women prone to stillbirth, for example. Bhagat's wife is pregnant again, and Sanichari needs the herb for her. She has to collect it with her hair untied at the time when the sun has just set and the sky is faintly lighted. Nobody goes there even in daytime, and everybody knows that after dark the burial stones wake up and wander about the field whispering to each other.

Sanichari and Pahan are the only ones who go there—Sanichari for her herbs and roots; Pahan to figure out if the stones are more restless than usual, if the spirits are upset about something improper going on in the community. Sometimes he senses that the spirits of their long-dead Oraon ancestors are troubled. Burying the dead does not end the duty of the living to them. Whenever there is another death in a family, they are supposed to leave offerings of rice and salt at the ancestors' graves at the end of the period of impurity. Who knows how the descendants of those in the ancient graves are scattered now! But the spirits can't be expected to starve and be forgotten. They become unhappy in the other world. Pahan is responsible for the well-being of the living as well as the spirits of the dead. Because the living and the dead do not cease to be related to each other, Pahan has to go there from time to time to sense if the spirits are happy or upset.

He must be knowing. Sanichari, therefore, feels confident about making her postponed trip to the field to collect the medicine she needs for Bhagat's wife. She will treat her tomorrow. She sees Bhagat's wife on the way home and asks her to prepare, have the house and the cowshed cleaned and the ritual items of rice, betelnut, oil, hair of black she-goat, cow's urine, and a new iron key all ready. Bhagat's wife is heavy with the weight of her womb. She moans with discomfort, saying she is scared that she may not live. Of course, she will live. Sanichari asks her to move about. Her brother thinks she should go to the city hospital for the delivery, but her husband is unwilling. Sanichari agrees. In the hospital your baby gets changed for someone else's. She will be fine here in Sanichari's care, but let Sanichari not be forgotten afterward. Bhagat's wife promises a gold ring. But Sanichari wants a heifer, not a gold ring. Bhagat's wife promises her a heifer.

A heifer means milk and calves to rear for selling; it means dung to make fuel chips to sell to Bhagat's wife. With a cow, she can hope to raise her grandson. She walks home planning a future for the little boy based on the heifer that she has only been promised. She picks up the trowel to dig up the root she needs. The little boy cries "I'm hungry" as soon as he sees her. She gives him some of the puffed corn she just got from Bhagat's wife. Walking to the burial field, it again occurs to her how unchanged, like the sun and the moon, are the two phrases "I'm hungry" and "I'm still hungry" in their lives. She is sure those two phrases were just as common among the Oraons in ancient times when they used to bury their dead in that field. Then her thoughts turn to her own battle for survival against the constant threat of hunger. She has managed a she-calf to assure her grandson's life. Not bad for an old Oraon woman of Hesadi, a place where few manage to leave anything behind to remember them by except the burial stones and that too in ancient times. Sanichari is going to leave her grandson a cow, a source of living for him.

She reaches the field dreaming of the future to come. The stones stand in a dark cluster against the fading light of the sky. Two big rocks tower like parents in the middle of a number of smaller rocks of varying shape. The field is almost dark now, but she knows exactly where to dig. The thin Jilad creek flows through that cluster of rocks, giving life to the plants with tiny sprays of white flowers at the base of the rocks. It's darker at the base of the rocks, but she knows where the plants are and starts digging. Instantly the solid dark of the monolith seems to move and from it springs out a terrible female shape, with wild hair and raised arms, bellowing like a tormented animal. It picks up a stone and aims at Sanichari, who is paralyzed with shock and fear. But soon her survival instinct returns, and she manages to climb down and run. She hears the footsteps pursuing her, the witch running after her. She hears the howl that shatters the deserted field and the somber sky, and she senses the ancient burial rocks of the Oraons move. She stumbles and falls, feeling the fingernails of death on her back before she loses consciousness.

She would have died where she fell but for a coincidence. That same evening Mathur happens to come to Hesadi to see his friend Pahan. He has brought a bottle of distilled liquor for him. He has planned to stay the night with Pahan and ask him more about his ancestor Gidhna Oraon.

"But I have already told you about the battle that Gidhna waged against the white men."

"You didn't tell me that you're his great-grandson."

"What's the point of telling that?"

"What's the point of hiding that?"

Pahan's eyes glaze for a moment with a tribal's ancient suspicion of all nontribals; then he talks. "Gidhna Oraon was hanged; his brother Kalna shot dead. My ancestors had to flee from their original home. I can't risk talking about it."

"But there's no risk any more."

"For us it's always risky. You won't understand it. Why do we have to discuss it anyway? Let's drink and smoke the bidi that you've brought."

Mathur also wants to talk to Sanichari tonight and find out from her what she knows and thinks about this witch scare. She should be back soon. Where's she? She's gone to Jilad's field. Isn't she afraid of the witch? Perhaps she isn't. Pahan is cautious in his answer. But Mathur does not seem very interested in the subject and says that maybe there's no witch. Maybe Hanuman Misra made it all up to harass them.

The Brahman priest! The big shot whom the police officer and the politician from Patna all go to see and touch his feet. Planting false rumor? They both laugh. Pahan knows Mathur's trick. It is to see if Pahan agrees with what he himself thinks. Pahan is no less shrewd.

They talk and wait for Sanichari. They send for her and learn that she has not returned. Pahan becomes increasingly worried. Nobody wants to follow even Pahan to Jilad's field at night. Finally he sets off with Mathur to look for her.

They find her lying unconscious near the creek, with scratch wounds on her back and footprints on the sand beside her. Both are stunned. Mathur asks Pahan to show the way with the flashlight; he will carry her on his back. Before he finishes saying it, a strange laugh rises from where the creek joins the river, followed by an inhuman scream rending the field and the sky.

Later, Mathur cannot remember exactly how he and Pahan managed to come back carrying the body. All he remembers is the laugh and the scream pursuing them and how he fought the urge to put the body down and turn back with the flashlight to find out.

Back in the village, they lay Sanichari down at Pahan's place. Mathur watches Pahan's face grow ashen with fear as he tends to her. The old timidity is returning, the belief in the power of Hanuman Misra. Pahan breaks his grim silence only to curse himself for having doubts about the witch. Mathur wants to go back with his flashlight and look for the witch. But he does not, sensing the grim mood around him. Pahan gets up and strikes the leather drum, his face set in determination. The terrifying signal of danger echoes through the night. The menfolk gather with torches in their hands and stones in the folds of their loincloths. The women clasp their children and bar the doors. No one looks accusingly at Pahan. But Pahan's face is pained, and his eyes angry.

In the report that he has been writing, Mathur described this witch-hunt. He wrote that even though he was with them, he knew that he could not possibly feel what was going through their minds, that he was only a spectator, watching an exotic drama being played out.

They check the footprints on the sand of the creek and follow them into the forest beyond it. The men shout as they advance with their torches held up. Pahan walks ahead, very agitated, his arms raised, shouting and looking. Suddenly he stops and shouts, "There!" They all stop and see in front of them something standing on a stone and swaying. Mathur at first thinks it is a bear. Bears can stand on hind legs. The deep scratches on Sanichari's back could have been made by a bear.

But it is definitely not a bear that is standing on the stone! It bellows the way a buffalo does when being branded, but the voice is definitely human. It growls angrily and starts throwing stones at them. The men drop their torches and are about to run. Pahan shouts at them, "Don't! Nobody runs back. It will kill anyone who runs back. We must drive it away the way they drove it away from Murhai."

They pick up their torches and lurch forward, hurling stones, with courage drawn from desperate fear. Though frantic, they try to follow the instruction about merely driving away, not killing, the witch.

Mathur later wrote down that he felt as if he was whisked from this century into a stone-age battle. He was in the battle, and yet he was not. He was also observing himself, an academic who even in the midst of a battle could instinctively stand apart and judge it, analyze it for his own purpose of obtaining a Ph.D.

The battle goes on, and soon they are possessed with the cruel excitement of a pack attacking a lone one. Now and then a flaming torch is thrown up in the air. In one of those moments of enlarged flare, Mathur catches a glimpse of the witch. He sees that she is a dark naked young woman, her belly horribly swollen. She seems to have run out of stones and gets off the rock and starts running into the forest, again bellowing like a buffalo. The men are throwing big stones now, forgetting the injunction about not shedding the witch's blood. They chase her until she is well inside the forest. They turn back, excited and triumphant. Pahan orders an all-night vigil at his place. All must stay up, for the one who falls asleep will become the witch's prey. Tomorrow he will worship the deity. It is exactly the way they spent the night of witch-hunt in Murhai, except that there the illicit lovers, who happened to spot the witch first, ran away from the village, also because of the witch's curse, in the villagers' opinion.

They return to the village very late at night. The party starts with drinking home-brewed liquor. Surrounded by the strange excitement, Pahan tells Mathur about another incident, involving a he-witch. Then Mathur sits silently, listening to the drunken singing and thinking. It is a song of Holi, the festival in which the young smear each other with color and often fall in love, also the day of their annual hunting festival. The girl in the song is waiting for the boy who has stolen her heart that day to return from the hunt. The evening approaching, she is waiting by the river to help him carry the deer he must have got.

Mathur thinks about how his own perspective has changed in the course of the night's events. He has realized that no matter whether the witch is real, these people's emotional reactions are very real—the fear and the vengeful anger arising from fear. It is also disturbing that the hold of Hanuman Misra's priestly power is now being restored in their minds, even though they are not Hindus.

He recalls the evening's stone-age battle and his glimpse of the witch. She was quite ferocious in the face of such a mob attack. Why had no one stopped to ask why the stones hurt her? Fire and iron are supposed to be antidotes against witches. Now stones? His thoughts turn to folk beliefs about witch power—the list of harms they can do like curdling milk, ruining crops, killing domesticated animals, dispersing rain clouds, entering the wombs of pregnant women to eat the fetuses, possessing menstruating women to turn them into witches—beliefs not just of these people. The women in his family, his mother, for example, believe these. His father makes money in the lumber business; they live in town; he and his brothers went to college. Yet he lives daily with the practice of rituals based on the assumed presence of witches and evil eyes. He begins to despair at the contradictions in his life, wondering if his rational, educated consciousness is only a veneer. How else could he live with the observance of rituals based on blind beliefs?

As if reading his thoughts, Pahan tells him that educated city folks like him dismiss witches because they do not know how someone very familiar can turn into a demon. Pahan tells him of the case of his uncle Gidhna, not the Gidhna Oraon who fought the British. "Who knows why his parents named him Gidhna, when nobody dared to touch that name for such a long time?" He brought up little Pahan after his father had been killed by a tiger. He was a good man. Then something went wrong within him. His wife ruined his mind by sending their two sons away to work in coal mines, with the help of her brother. His sons earned cash, rented a room in a concrete house, and his wife left him to live with them. Pahan begged his uncle to come and live with him. But he didn't want to be dependent. "Eat your own food, but stay with me," the young Pahan had asked. But he refused. He said that his pain in old age must be a punishment for being good and god-fearing all his life. So he wanted to have nothing to do with either god or his nephew who was then an apprentice priest. One year it had rained so much that the timid Kuruda river became like a rogue elephant. The Pahan to whom he was apprenticed asked him one day to spy on his uncle and find out what he did at dead of night lighting the lamp. He found out that his uncle got up, lighted the lamp, and conversed with someone invisible. When he asked uncle whom he was talking to, he answered that he was talking to his wife. He was very drunk. When he reported this to his Pahan, it seemed to confirm whatever was worrying the latter. Why did his uncle spend entire nights away from home? Soon, strange deaths started occurring in the village. Pahan's wife stubbed her toe and died foaming in the mouth, with her body bent back like a bow. Someone drowned in the river. Several small children died suddenly, convulsing and hiccuping for no apparent reason. So Pahan got some villagers together late one night and showed them Gidhna leaving the village, walking in the direction of Jilad's field, and coming back in the morning. Pahan had figured out that every night he went to Jilad's field, some strange death occurred the following day.

Mathur asks what happened then. The Pahan held a trial. Asked to explain his nightly trips, his uncle Gidhna said that as he was disillusioned with deities, he went to the burial ground to ask the spirits why his life was ruined, why he was deserted in old age by his able-bodied sons and his wife. He said that he was angry with the deities. To Mathur, it is the tormented mind of an unfortunate man. To the tribunal, it was definite proof that he was damned, in league with the witch. That night they gathered a pile of dry twigs and branches to block the door of his uncle's hut and set fire to it with him inside. Pahan puffs at his bidi remembering how he felt as a young man watching the entire village burn his uncle alive. His heart flapped like a captured pigeon's wings as he heard his uncle scream inside. They held him back as he struggled to run to the burning hut. A flying spark touched Sanichari's cheek and left a scar.

Then? Then the strange deaths stopped. And then? The police came. They camped for two days to question the villagers. They ate the chickens and drank the liquor they made the villagers provide, and then they too left. It ended there; his wife and sons never asked about him.

The night of fear and revelry is almost over. Mathur and Pahan lie down on the grass mats on which they sat the whole night talking and listening. Pahan has a day of worship ahead. He also has to make sure that goats and cows are not taken to the burial field to graze and defile the rocks. Mathur has to return to Tohri, but he will be back soon to follow up on the witch. The songs are still going on, and the Holi song is back. Mathur listens to the boy's side now. Back from the hunt, he is looking for the girl who has stolen his heart earlier that day; he looks for her along the edge of the forest, and finally finds her by the river, her feet wet, her face flushed, and flowers in her oiled black hair.

5

A few days after the Hesadi incident, three old men arrange to meet at the marketplace, the three Pahans of Kuruda, Hesadi, and Murhai.

They talk about Sanichari's death, how she bled and how her wounds became septic. Mathur took her to the town hospital, where the doctor said that she had a disease that prevented the healing. What do the doctors know? No one lives after being scratched by the nails of death. Who is taking care of her grandson now? Hesadi's Pahan is because Sanichari was like his sister, as he grew up on her mother's milk. And the little boy has nobody else left.

Then they come to the question of organizing a joint witch-hunt. Instead of living in fear waiting for the witch to show up, why not gather the young men of the three villages together to hunt for the witch? Hesadi's Pahan feels the respectful eyes of the other two men rest on him, wrinkled and in loincloth like themselves. They seek his verdict. The respect is the heritage of his ancestors Gidhna and Kalna, whose names are in a song known to all the Oraons, a song that compares their names to the leaves of trees, bound to grow back every time they fall off. His answer is no. They can't send their young men, sons of someone or other, to risk their lives. The other two agree. They exchange a few mundane items of news—whether the brick factory and the coal mine are still closed. Murhai's Pahan has heard from his son that Hanuman Misra has bought up both and is going to restart them this winter. In that case, they must make sure that their young men get the jobs. They could appeal to the officer of the Tribal Welfare Department in Tohri. The Pahan of Hesadi could ask Mathur to talk to the officer on their behalf.

Mathur promises to talk to the officer and to Misra about giving them priority in hiring.

Nationalization of mining has not affected the many surface mines operated in this remote region. During 1970 and 1971, at the peak of labor unrest and urban terrorism in West Bengal, many of those with money and businessmen who closed down their firms in the state, shaking their heads about industries being threatened by leftism, quietly invested in the surface mines in southeastern Bihar. They hire the tribal and outcaste labor at nominal wage to dig with pickax and shovel and load the coal hauled away to cities and industries. Brick kilns are very profitable, too. The clay in the area makes excellent bricks, and labor is very cheap with the people so poor and the sources of employment so few.

Mathur makes inquiries about Hanuman Misra's latest acquisition of property. Hanuman Misra now owns not only the temple in Tahad, a big moneymaker by itself, and a lot of farmland and orchards, but also quite a few surface collieries. Now he can say that he truly controls the area. Mathur goes to talk to him. The priest explains to him with genuine sadness that only for his sons is he forced to acquire coal mines and brick kilns; Western education is at the root of the problem of priests' sons refusing to follow the hereditary occupation. "Look at yourself," he says, "look at how you've turned away from your father's business." Mathur asks whether he will hire the locals in his mines and kiln. He would like to, Lord Vishwanath willing.

On his next visit to Hesadi, Mathur tells Pahan what he found out about the mines and the old kiln to be reopened, about his talk with Misra. "Where exactly is the kiln?" Pahan asks.

"Near that cave three villages away from Hesadi, just before village Tura."

"What's the place like? Is it true that one can find deer there?"

"Do you want to go there to hunt deer?"

"Who wants to go so far? Besides, that cave area is no good. It's evil and scary after dark."

"Well, the witch hasn't turned up there."

"The witch has not turned up anywhere else lately. Everything is so confusing about this witch. Poor Sanichari died because of all this confusion."

Pahan asks Mathur to bring his gun along next time he comes to Hesadi. Maybe they can kill the leopard that seems to be taking some of the dogs of the villages before it enters a village to take goats and people. And yes, perhaps Mathur could get some kerosene for them. Pahan will send two boys to bring the kerosene back. Mathur takes leave.

Within a few days, two Hesadi boys come to Mathur in Tohri. They will take back the two cans of kerosene that Mathur has procured. Pahan wants Mathur to bring along some nails, rope, and some of his red medicine, an all-purpose healer of cuts and burns, in Pahan's view. Sanichari's grandson has been scalded by hot water. Mathur is also to take along the gun and some bullets. Why? Has anyone actually seen the leopard? No, but three dogs have disappeared from Dhai village one after another, and vultures are seen flying over the forest near that village.

Packing a large bottle of mercurochrome, Mathur smiles to himself about the incongruity in Pahan's thinking. He does not believe in modern medicine and injections, but he faithfully remembers that Mathur's mercurochrome once healed a bad blister wound in his foot. More recently he had taken antibiotics from Mathur for a gum sepsis. He had actively supported Mathur's idea of getting Sanichari to the hospital. From his entirely different worldview, he seems to be eclectically accepting the superiority of science in certain matters. Perhaps even in the current witch affair he will sometime reveal a rational attitude. But, then, has Mathur's own rational attitude enabled him to explain all of what is going on?

Mathur asks his wife for some of their boy's old clothes, which she saves to barter for new pots and pans from the vendor. She hands him a bundle without question. Even after two children, their relationship is very close. She never complains about his choice of the low-paying teaching job over the

ready money of his father's business. In fact, her affection for him is en-
hanced by the rest of his family's lack of understanding about him. He
notices the slight wilt in her face as he takes leave. She must be on a fast to
worship for his welfare. He is not in any danger. Why does she have to fast
and pray? "Because you're going into the witch's domain, thrown in fire by
the white man himself sitting safely in Patna." Mathur says, "When I finish
my dissertation, I'll take you away from this place, to America."

Perhaps at the time Mathur does have such a dream about the direction of
his efforts, his field study, but soon his dream would be jolted by an unexpected turn of events. Later on, he would stop having that dream. He would
continue teaching, and he would still be visiting Pahan in Hesadi even
though quite aware that he is no longer motivated to write a thesis on the Kol
uprising led by Gidhna Oraon. He would keep using that excuse to see
Pahan because he has grown very fond of him. They have grown attached to
each other, the way the railway tracks and the river running alongside become attached to each other without uniting. It would be disastrous for both
and for others if their minds ever unite. The curious reader will be relieved to
know that their mutual attachment continues to run parallel.

Mathur comes to Hesadi with the mercurochrome, the bundle of his son's
old clothes, nails and rope, some bidi, and his hunting rifle and bullets. He
treats the festering burn on Sanichari's grandson. With the rope and the nails
he helps make a flat hammock in Pahan's porch for sitting. He helps him
distribute the kerosene and receives thanks from the villagers. Next morning
he starts with a bunch of youths to hunt the leopard, promising to include the
rest of the village in a picture taken with the dead leopard.

Three villages beyond Hesadi is a cave, then the unused brick kiln, and
after that Tura village of the Munda tribals.

Tura is a very small village beside Kuruda river, with the forest on the
other side of the river. Village dogs come to drink at the river, and when they
disappear it means that a leopard is near the edge of the forest. The vultures
circling overhead confirm that. Mathur asks the boys to be silent because
leopards are very shrewd. He feels excited as they enter the forest, silently
stalking through the cool shade of the dark green canopy. His mind feels very
light, except for the worry about snakes.

They reach a spot where the forest is thin, with a few storm-felled trees
lying about. Sitting on one of those trunks is . . . the witch, eating a dog leg.
His heart starts pounding like a hammer. The boys turn back and run. The
witch looks up, and her mouth opens wide with that terrible bellowing
scream. When she stands up, Mathur sees the naked body with an enormously swollen middle. Instinctively he covers his eyes and turns around,
dropping the gun in the process. Then he starts to run. Stopping to look
behind, he sees the witch running after him, but slowly and laboriously. He

resumes running, with a totally different kind of panic and urgency this time.

The boys have assumed from the howl that the witch must have caught Mathur. So they do not slow down for him. Because he is an excellent runner, he manages to catch up with them. Frantically he tries to tell them that she is a woman, not a witch. But they do not even listen to him. They are transformed by terror into savage killers. Wild-eyed and shouting alarm, they run to Dhai village, asking its menfolk to get ready for the witch-hunt. They keep running and doing the same in the other villages. Bands of men join them, and the enlarging horde runs back toward the forest.

Mathur, completely ignored by them, follows helplessly. He is not part of this drama; he cannot stop it; he cannot turn back. So he goes along, listening to them talking in the primeval solidarity of panic and aggression: "That's why the clouds can't gather to make rain! That's why there are no fruits in the forest! No fish in the river! The air is heavy with poison!"

Listening to them Mathur suddenly understands a crucial and terrible truth about their life. He sees that these people have no place at all in the economic world. They are left out of all the economic progress surrounding them—the steel industry and the coal mines, the lumber business, the railways, the grain-laden irrigated lands. They are totally excluded from the man-made bounty and control of technology and abandoned to nature at its most fickle. Unwanted by the rest of the country, they would be wiped out if nature turns against them. So when nature's breasts turn dry, they blame it on the witch because they don't understand their man-made deprivation. Mathur understands what makes them angry, but he also knows that he cannot think like them. The chasm between him and them cannot be bridged: the gulf between those holding the gun and those at whom it is pointed, between the caste Hindus and the tribals. No magic can ever unite the firing squad with its target.

Tribesmen from all the villages have collected, carrying sticks and stones. It is almost noon when the Pahan of Hesadi joins them near the edge of the forest, and then nearly a hundred armed men, shouting and advancing, enter the forest. The witch gets up from the log and tries to get away. She seems to have difficulty running. She keeps stumbling. They hear her alternate between angry animal bellowing and painful human screaming. Somebody shouts that she is going to the river. Where is she going? She must be heading for the cave. They follow her shouting.

Out of the forest, she is crossing the shallow waters. They see her dragging herself, halting and looking back, clutching her stomach every now and then, but moving on awkwardly.

"Throw stones! Careful! Don't spill the blood!"

The witch bends over to pick up a stone. They stop. Then instead of turning to throw the stone at them, she suddenly dashes for the cave.

"Don't let it escape in there!"

The mob gathers in front of the cave. The Pahan of Dhai accuses the men from other villages of driving the witch into their life. He is not letting them get away with it. The men become belligerent: "How will you stop us?"

"Kill you."

"We can kill too."

The Pahan of Hesadi intervenes, "Stop it. We're all in danger."

"What shall we do?"

"We must get her out of the cave and drive her away."

"How?"

"How do you get the fox out of a hole?"

"Smoke it out. . . . Start the fire!"

"Don't burn her! You know we'll be ruined then."

"We'll smoke her out, and then we'll drive her away."

"Be sure to drive her away in the direction of the forest, not in the direction of our village," warns the Pahan of Tura.

Mathur watches the killer crowd in action. With ferocious intensity and swift efficiency they cut shrubs and branches and gather them in a pile at the mouth of the cave. Someone from Dhai quickly fetches some kerosene and sprinkles it on. The Pahan of Hesadi lights it with his flintstones.

Flames lick through the pile. The air breathes out heat. Green branches hiss and crack as they cook. The smoke flows toward the cave. They step back and watch, craning their necks, savage excitement in their faces and eyes. The Pahan of Hesadi is swaying on his feet, perhaps chanting something. Then they all are swaying and chanting "out! out!" Mathur realizes that he too is swaying with them. It must be the primitive in his subconscious. He holds onto a branch to steady himself.

"Look!" someone shouts.

A gigantic coil of smoke suddenly strikes out of the pile and slithers into the cave like a python. Even the outside is now darkened with smoke.

They hear a female voice screaming in terrible pain. The scream stops abruptly. The total silence is then broken by an incredible sound, the pure and helpless cry of the newborn.

The men are paralyzed, confused, scared. The dreamlike unreality is shattered by the cry of the Pahan of Tura. "No!" He grabs a cut branch and drags it into the fire, making way through the fire to get into the cave. They try to hold him back. He fights himself loose, bites the hands that try to pull him back, and runs barefoot over the embers into the cave. Then they all hear his cry echo inside the cave, "Somri, Somri!"

Mathur wakes up from his daze and comes forward. He too, though not barefoot, walks across the burning wood into the cave. He sees nothing in the dark inside and stands surrounded by the smell of bat droppings and flapping bat wings. Then he dimly sees the Pahan of Tura kneeling on the floor before a naked woman with a baby between her legs attached to the umbilical cord.

"It's my daughter!" The Pahan of Tura seems to be talking to the floor. Then he looks up into the dark and says, "My mute and dumb daughter! Her body has grown, not her mind. I had sent her to work, the work of cleaning the cowshed of Hanuman Misra's house in Tahad."

"When was that?"

"It's almost a year now. She has been missing for the last five or six months. Misraji said that she left the job. I searched for her everywhere. Later I learnt that his son had dirtied her. When I went back to ask about it, he had me beaten up. Then he started this witch scare! I have never suspected that it is my Somri whom we've been hunting down all along as the witch!"

"She is no witch!" Mathur turns around at the bewildered voice and sees the Pahans of Hesadi and Murhai standing behind him. The Pahan of Tura shakes his head and weeps, saying that if they are going to kill her they should also kill him and the baby.

The Pahan of Hesadi now speaks firmly, "She's no witch. You get up. Let someone go and call the women." He turns to Mathur. "Take your shirt off and give it to her father. He can stay with her. You and I can't."

The Pahan of Hesadi comes out of the cave and addresses the crowd, "I'll explain to you later. Somri, the daughter of Tura's Pahan, has given birth. Some of you run to the village and ask the women to come."

"Where's the witch?"

"Ask the Brahman in Tahad. After his son ruined her, he threw her out. Then he told us that there's a witch, that we must stone her away."

"What are you saying?"

"Do you think the great-grandson of Gidhna and Kalna would say something like this without being sure?"

Nobody asks any further questions. Very rarely does he invoke his legendary ancestors' names to secure allegiance of the people clad in loincloth like himself. They get busy doing as he said.

The women come; they cut the umbilical cord and clean the baby. Those who had desperately tried a short while ago to stone her, to smoke her out of the cave, now cut branches to make a stretcher for her. The women carry her out, covered with Mathur's shirt. Somri watches their faces with apprehension, but she sees no more vengeance in their eyes. The men keep their eyes averted from hers. Carefully, they lay her down on the stretcher and start their journey back with her. The Pahan of Tura picks up a leafy branch and walks alongside the stretcher, shielding her face and the baby from the hot sun.

After taking them home, the men leave in groups and head for their own villages. Mathur and the Pahan of Hesadi walk through the forest to pick up the gun Mathur had dropped earlier. Mathur remains silent throughout their journey back to the village, and Pahan mentions only two things in the whole time.

"She was driven by hunger to eat raw meat," he says.

"I want you to go to Hanuman Misra and take back our appeal. We won't work for him, not one of us. We won't let him bring outside coolies."

Mathur nods silently to Pahan's words.

Both feel the profound peace around them, the air sweet as ever and the forest green and cool as ever. With the oppressive cloud of terror lifted from his mind, the Pahan of Hesadi realizes that nature is not at all different from any other drought year. Only his fear made him think otherwise. He speaks again to stress his resolve, "We won't work for him. We won't let anyone else work for him either."

Mathur nods again, as tears roll down his cheeks. Pahan asks him why he is crying. Mathur does not know how to explain to Pahan, worlds apart from himself, what it is in all that happened that makes him cry.

Crossing the forest, they wade the muddy riverbed, toward Hesadi.

Giribala

Mahasweta Devi

Giribala was born in a village called Talsana, in the Kandi subdivision of Murshidabad district. Nobody ever imagined that she could think on her own, let alone act on her own thought. This Giribala, like so many others, was neither beautiful nor ugly, just an average-looking girl. But she had lovely eyes, eyes that somehow made her appearance striking.

In their caste, it was still customary to pay a bride-price. Aulchand gave Giri's father eighty rupees and a heifer before he married her. Giri's father, in turn, gave his daughter four tolas of silver, pots and pans, sleeping mats, and a cartload of mature bamboo that came from the bamboo clumps that formed the main wealth of Giri's father. Aulchand had told him that only because his hut had burned down did he need the bamboo to rebuild it. This was also the reason he gave for having to leave her with them for a few days—so that he could go to build a home for them.

Aulchand thus married Giri, and left. He did not come back soon.

Shortly after the marriage, Bangshi Dhamali, who worked at the sub–post office in Nishinda, happened to visit the village. Bangshi enjoyed much prestige in the seven villages in the Nishinda area, largely due to his side business of procuring patients for the private practice of the doctor who was posted at the only hospital in the area. That way, the doctor supplemented his hospital salary by getting paid by the patients thus diverted from the hospital, and Bangshi supplemented his salary of 145 rupees from the sub–post office with the commission he got for procuring those patients. Bangshi's prestige went

"Giribala" was first published in the magazine *Prasad* (Autumn 1982); reprinted in *Bortika* (January–June 1985), 118–35, a magazine edited by Mahasweta Devi.

up further after he started using the medical terms he had picked up from being around the doctor.

For some reason that nobody quite recalled, Bangshi addressed Giri's father as uncle. When Bangshi showed up on one of his patient-procuring trips, he looked up Giri's father and remarked disapprovingly about what he had just learned from his trip to another village, that he had given his only daughter in marriage to Aulchand, of all people.

"Yes. The proposal came along, and I thought he was all right."

"Obviously, you thought so. How much did he pay?"

"Four times twenty and one."

"I hope you're ready to face the consequences of what you've done."

"What consequences?"

"What can I say? You know that I'm a government servant myself and the right-hand man of the government doctor. Don't you think you should have consulted me first? I'm not saying that he's a bad sort, and I will not deny there was a time when I smoked *ganja* with him. But I know what you don't know—the money he gave you as bride-price was not his. It's Channan's. You see, Channan's marriage had been arranged in Kalhat village. And Aulchand, as Channan's uncle, was trusted with the money to deliver as bride-price on behalf of Channan. He didn't deliver it there."

"What?"

"Channan's mother sat crying when she learned that Aulchand, who had been living under their roof for so long, could cheat them like that. Finally, Channan managed to get married by borrowing from several acquaintances who were moved by his plight."

"He has no place of his own? No land for a home to stand on?"

"Nothing of the sort."

"But he took a cartload of my bamboo to rebuild the hut on his land!"

"I was going to tell you about that too. He sold that bamboo to Channan's aunt for a hundred rupees and hurried off to the Banpur fair."

Giri's father was stunned. He sat with his head buried in his hands. Bangshi went on telling him about other similar tricks Aulchand had been pulling. Before taking leave, he finally said, perhaps out of mercy for the overwhelmed man, "He's not a bad one really. Just doesn't have any land, any place to live. Keeps traveling from one fair to another, with some singing party or other. That's all. Otherwise, he's not a bad sort."

Giri's father wondered aloud, "But Mohan never told me any of these things! He's the one who brought the proposal to me!"

"How could he, when he's Aulchand's right hand in these matters?"

When Giri's mother heard all this from Giri's father, she was livid. She vowed to have her daughter married again and never to send her to live with the cheat, the thief.

But when after almost a year Aulchand came back, he came prepared to stop their mouths from saying what they wanted to say. He brought a large taro root, a new sari for his bride, a squat stool of jackfruit wood for his mother-in-law, and four new jute sacks for his father-in-law. Giri's mother still managed to tell him the things they had found out from Bangshi. Aulchand calmly smiled a generous, forgiving smile, saying, "One couldn't get through life if one believed everything that Bangshi-*dada* said.* Your daughter is now going to live in a brick house, not a mere mud hut. That's true, not false."

So, Giri's mother started to dress her only daughter to go to live with her husband. She took time to comb her hair into a nice bun, while weeping and lamenting, partly to herself and partly to her daughter, "This man is like a hundred-rooted weed in the yard. Bound to come back every time it's been pulled out. What he just told us are all lies, I know that. But with what smooth confidence he said those lies!"

Giri listened silently. She knew that although the groom had to pay a bride-price in their community, still a girl was only a girl. She had heard so many times the old saying: "A daughter born, To husband or death, She's already gone." She realized that her life in her own home and village was over, and her life of suffering was going to begin. Silently she wept for a while, as her mother tended to grooming her. Then she blew her nose, wiped her eyes, and asked her mother to remember to bring her home at the time of Durga puja and to feed the red-brown cow that was her charge, adding that she had chopped some hay for the cow, and to water her young *jaba* tree that was going to flower someday.

Giribala, at the age of fourteen, then started off to make her home with her husband. Her mother put into a bundle the pots and pans that she would be needing. Watching her doing that, Aulchand remarked, "Put in some rice and lentils too. I've got a job at the house of the *babu*. Must report to work the moment I get back. There'll be no time to buy provisions until after a few days."

Giribala picked up the bundle of rice, lentils, and cooking oil and left her village, walking a few steps behind him. He walked ahead, and from time to time asked her to walk faster, as the afternoon was starting to fade. He took her to another village in Nishinda, to a large brick house with a large garden of fruit trees of all kinds. In the far corner of the garden was a crumbling hovel meant for the watchman. He took her to it. There was no door in the door opening. As if answering her thought, Aulchand said, "I'll fix the door

---

* *Dada*, meaning elder brother, is also used to refer politely to or to address a friend or acquaintance older than oneself, but not old enough to be referred to or addressed as uncle.

soon. But you must admit the room is nice. And the pond is quite near. Now go on, pick up some twigs and start the rice."

"It's dark out there! Do you have a kerosene lamp?"

"Don't ask me for a kerosene lamp, or this and that. Just do what you can."

A maid from the babu's household turned up and saved Giri. She brought a kerosene lamp from the house and showed Giri to the pond, complaining about Aulchand and cautioning her about him. "What kind of heartless parents would give a tender young girl to a no-good ganja addict? How can he feed you? He has nothing. Gets a pittance taking care of the babu's cattle and doing odd jobs. Who knows how he manages to feed himself, doing whatever else he does! If you've been brought up on rice, my dear, you'd be wise enough to go back home tomorrow to leave behind the bits of silver that you have got on you."

But Giri did not go back home the next day for safekeeping her silver ornaments. Instead, in the morning she was found busy plastering with mud paste the exposed, uneven bricks of the wall of the crumbling room. Aulchand managed to get an old sheet of tin from the babu and nailed it to a few pieces of wood to make it stand; then he propped it up as a door for the room. Giri promptly got herself employed in the babu household for meals as her wage. After a few months, Aulchand remarked about how she had managed to domesticate a vagabond like him, who grew up without parents, never stayed home, and always floated around.

Giri replied, "Go, beg the babus for a bit of the land. Build your own home."

"Why will they give me land?"

"They will if you plead for the new life that's on its way. Ask them if a baby doesn't deserve to be born under a roof of its own. Even beggars and roving street singers have some kind of home."

"You're right. I too feel sad about not having a home of my own. Never felt that way before, though."

The only dream they shared was a home of their own.

However, their firstborn, a daughter they named Belarani, was born in the crumbling hovel with the tin door. Before the baby was even a month old, Giri returned to her work in the babu household, and, as if to make up for her short absence from work, she took the heavy sheets, the flatweave rugs, and the mosquito nets to the pond to wash them clean. The lady of the house remarked on how she put her heart into the work and how clean her work was!

Feeling very magnanimous, the lady then gave Giri some of her children's old clothes, and once in a while she asked Giri to take a few minutes' break from work to feed the baby.

Belarani was followed by another daughter, Poribala, and a son, Rajib, all born in the watchman's hovel at the interval of a year and a half to two years. After the birth of her fourth child, a daughter she named Maruni,* she asked the doctor at the hospital, where she went for this birth, to sterilize her.

By then Aulchand had finally managed to get the babu's permission to use a little area of his estate to build a home for his family. He had even raised a makeshift shack on it. Now he was periodically going away for other kinds of work assigned to him.

He was furious to learn that Giri had herself sterilized, so furious that he beat her up for the first time. "Why did you do it? Tell me, why?"

Giri kept silent and took the beating. Aulchand grabbed her by the hair and punched her a good many times. Silently she took it all. After he had stopped beating because he was tired and his anger temporarily spent, she calmly informed him that the Panchayat was going to hire people for the road building and pay the wages in wheat.

"Why don't you see your father and get some bamboo instead?"

"What for?"

"Because you're the one who has been wanting a home. I could build a good one with some bamboo from your father."

"We'll both work on the Panchayat road and have our home. We'll save some money by working harder."

"If only we could mortgage or sell your silver trinkets, ..."

Giribala did not say anything to his sly remark; she just stared at him. Aulchand had to lower his eyes before her silent stare. Giri had put her silver jewelry inside the hollow of a piece of bamboo, stuffed it up and kept it in the custody of the lady of the house she worked for. Belarani too started working there, when she was seven years old, doing a thousand odd errands to earn her meals. Bela was now ten, and growing like a weed in the rainy season. Giri would need the silver to get her married someday soon. All she had for that purpose was the bit of silver from her parents and the twenty-two rupees she managed to save from her years of hard work, secretly deposited with the mistress of the house, away from Aulchand's reach.

"I'm not going to sell my silver for a home. My father gave all he could for that, a whole cartload of bamboo, one hundred and sixty-two full stems, worth a thousand rupees at that time even in the markets of Nishinda."

"The same old story comes up again!" Aulchand was exasperated.

"Don't you want to see your own daughter married someday?"

"Having a daughter only means having to raise a slave for others. Mohan

---

* Literally meaning a girl likely to die; the name is perhaps intended to repel death, following the belief that death takes first the lives people want to cling to most.

had read my palm and predicted a son in the fifth pregnancy. But, no, you had to make yourself sterile, so you could turn into a whore."

Giri grabbed the curved kitchen knife and hissed at him, "If ever I hear you say those evil things about me, I'll cut off the heads of the children and then my own head with this."

Aulchand quickly stopped himself, "Forget I said it. I won't, ever again."

For a few days after that he seemed to behave himself. He was sort of timid, chastised. But soon, probably in some way connected with the grudge of being chastised by her, the vile worm inside his brain started to stir again; once again Mohan, his trick master, was his prompter.

Mohan had turned up in the midst of the busy days they were spending in the construction of a bus road that was going to connect Nishinda with Krishnachawk. Giri and Aulchand were both working there and getting as wages the wheat for their daily meals. Mohan too joined them to work there, and he sold his wheat to buy some rice, a pumpkin, and occasionally some fish to go with the wheat bread. He had remained the same vagabond that he always was, only his talking had become more sophisticated with a bohemian style picked up from his wanderings to cities and distant villages. He slept in the little porch facing the room occupied by Giri and her family.

Sitting there in the evenings, he expressed pity for Aulchand, "Tch! Tch! You seem to have got your boat stuck in the mud, my friend. Have you forgotten all about the life we used to have?"

Giri snapped at him, "You can't sit here doing your smart talking, which can only bring us ruin."

"My friend had such a good singing voice!"

"Perhaps he had that. Maybe there was money in it too. But that money would never have reached his home and fed his children."

Mohan started another topic one evening. He said that there was a great shortage of marriage-age girls in Bihar, so that the Biharis with money were coming down for Bengali brides and paying a bundle for that! He mentioned that Sahadeb Bauri, a fellow he knew, a low-caste fellow like themselves, received five hundred rupees for having his daughter married to one of those bride-searching Biharis.

"Where is that place?" Aulchand's curiosity was roused.

"You wouldn't know, my friend, even if I explained where it is. Let me just say that it's very far and the people there don't speak Bengali."

"They paid him five hundred rupees?" Aulchand was hooked in.

"Yes, they did."

The topic was interrupted at that point by the noise that rose when people suddenly noticed that the cowshed of Kali-babu, the Panchayat big shot, was on fire. Everybody ran in that direction to throw bucketfuls of water at it.

Giri forgot about the topic thus interrupted. But Aulchand did not.

Something must have blocked Giri's usual astuteness because she suspected nothing from the subsequent changes in her husband's tone.

For example, one day he said, "Who wants your silver? I'll get my daughter married and also my shack replaced with bricks and tin. My daughter looks lovelier every day from the meals in the babu home!"

Giri's mind sensed nothing at all to be alerted to. She only asked, "Are you looking for a groom for her?"

"I don't have to look. My daughter's marriage will just happen."

Giri did not give much thought to this strange answer either. She merely remarked that the sagging roof needed to be propped up soon.

Perhaps too preoccupied with the thought of how to get the roof propped up, Giri decided to seek her father's help and also to see her parents for just a couple of days. Holding Maruni to her chest and Rajib and Pori by the hand, she took leave of Belarani, who cried and cried because she was not being taken along to visit her grandparents. Giri, also crying, gave her eight annas to buy sweets to eat, telling her that she could go another time because both of them could not take off at the same time from their work at the babu's place, even if for only four days, including the two days in walking to and from there.

She had no idea that she was never to see Bela again. If she had, she would not only have taken her along, but she would also have held her tied to her bosom, she would not have let her out of her sight for a minute. She was Giri's beloved firstborn, even though Giri had to put her to work at the babu household ever since she was only seven; that was the only way she could have her fed and clothed. Giri had no idea when she started for her parents' village, leaving Bela with a kiss on her forehead.

"A daughter born, To husband or death, She's already gone." That must be why seeing the daughter makes the mother's heart sing! Her father had been very busy trying to sell his bamboo and acquiring two *bighas** of land meanwhile. He was apologetic about not being able in all this time to bring her over for a visit, and he asked her to stay on a few more days once she had made the effort to come on her own. Her mother started making puffed rice and digging up the taro root she had been saving for just such a special occasion. While her hands worked making things for them to eat, she lamented about what the marriage had done to her daughter, how it had tarnished her bright complexion, ruined her abundant hair, and made her collarbones stick out. She kept asking her to stay a few more days, resting and eating to repair the years of damage. Giri's little brother begged her to stay for a month.

* One *bigha* is roughly one-third of an acre.

For a few days, after many years, Giri found rest and care and heaping servings of food. Her father readily agreed to give her the bamboo, saying how much he wanted his daughter to live well, in a manner he could be proud of. Giri could easily have used a few tears and got some other things from her father. Her mother asked her to weep and get a maund of rice too while he was in the giving mood. But Giri did not do that. Giri was not going to ask for anything from her loved ones unless she absolutely had to. She walked over to the corner of the yard, to look at the hibiscus she had planted when she was a child. She watched with admiration its crimson flowers and the clean mud-plastered yard and the new tiles on the roof. She also wondered if her son Rajib could stay there and go to the school her brother went to. But she mentioned nothing to her parents about this sudden idea that felt like a dream.

She just took her children to the pond, and, with the bar of soap she had bought on the way, she scrubbed them and herself clean. She washed her hair too. Then she went to visit the neighbors. She was feeling lighthearted, as if she were in heaven, without the worries of her life. Her mother sent her brother to catch a fish from the canal, the new irrigation canal that had changed the face of the area since she last saw it. It helped to raise crops and catch fish throughout the year. Giri felt an unfamiliar wind of fulfillment and pleasure blowing in her mind. There was not the slightest hint of foreboding.

Bangshi Dhamali happened to be in the village that day, and he too remarked on how Giri's health and appearance had deteriorated since she went to live with that no-good husband of hers. He said that if only Aulchand were a responsible father and could look after the older kids, she could have gone to work in the house of the doctor who was now living in Bahrampur town, and after some time she could take all the children over there and have them all working for food and clothing.

Giri regarded his suggestion with a smile, and asked him instead, "Tell me, dada, how is it that when so many destitute people are getting little plots of land from the government, Rajib's father can't?"

"Has he ever come to see me about it? Ever sought my advice on anything? I'm in government service myself, and the right-hand man of the hospital doctor as well. I could easily have gotten him a plot of land."

"I'm going to send him to you as soon as I get back."

It felt like a pleasant dream to Giri, that they could have a piece of land of their own for a home of their own. She knew that her husband was a pathetic vagabond. Still, she felt a rush of compassion for him. A man without his own home, his own land. How could such a man help being diffident and demoralized?

"Are you sure, Bangshi-dada? Shall I send him to you then?"

"Look at your own father. See how well he's managed things. He's now almost a part of the Panchayat. I don't know what's the matter with uncle, though. He could have seen to it that Aulchand got a bit of the land being distributed. I once told him as much, and he insulted me in the marketplace, snapped at me that Aulchand should be learning to use his own initiative."

Giri decided to ignore the tendentious remark and keep on pressing Bangshi instead, "Please, Bangshi-dada, you tell me what to do. You know how impractical that man is. The room he's put up in all these years doesn't even have a good thatch roof. The moon shines into it all night and the sun all day. I'm hoping to get Bela married someday soon. Where am I going to seat the groom's party? And, dada, would you look for a good boy for my daughter?"

"There is a good boy available. Obviously, you don't know that. He's the son of my own cousin. Just started a grocery store of his own."

Giri was excited to learn that, and even Rajib's face lit up as he said that he could then go to work as a helper in his brother-in-law's shop and could bring home salt and oil on credit. Giri scolded him for taking after his father, wanting to live on credit rather than by work.

Giri ended up staying six days with her parents instead of two. She was about to take leave, wearing a sari without holes that her mother gave her, a bundle of rice on her head, and cheap new shirts and pants on her children. Just then, like the straw suddenly blown in, indicating the still unseen storm, Bangshi Dhamali came in a rush to see her father.

"I don't want to say if it is bad news or good news, uncle, but what I just heard is incredible. Aulchand had told Bela that he was going to take her to see her grandparents. Then with the help of Mohan, he took her to Kandi town, and there he got the scared twelve-year-old, the timid girl who had known only her mother, married to some strange man from Bihar. There were five girls like Bela taken there to be married to five unknown blokes. The addresses they left are all false. This kind of business is on the rise. Aulchand got four hundred rupees in cash. The last thing he was seen doing was, back from drinking with Mohan, crying and slobbering, 'Bela! Bela!' while Kali-babu of the village Panchayat was shouting at him."

The sky seemed to come crashing down on Giribala's head. She howled with pain and terror. Her father got some people together and went along with her, vowing to get the girl back, to break the hands of the girl's father, making him a cripple, and to finish Mohan for good.

They could not find Mohan. Just Aulchand. On seeing them, he kept doing several things in quick succession. He vigorously twisted his own ears and nose to show repentance, he wept, perhaps with real grief, and from time to time he sat up straight, asserting that because Bela was his daughter it was nobody else's business how he got her married off.

They searched the surrounding villages as far as they could. Giri took out the silver she had deposited with the mistress of the house and went to the master, crying and begging him to inform the police and get a paid announcement made over the radio about the lost girl. She also accused them, as mildly as she could in her state of mind, for letting the girl go with her father, knowing as they did the lout that he was.

The master of the house persuaded Giri's father not to seek police help because that would only mean a lot of trouble and expense. The terrible thing had happened after all; Bela had become one more victim of this new business of procuring girls on the pretext of marriage. The police were not going to do much for this single case; they would most probably say that the father did it after all. Poor Bela had this written on her forehead!

Finally, that was the line everybody used to console Giri. The master of the house in which she and Bela worked day and night, the neighbors gathered there, even Giri's father ended up saying that—about the writing on the forehead that nobody could change. If the daughter was to remain hers, that would have been nice, they said in consolation, but she was only a daughter, not a son. And they repeated the age-old saying: "A daughter born, To husband or death, She's already gone."

Her father sighed and said with philosophical resignation, "It's as if the girl sacrificed her life to provide her father with money for a house."

Giri, crazed with grief, still brought herself to respond in the implied context of trivial bickering, "Don't send him any bamboo, father. Let the demon do whatever he can on his own."

"It's useless going to the police in such matters," everybody said.

Giri sat silently with her eyes closed, leaning against the wall. Even in her bitter grief, the realization flashed through her mind that nobody was willing to worry about a girl child for very long. Perhaps she should not either. She too was a small girl once, and her father too gave her away to a subhuman husband without making sufficient inquiries.

Aulchand sensed that the temperature in the environment was dropping. He started talking defiantly and defending himself to her father by blaming Giri and answering her remark about him. "Don't overlook your daughter's fault. How promptly she brought out her silver chain to get her daughter back! If she had brought it out earlier, then there would have been a home for us and no need to sell my daughter. Besides, embarrassed as I am to tell you this, she had the operation to get cleaned out, saying, 'What good is it having more children when we can't feed the ones we've got?' Well, I've shown what good it can be, even if we got more daughters. So much money for a daughter!"

At this, Giri started hitting her own head against the wall so violently that she seemed to have suddenly gone insane with grief and anger. They had to grapple with her to restrain her from breaking her head.

Slowly the agitation died down. The babu's aunt gave Giri a choice nugget of her wisdom to comfort her. "A daughter, until she is married, is her father's property. It's useless for a mother to think she has any say."

Giri did not cry any more after that night.

Grimly, she took Pori to the babu's house, to stay there and work in place
of Bela, and told her that she would kill her if she ever went anywhere with
her father. In grim silence, she went through her days of work and even more
work. When Aulchand tried to say anything to her, she did not answer; she
just stared at him. It scared Aulchand. The only time she spoke to him was to
ask, "Did you really do it only because you wanted to build your home?"

"Yes. Believe me."

"Ask Mohan to find out where they give the children they buy full meals
to eat. Then go and sell the other three there. You can have a brick and
concrete house. Mohan must know it."

"How can you say such a dreadful thing, you merciless woman? Asking
me to sell the children. Is that why you got sterilized? And why didn't you
take the bamboo that your father offered?"

Giri left the room and lay down in the porch to spend the night there.
Aulchand whined and complained for a while. Soon he fell asleep.

Time did the ultimate, imperceptible talking! Slowly Giri seemed to accept it. Aulchand bought some panels of woven split-bamboo for the walls.
The roof still remained covered with leaves. Rajib took the work of tending
the babu's cattle. Maruni, the baby, grew into a child, playing by herself in
the yard. The hardest thing for Giri now was to look at Pori because she
looked so much like Bela, with Bela's smile, Bela's way of watching things
with her head tilted to one side. The mistress of the house was full of similar
praise for her work and her gentle manners.

Little Pori poured her heart into the work at the babu household, as if it
were far more than a means to the meals her parents couldn't provide, as if
it were her vocation, her escape. Perhaps the work was the disguise for her
silent engagement in constant, troubling thoughts. Why else would she
sweep all the rooms and corridors ten times a day, when nobody had asked
her to? Why did she carry those jute sacks for paddy storage to the pond to
wash them diligently? Why else would she spend endless hours coating the
huge unpaved yard with rag dipped in mud-dung paste until it looked absolutely smooth from end to end?

When Pori came home in the evening, worn out from the day's constant
work, Giri, herself drained from daylong work, would feed her some puffed
rice or chickpea flour that she might happen to have at home. Then she
would go and spend most of the evening roaming alone through the huge
garden of the babus, absently picking up dry twigs and leaves for the stove
and listening to the rustle of leaves, the scurrying of squirrels in the dark. The
night wind soothed her raging despair, as it blew her matted hair, uncombed
for how long she did not remember.

The gentle face of her firstborn would then appear before her eyes, and she
would hear the sound of her small voice, making some little plea on some
little occasion. "Ma, let me stay home today and watch you make the puffed

rice. If they send for me, you can tell them that Bela would do all the work tomorrow, but she can't go today. Would you, Ma, please?"

Even when grown up, with three younger ones after her, she loved to sleep nestled next to her mother. Once her foot was badly cut and bruised. The squat stool that the babu's aunt sat on for her oil massage had slipped and hit her foot. She bore the pain for days, until applying the warm oil from a lamp healed it. Whenever Giri had a fever, Bela somehow found some time in between her endless chores at the babu household to come to cook the rice and run back to work.

> Bela, Belarani, Beli—
> Her I won't abandon.
> Yet my daughter named Beli,
> To husband or death she's gone!

Where could she be now? How far from here? In which strange land? Giri roamed the nights through the trees, and she muttered absently, "Wherever you are, my daughter, stay alive! Don't be dead! If only I knew where you were, I'd go there somehow, even if I had to learn to fly like birds or insects. But I don't know where you were taken. I wrote you a letter, with the babu's help, to the address they left. You couldn't have got it, daughter, because it's a false address."

Absently Giri would come back with the twigs, cook the rice, feed Maruni, eat herself, and lie down with her children, leaving Aulchand's rice in the pot.

The days without work she stayed home, just sitting in the porch. The days she found work, she went far—by the bus that now plied along the road they had worked on a few years ago, the bus that now took only an hour and a half to reach Kandi town. There, daily-wage work was going on, digging feeder channels from the main canal. The babu's son was a labor contractor there. He also had the permit for running a bus. Giri took that bus to work.

There, one day she came across Bangshi Dhamali. He was sincere when he said that he had difficulty recognizing her. "You've ruined your health and appearance. Must be the grief for that daughter. But what good is grieving going to do after all?"

"Not just that. I'm now worried about Pori. She's almost ten."

"Really! She was born only the other day, the year the doctor built his house, and electricity came to Nishinda. Pori was born in that year."

"Yes! If only I had listened to what you said to me about going to work at the doctor's house and taken the children to town! My son now tends the babu's cattle. If I had gone then, they could all be in school now!"

"Don't know about your children being able to go to school. But I do know that the town is now flooded with jobs. You could put all your children to work at least for daily meals."

Giri was aware that her thinking of sending her children to school annoyed Bangshi. She yielded, "Anyway, Bangshi-dada. What good is it being able to read a few pages if they've to live on manual labor anyway? What I was really going to ask you is to look for a boy for my Pori."

"I'll tell Aulchand when I come to know of one."

"No. No. Make sure that you tell me."

"Why are you still so angry with him? He certainly made a mistake. Can't it be forgiven? Negotiating a daughter's wedding can't be done with the mother. It makes the groom's side think there's something wrong in the family. When it comes to your son's wedding, the bride's side would talk to you. It's different with the daughter."

"At least let me know about it all, before making a commitment."

"I'll see what I can do. I happen to know a rickshaw plier in Krishnachawk. Not very young, though. About twenty-five, I think."

"That's all right. After what happened to Bela, the groom's age is not my main concern."

"Your girl will be able to live in Krishnachawk. But the boy has no land, he lives by plying a rented rickshaw, which leaves him with barely five rupees a day. Makes a little extra by rolling bidis at night. Doesn't have a home yet. He wants to get married because there's nobody to cook for him and look after him at the end of the day."

"You try for him. If it works out, I'd have her wedding this winter."

The total despondency in her mind since losing Bela suddenly moved a little to let in a glimmer of hope for Pori. She went on hopefully, saying, "I'll give her everything I've got. After that, I'll have just Maruni to worry about. But she's still a baby. I'll have time to think. Let me tell you Bangshi-dada, and I'm saying this not because she's my daughter, my Pori looks so lovely at ten. Perhaps the meals at the babu house did it. Come dada, have some tea inside the shop."

Bangshi sipped the tea Giri bought him and informed her that her father was doing very well for himself, adding to his land and his stores of paddy, and remarked what a pity it was that he didn't help her much!

"It may not sound nice, sister. But the truth is that blood relation is no longer the main thing these days. Uncle now mixes with his equals, those who are getting ahead like himself, not with those gone to the dogs, like your man, even if you happen to be his daughter."

Giri just sighed, and quietly paid for the tea with most of the few coins tied in one end of the sari and tucked in her waist. Before taking leave, she earnestly reminded Bangshi about her request for finding a good husband for Pori.

Bangshi did remember. When he happened to see Aulchand shortly after that, he mentioned the rickshaw plier. Aulchand perked up, saying that he too was after a boy who plied a rickshaw, though his did it in Bahrampur, a bit further away but a much bigger place than Krishnachawk. The boy had a fancy beard, mustache, and hair, and he talked so smart and looked so impressive in some dead Englishman's pants and jacket he had bought for himself at the second-hand market. Aulchand asked Bangshi not to bother himself any more about the rickshaw plier he had in mind.

Next time Giri saw Bangshi, she asked him if he had made contact with the rickshaw plier in Krishnachawk. He said that he had talked with Aulchand about it meanwhile and that she need not worry about it.

Aulchand then went looking for Mohan, his guide in worldly matters. And why not? There was not a place Mohan hadn't been to, all the nearby small towns in West Bengal that Aulchand had only heard of: Lalbagh, Dhulian, Jangipur, Jiaganj, Farakka. In fact, Aulchand didn't even know that Mohan was now in a business flung much further, procuring girls for whorehouses in the big cities, where the newly rich businessmen and contractors went to satisfy their newfound appetite for the childlike, underdeveloped bodies of Bengali pubescent girls. Fed well for a few months, they bloomed so deliciously that they yielded back within a couple of years the price paid to procure them.

But it was very important to put up a show of marriage to procure them. It was no longer possible to get away with just paying some money for the girl. Any such straight procurer was now sure to get a mass beating from the Bengali villagers. Hence, the need for stories about a shortage of marriage-age girls in Bihar and now the need for something even more clever. The weddings now had to look real, with a priest and all that. Then there would have to be some talk about the rituals that must be performed at the groom's place according to their local customs to complete the marriage, and so with the family's permission they must get back right away.

The "grooms from Bihar looking for brides in Bengal" story had circulated long enough. Newer tactics became necessary. The local matchmakers, who got a cut in each deal, were no longer informed enough about what was going on, but they sensed that it held some kind of trouble for their occupation. They decided not to worry too much about exactly how the cheating was done. They just took the position that they were doing what the girl's parents asked them to do—to make contact with potential grooms. They played down their traditional role as the source of information about the groom's family and background.

The girls' families too decided to go ahead despite the nonperformance of their usual source of information. Their reason for not talking and investigating enough was that the high bride-price they were offered and the little dowry they were asked to pay might then be revealed, and, because there was no dearth of envious people, someone might undo the arrangement. In some cases, they thought that they had no choice but an out-of-state groom because even in their low-caste communities, in which bride-price was customary, the Bengali grooms wanted several thousands of rupees in watches, radios, bicycles, and so on.

Since the incident of Bela, Kali-babu of the Panchayat refused to hire Aulchand on the road project or any other construction under the Panchayat. Aulchand found himself a bit out of touch, but, with plenty of free time, he went away for a few days trying to locate Mohan.

Mohan, meanwhile, was doing exceedingly well considering that he never got past the fourth grade in school. He had set up another business like a net around the block development office of Nishinda, to catch the peasants who came there for subsidized fertilizers and loans, part of which they somehow managed to lose to Mohan before they could get back to their village. Mohan was an extremely busy man these days.

He firmly shook his head at Aulchand's request, saying, "Count me out. Mohan Mandal has done enough of helping others. To help a father get his daughter married is supposed to be a virtue. You got the money. What did I get? The other side at least paid me forty rupees in broker's fee. And you? You used your money all on bamboo wall-panels. Besides, I'm afraid of your wife."

"She's the one who wants a rickshaw plier in a nearby town."

"Really?"

"Yes. But listen. You stay out of the thing and just put me in touch with a rickshaw plier boy in a big town like Bahrampur. My daughter will be able to live there; we'll go there to visit them. I'd like nothing better. Bela's mother too might be pleased with me."

"You want to make up with your wife this way, right?"

"I'd like to. The woman doesn't think of me as a human being. I want to show her that I can get my daughter married well without anyone's help. Only you can supply me that invisible help."

Mohan laughed and said, "All right. But I'll not get involved. I'll just make the contact, that's all. What if the big-town son-in-law has a long list of demands?"

"I'll have to borrow."

"I see. Go home now. I'll see what I can do."

Mohan gave it some thought. He must be more careful this time. He must keep the "groom from Bihar" setup hidden one step away and have a rickshaw plier boy in front, the one who will do the marrying and then pass her on. Aulchand's plea thus gave birth to a new idea in Mohan's head, but first he had to find a rickshaw plier boy. Who could play the part? He must go to town and check with some of his contacts.

Talking about Pori's marriage did reduce the distance between Giribala and Aulchand. Finally, one day Mohan informed Aulchand that he had the right match. "How much does he want?" Aulchand asked.

"He's already got a watch and a radio. He plies a cycle-rickshaw, so he wants no bicycle. Just the clothes for bride and groom, bed, shoes, umbrella, stuff like that. Quite a bargain, really."

"How much will he pay in bride-price?"

"One hundred rupees."

"Does he have a home for my daughter to live in?"

"He has a rented room. But he owns the cycle-rickshaw."

Aulchand and Giri were happy. When the future groom came to see the bride, Giri peeked from behind the door, studying him intently. Big, well-built body, well-developed beard and mustache. He said that his name was Manohar Dhamali. In Bahrampur, there was indeed a rickshaw plier named Manohar Dhamali. But this man's real name was Panu. He had just been acquitted from a robbery charge, due to insufficient evidence. Aulchand didn't know about this part. After getting out of jail, Panu had just married a girl like Poribala in Jalangi, another in Farakka, and delivered them to the "groom from Bihar" gang. He was commissioned to do five for five hundred rupees. Not much for his efforts, he thought, but not bad with his options at the moment. Panu had plans to move further away, to Shiliguri, to try new pastures as soon as this batch was over and he had some money in hand.

At the time of Bela's marriage, no relative was there, not even Giribala. This time, Giri's parents came. Women blew conch shells and ululated happily to solemnize each ritual. Giri, her face shining with sweat and excited oil glands, cooked rice and meat curry for the guests. She brought her silver ornaments from the housemistress and put them on Pori, who was dressed in a new sari that Giri's mother had brought. Her father had brought a sackful of rice for the feast. The babu family contributed fifty rupees. The groom came by bus in the company of five others. Pori looked even more like Bela. She was so lovely in the glow on her skin left from the turmeric rub and in the red *alta* edging her small feet.

Next day, with the groom she took the bus and left for the town.

That was the last time Giri saw Pori's face. The day after, Aulchand went to the town with Rajib and Giri's young brother to visit the newly married couple, as the custom required. The night advanced, but they did not return. Very, very late in the night, Giri heard the sound of footsteps of people coming in, but silently. Giri knew at once. She opened the door, and saw Bangshi Dhamali holding Rajib's hand. Rajib cried out, "Ma!" Giri knew the terrible thing had happened again. Silently she looked on them. Giri's brother told her. There wasn't much to tell. They did find a Manohar Dhamali in the town, but he was a middle-aged man. They asked the people around and were told that it must be another of Panu's acts. He was going around doing a lot of marrying. He seemed to be linked with some kind of gang.

Giri interrupted to ask Bangshi, "And Mohan is not behind this?"

"He's the mastermind behind this new play."

"And where's Rajib's father? Why isn't he with you?"

"He ran to catch Mohan when he heard that Mohan got five to seven hundred rupees from it. He left shouting incoherently, 'I want my daughter. I want my money.'"

Giri's little porch was again crowded with sympathetic, agitated people, some of them suggesting that they find Mohan and beat him up, others wanting to go to the police station, but all of them doing just a lot of talking. "Are we living in a lawless land?" Lots of words, lots of noise.

Close to dawn, Aulchand came home. Overwhelmed by the events, he had finally gone to get drunk and he was talking and bragging, "I found out where he got the money from. Mohan can't escape Aulchand-sardar. I twisted his neck until he coughed up my share of the money. Why shouldn't I get the money? The daughter is mine, and he'll be the one to take the money from putting her in a phony marriage? Where's Pori's mother? Foolish woman, you shouldn't have done that operation. The more daughters we have, the more money we can have. Now I'm going to have that home of ours done. Oh-ho-ho, my little Pori!"

Aulchand cried and wept and very soon he fell asleep on the porch. Giribala called up all her strength to quietly ask the crowd to go home. After they left, Giri sat by herself for a long time, trying to think what she should do now. She wanted to be dead. Should she jump into the canal? Last night, she heard some people talking, correctly perhaps, that the same fate may be waiting for Maruni too.

"Making business out of people's need to see their daughters married. Giri, this time you must take it to the police with the help of the babu. Don't let them get away with it. Go to the police, go to court."

Giri had looked on, placing her strikingly large eyes on their faces, then shaking her head. She would try nothing! Aulchand got his money at his daughter's expense. Let him try. Giri firmly shook her head.

Bangshi had remarked before leaving, "God must have willed that the walls come from one daughter and the roof from the other."

Giri had silently gazed at his face too with her striking eyes.

After some time, Aulchand was crying and doing the straw roof at the same time. The more tears he shed, the more dry-eyed Giri became.

The babu's elderly aunt tried to console her with her philosophy of cliches, "Not easy to be a daughter's mother. They say that a daughter born is already gone, either to husband or to death. That's what happened to you. Don't I know why you aren't crying? They say that one cries from a little loss, but turns into stone with too much loss. Start working again. One gets used to everything except hunger."

Giri silently gazed at her too, as she heard the familiar words coming out of her mouth. Then she requested her to go and tell the babu's wife that Giri wanted to withdraw her deposited money immediately. She went to collect the money. She put it in a knot in her sari and tucked the knot in her waist.

She came back and stood by the porch, looking at the home Aulchand was building. Nice room. The split-bamboo woven panels of the wall were neatly plastered with mud and were now being topped with a new straw roof. She had always dreamed of a room like this. Perhaps that was wanting too much. That was why Beli and Pori had to become prostitutes—yes, prostitutes. No matter what euphemism is used, nobody ever sets up home for a girl bought with money.

Nice room. Giri thought she caught a flitting glimpse of Aulchand eyeing little Maruni while tying up the ends of the straw he had laid on the roof. Giri silently held those striking eyes of hers steadily on Aulchand's face for some time, longer than she had ever done before. And Aulchand thought that no matter how great her grief was, she must be impressed with the way their home was turning out after all.

The next morning brought the biggest surprise to all. Before sunrise, Giribala had left home, with Maruni on her hip and Rajib's hand held in hers. She had walked down to the big road and caught the early morning bus to the town. Later on, it also became known that at the Nishinda stop she had left a message for Pori's father with Bangshi Dhamali. The message was that Giri wanted Aulchand to live in his new room happily forever. But Giri was going away from his home to work in other people's homes in order to feed and raise her remaining children. And if he ever came to the town looking for her, she would put her neck on the rail line before a speeding train.

People were so amazed, even stunned by this that they were left speechless. What happened to Bela and Pori was happening to many others these days. But leaving one's husband was quite another matter. What kind of woman would leave her husband of many years just like that? Now, they all felt certain that the really bad one was not Aulchand, but Giribala. And arriving at this conclusion seemed to produce some kind of relief for their troubled minds.

And Giribala? Walking down the unfamiliar roads and holding Maruni on her hip and Rajib by the hand, Giribala only regretted that she had not done this before. If she had left earlier, then Beli would not have been lost, then Pori would not have been lost. If only she had had this courage earlier, her two daughters might have been saved.

As this thought grew insistent and hammered inside her brain, hot tears flooded her face and blurred her vision. But she did not stop even to wipe her tears. She just kept walking.

The Daughter and the Oleander

Hasan Azizul Huq

It is a cruel winter night, with a sheet of frost descending from the clear sky. The moon is a lifeless cold bloom above the fronds of the coconut tree. In the slight wind, a large banana leaf turns slowly, heavily, showing its topside and its underside, back and forth.

Further away, at the crossing of the road that goes to the marketplace, the tin roof of Rahat Khan's house is glittering with frost in the moonlight.

A fox puts its forepaws up on the porch of the hut of Kanu's mother and howls. Then, all at once, a chorus of howls rises from the bushes, from the piles of bricks and the deserted crumbling huts along the sides of the brick-paved path leading to the school. From northeast of the village rise many voices shouting, "Chase it! Chase it! Quick! Quick!" The sudden noise seems to send a shiver in the ghostly patches of darkness in the deserted cold night. The moonlight, too, sparkling steadily on the tin roof until then, seems startled by the noise.

The robber fox now appears on the market road with the chicken in its jaws. The dying chicken thrashes its wings, casting a fluttering shadow on the road. The fox's shadow in the moonlight looks like a wolf's shadow. It looks up at the moon, pauses to consider something, then crosses the road

Written in 1966, "Atmaja O Ekti Karabi Gachh" appears in Hasan Azizul's collection *Atmaja O Ekti Karabi Gachh* (1967; reprint, Dhaka: Muktadhara, 1981), 9–17. Although the 1947 Partition of Bengal is never directly mentioned, its effects in the demoralization, destitution, and uprooting of the people can be seen in the plight of the individuals this story portrays. The old man, who is introduced only near the end of the story, is the head of a Muslim family that was transferred from West Bengal to East Bengal (Pakistan) in accordance with the property exchange arrangements between immigrants. Whether the main character's own impoverished family was likewise displaced by the Partition is not certain, but he is in any case a victim of East Bengal's economic stagnation following the Partition.

and goes in the bushes beside the school road. Chandmani's folks soon appear on the road, carrying sticks and shouting like thugs, "Where did the bastard go?"

The sheet of frost keeps rolling down from the sky.

Inam, the eldest of the Sirdar sons by the younger wife, walks up the bridge over the still water. He peers down at the reflection of his face on the silvery surface, scanning it for details, the eyes and the nose, while listening to the eerie sound of frost, the shiver of breeze, the light crackle of a few peanut shells swept up. The shiny leaves along the side of the canal seem dripping wet with liquid moonlight. A branch of the jackfruit tree sticks out to the east, waving awkwardly. Somewhere in the distance finger cymbals start up a musical soiree.

Inam crosses the bridge, wades through the dusty stretch, and stands by the side of the nearly dry river. He waits, watching the path that looks like a white snake in the pale moonlight. Soon moving shadows fall upon the path, with noisy voices. Inam sees the big body of Feku, like that of a flabby old tiger, followed by Suhash.

They are talking but not about why they are meeting here so late in the winter night. Suhash is raving about the *loochi* and the sweets he once had when he went with the groom's party to his uncle's wedding. The transistor radio under Feku's arm is playing a song they are obviously not listening to. The plaintive, beautiful voice of Kanika goes on, in the bitter cold beside the dry river, singing about the pains of the night alone. Strangely, it doesn't seem to disturb any of the birds sleeping in the trees, but it disturbs Inam. "Turn off the radio," he says gruffly as soon as they come close.

"There you are." They see him and stop. Suhash grins so wide that his teeth, black with smoking, jut out of his mouth. It adds to Inam's irritation. "Stop the radio."

"Nobody can hear it. Even if they do, nobody would come out here," Feku says.

"That's not the reason. The song bothers me."

Feku flips off Kanika's voice and hands the radio to Suhash, saying, "Hurry up now, or he will fall asleep."

"Who?" asks Suhash, taking the radio.

"The old man. Who else! As soon as the evening sets in, the old man with his infernal cough goes to sleep." Feku finishes his remark by spitting on the dusty ground.

As they walk away, the wind rises a little, perhaps from the dried river bed, sounding with the rustle of dry leaves. They pass by the Kazis' backyard and hear the splash of a fish leaping in the tank. Through gaps in the fence of Khan's yard, they see the boiling of paddy going on in there, and the briefly illuminated pretty faces of the Khan women as the fire is stoked.

"Aren't you going to school these days?" Suhash asks Inam.

"No."

"So you aren't going to finish studying?"

"What good is studying?"

"You want a proper job, don't you?"

"Sure! Jobs are hanging in the trees, waiting to be picked as soon as I finish studying."

Suhash doesn't say anything else to drag out the pointless conversation. He just turns the dial of the radio, making flitting random noises, while his clumsy big shoes scatter the dust of the path.

Inam smells dry earth in the dust in his breath.

It brings back the memory of afternoons on market days and of fish. From fish his mind moves to the river, the river almost dried now, patches of sand bank risen on its bed, people returning in bullock carts piled up with the river's sand. His mind sees the tall white plumes rising from the clumps of pampas on the other side of the river. On this side of it is the school building, with the big *sajne* tree, and the little birds in the tree swinging their long tail feathers. He hears the sound of an iron rod clanging on a piece of iron rail, instead of the school clock since it broke, followed by the rush of people. The stupid joker of a headmaster, followed by the teacher Tarapada, with his wrap twisted like a fat rope and laid over his shoulder, his mouth with the broken teeth and the froth of constant talking. These images flit by Inam's mind, like a shower of dry yellow leaves set loose from the high branches of the *neem* tree by the southern wind. They flit by as if he were the naked lone boy watching the train run across the bridge and cut through the wide open field.

With the train of images gone, Inam becomes aware of Suhash babbling again about that trip with his uncle's wedding party. Feku does not seem to be listening to a single word of it. He stops to light a cigarette. The fire at the tip of the match, dull yellow by the moonlight, reveals Feku's ugly face, the cut on his forehead, his round chicken eyes, and the lower lip, black and hanging like that of a horse. "Want one?" Feku offers, and Suhash stops talking just long enough to take one and light it and immediately picks up his story. "We had to go there by a steamboat down the Madhumati river. One couldn't even see if there was any village by the river. It was so dark, and there was so much jungle—felt like we were in the Sundarbans or something, you know?"

It seems to Inam as if Suhash has been telling this story since yesterday and will go on and on until the end of tomorrow. Why can't the stupid barber save a few words? His unbearable story has a hundred branches— the description of his uncle's looks, the search for a bride, the one finally chosen, the quarrel that broke out between the bride's uncle and the groom's father, the trouble about renting a silk kaftan from the laundry on the day of the wedding. He isn't going to leave anything out. Inam is furious now. "Tell me, why on earth did your uncle have to get married?"

Suhash ignores him and goes on, "In the morning, the Madhumati river was bright and shiny under the sun. My elder uncle slipped when getting off the boat and fell smack in the mud. And, oh, the younger sisters of my aunt-to-be! I can't describe their fantastic beauty."

"Where does your uncle live? Let me know when any of his sisters-in-law come for a visit," Feku comments, just to say something.

"No chance, you understand?" Suhash answers, languid with pleasure.

"I see! Is that why you make five trips a month to the place of your uncle's in-laws? I understand. It doesn't cost any money there. Nice life you got." Feku winks at Suhash.

Rahat Khan's glittery tin roof is no longer visible. Nor is the bridge. The dried riverbed is far behind. The agitation at Chandmani's house has died down. They are recovering from the grief over the lost chicken. Tomorrow, the poor thing's shiny feathers, yellow feet, or part of the beak will be found somewhere near Mr. Basu's brick kiln or on the broken landing of the dilapidated part of the Sarkar house. The folks in there are quiet now, in bed after supper, except for the old woman, sitting and rubbing oil from the lamp into her chapped feet, while the lamp somehow keeps lingering on. "So cold here! Ho, daughter-in-law, give me another rag quilt. I'm dying with cold." The old woman keeps begging, while her daughter-in-law sleeps inside like Kumbhakarna, and her son mumbles, "Who knows why she doesn't die!" The old woman makes another loud plea, but the sound of a sudden wind rises in the night and obscures her trembling voice.

So goes life.

Feku's thick lips are shut tight. Suhash absently turns the radio on and immediately off. Inam walks with his head bent forward, as if he is trying very hard to think.

They leave the dirt path, knock the dust off their shoes on the grass, and turn into the narrow lane. Immediately, they are swallowed by its dense darkness and get the lashing of a vine like a whip. Feku opens his lips with a dirty curse at the vine. Then he calmly starts talking to them about what is on his mind. "Who knows why I'm getting caught so often these days?"

At this, Suhash's eyes light up with curiosity. "Can I ask you something? If you promise not to get angry." Without waiting for Feku's permission, he asks, "Tell me how you manage to take so much beating. I feel faint when I get a slap from my elder brother."

"One has to learn how to take the beatings, my dear. One has to learn it from the experts, the way one gets an education by attending school every day."

Inam is again unbearably irritated, "As if schools gave birth to education like babies! Those bastard teachers . . ." Inam uses an unprintable epithet.

Feku goes on telling Suhash, "If you're an idiot and if you don't know how to take the beatings, then you don't go anywhere near someone's pocket in a public place, even if money is sticking out of the pocket and staring straight at you."

Inam suddenly feels depressed at the mention of money. The other day, encouraged by the driver Tendu's tips, he had tried putting his hand in the pocket of a stern-looking man in the bus. The paper in there rustled so loud, and suddenly there seemed to be an ear-splitting noise followed by a growl in the man's throat. Actually, the man was only clearing his throat. So Inam has no money. He could get money by stealing some coconuts that his family sells in order to buy rice, but it is more painful to starve and go without rice.

The darkness over the path is thick like tar. Overhead, the vines have spread their tangled web from one side to the other. Feku, busy talking, steps on Suhash, making him scream with pain, to which Feku merely says, "Don't drop the radio," and goes on. "You won't believe what happened the other day. The bus was packed with people, and it was going at a speed of forty to fifty miles. Money was sticking out of a man's side pocket. As soon as I got my hand near it, he grabbed my hand. Then came the beating. My god! They fell on me the way they fall on a dead cow thrown in the skinning ground. See, the gash on my forehead is still not healed."

Now it's the ruffian's turn to chatter, Inam says to himself.

As Suhash suddenly turns the transistor radio on in the midst of the story, a weird sound bursts on the cold and silent darkness. "The son of a bitch is singing classical," Suhash spits and tunes in someone singing, "You've come into my life." A dog comes out of one yard and tries to bark, but realizes that it is too cold to put the energy into barking; instead it comes to Inam and stands by his side wagging its entire behind. "The son of a bitch wants to warm up," Feku remarks, and then goes on talking about how his life is ruined, the ones who ruined it, the tricks of picking pockets, his own special tricks and success, about failure and getting beaten up. "What else can I do? If I had some education, then—"

Inam feels his impatience rise, and he says, "Piss on education."

Feku thinks for a minute and gives a considered answer, "Let's stand on a high spot and piss on everything. But where's the work? Work on land one doesn't have? Start a business with no money? What can I do?"

The birds in the trees, huddled inside the mist and frost, make little muffled sounds, strangely different from the singing and cooing they do all day. A cat crosses their path, revealing only its glowing eyes. Suhash, Feku, Inam are silent now. Suhash puts the radio under his armpit; Feku wraps his muffler over most of his face; Inam rubs his hands trying to warm them.

In the house to the right lives the Pal family. They make clay pots and containers, but he always announces himself as "Mr. Pal" when he goes to someone's place. The house has lost large patches of the plaster coating, and it is in disrepair, because the house really belonged to the Sen family before they left East Pakistan for India in the fifties. Inam tears a fragrant leaf off the lemon tree he passes by and watches the cold porch. He smells burnt clay and sees the huge blackened clay containers scattered about the yard. Strange groanings from sleepy voices come through the gaps in the broken door.

"Everybody is asleep," Suhash says, and Feku agrees with a grunt.

"We shouldn't have come tonight, so late," Suhash says. "I'm afraid."

Feku mimics him in irritation, "Afraid! Little boy! Want to drink some milk?"

Suhash ignores it and goes on about his fear. "The sight of the old man scares me. One moment he looks as if he is about to die; the next moment he looks as if he is going to kill us all! Have you seen the look on his face when we enter the inner part of his house?"

"Yes, I've seen, and stop your stupid worry," Feku spits with contempt. "Try to catch the look on his face when he takes the money."

Inam rages in his mind, wishing to kill that bastard Feku.

But Feku's remark changes Suhash's mood. He joins Feku with salivating images, "The girl feels like the taste of the soft pulp inside a young coconut. Isn't that right?"

Inam silently rages again, wishing to kill this one too.

Those two are now laughing and giggling, talking and warming up. They go past the house of the doctor, his fat and fair body sitting inside made visible by the little circle of dim light from a kerosene lantern. Then the pond, a single dry leaf whirling noisily on its paved steps. Then the empty field, covered with a stubble of dead grass, now bathed in the milky mixture of moonlight and mist. Behind them the *jaam* tree stands like a huge black figure, and behind that everything else is a uniform black mass. They walk on, past some open space and land overgrown with weeds, then the godown of betel leaves, then the marsh lined with the tall grass and white plumes of *kaash*. At this point, to the right, is the gate made of bamboo pieces hung with rope. The yard inside is very empty, with almost nothing growing in it.

Inam has fallen behind, quite a bit behind them now. He looks as if he is considering whether to turn back and may in fact do so at any moment. The faint red glow of a dimmed lantern makes the window and its bars visible. A pair of glowing eyes flitting by the marsh gives away the fox. An old branch creaks overhead as the hawk perched on it moves and neighs like a horse.

Feku has lifted the bamboo poles strung along the rope and is signing to Suhash to come along, but Suhash seems immobilized, standing uncertainly with the transistor in one hand and the other hand over his mouth.

Inam suddenly comes forward and asks Feku for money. "Just two rupees. I'll give it back tomorrow."

Feku lets go of the poles to sneer at him, "So, you came for the fun without the money to buy it?"

Inam sees in his mind the golden brown arm, its downy sheen lit up by the dim light. The arm touches the head, smoothes the hair, and wipes the trace of hair oil on the fingers on the sari. Though Inam bought her the cheap mill sari, he couldn't take it off her to return it for the money now. Desperately, he pleads, "Just two rupees, I'll give it back tomorrow."

Feku grinds his big teeth. "I have just two rupees in my pocket, not that many jumping around there to spare."

Inam seems to become wild, as if with some kind of pain. "Suhash, then you give it to me. I promise to give it back tomorrow. I swear in the name of your goddess Kali, I will. I will."

He seems tormented by a restlessness suddenly turned loose inside.

Suhash gangs up with Feku to sneer at him, "All the way he has come with us quietly, without a word about it." Then he turns to Inam with his ugly smile, "You're so stupid! I swear I have only two rupees that I stole from my brother's pocket. Here, search my pocket."

After this, Inam seems to calm down, just as suddenly.

Suhash and Feku stand together by the bamboo gate and wait.

The old man's face now appears, pressed against the wooden bars of the window; he asks, "Who's there?" Then the reddish light moves away from the window, and the broken door opens noisily; the man emerges with lantern in hand and comes across the barren yard toward the gate. His long shadow falls across the yard. His withered legs are like thin sticks under the knee-high wrap around his waist. He stops beside the bushy oleander and holds the lantern up. Its dim light shows the face crisscrossed with lines like the parched earth before the monsoon. With cold eyes he watches Inam, Suhash, and Feku. Watches them for a long time, piercing them with glowering eyes.

Finally, with a trembling hand, he raises the wick of the lantern and says, "Oh, it's you! Come in. I was wondering who would come at this hour. Who would care to come to this place at any time? I wasn't really sleeping. Sleep doesn't come easily at this age, you know," and so on. He goes on uttering pointless words. "Come inside. It's cold out there. Isn't the inside cold too? All the same, in or out. For those who had to leave their homeland, inside and outside are the same . . . Makes no difference."

As they go in, a leafy branch of the oleander suddenly sways against a draft of wind. The cold hard floor inside makes Inam aware of the pain in his heels now out of his shoes.

Inside, the age-blackened planks of a bedframe lie bare, without a bed. Sleeping chickens cackle faintly somewhere inside. From outside comes another collective howling of foxes and then the sound of wind rising from the dried riverbed. The old gentleman sits in the broken chair, the lantern on the ground beside him. The three of them sit close together on the bed platform.

The old man is breathing his asthmatic breath. The flow of his pointless clever words has stopped, and he is breathing hard through his mouth.

White stubble has covered his sunken cheeks and chin. Fingers of the bony hands, their veins sticking out, grip the chair's armrests. The nails haven't been clipped for ages. The mucus collecting in his throat makes his breathing impossible. Inam wants to get a tube and clear the mucus. But the man recovers enough breath to resume his meaningless chatter in a creaky voice, "How are things with you? Everything all right? Regrets, laments are quite useless. It's time to die, don't you agree? Suppose I pop off suddenly. Then? For me, it's freedom, I go off with joy. Let the old woman take it, let her fend for herself and her brood. . . . It's nice of you to come now and then to check on us. You aren't fussy about the time to come and see us. You're the only ones we can count on. My wife always praises you."

Feku is now visibly unnerved. He watches the old man's face, trying to guess the situation, and his big body is visibly cowering. Suhash stares with round eyes, thinking, "Won't be surprised if the old man kills us. Why did I come here tonight!"

The old man goes on, "We'd have starved in this jungle, if we couldn't count on you. We would never be able to raise food from the land in the yard. We were never good at it. You people are. We are from a dry area, you know? Everything is different there, the way of life. We'd have starved here if it weren't for you young men! My children adore you! My daughter Ruku is preparing to make tea for you . . ."

His voice is cut off by a lump of mucus, and a coughing fit makes his eyes nearly pop out. The man who talked nonstop a moment ago now seems about to die.

Suhash and Feku simultaneously speak up, "We don't want any tea."

The coughing subsides, and the old man says, "So you don't want tea? That's all right."

The wind from the riverbed is suddenly heard swishing the massive top of the banyan tree and sweeping closer, carrying with it the sound of the finger cymbals and the tabla drums accompanying some song about Visakha and *tamal* trees, and then it sweeps away carrying the music along with it. Now the dry rustle of rupee notes being handled inside Suhash's wrap is heard. Feku takes the two rupees from Suhash and the two from his own pocket, thinks for a minute while crumpling them in his large fist. He hesitates, seems scared, but finally leans to the old man, holding out his hand and saying, "This is from me and Suhash."

The old man is so startled by this that he seems about to fall off his chair. Its legs totter and knock on the floor back and forth. "You're giving me, you and Suhash? Who knows how much more I've to take from you fellows! Who knows if I can ever repay all these loans!"

Suhash stands up, ready to move but not sure which way.

The old man looks up, "Are you leaving? So soon? Ruku will be upset. You didn't let her make tea for you, and now if you leave without seeing her, she may never talk to you again. Wait a minute here . . ."

The old man starts for the inner quarter, leaving the lantern behind. His shadow gets smaller and smaller, then disappears. The sleepy chickens cackle a little and stop. An old woman's voice says something. It is followed by an angry brutal shout, "Shut up, bitch. Shut up!" Then all is silent again.

The old man comes back, his head bent, his shoulders drooping. He comes close to them and whispers, "You can go in now and talk to her. She is in the side room. Inam, you stay here with me. You don't have to leave. Let's have a chat."

The old man tries hard to carry on his monologue. He is very cold, shivering, even with his wrap wound tightly around him. Still, it is not so much the cold as the mucus swelling in his throat that gets in the way of his frantic talking. Shivering and struggling for breath, he goes on and on, "When I came here, you know, when I came here, the first thing I did when I came here was to plant an oleander . . ."

He pauses, and just then they hear the sound of sobbing, the old woman sobbing away hopelessly. And the sound of bangles tinkling and sari rustling. Inam feels in all his senses the soft smooth golden brown body. He also hears Suhash's obscene giggle, and the old man going on again, "I then planted the oleander, you know?"

The old man pauses, listens to the sob and the laughter, and goes on, "Not for its flowers, you know, but for its seeds. The seed pods of oleander make good poison, very potent."

Another wave of disconsolate sobbing comes from the dark inside.

The old man loses track of his story, as his face floods and his voice drowns. He weeps, stupidly repeating, "First thing I did was to plant the oleander, you know, Inam, for its bitter seeds . . ."

Inam suddenly breaks out, screaming viciously at the old man, "Now you are crying? Why on earth are you crying now? Why are you crying now?"

In Search of Happiness

Hasan Azizul Huq

The cool shadow is calling me! Kumkum wonders, leaning over in her bed, the pillow under her chest, looking out the window at the paved side of the well under the grapefruit tree. She hears the shrill cry of the hawk in the sky announcing its noontime domain. A dirty crow comes in the paved area by the well in the shade of the citrus tree to bathe in the little pool of dirty water. Kumkum watches it bathe happily, wet its throat and the wings, and fly to a branch to comb its head with its claw, totally contented.

Right then Kumkum feels the strange agony resurface, like a howl of despair tearing her inside into pieces, as if the flip side of a new coin with the imprint of happiness she has been watching intently has quite unexpectedly turned into the imprint of unhappiness and is staring at her.

The bewildering switch of feeling disturbs her, puzzles her. And she resorts once again to looking through the past for an explanation, like rummaging through a box of old letters. But as soon as she starts remembering, she feels the warm breath of things from the past, reassuring and comforting like the touch of an old favorite sari or an ornament of one's dead mother. How curious! One moment she is drowning in a flash flood of unhappiness, but, when she searches for its cause in her life, she cannot find it anywhere in her memory of her childhood and early youth.

Waves of unhappiness with no cause, no source, no root in what she knows to be her life!

Kumkum gets up from the bed and stands by the window, absently watching the midday stillness in the yard. The cooing of the dove in the mango tree on the south side of the yard pulls her consciousness back to the

---

"Sukher Sandhane" appears in Hasan Azizul's *Atmaja O Ekti Karabi Gachh* (1967; reprint, Dhaka: Muktadhara, 1981), 62–67.

present, her immediate environment. But still she stands there, her face
pressed to the window bars, just lingering at first and then slipping back into
the puzzled wondering. The afternoon seems to stand still.

Kumkum, twenty-two years old, is getting tired of trying to make sense of
her feelings of happiness and unhappiness, and she is frustrated at not being
able to understand the reasons for either. The reasons seem to elude her, the
feelings too fleeting to catch hold of and figure out, or else as soon as she
reaches out for something that looks like happiness, a terrible feeling of
emptiness or an unbearable dislike seems to replace the longing. And the
pain resurfaces. The headache becomes so bad that she has to lie down at a
totally inappropriate time. This has been going on for a while and getting
worse. The unhappiness, unbearable but inexplicable, and the pain of
headache have even made her lose consciousness a few times.

When the trouble had first appeared, her husband Rajib raised his eyebrows, creasing his fair forehead. He held her in his arms, as if he could cure
it with a caress, and half-taunted her, "You seem to be developing hysteria!"

"Don't know what's the matter with me," Kumkum said in an agonized,
strained voice. "I never felt sick like this before. When I was in school, I used
to get headaches and had to wear glasses. Then they went away; they came
back for a while when I was in college. Once I threw a pebble into the
darkness of a well that had dried up. I distinctly heard the strange, unnerv-
ing sound of the pebble hitting its unseen dry bottom, deep down somewhere.
Ever since then I feel terribly empty from time to time, and I remember that
sound."

"This is just a silly mania. Women are good at contracting manias. But
such things ought to go away after marriage."

Rajib said it so authoritatively that Kumkum felt guilty for her troubled
feelings. Rajib tried to put her at ease by dismissing the problem. "No need
to worry. It will go away on its own."

Perhaps that is why the problem stayed on instead of going away. The
symptoms started occurring regularly and increasingly showed a definite
pattern. For example, Rajib returns early from his office with a packet in
hand. He takes the pretty rust red sari out of the packet and surveys Kumkum's smooth young body. Kumkum sees the lust in his eyes and pretends
that she is very happy, that she has not been having a splitting headache all
day. But after dressing up in the new sari, while she waits like a princess to
please him, the headache becomes so bad that it knocks her out. Then Rajib
finds it very hard to treat her body, all decorated for his pleasure, like that of
"the sleeping beauty." The poor man cannot help behaving like an animal,
forgetting his education and civility.

As a result, he has now stopped coming home straight from work as he
used to not so long ago. Many times he would come home even before the
office hours were over because in the midst of work and people he would

suddenly remember being in Kumkum's body; and he would be aroused and flustered enough to drop everything and come home to make love to her. The same man is now coming home late, rarely before eleven.

The sun begins to mellow, and the afternoon grows in the terrace. Late afternoons like this are supposed to be for their intimate sharing. "This is why I took this flat outside the crowded town, in this quiet area," Rajib had said smiling at her, "so that I can come home any time to be with you and caress you." They bought their beautiful bed and steel cabinet, the book-shelves, the dressing table—all the things in the realm of Kumkum's dream. By decorating their home with their cherished objects, this young couple of twenty-seven and twenty-two started on their "happily ever after" plan of life.

But somehow, imperceptibly, dullness set in, like the dust of daily life collected on storage boxes and trunks, over tins of rice and biscuits. In each carefully acquired item of their arrangement for a happy life, weariness entered invisibly and started eating away, boring holes like those in moth-eaten woolens.

"You must tell me what the problem is, exactly what is this sickness of yours. What can I do if you don't explain it?"

But Kumkum is unable to give Rajib any concrete explanation, except her vague reference to the sound of a pebble hitting the bottom of a dried up well. So Rajib does not come home before eleven at night.

Kumkum has been standing at the window turning these thoughts and absently watching the slowly maturing afternoon. I must stop thinking useless thoughts, she prods herself to resolve, otherwise I'll go crazy. She picks up her change of fresh clothes and starts for the well for the midday bath.

The shaded side of the well is absolutely silent now. She stands still in the shade of the citrus tree listening to the silence around her. Under the side with the leafiest branches, the shade is dark and unbroken; under the side with the thinning branches, the pattern of light and shade keeps agitating silently. Kumkum hangs the fresh clothes on the fence around the bathing area and peeks into the well. The sight of the dark cold water in its depth makes her whole body thirst and shiver with anticipated pleasure. When she goes in the bathing enclosure and closes the little door, she suddenly feels lonely, cut off. Then by the time she has taken her clothes off and slipped into absentmindedness, she hears the yard and the side of the well change from sleepy silence to a world of sounds. The lone crow caws, the dove coos, the wind stirs, and the dry leaves fall to the ground. She feels very peaceful listening to the natural world suddenly awaken all around her. She feels perfectly relaxed knowing that her naked body is seen by and in tune with the sky, the tiny creatures, and the plants. She puts a centipede down on her palm and creates a flood in front of it; she watches a grasshopper rub its head between its front legs; and she stands very still so as not to disturb the but-

terfly that just flew in to sit on her hair. She opens herself up before the
nontalking natural world and feels happy being at one with it.

When she comes back inside the house after her bath, she is surprised to
see Rajib back and lying on the bed with his hand over his eyes. She notices
his fair forehead and the sharp nose under the fingers covering his eyes. He
has not changed from office clothes, has not even taken his shoes off. Seeing
him like this suddenly reminds her of the first time she saw him, dressed for
the wedding. It had seemed that she was marrying a prince from a fairy tale,
almost incredible that she was going to have the beautiful young man all to
herself for the rest of her life!

"Are you feeling unwell? You're back so early today?"

Rajib just glances at her in response. Two months earlier she would have
been glowing with happiness at his coming home early. And Rajib, without
waiting for her question, would have bubbled forth his excuse, "I didn't feel
like working in the office today. Frankly I wanted to be with you right away."
Today he does not bother to say anything. It must be that he is feeling unwell, perhaps with a headache.

Kumkum recovers from the tentative blush of happiness at his untimely
return and asks him if he has a headache.

"You shouldn't have come home in the sun then!" she says, looking at
him with sympathy.

Rajib looks at her sternly. "Why haven't you eaten lunch yet?"

"I'm about to."

"What were you doing so long? I left after lunch at ten in the morning. It's
three-thirty now! What were you doing all this time that you did not manage
to eat lunch yet?"

The tone of Rajib's voice is so hard that it sounds as if he does not really
have a headache, as if he has come home at this hour just to catch her in her
irresponsible anomie and scold her. Kumkum is at a loss for words. Rajib
looks at her accusingly, as if by spending the day absentmindedly without
eating lunch, she has tried to demonstrate her displeasure with him. She
leaves for the kitchen to eat and returns to her puzzled wonderings as she
puts the lumps of cold rice mixed with vegetable curry in her mouth and
almost forces them down her esophagus.

I don't understand myself, this young woman named Kumkum! When I
was little, in frocks, and ran after the butterflies and recited poems at the top
of my voice, I did not know what happiness meant, what it was supposed to
be. But I was happy then. I was immersed in happiness, in warm, thick
happiness!

Kumkum looks out the kitchen window at the tiny bird hopping and playing by itself in the wild *ata* tree. When one is happy, she concludes, one does
not know it. Because happiness is something that disappears the moment one

is either conscious of it or consciously seeks it. Time, the present time, enters everything and sets its teeth into everything and tears it all up. But the past remains pristine; memory imperceptibly covers everything in the past with a soft film of happiness.

Kumkum pulls her straying thoughts back to order. When I became older, I started dreaming about happiness, especially when I was in college. Amazingly, all the things that I dreamed of as important for happiness have come to me. I have got Rajib, I have known affluence, I have arranged all my dream objects in our home, although the cabinet is made not of teak but of jackfruit wood and the clothes rack is on the cheap side. On the whole, everything I dreamed of has come true. But the happiness I felt when I was dreaming of them seems to have disappeared as soon as I got them. The things that made me happy in the dream do not seem to do so in reality.

When Kumkum finishes eating and comes out of the kitchen, the sunlight has begun wilting. She stands in the yard watching the sky turning pale and the birds starting to fly about in the sky. A beautiful late afternoon before the dusk sets in. It seems to Kumkum that if there is any happiness in her life now it is what she feels when quietly watching the sky, the squirrels in the ata tree, listening to the soft hum that she hears rising from the bosom of the earth when she stands naked in the midst of the nontalking world. She decides that this is what happiness is—the peaceful feeling of being in tune with nature—and wants to have this feeling all her life. Having resolved this, she turns to go in the bedroom, the cave of unhappiness. On the wall outside near the door she notices a house lizard, obscenely big, stalking a tiny insect, taking aim with its lidless eyes. Kumkum stops short. She feels the agony rise from under her chest. Beads of sweat collect on her forehead as she watches the lizard and the insect unaware of its stare. The lizard stealthily moves closer, an obscene wave travels down its curved back toward the tip of its tail. The lizard is now very near the insect and absolutely still, its cold metallic stare fixed like dots of copper. Kumkum turns her eyes to the sky and the yard and finds that nature too is looking on, unblinking! She cannot bear the tension, and, as soon as the lizard leaps for the insect, she utters a cry and runs inside.

There, Rajib is sitting on the bed, watching Kumkum. She holds the back of the chair to steady herself. Then she touches the smooth surface of the table, the bookcase; she slowly walks around the room touching the objects of her dream, as if seeking protection from each of them. And in the midst of all the dream furniture warped by the cruel teeth of the present and turned into inert things dulled by the boredom of her existence, she sees that Rajib is holding her in his arms and staring at her, totally bewildered. And then, the young woman cannot see anything any more, as she is swallowed by the dark waters of her unhappiness rising from the depths of her own existence.

Through Death and Life

Hasan Azizul Huq

There was a sudden wind in the sky.

Karam Ali looked up and saw the gray clouds silently coming up the horizon, like a herd of buffaloes.

He called his son, "The rain is coming! Hurry up, *bap jan!*"

Then he walked quickly into the cowshed and stood for a minute watching the two animals. The white bullock's tail twitched restlessly. The lame old cow lay on the layer of straw in the far corner, her huge dark eyes gazing into the darkness. The dog got up from the pile of cinder near the porch, shook its body, and raised its muzzle to sniff at the flow of damp air.

Karam Ali stepped out of the cowshed and stood on the porch outside looking across the flat landscape at the sad, brooding marsh, its still water turning shiny like polished silver that flashed at his dull yellow eyes. He narrowed his eyes, and the marsh at once appeared far removed, like a picture framed within the greenery of the distant villages. He turned his eyes back to the dim porch. Scanning about, he noticed his seventy-five-year-old mother engrossed in making a broom out of a bunch of dry stalks.

Within this short time, the ranks of dark clouds had marched above the horizon and occupied the entire sky. He could now hear the deep rumble rolling across the sky, back and forth, like giant barrels across a cement floor. He saw the black clouds turn smoky as if boiling inside. As he watched the coming of rain, the vaults of his memory packed with the countless oncomings of monsoon with all their sensations spilled forth into his vision, his senses: The damp air whipping wildly; the powerful clouds darkly hanging low overhead; the marsh, ageless like the earth, its black plant-soaked water

"Amrityu Ajiban" appears in Hasan Azizul's *Atmaja O Ekti Karabi Gachh* (1967; reprint, Dhaka: Muktadhara, 1981), 68–90.

taking on the curiously still and bottomless look, forming a stark somber background for the ducks in it and the lush green growth all around it; the monstrous hunger at the end of the morning's work. All these images and sensations were vividly flitting across the pupils of his dim, yellowish brown eyes.

To disentangle himself from this enchanted web, Karam Ali tried to survey the porch. His eyes fell on his mother's rheumatic old knees, swollen like purple eggplants. Because his eyes refused to move and stayed glued to those grotesque knees, he stood there helplessly, distressed, his fingers scratching his graying beard. Just then there was an incredibly brilliant flash. It revealed, just for an instant, the minutest and the most hidden details in the surroundings, before the sky broke out in an ear-shattering roar.

The thunderclap tore open a chamber of memory stored from his childhood. He stood there remembering, while staring at his mother's crumbling room by the slope of the yard, and listening to the drops of murky water dripping from the old thatch of the roof. His eyes, glassy with the detachment of immersion in memory, drifted across the cowshed, the cow chewing her cud in there, the shining surface of the marsh, and the villages arranged around it as if in a picture, while his mind dove into the joyless days of his childhood: plodding along with a ruthless old man toward the wetlands; working on some unfamiliar land all morning, afternoon, and evening, with the constant feeling of gnawing hunger. While he stood transported into the monsoon of his childhood, the steaming sky above started to rain in large drops. The marsh now looked hazy, and the sound of falling rain pervaded everything.

His mother went inside, dragging her painful legs, and his son Raham Ali finally came out, burping loudly after his morning meal, the veins distended over his swollen belly. "We'll go when the rain slows, bap jan," he said, and stood under the thatch in the porch staring up at the sky.

Raham's mother now emerged in Karam Ali's line of vision, walking through the darkly shaded mango and *jaam* trees, then among the slender areca nut palms dancing joyously in the wind and rain. She was carrying in her hands a lump of cow dung that was beginning to wash down. The sari she wore was raised above her knees, but she had her head covered with it, and she was carefully sheltering the wet lump of cow dung and sloshing like a fox through the rain. Near the yellow pile of cut grass, she slipped and then got up looking really awful—all wet with cow dung on her face. Karam Ali could find nothing to say or do about this accident except, "There goes the cow dung, after all the work to bring it home!" And perhaps to commiserate with her, he stepped out of the storage shed into the wind-whipped rain and stood getting wet while calling his son, "Let's go now, bap jan."

Twenty-year-old Raham, seeing that he could not delay it any longer, jumped down onto the yard, went into the shed to pick up the two hoes

stored among the piles of old tin cans and worn-out straw mats, and joined
his father in the rain. Karam Ali watched the large drops fall on his son's jet
black firm body, and as he walked to his father in long but unhurried strides
through the downpour, the essence of this life—the life that is so hard and yet
so soft—seemed to be flowing down his body like a song. This ancient life of
the land of rivers, the life in the cruel heat and the soaking rain in this land of
the Padma, the Meghna, and the Dhaleswari, was now a song in the dripping
dark body of his young son.

The wind started lashing harder, and the rain became so dense that he
could no longer see the villages around the marsh. Raham's mother had
given up on the cow dung and, having washed her hands, was now trying to
wring the water from the upper half of her sari. The sight of her shriveled
body, from the corner of his eyes, so embarrassed and disconcerted Karam
Ali that he forgot what he was going to ask her for. Raham Ali remembered
and asked his mother to pack his father's tobacco things. Raham Ali might
not remember when he suckled on his mother's breast, but the memory must
be there glowing like a gem somewhere inside his subconsciousness, beyond
the darkness of custom, so her bare chest did not embarrass him.

As they waited in the rain for the tobacco, Raham Ali's mind dipped into
the cool dark water of the marsh and imagined in the sound of rain the sound
of dew on the leaves in the early hour of dawn when they left home to work in
wintertime. But Karam Ali's mind was now confined to the old injured cow
in the cowshed, hopelessly waiting for death.

When they finally left, the morning was darkened with rain. The smoky
sky growled from time to time, sending slight shivers in the tree-enveloped
darkness of the deserted path. The loose dirt of the path had turned into
muddy mounds among the puddles from the dripping leaves. The wet vines
constantly clung to their feet or lashed at them. They were almost at the end
of their neighborhood. From there the huts, all with the thatched roof sloping
down all around to the level of the porch, looked like the backs of big turtles.
They left the path and started cutting through the orchard, the clusters of
areca nut palms and the uncultivated fields laden with soggy grass. As soon
as they cleared the dark green circle of the village and came out near the
marsh, a bright green scenery opened up before their eyes. The view of the
huge marsh with its sky, its little ducks, and all the vivid details was so
different from the tree-covered village paths, and the change was so abrupt
that it felt like a shock.

Karam Ali now studied the uncultivated fallow plot he was going to prepare for plowing this time. In the part he had cleared the day before, the
wilted green weeds lay in heaps, and the cleared ground was tamped down
by the rain. Once the rain stopped and the wind subsided, a strange silence
hovered over the marsh. The ten ducks—black, white, brown—were floating

almost motionlessly. The glassy surface showed not only the big sky but also the quick little lines traced by the movements of water insects. The shiny mirror was surrounded by patches of fields, in all sizes and shapes, gently oozing with the fresh green of paddy seedlings. Then the color of the water started to change, reflecting the renewed gathering of gray clouds since the wind died down.

The sky was ready again. As it waited in grave silence, one could even hear the skitting of water insects on the black crystal surface. Karam Ali was so enchanted with the calm that he was seeing his fallow plot of land as if it was already cleared, its uprooted damp weeds gone into the marsh, its uncluttered soil already spaded into chunks turned over on their backs, as if those chunks had steadily soaked in rain for days and become sweetly soft like milk-soaked bread. In a quick succession of effortless images, he could see his little fallow plot in the vast flatland float in the air above ground as a lush green field of growing seedlings, transformed like a beautiful daughter once born out of one's very own blood.

Karam Ali stirred out of his dream with a sigh and returned to work on the half-cleared land. He asked Raham to put the weeds they had cut the day before in piles along the edge of the plot of land and proceeded with the hoe to tackle the thicket of weeds and vines in the middle at the base of the single coconut tree. He entered the dense growth that reached up to his neck.

Simultaneously with the first strike, he heard it. A sharp loud hiss went up the very instant the hoe came down! He was sure it was not the involuntary sound of his own exhalation. Because it was a distinct moment before the blade of the hoe came down to the ground that Karam Ali heard the hiss, angry yet somber and dignified, and at once he saw a smooth coil of golden yellow vine swiftly uncoil. The very next moment the dazzling form of the snake was swaying against the panorama of the darkly clouded sky, the softly overflowing green of baby paddy and the glistening expanse of water.

Suddenly his entire life up to that point seemed engulfed in the blank darkness that precedes one's birth. The reel of memory unraveled, and his past tumbled away like a kite caught in rough wind. The future also disappeared from his mind, the future of constant labor and deprivation. Even the immediate present embodied in the surrounding landscape became dim and unfocused, as he watched, with the acute concentration of his peasant life, the cobra steadily swaying two and a half yards away from him. He watched the huge hood and on it the dazzling mark that was as clear and brilliant as the sun on an autumn morning. Karam Ali tried to look into its eyes but soon gave way to the steady stare, cold and sad, and he could not find the courage to look at them once more.

Was he terribly afraid? Did he feel the choke hold of fear? Anxiety tearing at his guts? He did not feel anything he had known before. He felt no anxiety, no fear, no hatred, no nausea, no love, no affection. He only saw his destiny, his whole life, and the constancy of relentless struggle, without respite, without excitement, the struggle in which defeat was everpresent yet hesitant in the face of his tenacity. The dazzling white mark on the outspread hood seemed pulsating with complex motion, and he observed in it the intricate tangle of threads that seemed to be weaving his past and his future, his life and his death.

Suddenly the ducks screamed all at once, and a flash of lightning illuminated the shades of wet green of the plants and trees all the way up to the horizon. For a moment he glimpsed the expansive waters of the marsh, along with two overturned little boats, and in that moment he also heard the faint sound of people, birds, animals from the direction of the village. Then the moment of sight and sound sank away from Karam Ali's consciousness, totally controlled again by one nameless acute sensation like the sting of a wasp.

The cobra was still swaying gracefully before him, the glistening forked tongue casually darting out. The swaying hood seemed to be slowly receding. Then before his startled eyes, it rose to an enormous height, towering above the trees in his line of vision. The immaculate hood seemed to have expanded to the size of a pond, and the brilliant mark atop seemed to depict in its bold design all the desires and dreams ever felt in his life. Then the powerful jaws opened under the hood, the dark cavity seemed to be holding for a moment all the worn-out lives of the villagers and their constant, ageless struggles, unwavering like the creator himself, before they were going to be crushed with a merciless crunch.

The hood suddenly came lower and toward him. Karam Ali was calm, ready, his hand resting on the handle of the hoe. It slowly lowered its head and, ignoring him completely, left with the utmost grace and regal dignity, along the edge of the tilled field and the shallow edge of water, its golden color slowly changing into ochre and then brown in the pale light from the gray sky until it went out of sight.

Karam Ali now wanted to go home. The ducks were out of the marsh, drying their wings, all except one duckling still merrily dipping for snails. The large brown duck stood still on one leg, its bill tucked under its feathers. As he watched the ducks and the marsh, he suddenly felt himself choking with the pressure of an enormous fear.

Frantically he called Raham Ali, asking to go home. Raham Ali was absorbed in work, facing away from his father, and he did not at first hear his father's parched, faint voice. The marsh seemed to pick up the mysterious foreboding in Karam Ali's mind, magnified it many times and threw it to the gloomy sky. It was then that Raham Ali heard his father's desperate voice, "I don't feel well, bap jan. Leave the work now. We'll do it later, in the afternoon."

Raham Ali turned around surprised. They had barely started working. But then he saw the terror in his father's face.

"Did you see him, Raham?"

"Who are you talking about?"

Karam Ali's answer sounded like the dreamy chant of someone in a trance, "You didn't see him? You didn't see the one that has lodged in my fallow land! Where were you all this time that you didn't see him?"

Raham Ali was now keen to take his suddenly incoherent father home. Raham Ali scared easily—when it thundered in the dark, when the wind suddenly stopped and made the water feel deeper, when strange fish came out of the water and raced over the surface like a train with their backs arched. Karam Ali scared him now. He picked up the hoes and started back.

Their bare feet went splashing in the ankle-deep water. Soon they were back to the darkly shaded path, filled with the sound of big drops falling on leaves from other leaves, the drenched orchard, the huts like the backs of turtles against the sky. Soon they could see the crumbling room of Karam Ali's mother through the hedge formed by a row of withered banana leaves. Karam Ali spotted her standing fixed in a spot there, her knees swollen like turnips and not letting her move on her legs, but her hands were frantically waving skyward in bizarre gesticulation. He could faintly hear her voice; it was worked up about something. He could not make out what she was saying, but it did strike him that she looked like an ugly witch as she wildly moved her arms standing in one spot. He could also see many people milling about in his yard.

As they got closer, he saw almost a crowd gathered in front of the cowshed. Then Raham Ali's mother came out screaming and tearing her hair, her leathery breasts bared and with hardly any clothes on. "We're ruined. Allah, we're ruined!"

"Shut up! What's the matter?" Karam Ali shouted at her as he walked past her toward the cowshed.

The people gathered near the cowshed made way for him, solemnly and silently, with profound sympathy. He went in and saw his young healthy white bullock lying on its flank, perfectly still, taking up almost the entire floor, his legs stretched out and his moist, black, gentle eyes set in a fixed stare. A trickle of tears left its mark rolling down to the edge of the mouth, where some white foam had collected. Karam Ali stood there, staring at the sad posture of the large, beautiful animal.

The old cow sat in her corner, gently swishing her tail. He watched a large blue fly settle on the lifeless bullock's face and vigorously rub its legs together. He could also hear the quiet breathing of all the people standing behind him near the porch, the soft breathing from many faces over his shoulders, under his arms, close to him and away from him. Their eyes were moist, and their bare ribs moved feebly as they breathed and mourned silently. Many had come directly from work; some perhaps dropped their work and ran here, the tools still in their hands. They were all tired from their day's labor in others' fields. They were filled with sadness and sympathy and tormented by the fierce churning of their empty bellies! The rain-soaked air stirring the trees and blowing over the silent gathering made their silence oppressive.

Someone spoke in the emotionless voice of an announcer, "It's snakebite."

The sudden pronouncement opened the floodgates, turned on the silent voices, and thousands of words spoken in low voices seemed to heave like a wave, back and forth, across the gathering.

"Check to see if the hair can be pulled off the skin easily."

Karam Ali stared blankly at the tuft of white hair someone was holding like a bunch of fine grass.

"Look! It's true. It is snakebite! What can one do? What can one say?" The man who said this started sobbing.

Crying is so infectious that all those men in no way related to Karam Ali, except that they went every morning in search of work, and, if hired for the same field, they worked together addressing each other as uncle and nephew, or they cultivated someone else's land from sunrise till sunset for a share of the crop because they did not own even a sixteenth of an acre, all those sharing with Karam Ali only the bitter struggle to survive, were silently wiping the tears from their eyes.

At this point, Karam Ali felt a sudden jolt in his head. Someone grasped him as he was about to fall. The dark, workless days were circling before his eyes, as he suddenly remembered that he owned less than a sixteenth of an acre, not enough for more than a month of food in a year. His pair of bullocks got him work tilling others' fields that earned him a share of the paddy to live on for the rest of the year. Now that his white bullock was gone, how was he going to work, how was he going to live? "Will anyone tell me what I can do now?" The question turned round and round in the damp wind, hitting him like a hammer, and his heart alternately stopped cold and jumped back beating wildly.

Raham Ali's mother was crying and lamenting about why the snake did not bite her instead, et cetera, stupid words that would have sounded ridiculous if the situation were not so sad. Karam Ali's mother had calmed down and sat silently by herself, dejected, looking on with eyes clouded with days of old yellow mucus.

Raham Ali suddenly made the scene melodramatic by screaming in a forced, distorted voice, clutching at his ribcage. It sounded as if his inside were overloaded, his emotions dammed up too high, as if a vein had burst under the strain, filling his throat and mouth with the hemorrhage, which was choking him and which he was now desperately trying to empty. His crying was wordless, a sheer scream. Perhaps pain really has no language, and perhaps that was why Raham's wordless crying finally smeared everything with pain. The gray sky and the damp air, leaden with pain, bore down on the gathered people. Even the calmly dead bullock seemed touched by the scream, and its black tongue inertly leaned out the side of its lax mouth.

Later that evening Karam Ali stood alone by his porch looking toward the marsh. It was turning black with the early nightfall. The fields with paddy looked like crude patches of ink against the charcoal sky. The rain started again, and as he stepped back under the thatch, the inky marsh merged into its now totally inky surroundings. Karam Ali sat by the roof post wondering if his mother's room would survive the night's rainfall. He saw the dim lamp in her room. She was talking to herself, talking to Allah, and doing this and that in between, pulling out the old quilt, placing clay pots under the leaks in the roof. She was doing these things with difficulty, unable to straighten her knees.

Where was Raham Ali meanwhile? Inside the dark hut? Karam Ali had forgotten about him. Would he rather have lost Raham instead of the white bullock? All the time that he was thinking of his only treasure dead on the floor of the dark cowshed, obliterating his future and replacing it at a blow with starvation and certain death, all this time he had forgotten about Raham. He now came out of the room and sat by another post.

After a long time listening to the hard rain and harder wind, Raham Ali was softly calling, "bap jan, bap jan!" Karam Ali did not quite hear him, which made the boy feel that terrible pressure rise again in his chest. He got up and stood close to Karam Ali, whispering, almost to himself, "You've no money, bap jan, no money at all. The white bullock is gone, and you can't buy another. How are you going to keep the lease to sharecrop this year? We're going to die this time, bap jan."

Karam Ali suddenly sprang up like a released bow and pulled Raham with both hands to his chest with the eagerness of a thirsty man taking water. "Death this time, bap jan. The rain just started, and the landlord will take away the land the moment he hears that I lost my bullock. I was going to ask him for a paddy loan out of my share. Now we've to find wage-labor starting tomorrow. How much rice can we buy with the wage?"

"We didn't even know when the snake struck the bullock, bap jan. We didn't know at all. Couldn't even try to treat him. Nobody ever saw the snake around here!"

Karam Ali had calmed down and silently watched the darkness, the fireflies, the rain, the waving treetops. He was thinking of the solitary marsh, immense and mysterious, beyond the waving treetops, silently juggling life and death. It tossed life to the sky to catch death and then threw death to the sky to catch life. Life sank to the tar-black bottom of the marsh. It settled there, glowing like a rare priceless gem, radiating the essence of all the struggles of human life so far. The irradiated glow lingered like affection in the grass, the wind, the paddy, and the soil. The glowing jewel held life—all vibrant, energetic, and rhythmic. The marsh gravely watched this glowing, pulsating behavior of the light that it enveloped in its darkness. Then it gripped the light, tighter and tighter, choked the throbbing life, the struggles of Karam Ali and all others like him. It became the antagonist of all human striving, the ruthless destroyer, disrupter, and it received death instead. Then it tossed death away and received life again back to its bosom. It held not only life but also death, which sometimes hovered like a dark mountain in the distant horizon and sometimes sat on your chest strangling you. The tornado sometimes whirled across the sky away from the village, and sometimes it roared down on it, churning and crushing it.

For a moment Karam Ali felt the warm breath of Raham sitting close by, but then his mind drifted back to the swaying hood of the mysterious cobra. The one that Raham Ali was puzzling about, the one that killed his bullock, and whom nobody had seen around the village. As soon as the hood came up, the glowing life at the heart of the marsh went out. Karam Ali could clearly see, as if in slow motion, its hidden monstrous movements. He saw first the shiny black lips rise out of the marsh, then the pair of cold joyless eyes, and the split tongue darting like a rapier, spitting blue poison. Then suddenly the spread-out hood shot up toward the sky and became enormous, the size of a large pond, with the terrifying, dazzling mark on top. Slowly it opened its jaws, revealing the horrible cavern inside, and in it went the white bullock, Karam Ali's newly leased land, the field of his green dream, his home, and then Raham with his mother and Karam's mother too. He could no longer see the white mark on top nor the rapierlike flashing tongue, only the dark cavernous mouth. He saw the whole village with all its people, trees, plants, and soil shrink in scale as it was sucked into that cavern. When everything went in, the teeth flashed, and with a crunch, ear-shattering like a thunderclap, the two rows of teeth clamped shut.

It was late in the night. The rain had stopped, the wind died down, and it was steaming hot. The sky was becoming faintly lighted. Karam Ali heard someone calling his name. He could not understand who it could be. A man was calling him insistently in a rough voice, and the light from his flashlight darted pointlessly from the bush to the washed treetops to the cloudy sky. "Are you home, Karam Ali? Do you hear me?" Karam Ali went across the porch and craned his neck, asking who it was. Before Karam Ali managed to see him, the man turned the flashlight on his eyes, following the bad habit of most village people. Karam Ali, squinting, asked again who it was. The man ignored his question and said that he had to come after hearing what he heard because it was too serious to wait.

Now Karam Ali knew who it was and quietly said, "Come in." As they stepped on the porch, Raham Ali came out with a stool and a soot-covered lantern. The checked fabric of the *lungi* the man was wearing, the expensive but dirty shirt, the charcoal black skin, and the graying hair above the thick neck now became visible. After he had sat on the stool, Karam Ali sat on the floor below and fanned himself with the *gamchha* that was always on his shoulder. The man started talking like a great thinker, his eyes dramatically closed and the brows frowning, about how sad it was that the poor animal had to die like that, especially at this time, before Karam Ali could do any plowing.

When he paused, Karam Ali said nothing, and the man went on, "What can we do now? You can't bring the bullock back to life!"

"No, I can't," Karam Ali said vaguely.

"So what are you going to do? Will you buy another bullock?"

"Even if I sell myself, it won't be enough for buying a leg of one."

"Then? Buying one leg isn't going to help either."

The man paused again. Karam Ali said nothing. The man went on, "I'm not exactly a landlord, Karam. I feed my family with the share of the crop. Now that you can't till that land, I can't leave it with you."

"What can I say?"

"Then I have to say it. Let go of the land for this time. Next year when you get your bullock, you'll get it again. I won't lease it to anyone else without offering you first."

Karam Ali saw the steel blade coming down to his neck, his neck held down in the sacrificial U-frame by the man sitting on the stool. He felt as if he were drowning in the clammy waters of the marsh. He struggled one last time for breath.

"If you take away the land, you'll starve us to death."

"What good will the land do you if you can't plow it?"

"I'll manage. You'll see." He got up, begging him. "You'll see. I'll somehow raise the money and rent the bullock. The rain has just started. Give me a few more days. If I can't do it, I'll return the land to you."

"All right, Karam Ali. But if you don't start plowing before this week is over, you can't have it. Don't forget that I have to live too."

The man got up and left, showing himself out with his flashlight.

Karam Ali looked up and saw the marsh now lying very still in the horizon. Then the southwest corner of the horizon stirred a little, and an enormous presence, colorless and bodyless, spread through the sky in large patches, moving slowly at times like an elephant's trunk, at other times shooting in fine, raylike luminous arrows. Down below on earth it revealed spots of inert darkness, as in the eye of the fish; it revealed the growth of the paddy by the night and the water lilies slowly waking. This awesome appearance seemed to hold in its abundant folds the endless life, the deathless death, the rows of valiant fighters ready with their weapons as well as the rows of enemy facing them.

"Bap jan, what are you going to do now, bap jan?" Raham Ali was asking insistently like a child. Just like when he was little and got a thorn in his foot—instead of trying to pull it out, he kept calling his father.

Karam Ali did not answer. The boy then quietly said, in a way that was at once a solemn command and an eager plea, "Listen, bap jan! I can pull the plow in place of the white bullock. Can't I, bap jan? The old cow on one side of the plow and me on the other? Why can't we do it, bap jan? The ground is now soft with rain. You know I can do it. Don't turn me down, bap jan."

In Karam Ali's weary eyes the dim sky seemed to blaze forth as if with fireworks, as he finally broke into long, silent weeping. With his face lowered into his hands, he cried without restraint. Through the streaming hot tears he said over and over, almost singing it like a refrain, "What a terrible thing to say, bap jan."

After having made his proposal, Raham Ali suddenly felt confident, as if transformed into old Karam Ali's father, scolding him, urging him on. "What else can you do? Have you money for another animal? You want to lose the land and have us suck our thumbs this year? We have to cultivate the leased land and weed and plant our own plot. You understand?"

The sleepless night was nearly over. Karam Ali crouched on the mud floor of the dark kitchen for breakfast. He waited with his head between his knees, while Raham washed his hands and face outside, and Raham's mother, her head covered with her sari, looking like a very old new bride in the lamplight, served yesterday's rice on clay platters. At the sight of the pile of coarse grains of brown rice with two bright red chilies on the side, his stomach churned ferociously, making him forget the night of disaster.

"Where's mother? Sleeping?"

"Yes, she's asleep."

"Did she eat?"

"Not yet. She will after you two finish."

Raham Ali came in, and they ate silently. His sudden rush of energy left Raham Ali after the meal. The clouds had cleared from the night sky, and its cool fresh air dropped the heavy curtain of sleep over his tired mind, limbs, and his suddenly full stomach. He unrolled the mat, lay down, and started snoring.

Karam Ali walked back and forth on the porch listening to his son's snore. He felt sleep creeping over himself. But he wanted to take a last look, as he didn't have much time left. Abruptly he stepped out of the hut into the empty yard. There he stood for a moment, feeling the silence of the deep forest wrapped around the village and its paths, its orchards, and the boughs of its massive trees. The darkness had thinned a little, and the still dark slate of the cloudless sky held out countless stars shining clearly. There was no sound from the kitchen any more. Karam Ali walked uncertainly over to the cowshed and tiptoed in. At first he saw nothing in the dark inside. Then the old cow probably woke up, and its loud sighs seemed to ruffle the darkness. Slowly he saw the white shape of the bullock, in the same sad posture with legs stretched out and head sideways. The image seemed to be gently rocking against the darkness. With a draft of wind, the image floated up in the air like a feather and floated down to rest again on the ground when the wind was gone. Karam Ali crouched beside it. Putting his hand on the conch-white soft neck, he wept. The floating peaceful image he had seen before was now blurred and lost to his weeping eyes.

The light of a lamp fell across the entrance of the cowshed, and he turned around to see Raham's mother, incongruous in a demurely wrapped blue sari, holding up the lamp and intently watching him and the white bullock. In the orange light and the gushing black smoke of the oil lamp, her hollowed thin face looked ghoulish, with her eyes sticking out of her forehead. Yet there was something so touching about the way she held up the lamp and looked at him with concern that Karam Ali broke down.

"What am I going to do now, Raham's mother? Can you tell me?"

"Crying won't bring it back."

"No crying will ever bring it back."

"Why are you crying then?"

"Because I don't know what to do."

Quietly, unexpectedly, like the sound of sweet drizzle on a sultry parched afternoon, Raham Ali's mother made the same proposal her son had made a short time ago.

"Tell me, can't you use me? I've seen you use the milk cow once in a while in the absence of a bullock. Use me the same way. I have borne Raham; I have carried your household all these years. I can do it, you'll see."

Karam Ali listened with dry eyes, in amazement and in distress.

When the sun was bright and warm, they took the carcass out to the disposing field. Within ten minutes, the skin had been taken off, and the raw red flesh lay glowing like a pile of live embers. From there Karam Ali and his son went to his half-cleared uncultivated plot.

The marsh at that time was smiling and truly enchanting. A long streak reflecting the slanted rays on the black water glittered like the silvery back of some magic fish, and the spot reflecting the sun itself shone like molten silver, rippling softly in the light wind. Even as his eyes hurt, he could not help looking at that pool of silver. When he could not bear the dazzle any more, he turned his eyes away to the patchwork of fields with soft green paddy. He looked lovingly at his own little plot in the wetland, where the seedlings had risen half an arm's length and fluttered from time to time at the touch of the breeze. He wanted to gaze at it for a long time. Then he remembered what Raham and his mother had proposed to him.

His mind roamed through the villages along the marsh toward the marketplace. The Sunday market was full of people coming and going. Karam Ali stood in the middle of the milling crowd and watched the spot that on other days stayed empty, except for the crows and the kites scrambling for a bone or some bit of refuse or a few vultures sitting over a dead cat or dog, and a few doves cooing in the single tall tree. That spot was now packed with cattle, white and black and in all colors, waiting patiently. He could almost see the large ears pricked up, the tails swishing and small areas of hides twitching to shake off the flies. Standing beside his ridgelike uncultivated plot with the partially cleared dense growth of weeds, Karam Ali could even see the brokers going back and forth, and he could even hear them haggling over the price.

Raham Ali's voice woke him up. "If we don't finish clearing it today, bap jan, we won't be able to plant it this season."

Karam Ali absently asked if he thought the marsh was going to reach as far as this plot so the growing paddy would receive water. It might, Raham said, as the rain had only started; perhaps later on, before the two months of rain were over.

Karam Ali walked to the clump of weeds at the foot of the coconut tree, his eyes searching for the ancient, powerful creature in the little puddles shining with light in the folds of the dark soil. He was looking for the indomitable snake, as old and powerful as the earth, as steady in the endless course through time, and as gently covered by time with layers of moss.

He knew that even if he did not find it now, it might appear suddenly at a time and in a place that he could not foresee. Like the passage of time, one could lose track of it as easily as one could come upon it. As the constant companion of time, it existed not only in the real world but also in one's consciousness and one's subconsciousness. It could never be overcome, although one's destiny was to constantly struggle against it, forever sharpening and resharpening whatever weapons one had and whatever technique one could learn, no matter how many times one was defeated. In death itself, at the end of all the struggles, one would perhaps return to it, finally stand face to face with it. Perhaps that was why the snake seemed inscrutable and arbitrary like death. Perhaps that was why one invariably thought of it when there was a flood, or a tide of salt water entered the field burning the sweet paddy, or a snake struck, or a lightning bolt hit, or the lease of a little land was lost. One always thought of it, for it moved silently with the ceaseless circular motion of life.

Karam Ali thought while his hands pulled out the weeds. The twisted cordlike muscles of his thin arms, black and glistening with sweat, seemed to be made not of flesh, but bluish steel. With so much rain the day before, and the sun now out full blast, it was getting very hot and humid with steam rising from the ground. Raham Ali was frequently going behind the bush to smoke or maybe to snatch a bit of rest. The patch of melted silver in the marsh had been slowly moving from west to east, closer to them.

Karam Ali stood in the tiny shade of the coconut tree, leaning forward on the handle of his hoe. His ridgelike strip of land was now almost cleared of weeds. Raham Ali had already piled the uprooted weeds neatly along its edge and spaded part of the land about three inches deep. Karam Ali was feeling thirst and hunger, and he tried to suppress them by thinking hard if he could expect to prepare the fallow land in time for planting this season. It seemed very unlikely, and because the planted plot he owned would yield no more than twelve maunds of paddy, it would be absolutely necessary for him to find some way to retain the leased land. Seeing his father resting from work, Raham Ali thought he must be wanting a bidi any moment now and came forward to offer him one.

Karam Ali saw his son coming toward him, and just as he shielded his eyes from the sun with one hand to look at Raham's face he saw the cobra resting in a cool trough along the side of the bush. Its color that was so bright the day before appeared brownish this time, blending with the earth, as it lay renewing its ancient bond. Although the dappled light made it look like some ordinary spotted creature, it took Karam Ali no time at all to recognize it. Perhaps he recognized it even before he actually saw it.

When Raham Ali came near, Karam Ali slowly and calmly pointed his finger, as if he was indicating to his young son the writings of fate on his own forehead. Raham Ali did not see it at first, so still and blended with the earth it was. Then a quiver ran down his body like an electric current and he stiffened up, but only for a moment did he stand still.

Raham Ali suddenly shed the bluntness of plodding patience that the coming of age was forming in his chin, forehead, the lines of his lips, and the fuzzy hair on his face. The quiet, sad, unamused determination that life had been sculpting in his limbs and his demeanor suddenly dropped away. He seemed to have returned to his childhood; his pupils dilated with excitement, and all his muscles were eager for quick activity. For a while he ran about the field wildly, pointlessly, like an inexperienced colt. Then, behaving like a thoughtless idiot, his feelings totally out of joint with all that he had learned and experienced, he picked up the hoe and ran back to the spot.

Karam Ali stood watching him, unperturbed by his wildness. He felt quite

HASAN AZIZUL HUQ

sure that nothing startling would happen. Something sad and grievous might happen, but even that possibility did not move him because if something terrible was going to happen then its beginning was already made—perhaps the previous day when he first encountered it, perhaps earlier, much earlier, through all his conscious life, in its complex twists and dark turns, in the self-wasting struggle to survive. Perhaps everything in his life since the beginning, even when apparently unconnected, really formed stages in that inexorable process. Perhaps it was there in last evening's tragedy. Perhaps it would be present in still another death, in still another loss.

Raham Ali was now approaching it cautiously; his crouching body bristled with tension, his muscles taut. With the hoe raised over his head with both hands, he was very close to it; but it still lay there as motionless as before.

Karam Ali looked away in the direction of the marsh. The afternoon was rapidly waning, he thought, and they should be starting back home soon!

Raham Ali now had it within his striking reach. He straightened a little and took aim. With a white flash of reflected light Raham Ali's hoe came down.

At once, in that fraction of a second, there was a deafening hiss, an incredible roar of a whistle. Quicker than lightning, it was up on the tip of its tail, its huge hood hovering at the level of Raham Ali's head. With cold metallic eyes it watched him for a while. Then it lowered its head and went away. The boy stood there astonished, scared, chastised, sad. Karam Ali came to him and said, "Nobody can kill it. Nobody ever could kill it."

Thus ended the incident.

Raham Ali came home and told his mother of the extraordinary snake and, quickly finishing his meal, went out to tell the neighbors about his encounter. Who knows how he told the story in all the places he went that evening! Maybe he visited them in their homes, starting his story in different ways, sitting on a mat or a stool in some case, in some other case perhaps taking aside his primary listener to the edge of the porch. However, in all his descriptions, far more eloquent than the words spoken were the gestures of his hands and his eyes, alternately startled, terrified, amazed. With his mobile eyes and the details of the incident, he went on depicting the snake, its immense hood, lightning speed, cruel anger, infinite power, and amazing mercy. To make his description true and vivid, he also highlighted fragments of the environment in which the incident took place. Images of the midday sun, the shade of trees, the slightly trembling surface of the marsh, the patchwork of paddy seedlings were conjured up with his sparse but lively village language.

Thus, very soon, even before the evening was over, the invisible snake occupied the minds of everyone. In its unhurried, but swift and certain way, the immensely long body of the snake soon held the village gripped in its coils. Imperceptibly, as always, it appeared looming in the collective consciousness that was as age-old and permanent as the earth. The villagers always read in it their struggle, their life as well as death. Sometimes it sprang on them suddenly; at other times it let them prepare to face it. Now, as the night fell, it was on every mind. They were not angry at all, only determined, united in their individual resolve, their consciousness sharpened like spearheads.

At the break of dawn, with the same spontaneous unity with which they worked every day, tended their family needs, maintained the plows, animals, and weapons, nurtured the tradition in their social life, they went to Karam Ali's hut. They called father and son out and told them that together they mush finish it off before going to work that day.

"We can't postpone it; death mustn't be allowed to dwell near home."

Nobody spoke after this statement, whether in agreement or in disagreement; they silently contemplated whatever tool or weapon they carried. The group had few of the elderly but many young men and many more boys and adolescents. Perhaps the elders, like Karam Ali, believed in the futility of such enterprise. A young man named Tanna suddenly raised his stick and said, "It must be the same one that killed your bullock, uncle."

Karam Ali was philosophical. "Perhaps it was, if it so willed," he thought, but Tanna's sudden utterance of the implicit common thought seemed to produce a current of shiver all around.

So they left together. As long as the thought of the snake stayed like background music in their minds, they talked about other things like the rain, the crops, the work of cultivation, hardships and wants, fate, and the markets. These themes always struck a responsive chord in their minds, for these they had always heard their elders talking about until they permeated the village paths, the dark under the gigantic tamarind tree, the paved steps down to the pond, their entire environment at home and outside. As these themes had over the countless years dissolved into their consciousness, they could think of nothing else to talk about, no other expressions to use. But as soon as they reached Karam Ali's uncultivated strip of land, all conversation stopped, and, although they shared the same goal with the same determination, they forgot even each other in their acute individual concentration. Once on the land, they marched through it end to end a number of times but did not find it. Then, as if searching for some lost personal treasure, each silently went about checking the troughs and the folds of earth, carefully turning the heaps of cut weeds, probing in the tangle of the standing weeds. In this way, they became mentally and physically separated from each other, and even the invisible presence that focused their minds and held them together seemed to be disappearing. All the while, Karam Ali stood by himself, leaning on his hoe, watching the group slowly dissipate.

When the group had disintegrated—the boys playing, the young men talking, and many busy thinking their personal thoughts—a column of wind suddenly came down from the sky, and just then it appeared.

Against the backdrop of the shimmering marsh and the shaded villages beyond, its powerful form, slim and golden yellow, swayed in the most enchanting manner, as if inviting them to come closer. They approached it, tuned to the music of its graceful swaying, mesmerized by its cold eyes, totally forgetting the weapons held in their limp hands. They gathered in front of it, watching it with acute concentration.

Karam Ali then noticed that the marsh behind the towering hood was sending up a black cloud, which quickly expanded and spread across the sky, turning the marsh lead-colored and absolutely still. Immediately, the snake changed its color from golden yellow to dull clayish brown, and its shape from slim beauty to obese monstrosity—extremely old and unimaginably heavy. Karam Ali closed his eyes, for he could no longer keep looking at the huge shape, the heavy brownish hood and the gaudy white mark on it. As soon as he closed his eyes, he heard the air come alive with the cruel hiss, followed by total silence.

When he opened his eyes, he saw the sprawling body of Sadeq, the fair and angelic boy of fourteen, felled by the gigantic cruel force. The boy's thin little hand still held a small stick, and a trickle of dark blood was flowing down his neck. Having leveled Sadeq to the dust, it was now leaving unhurriedly, completely ignoring the blows of sticks falling after it. Karam Ali, determined to confront it once and for all, stepped over and firmly brought his hoe down aiming at the middle of its body. Instantly increasing speed, but not disappointing Karam Ali entirely, it left behind about four inches off its tail, as if out of kindness and consideration for him.

In the afternoon, Karam Ali went out alone, as he did not find the courage to take Raham along. What he wanted was accomplished rather quickly. He did not have much trouble persuading his landlord about it.

"You've seen my little plot in the wetland. You've to agree there are few plots as nice over there."

He paused and added, "But I don't want to sell it. That's all I have left. I would never sell it. You keep my land this year for three hundred rupees. Its crop is yours. After the harvest is over, I'll bring the money back and take my land."

"How do you think you can repay the money once you let go of your land?"

"How can I keep the lease from you without the money? I must buy a bullock. I can't survive without cultivating your land."

In a few minutes the landlord agreed to his proposal, and Karam Ali was in a good mood on his way home. The rain started almost as soon as he began walking back home, and soon it turned into a wind-whipped downpour.

Walking home in the rain, he intensely argued with his absent son, "What is it to you if I sell my land? Son of a bitch, is it your father's land that it should be any of your business? So what if the last bit of land is lost? If I don't buy the bullock, if I can't lease the land to sharecrop, what are you going to live on the whole year? Sucking on your thumb?"

Soon he was so thoroughly soaked that his agitation seemed to calm down. He was now whispering to him softly through the rain, through the cold blowing wind, through the roar of the sky.

"Bap jan, don't be sad. I really didn't sell it. I'll bring you back the land right after harvest, in the month of Magh when I pay him back. I promise I will!"

It was raining so hard that he had no need to wipe his tears, because they were steadily washing away. He looked at the marsh. It was steamy like a boiling cauldron, busy making slate-colored clouds in the shape of mountains and pushing them upward. Karam Ali just managed to reach the coconut tree beside the stack of hay in front of his hut.

Raham Ali saw his father coming, totally drenched, pushing with his hands through the heavy curtain of rain till he reached the coconut tree. That very instant, a blinding white light flashed through the sky and the air. After an unbearably long pause, a ferocious noise seemed to crack open the earth in that part of the village, and then it stomped away toward the marsh with the ground trembling in its wake.

Karam Ali was still standing under the coconut tree, leaning against the pile of straw. He looked horribly ugly, without a trace of his graying hair and beard, his eyebrows, and eyelashes. Raham Ali came out of the hut, and gently, with great affection, he took the body of his father in his arms. He walked back to the porch and carefully laid his father down in a dry spot. Raham Ali had no tears in his eyes.

The afternoon outside was now turning dark with the rain.

A Day in Bhushan's Life

Hasan Azizul Huq

It was an afternoon in April. Bhushan had walked home in the hot sun a little while ago, but he had to come out again shortly after to go to the market. He kept watching the sky impatiently. The sun was still burning hot—the shadows of the tall trees on the west side of the canal still had not reached the water.

But he could not wait any longer for the sun to mellow. He had to leave in his small dugout, and he was trying to ply it close to the west bank of the canal so as to get a bit of shade on his head and face. That was very hard to maintain, and with every little slant and veer of the boat, the merciless heat and glare struck his face directly. The sun made those parts of his oily face that were not covered with hair look abnormally shiny, revealing the ultimate ugliness a human face could possibly assume. He was in a bad temper and cursing fiercely, hurling the foulest of epithets not just at the cruel sun at half past two on an April afternoon but at anything he happened to see.

Yet if only he would shut his mouth, he would look absolutely meek and harmless. With his little eyes sunk under his forehead, blinking timidly, he would normally be talking very politely, saying that his name was Bhushan Das, but not the kind of Das known as Rishis.* In his normally shy manner, this is his way of saying that his occupation is neither skinning animals nor working with leather.

Bhushan is a peasant by occupation. The only kind of work he has done in all the fifty years of his life is cultivating land. His occupation is stamped on his every muscle, written all over his body; anyone can see that he is a

"Bhushaner Ekdin" appears in Hasan Azizul's collection *Namheen Gotraheen* [No Name, No Lineage] (1975; reprint, Dhaka: Muktadhara, 1985), 9–20.
* Descendants of the untouchable sage Valmiki.

peasant. All his muscles are twisted and tightly knotted like ropes; his calf muscles are so condensed that they look like iron balls; and from each ankle a twisted vein stands out all the way up to the back of his knee and above. All his life he has worked on land, day after day, planting the seeds, weeding the fields, harvesting the crops, carrying them in headloads to the storage stacks.

Yet the fact remains that he owns very little land, apart from his home and an acre and a half next to it. In relation to his near-landlessness, Bhushan would say that his forefathers had a lot of land, that they were almost landlords. Once he had stated that, Bhushan's beady eyes would blink and watch the distant horizon and then focus closer and examine the little land he actually owned.

Bhushan's bones are large compared to his body, the palms of his hands like big paws, flattened out by so many years of gripping and driving the plow and shoveling the soil. The years of carrying headloads seem to have pushed his head down into his shoulders, leaving very little in the form of a neck. His head—anyone could recognize Bhushan from a distance by his strange head—is like a big squat vat sitting atop his body; and it is covered with coarse, wirelike graying hair that he never bothers to comb. The slightly longer tuft of hair sticks out a bit higher than usual at the back of his head, giving his hair the appearance of a wig with a handle by which it could be pulled away, perhaps to reveal a scalp made of iron.

Bhushan was plying slowly. The canal was sunk much lower than the flatlands on its two sides. The water level in the canal was low, close to its bottom, so low that its banks looked high, and Bhushan had to tilt his head back to see the dried-up flatlands that stretched to the horizon, almost unbroken except for the few trees. The sides of the canal itself were lined with leafy trees and shrubs, from one of which came the strong fragrance of some wild flower. The hidden fragrance he just smelled did not soften his temper. He was engrossed in cursing loudly, "The son of a bitch comes home just to eat, like a pig. Nobody can save you from what you have in store; and you've a lot in store today. I'm going to kill you today!"

While cursing, he kept cocking his head toward the burning sky. It was one of Bhushan's mannerisms. Even when working on the land, he would from time to time quite pointlessly lift his head to the sky or to the horizon, hold it like that for some time, and then lower it back to work. Only he knew what he thought of in those moments.

He had reasons to be in such a bad mood that day. He could see the stacks of harvested paddy waiting in clusters on the fields in the flatlands. He could see the flocks of birds eating the seeds, but he did not have a fistful of paddy in his home. Repaying the money he borrowed from the landlord last planting season took away most of his share of the crop that Bhushan has raised on the land he cultivated as a tenant. He did not even have a batch of straw left to feed his starving plow-bullocks. His son would not stay home for even five minutes so that Bhushan could ask him to take the bullocks out to graze.

Bhushan had gone out in the morning in search of daily-wage labor. He did find some—the work of mending the bamboo fence of the Malliks' yard. He was working there quietly by himself, when three young men approached him. Bhushan was surprised to see them carrying rifles like policemen, although two of them did not even wear shirts and wore their *lungis* above their knees like peasant folks. Bhushan knew them; they were boys from the next village. He had seen them walking to school when they were little, and then they started doing farm work, the kind of work Bhushan himself did. Bhushan could not recognize the third one, who wore a shirt. They came to him, and one of the bare-chested boys addressed him, "What are you doing, uncle?" Bhushan was so startled and unnerved that he could say nothing at all. He just stared at them. They said to him, "You must come with us, you know. You must learn to hold the rifle and fight like we are trying to."

One bare-chested young man then pointed his rifle to the sky, and there was the sound of a terrible crack that made Bhushan almost jump up, and his sickle fell from his hand. "Why are you upsetting me, making such a terrible noise?" Bhushan asked in a shaken voice.

The young man in a shirt now spoke to him. Bhushan could see the pale irises, the eaglelike look of his eyes, and the puckered sides of his nose. "Bhushan, you must fight to make your country independent, your very own. We're not going to be part of Pakistan any more."

Bhushan had heard of troubles in the cities, mostly in Dhaka, where many were killed, and some in Khulna, too. He had only heard about those happenings, but he had not paid much attention, thinking that it must be one of those endless troubles that always plagued the country in one distant place or another. Now he was frightened out of his wits seeing the rifles and the terrible noise they made in the hands of ordinary peasant boys he had seen since they were children.

Brashly they said, "You all have to come with us and learn to use the rifle. Will you be able to hold the rifle? What do you say?"

The shirted young man stepped closer to Bhushan and said to him, "Listen. If you people are going to remain afraid, then nothing will come of it. You—the sixty million peasants in this country, all of you who till the land— must hold the weapons. Those bastards have been sucking us and our homeland dry. Now they are killing us freedom fighters by the drove with their modern weapons in the big places like Dhaka and Khulna. If you don't learn to wield weapons and fight back, they are going to be here too to finish you off. If you think you can stay out of harm's way by hiding in the village, you are wrong."

With this, the three boys left him staring after them.

Bhushan could not quite understand what was going on here. Guns, which he was used to seeing only in the hands of the police, were now held by shirtless peasant boys. It seemed to him very disturbing and terrifying.

With one and a half rupees for the whole morning's work, he came home at noon for food, with the sun directly overhead beating mercilessly down. When he got home, he was furious to see the two bullocks still tethered in the same spot where he had left them at dawn. His wife brought him some left-over rice soaking in water, leftover from what he had for breakfast, which was leftover from the rice cooked the day before. She had nothing at all to cook for lunch. His two little boys were asleep naked in the yard under the broad-leafed *pituli* tree, which offered the only bit of shade around noontime in both his yard and the adjoining land, all of which was scorched by the sun with nothing else growing on it.

Bhushan asked his wife where his eldest son Haridas was. She said that she did not know where he had been since morning. At this, Bhushan's sunken eyes flared up and he started cursing, "I'm going to kill that pig. I'm going to bury that bastard in the mud of the canal as soon as I catch him today."

He could not do anything about the bullocks not being fed. He had no feed, and his son was not there to take them grazing. The animals looked at him as soon as he came home, their dark eyes lit up with hope. He asked his wife to see if she could feed them something, anything.

"Where am I going to find food for them?" his wife asked.

"Don't answer back to everything I say. Try and see if you can do it."

With that, he left home again and walked in the sun to his dugout *shalti*. The muddy water of the canal was heated by the whole day of April sun. Even the air, with the waves of heat, felt like convection from a furnace. He could hear the crackle of dry grass burning in the fields above the canal. He lifted his head and absently watched the distant horizon across the dried-up flatlands. It was shimmering with the hot air from the ground rising into the intense light. Beyond the shimmering haze, the villages were fixed in a dark green wavy pattern. He was thinking of what he saw in the morning, the shirtless boys carrying guns. He could not understand what was happening. Fifty years ago he was born in one of those villages, along the edge of the vast flatland crisscrossed with channels that cut it both lengthwise and diagonally. He was born in one of those huts thatched with leaves and surrounded by a few fruit trees and shrubs and vines, in one of the homes of peasants and fishermen that made up a village. He heard many times that many things had changed since then, in the fifty years that he had lived, but he had no personal experience or knowledge of those changes.

He tried to remember his own childhood. There was a big mango tree on the east side of the yard. He could even see himself, a naked little boy, with nothing on except the black cord with a bead around his waist, asleep under that tree. He remembered his father's moustache, big and drooping and bushy with black and white hair. He could even recall his long-dead father's face, and perhaps in an effort to recall it more clearly he looked up harder across the flatland toward the dark green patches against the horizon. He noticed that the sun had mellowed a little, and the leafy big trees along the side of the canal were beginning to stir and send out a breeze. As the boat glided close to the bank, he saw that new leaves were coming out in old trees, and passing under the *jaam* tree, he heard the noise of wind rustling in the vines that were hanging down into the canal water.

Bhushan could not figure out what had changed in the country.

"I don't see any difference. The flatlands are the same as ever. As always, only god knows who owns those fields. I'm doing exactly the same work my father did. Even the jaam tree hasn't changed. Not even the bastard Haridas . . ."

Bhushan gravely shook his weirdly squat head; and the shake made his coarse hair fall evenly over his head. He had stopped cursing, and with a puzzled, worried face he silently plied the boat. He pulled absently at a tall grass along the canal's side. Immediately, the grass itself seemed to hiss and transform into the hood of a snake swaying before him. Bhushan saw a venomous, spirited young cobra, reddish in color, swinging from a *jamrul* tree, and the light of the setting sun shone in its eyes as two bright dots. He recalled that his father had died of snakebite, within two hours, before he could be treated. Bhushan raised the oar and with one blow smashed the snake's middle. It was still hissing angrily. The boat veered off the side of the canal. Bhushan's square face tightened up with anger and the satisfaction of revenge; the muscles on his jaws were twitching, and his beady eyes were shining with eagerness. He pulled the boat back to the side of the canal and smashed the snake again.

As his boat approached the marketplace, he looked back to see the canal appearing like a thin strip of silver, winding away through the empty and uninhabited stretches of the flatland. He had crossed that distance so many times going back from the market, but today he felt strangely afraid. By the time he would be heading back from the market, it would be almost night. He worried whether he could manage the trip back alone, in case he did not find Haridas in the market. It had never felt like a problem to him before.

He rowed halfway along the marketplace and tied the boat at the back of Ratan's grocery store. He piled on his head the plantains, the two white gourds, and the bunch of gourd leaves and started up the steep shortcut to the vegetable market north of the store.

He slipped several times coming up the steep path lined by thorn bushes. It took him a while, and he was panting when he reached the top, near the vegetable market. He was late today; the place was full of people, all the able-bodied men from the surrounding villages seemed to have gathered there. It seemed unusually crowded, and the noise made by the voices hit his ears like a high-pitched drone when he reached the top.

Suddenly he spotted Haridas in the tea shop directly in front of him, talking and laughing. Bhushan was trembling with anger; his eyes glowered, and his face now became totally square with the jaws clenched. He seemed about to jump on Haridas like a tiger but stopped short remembering the load held on his head by both hands. He quickly put the vegetables down on the ground and started for Haridas. Standing on the step to the shop, he summoned Haridas, "Come here, you pig, bastard, scum. You and I will settle things once and for all today."

Haridas's face dropped at the sight of Bhushan, and fearfully he started toward his father. Bhushan stood there, as if ready to tear off Haridas's head as soon as it would come within his reach, when he heard a rumbling noise come up from the canal side. Bhushan knew the sound. It was the sound made by the water when a motor boat came ashore. But no motor boat ever came into this canal!

Haridas by then was standing in front of him, but Bhushan stood puzzled, transfixed. Instantly, there was the sound of an explosion that shook the whole marketplace. Bhushan saw the huge tamarind tree shake all over, and the crows in it fly out, cawing together and circling over the tree. The sound came again: an ear-shattering explosion, followed by a high-pitched, metallic sound made by some machine. The dhoti that Bhushan was wearing sarong-like around the lower part of his body slapped sharply at his legs with the blast of air from the explosion. He stood there, unable to move or turn, facing the bewildered Haridas.

He heard the noise of the marketplace stop completely. It was dreadfully silent. The abrupt silencing of the ceaseless hum of the market was accentuated and made unbearably heavy by a collective gasp of terror. The sound— a deep explosion, followed by a flying, high-pitched, metallic sound—was repeated some more times. After that, Bhushan could not hear the steady sound of the motorboat engine any more.

He heard another sound now, sort of like that made by the wings of a small bird flying close to the ground. Following this sound, he heard a blood-curdling scream of terror rise through the crowd in the marketplace. And then, following Haridas's terrified eyes, he turned around and saw a man appear on the bank of the canal, leaping up the steep path. The man was dressed in a khaki uniform, with a cap perched diagonally on his head. The man was very fair, very tall, and big like a hill. Bhushan looked at the man's eyes and immediately remembered the eyes of a tiger he had once seen in his youth near the Sundarbans. The man was shouting angry things that Bhushan did not understand except some words that sounded like *beiman*, *kafir*, *malaun*.* Bhushan's ears heard his angry words, and his eyes stared at the black stubby gun he held in his hands.

---

* Abusive epithets meaning ingrate, infidel, and idol-worshiper, respectively.

In a fraction of a second, the man seemed to be doubled. Bhushan saw another exactly like him next to him. Then he heard the sound of boots as more of them came up the path. Then they stood forming a line along the bank. Then, 'here was another kind of sound: a constant tat-tat-tat-tat. His ears were ringing from the sound. Haridas had moved away a step or two, but Bhushan stood in the same position, vaguely watching the sky and the light still lingering, shining on the trees. The steady tat-tat-tat-tat sound started again. It was then that Bhushan turned his head and saw people falling to the ground, slowly and smoothly, falling like clean-cut trees that seem to lie down slowly, unhurriedly, instead of crashing.

Then he saw the blood. Blood spurting, spilling and flowing, from heads, from legs, from shoulders and chests and abdomens. He did not quite hear the spurting and flowing blood make any sound like spurting and flowing water. He saw more batches of people falling down slowly, unhurriedly like clean-cut trees.

All this time Bhushan had remained almost immobile. Most people in the marketplace had not tried to move either. Now the terrified stillness of the people was shattered by the terrified movements of those not yet fallen, as they started screaming and running helter-skelter. Many stumbled as they ran blinded by fear; some stopped, looked at the canal bank, and then collapsed clasping their abdomens from which blood flowed with a vigorous gurgling noise.

Their blood was spreading slowly, collecting and then flowing along the unpaved path of the marketplace, the path smooth like cement with the constant walking and the months of heat. The flow of blood down the path was so rapid now that Bhushan could see the foam collecting and moving along. In patches, the blood spilled off the path and soaked the dried grass, leaving red drops dangling from the ends of the grass tips.

The rounds of tat-tat-tat-tat kept coming.

The slumped bodies of people were forming heaps, like sacks piling up, heaps that were growing larger with more bodies falling on them. Some falling bodies were vaguely waving their limbs, while some showed no movement except the tremor in the dilated pupils before they turned into fixed gazes. The dying just stared at the fading light of the April sky at dusk. Some stares were stony without emotions, some were tormented by pain, some had the look of being betrayed. Those still alive said prayers to the Almighty, and the collective sound of their individual prayers hummed through the air. In between the waves of the hum of prayers and moans, more people sat down or fell and joined the dying. One lay on his side with one leg folded, as if sleeping, with the jute bag full of shopping still slung from his shoulder. A very old woman, perhaps eighty years old, seemed to be oblivious to her cracked open chest as she seemed busy trying to tie back into her waist the loosened knot of her worn out, torn sari.

Bhushan by then had managed to drag Haridas by the hand and reached the tamarind tree to take shelter behind its trunk. From there he heard the tat-tat-tat going on, and he saw that few people in the whole marketplace were still on their feet. Most were slumped on the ground, dead in strange postures; only a few were still screaming, or moaning, or praying to god, or asking for water, or moving some limb. The dwarfish peasant folks that had filled the marketplace mostly lay on the ground, mowed down, and the bullets were now flying through the air making sharp whistling noises.

Bhushan saw a young woman, about twenty-five, trying to reach the shelter of the tamarind tree through the bullets whizzing by all around her. She nestled a dark, chubby baby in her bosom. She had almost reached the tree when there was the sound of a sharp snap. The woman stopped, with her hand on the baby's head. Bhushan saw the bright red blood pouring through her fingers, soon mixed with the white matter of the baby's brain now emptied into her palm. The young woman turned around, looked at the baby's face, and like a lunatic she shook the baby a few times with both hands and threw it away with a scream that no human voice would have seemed capable of. And then her hands tore away her dirty blouse. Bhushan saw her round breasts swollen with milk. She pointed to her chest and shouted, "Come on, sons of bastards. Shoot me here! Here!"

Next moment one of her swollen breasts burst open like a ripe cotton flower of a *shimul* tree. Her body was thrown off with a jerk. She fell under the tree and lay with her open eyes frozen in the fierce anger of her last moment.

In the midst of all this, Bhushan could also see that Haridas was standing a little away from him. He was going to grab him and pull him back, when Haridas suddenly kneeled to the ground. Bhushan turned and saw, right before him, within barely two feet, one of the men in khaki holding his stubby black gun. His huge fair-skinned face was dripping with sweat and red with anger. He was so close that Bhushan saw his eyes; he even smelled the sweat of his body. The man was shouting, "You *kamin*,* are you a malaun?"

At this point, Bhushan was seeing nothing else. The muscles of his hands tensed up his flat paws, as he considered the throat of the man. He stood looking at the man's neck, and he seemed to be undecided, till his body finally made up its mind, and sprang to the side of Haridas in a single stride of concentrated energy.

By then, Haridas was lying on the ground, his body quite still, only a bit of his fading life lingering in his eyes like a faint spark left in cooling embers. Bhushan crouched beside him, his face bent close to Haridas's face, and he talked to him with all the tenderness of a father for a son. "Haridas, my son, my darling son." With his rough peasant hands, Bhushan stroked the body

* Laborer, lowly worker.

of his dying son, and he kept singing to the boy, "Haridas, my dear son, my darling boy!"

Then there was a single odd crack, with which Bhushan's stubby pillarlike body shook a few times and became very still, releasing him from feeling anything any more.